HIS SAXON WIFE

THE SAXONS OF HYRSTOW

C.A. FRAY

DEDICATION

To Jill and Robyn.
You were my sisters in the trenches as this book fought its way
out of me. Thank you for your continued support and for
being the best friends a girl can ask for.
We leveled up this year, ladies.
"What's the best that could happen?"

A NOTE TO THE READER

Thank you for choosing to read *His Saxon Wife*.

This book contains scenes of gory violence, references to death in childbirth, loss of a spouse/parent, mental health issues, depressive thoughts and actions, discussion of suicide, vulnerable characters in grave danger, and references to sexual assault.

Please take care of your mental health if you choose to read.

THE SAXONS OF HYRSTOW BOOK TWO

HIS SAXON WIFE

C.A. FRAY

PROLOGUE

Northumbria

Beginning of September, 795 A.D.

Her death shouldn't have surprised him. Childbirth had been difficult with their other daughter, Æfflead. She'd almost lost too much blood that time. Despite knowing death was a possibility Branton felt the yawning fogginess of shock. That morning, they'd laid his wife, his heart, his Freda, to rest. Had covered her burial shroud with dirt until a mound in the churchyard was all that was left of her.

Tears stung the backs of his eyes as he held the squalling baby aloft. Freda's life, the price of its presence. His beautiful wife was now to have worms devour her milky skin, dirt absorb her midnight hair. His other children would be without a mother, and this one would never know her.

She'd not wanted another baby. She'd told him she was going to take herbs to help prevent more children. He'd been angry. Children meant joy and prosperity. He loved each of his little souls, and the thought of Freda not wanting more had cut him deeper than he liked.

It didn't matter. By the time he'd realized he loved Freda more than any future babes and apologized a few days later, her monthly bleeding had been absent. They waited, Freda anxious and Bran suddenly hopeful at the prospect of one more child. He might as well have put a knife into her himself.

Exhaustion climbed into him, made a nest in his bones.

Branton clutched the new babe to his chest, struck dumb about what to do. He should know. He and Freda had three other children. And yet, as the little girl wailed for food, he couldn't bring himself to care.

His eldest, Neil, had gone to fetch milk from the goat, his eyes heavy with sorrow. The other two, Ginnie and Æfflead, had been taken to Freda's mother's house. He needed to right himself, but his head felt far away.

Branton sucked a breath through his teeth at thoughts of what he would need to do to care for them. He'd never had to cook, nor clean, nor mend. He'd been with Freda his entire adult life. Even before they were wed, he couldn't remember life without her.

A memory flashed to mind of Freda, eight, long hair tangled around her face as she played tag with him, his friend Ridley and her younger brother Grahame. They'd shucked their chore of tending to her family's flock of sheep. The sky was the light blue of a robin's egg, unmarred by clouds. Freda, tired of being tagged by Bran, had scooped a stick from the ground and began whacking him in the legs with it. He'd stopped tagging her after that.

A grin poked through his beard. His whole life had been molded around getting Freda's attention and she'd answered twofold.

What would he do without her? Why in God's name was *he* the one left on this earth?

Neil banged through the hut's wooden door, milk pail in hand. The boy gave Bran a questioning look through his tears as he placed the pail on the large wooden table.

"The baby alright?" Neil asked, his thin mouth pinched into a frown. He had a smear of dirt on his forehead that hadn't been there before. It made Bran wonder how difficult it had been to procure the milk.

Stupidly, Branton looked down at the crying baby. The pathetic comfort he offered her hadn't helped and now she was red-faced. Her tiny hands were curled into fists that knocked the swaddling blanket clear. He knew he had to help, but time had slowed.

"Father?" Neil asked. He strode to where Branton sat in the great chair by the dwindling fire and held a cloth out to him. Branton had no idea where his son had retrieved it. With the amount of blood Freda lost, it seemed as if the midwife had used every available blanket and cloth in the household.

Before he could take it, the door cracked open. Emma

Baker poked her head inside. She'd been with Freda during her last moments, helping the midwife. Her daughter, Merthe, had been sent to the hall to find him when things went wrong.

Too late. He'd been too late.

He shouldn't have left the hut in the first place. The birthing bed was the women's domain but he should have hovered, should have *been* there. Bran cleared his throat, though he knew tears still ran down his cheeks like rivers that would never cease.

"Is the baby alright?" Emma asked, her light voice subdued. Sorrow ate at her features, making her pretty face seem ready to crumple at any moment.

Bran swallowed, wanting to answer, but his throat was like tinder. He drew in a breath and opened his mouth to try again but the sound that shuddered out of him was a gasp wrapped in a howl.

"Nothing's wrong with her. She's just hungry," Neil said, his tone sullen.

"May I help?" she asked, stepping inside and closing the door to keep the heat in.

She must've been exhausted. The birth had taken hours. Then the last rites, the burial, the cleaning. Emma had thrown herself into the care of Freda's after-life as if it would bring her friend back. She'd left Branton with the baby for a short time to clean herself and feed Merthe. A rusty stain still clung to the bottom of her skirt. It was all Bran could stare at as he wordlessly handed Emma the child.

She accepted the baby and settled herself into the

chair next to his. Neil brought the pail of milk and cloth to her.

"Is it clean?" she asked.

Neil nodded, his eyes narrowed.

"Thank you," Emma said. She settled the baby on her lap, then twisted the corner of the cloth and dunked it in the milk. The infant latched to the cloth as soon it was brought to her lips, sucking with all her might.

Relief washed across Neil's features as the baby suckled. It struck Bran that the child was now the closest connection Neil had to his mother.

Something in his chest crumbled. Freda was gone. The pain that had lanced through him at the news of her death seemed to fold into itself and grow, bottomless and aching.

His life was over, as hers was.

He would sustain for his children, and that was all.

Haligmōnaþ
(September)

Wintermōnaþ

(October)

Blōtmōnaþ
(November)

Ærra Gēola
(December)

Æfterra Gēola
(January)

Sōlmōnaþ
(February)

CHAPTER

ONE

Emma looked up from beneath her lashes at the miserable man she was marrying.

It would get better, she told herself. It was something she'd been telling herself for months.

Branton Cutter's bright blue gaze refused to meet hers. Instead, it remained stuck on the small bundle of dried herbs she clutched. He wasn't particularly riveted by it; rather, she suspected he couldn't bring himself to look at her face. Fern leaves turned crisp amid winter's season bracketed bunches of rosemary, thyme, and sage. Each piece in the bouquet represented well-wishes from those around them: longevity, good health, fertility. Emma's fingers itched to toss the bouquet into the fire.

Good health was fine, but longevity and fertility were laughable. From what she witnessed of the Cutter family these past months, Branton wished for nothing more than to disappear in his grief. There would be no children from this marriage, she was sure.

Wind blustered from the south, causing the small assembly of friends and family to hunker into their cloaks. Branton didn't flinch. His wide, muscled frame seemed out of place among those who came to bear witness to their vows beside the church. As Head Cutter of Hyrstow, he was used to long days against the elements, chopping down trees and hefting logs. A petty wind was nothing compared to the deep chasm of loss that had ripped through his life. All their lives.

Other than his lips tucking downward, Branton looked every bit a groom. He'd tamed his unruly, umber hair, trimmed his beard, and even his flaxen tunic appeared clean. Emma wondered who had taken the trouble to wash it. Between feedings for baby Tatswip, baking fresh loaves for the meal after the wedding mass, fending off Yrsa's attempt at helping with Æfflead's hair, and hoping her groom would show up to the nuptials, Emma didn't have time before the ceremony to tidy Branton's clothing.

In spite of herself, something deep and forbidden curled within Emma at the sight of her roughly hewn groom. Branton was to be hers. Not in spirit, perhaps, and certainly not in love, but as a partner.

Emma would finally have someone to rely on. She could stop paying the kingdom's widow tax. It stung having to scrape together her earnings these past years simply to remain unwed. The ability to put her income toward a proper dowry for her daughter, Merthe, was too sweet. She would face whatever Branton delivered as a husband if it meant a safety net for her child. All she had to do was marry him and continue to help raise his children. As she'd been doing since Freda's death months ago.

A now-familiar pang of sorrow hit her in the middle of her ribs. She pressed a hand to her stomach to ward it off. It didn't work.

"Emma Baker," Father Chisholm said, expectant, as if he'd said her name once before.

Emma tore her gaze from Branton's face, heat warming her ears at being caught staring. Had it been a happier occasion, friends would have joked about her not being able to tear her eyes from her groom. As it was, those gathered remained solemn.

"Yes?" She inclined her head in apology, properly cowed at the thought of drifting off during her marriage ceremony. The priest nodded in acceptance of her answer. Well, if *that* wasn't an indication how this marriage would go; she'd missed her own vows.

Merthe stood beside her, quietly resentful that Yrsa, a former Viking raider and now-wife to the chieftain, wasn't allowed to accompany them into the church for the customary mass after the ceremony. Neil, Branton's eldest, stood next to his father, jaw clenched, green eyes to the ground, while his sister, Ginnie, corralled the second youngest, Æfflead, with one hand and held baby Tatswip on her hip with the other. Despite her full hands, Ginnie looked at Emma as if she were the most beautiful woman the girl had seen. Emma had to resist the urge to duck her head beneath her stare, since she knew it was a lie. She'd never measure up to Freda's midnight hair and cherry lips, nor her wild, happy spirit.

"Indeed," Father Chisholm declared, a smile warming his thin lips as he nodded. He squinted against the watery sun peeking around one of the swollen clouds overhead. Someone coughed and more than one person shuffled among the small group, bending toward Emma and Branton like a crone against the cold. Snowflakes began to swirl from the sky.

The priest turned to Branton, infusing cheer into his tone as if to temper the common knowledge of Bran's displeasure.

"And do you take this woman, in health and illness, wealth and poverty?"

Branton, for his part, didn't miss a beat. His deep baritone carried through Emma's bones as he lifted his eyes to hers for so brief a moment Emma thought she may have imagined it, before locking onto the priest's face.

"Yes."

Their kin clapped, Grahame Shepherd offered a cheer, the children pasted smiles on their chilled faces, and Emma's insides twisted together like two hands wringing out laundry at the thought that she and Branton were now man and wife.

BEHIND THE CLOSED door of Branton's bedroom—now *their* bedroom—both Emma and Branton heaved long, exhausted sighs.

Emma placed her hand against the rough-grained wood, not yet able to look at her new husband. Branton seemed just as eager to collect himself after the long day. The slip of leather through cloth and the clunk of his short ax on the stout bedside table were the only sounds in the quiet room.

Steeling herself with a breath, Emma turned. The room was not unfamiliar. She'd assisted with Tatswip's birth, had brought blankets to the bed, fed Freda sips of water between laboring shouts. She'd made a vow to Freda in that very room, one that had redirected her own life.

A small ring of firestones stood in the right corner of the room. It was bright with flame and illuminated the large clothing chest in the far corner. The bed was a squat mockery directly across from her, once shared by Freda and Bran. It glared at her as if in protest she would dare lie in it with Branton now. To the left, a short table contained a three-pronged brush, and in the corner, another chest. Blankets in cheerful reds, browns, and greens hung on the wood planked walls to keep warmth inside. Beside the fire, a small huddle of blankets lay in the shape of a cot.

"D'you need anything?" Branton asked. Emma forced herself not to jump at the barrenness of his tone.

"I'm fine, thank you."

Emma clasped her hands in front of her to keep herself from fidgeting.

Branton stared at her, bearded jaw tightening. He'd loosened the laces on his tunic at some point in the evening. She'd been grateful he'd bothered to tidy himself for the ceremony. Lord knew that her cousin, Ingrid, and her husband, Paul, were apprehensive about the marriage. Emma was glad Branton's current appearance didn't give cause for further doubt.

Now, with him before her, Emma was suddenly at a loss. The children were abed. They were alone for what felt like the first time.

She forced herself to step forward, her heart beating like a sparrow's wings inside her chest. The plainness of his stare unnerved her more than anything. It was a hollow sort of look, as if he peered at her without really seeing. She could have been a piece of new furniture he wasn't sure what to do with for all the warmth in him.

"The day went well," she ventured, dropping her gaze to his throat. Thick muscle honed from hours cutting in the forest lay beneath the loosened leather string.

"It did," Branton said. The words were stale.

All the children had been polite, their friends had helped put on a nice dinner in the hall, and baby Tate had fallen asleep, milk-happy, a little while ago. She should have a few hours' reprieve before Tate had to feed again.

Emma pushed her hands to her thighs to rub the sweat from her palms. The fabric of her finest dress was smooth beneath her fingers. She loved the garment, spun with wool so fine the blue threads almost shimmered. And, up until that moment, she hadn't considered she would have to remove it in front of Branton.

Her mind grasped with weak fingers for anything to say.

Branton must have noticed her nerves because his eyes, the shade of a cloudless spring morning, roved over her. They touched on her hips, chest, neck before tearing away.

"The…uh…venison tasted…good," he offered, reaching up to run a hand through his hair.

"Indeed. The carrots were also done well."

Emma swallowed, though her throat felt like sand.

The carrots were done well? What type of statement was that? She and Branton were far from strangers. Before it all, they were friends.

As her fingers skimmed the smooth material of her dress, she suddenly wasn't sure what Branton wanted from his wedding night. Though theirs was a marriage of convenience, they hadn't discussed the repercussions.

Branton blew out a low breath through puffed out lips, shifting from one foot to the other.

"Thank you," he blurted, "for everything. With the baby. With Ginnie and Æffie. It was…nice. Today, I mean."

His hands hung at his sides as if he was forcing himself not to clench his palms into fists.

"You're welcome," she said, stopping herself from

offering a slight bow. This man was no lord. He was her groom.

Emma's gaze skittered toward the bed to their right. She didn't think he would, but if Branton desired to take her in the way of a husband, Emma supposed she would follow through on her vows to be a wife in every way that mattered.

It wouldn't be a hardship. She'd always thought Branton's roughly hewn features beautiful. His forehead carried the slightest crease of age that reminded her of the bark of the trees he felled. Heavy, dark brows gave a wide, wild shape to his face. Taller than she, though everyone was, Branton was not of such a height that she would have to painfully crane her neck to look up into his face. Broad shoulders held muscle so thick, she sometimes wondered how he bore the weight.

And she hadn't been with a man since Jon's passing, years ago. Even before her first husband had died of a coughing illness, they hadn't spent much time bedding one another. In the early days of their marriage, indeed, but after Merthe, no more children came and Jon's parents died, leaving him the sole baker to Hyrstow. Their marital joining was limited to special occasions or in the darkness of midnight wakings.

Emma itched the skin above her dress's neckline. She took a step toward the bed, her nose scrunching against the heat laying heavy in her cheeks. Before she could even think of what side to sleep on, Branton was in front of her, rough hands held partway up to halt her.

"I do not expect to bed you this evening."

Something in her middle churned. Branton continued, a pained look fixing his mouth into its ever-present frown.

"You are kind to have entered into this marriage, to agree to care for my children. I want you to know that you have nothing to fear from me as a man. You do not have to feel as if you owe me anything."

Emma's mouth formed a round 'O' before she snapped it shut and nodded. Suddenly, the back of her neck was too hot. She didn't know what to do with her hands. She placed them on her hips, then clasped them together, wringing to soothe the ache building in her chest.

Men and women needed physical release. It was common knowledge. And from what she knew of Bran's habits since Freda's death, he'd not been with another woman. She did not wish to pressure him into something he didn't desire yet wanted to allow him the knowledge of her understanding. Heat rippled up her chest to her cheeks as the next words dropped from her mouth like heavy stones.

"Thank you, Branton. I appreciate your kindness. Though I did agree to be your wife in every way."

The truth hung between them, heavy and thick, like a quilt warming over a fire. Everyone who knew her thought her mild and sweet, but Emma did not survive her own husband's death and subsequent years alone through meekness. She was straightforward when necessary, hard even. Three years of being Hyrstow's

Baker, commanding fair prices for her goods without a husband to back her, had created a tough shell.

The muscles in Branton's neck worked as he swallowed. He ran his hands over his thighs and the intensity of his narrowed gaze was something Emma forced herself not to flinch from. He was her husband, after all, and his eyes could drift over her body any time he pleased. She did, however, avoid his assessment by looking at the small fire warming the room.

The silence seemed to echo beneath the thatched roof and wooden walls as Branton considered her. Emma shuffled from one foot to another as he took her measure as a woman. She knew what he'd find. A slight frame, with a marked cut to her waist and flared hips, though she was none so buxom as Freda had been. Emma's brown hair seemed lackluster compared to Freda's raven strands and her skin a few shades darker than Freda's milk-white.

"I...you are a lovely woman, Emma. And I thank you for your commitment to our...arrangement."

Branton's softened tone may as well have been a slap against the cheek of a wayward child. Emma felt as if she were drowning in her own humiliation. Rejection. Her mind scrambled to save her pride. An explanation sprang to mind, not wholly shaped. Before she could rethink it, she stepped forward, her gaze locked on his middle. Even as she spoke, Emma felt as if she had left her body and was looking at the two of them from above.

"It is not what I wish for. It is just that, in the eyes of

the church, relations between a married couple promote good health."

His silence was like a scream. Heavens, she wasn't saying anything right.

Emma looked at his face then, though she wished she hadn't. Branton's cheeks hollowed as his jaw rippled. His gaze was like a layer of frost upon a summer pond.

"I love Freda." His deep voice cracked a little over the name.

He didn't see her nod of acceptance nor her attempt at a sympathetic smile because he made for the door, great shoulders hunched. Emma wanted to call him back, to explain how her unease had bungled up her words. Branton was through the main room and out the front door a moment later.

From the cradle, Tate began to cry.

Bran hadn't donned his cloak. He strode across the frozen field to the west of his land and halted before the sentinel trees swallowed him up. Amidst the nearly black night, winter's chill cut through flesh to bone. He relished it. Since Freda's death, he'd been a barren waste, keeping himself alive only to care for his children, which he didn't do well. He refused to feel anything other than the immediate needs of cold, hot, hunger, thirst. Anything else he'd shoved down so deep, he knew he would never feel anything again.

Until he saw Emma at the wedding ceremony.

He'd caught sight of her between the heads of her cousin, Ingrid, and Ingrid's husband, Paul, just before she was to walk up the short, makeshift aisle. The small smile she always wore had been exchanged for a firm line and a tented brow. Bran watched as she drew a deep breath through her nose, then let it out with a great puff of rounded cheeks. He'd seen her do it before, when she interacted with a customer who didn't take her seriously at market, or when she was frustrated with Merthe. Recently, he saw it when she thought no one was looking, usually when preparing a meal for his mother-starved children. Another time, when sorrow ravaged her delicate features after Ginnie had asked if Emma could take care of them forever.

It was a mark of her reluctance. A dive down into her own strength.

Despite her trepidation, Bran couldn't help noticing her beauty. He'd looked away as soon as she turned down the aisle to face him. However, he knew her hair was intricately woven into a crown atop her head, a ribbon of green fabric threaded through the strands. How could he not notice the way the ribbon brought out the rich brown of her thick-lashed eyes? From first glance, he knew her upturned lips, the color of a pink rose, appeared ripe enough to bite.

Through the entire day, he'd stood still as stone trying not to look upon her. She was utterly ravishing.

But, in their bedroom, with the pressure of a wedding night a weight on their shoulders, he'd had to look. Her slight frame clad in her best gown, a light blue showcasing her creamy skin, made his body thirst for the first time in months. Shame slammed into him half a heartbeat later.

The temptation had to be snuffed out and buried.

Emma was Freda's friend. His by extension. She'd helped with the squalling new babe and the constant needs of his children while he waded through the aftermath of his only love's death. She'd made meals and brought Merthe to play with the children and hugged his crying girls. She'd slowly taken over Fiona's cleaning and cooking efforts—a boon to his mother-in-law since she lived an hour's walk outside of Hyrstow. Now, Emma was his wife. There was no mystery, no question about their arrangement. He needed a caregiver. She needed freedom from the widow tax. That was all.

Footfalls crunched against the icy grass.

"Branton?" Emma's silvery voice came from behind him. It set his teeth on edge. He huffed out a breath, reminding himself to be civil. This was the woman who kept his family together when he couldn't.

He couldn't. Branton despised the thought, despite its truth.

Emma stood a few feet away, holding a lonely candle uplifted against the dark. She wore a cloak, hood up against the wind, and in her arm a bundle of something he couldn't discern.

"Here," she stepped forward, holding out the bundle. Branton remained still for a moment too long. He hadn't expected her to follow him. It was bitterly cold, and he thought her smart enough to leave him alone. With a grimace, he stepped forward to take it, eyes narrowed against her good intentions. With a pull, the fabric unraveled to reveal his cloak.

"I thought you might be cold."

Emma cupped her hand around the candle's flame as it quaked in the wind. The glow from it illuminated the point of her chin, the dimple that peeked out from her shy smile. Branton's throat suddenly felt tight. That she would care, after he'd been short with her...

"Thank you," he croaked. A strange feeling pressed upon his shoulders, causing him to straighten. Emma didn't have to bestow a sliver of kindness to him, yet here she was.

"You're welcome," she said. She did not leave. Instead, her mouth opened and closed, the curve of her pillowed lips slicing downward. Her delicate brows descended next.

Branton waited. He had nothing to say. No inkling of how to assert he couldn't share the bed with her. He didn't even sleep in it himself. He slept on the floor near the fire, huddled beneath a new blanket gifted to him by Yrsa. Though, for some reason, speaking the words aloud to Emma was almost worse than telling her they would not be man and wife in the carnal sense.

"Won't you come in? The children are asleep. Tatswip awoke, but she settled quickly. You must be cold. And it's so dark."

Surprise lit through him. Emma was babbling. Emma never babbled. In all the years of their friendship, she only did so when unease settled in her. She wanted him back in the hut, even after he behaved so rudely.

"I don't have to stay with you," Emma said. She took another step forward, lifting the candle to better see his face. Shadows clung to her hair, her shoulders. The bell of her hips was lost to darkness. "I know what it is to lose someone. I can sleep with the children in the other room."

Mortification was thick and hot in the back of his throat. Emma had been the one he could rely on these months past. Barely able to work, he'd holed up in his room, waning in and out of sleep. Emma had been unobtrusive yet vital to his family. He needed to work with her and remain apart. Even if the candlelight against the apple of her cheek made him want to slip his thumb across the flesh to see if it was as soft as it looked.

The errant thought had him shaking his head. Coupled with the wildness of the frosty night, the urge to touch her, to ensure she was real and not some forest nymph, caused his skin to tighten.

"What?" Emma asked, taking a step closer.

His words were rusty as they tumbled out. "Thank you. No. You may take the bed, if you so choose. I don't sleep in it."

She shivered. Whether from the cold or the chill of his words, Branton didn't know. They stood close enough that he caught the scent of the rosemary that had been in her bouquet. The cloak hung from his fingers. Darkness wreathed him from the forest behind. Fitting, for he felt one with the dark. It had claimed his soul, stripped him bare when Freda was wrenched from him. And now this woman, this thoughtful, beautiful woman stood in the frigid outdoors before him, offering him nothing but kindness and light.

It made him want to hurt something, someone. Most of all, himself.

"You should go back," he said, his tone as harsh as the coldness leaching into their skin.

Emma's gentle smile wavered. Bran was glad. She shouldn't see him as a good man. Shouldn't give him a look laced with such hope that said if she just gave him time, maybe he would grow into someone better. As if he could fold himself up into the man he once was, happy and arrogant, so secure. Regret for needing her and dooming her to a life of misery burned along his spine. He straightened to his full height.

She would have to stop looking at him like that.

"Branton?" Emma asked. Clearly, she had no survival instinct because she should have been afraid. She should have stepped away as an icy, cruel smile formed along his lips. He let it grow.

Rather than back away, Emma seemed to steel herself beneath his gaze. The curve of her full top lip hardened. Wind scraped them, and the candle was snuffed. Still, she persisted as if intent on making him snap.

"It's been a long day. I think you should come back now." There was no softness in her tone, only command.

Heedless of his size compared to her, she reached out, clasping his chilled forearm. The warmth of her hand was a brand on his skin. In months, save his children and a few hearty pats on the back from Ridley or Grahame, no one had dared touch him. Yet Emma was either so concerned for him, or so heedless of her own safety, she felt the need to push him to the brink of madness when he needed time alone. He nearly buckled beneath the weight of her trust in him.

He'd have to prove her wrong. She could help

everyone around her but not him. The only way he knew how to disgrace himself once and for all in her eyes was to destroy the image of the hurt widower she imagined him to be.

So quick Emma didn't have time to gasp, Branton gripped her arm and hauled her to him. He slid one hand beneath her cloak, anchoring it on her waist. The candle thumped to the ground. She could do nothing but grip his upper arm to hold herself steady. Christ, she was dainty. He could nearly fit his whole hand across the expanse of her lower back. He brought her flush to him. Soft, rounded breasts hugged him, and for a moment, Branton forgot he was trying to scare her away. A deep, unsteady craving for *more* struck him like an ax. More of the feel of this woman and her slight curves and the panting little breaths that puffed along his collarbone.

He stifled a moan he loathed himself for.

After a heartbeat, Branton could feel the shift of her head as her breath trailed up his neck. As if she looked up at him, unflinching.

"You do not scare me," Emma said. The sturdiness of her tone felt like a whip against his back. With a noise made low in his throat, he gripped her harder. Her skirts rustled against his legs, her cloak opening to him. Through her dress the points of her nipples chafed.

Awakened by the feel of a soft female body against his, desire rushed through Bran like a flash of fire in the night. It overtook sense. His lower half hadn't worked for the better part of a year. There had been no morning urges, no lustful thoughts of Freda. Apparently, until he wanted to strike fear into his new wife.

"I should. I am not the man I was. I am nothing. Save yourself misery and go back to the hut," he growled.

"You stubborn ass. This is not how we will treat one another. I am invested in this union, same as you, and though you think I am abhorrent, I have promised to care for you."

If only Emma could hear the lecherous thoughts clanging around in his head.

"You think I find you abhorrent?" A dark laugh escaped him, "It is quite the opposite, unfortunately."

She couldn't want this, want *him.*

Branton dared to roll his hips, showing her the evidence of his arousal. A sharp intake of breath stole through her. The slip of noise caused his blood to pound, scraping every sense to something raw. He had to let her go. She'd called his bluff and wasn't balking at his show of force. To act on the desire clawing at him was madness.

Then a moan escaped her, paired with the feather-light touch of supple lips against his throat. Branton froze. Something dormant in him clenched.

"Branton..." her breath against his skin caused his tenuous grasp on the situation to snap. He spiraled, his hate for himself, the desire for her and frustration that they *shouldn't* tossed him over the edge.

Suddenly, he was stalking toward the trees, spinning Emma to face away from him while shoving her against a trunk. Mindless, hard as stone, Branton rucked up her skirts, digging through the layers with one hand as he fumbled the laces of his trousers with the other. Emma braced her hands against the tree's trunk, harsh pants coming out as plumes of cold smoke in the frigid air.

Trousers be damned, he couldn't tear the laces free one-handed so shoved them down, his cock hot and hard against his palm as he guided it beneath Emma's skirts. The barrier of her undergarment was no match for his furious fingers. He yanked it down. When he felt the slickness of her entrance, he lost his last shred of sense. Quaking, he rubbed his cock against her wetness once before thrusting forward to the hilt.

Emma's sharp intake of breath matched his own as he stilled against the tight feeling of her sheathing him. Christ, she felt like hot salvation.

The pause of their joining lasted an eternity, if a moment. The need to move, to ram into her again and again yanked at him. Branton clenched his eyes shut to beat back the feeling of his bollocks tightening, ready to spill at how damn good she felt. Emma clamped around him harder than he could have imagined. Her hips warmed his hands where he gripped her. Then she was moving on him, inching away and thrusting back. It tore his restraint to shreds. With a roar Branton withdrew to the tip then rammed forward, surging inside Emma. Angry and overcome, he fucked her without mercy.

Somewhere in the back of his mind, he knew he was failing her. Their first time as man and wife in the snow, against a tree, and he wasn't even making it good for her. She pushed off from the trunk and ground her bottom into him, hiking up her legs to meet his power with hers. With every stroke, she gave it back to him, moaning until they became a writhing mass in the dark.

It didn't take long before Emma's inner muscles pulsed, gripping him with mighty strength. A moan slipped from her and release ripped through him, eating what was left of his soul. Bran couldn't help the way he rutted Emma into the tree, groaning incomprehensible nothings into the air as she milked him dry.

They stilled. Branton drew a deep breath through his nose. The cold air spread through his chest, clearing his head from the frenzy. Dread was an anchor pulling him under.

He'd committed the worst of sins.

He'd betrayed Freda.

He'd abused Emma.

Without care, he withdrew, turning to tuck himself into his pants. He didn't look at Emma as she straightened her skirts. Didn't think of how uncomfortable she likely was with his spend running down her legs in the dead of winter. Didn't ask whether he hurt her, which he no doubt did. Instead, he grit his teeth against the invisible whip of guilt.

Absolute silence descended. As if the animals and the wind had witnessed his transgression and decided to keep away. He could feel Emma turn to look at him.

He couldn't bear it.

"Don't follow me," was all he said as he stalked across the meadow leading to Hyrstow.

CHAPTER
THREE

Branton's hut would need a bread window. And an oven. The first was inconvenient, the second expensive. People didn't go around building bread ovens. It was why her hut, the one rebuilt after last year's Viking raid, had the only bread oven in Hyrstow. Emma would have liked to move Branton's family to her home where the oven was, but the small, one room square was tiny compared to the luxury of the two-roomed hut where the family resided.

Emma held Tatswip in one arm, gently bobbing her up and down, as she awkwardly stood in the doorway and passed two loaves of bread to Brunhild Smith. The bread was warm, fragrant with yeast. Brunhild tucked the loaves into the woven basket on her arm, folding the interior cloth overtop.

"Busy now, are you?" Brunhild nodded her graying head toward the baby. Tate stared back, a smile curving her tiny lips, drool slipping down her chin.

"Aye, I've been busy with Tate since her mother passed, but she's no burden," Emma said, hoping the statement would invite no more questions. She wanted to close the door to keep the heat inside and set the baby down so she could get Æfflead away from her bin of rye flour. The two-year old had taken a liking to running her hands through the silky grain. With Merthe and Ginnie gathering things from her hut to move into Branton's, Emma didn't have an extra pair of arms to move the girl away.

"Y'know, that young one getting into the flour should be helping. She could pour it into the bowl, sweep the floor after she's made a mess..." Brunhild went on, ignoring Emma's tense smile. That was often her trouble; Emma's face wasn't one that shot daggers. Instead, it invited conversation.

"Emma," the lilting voice of Yrsa came through the gate. Brunhild stiffened, crossing her arms as if to ward off the woman that strode up the path behind her. Emma pressed her lips together. After she helped defeat her clan, most people in Hyrstow accepted Yrsa as a resident of the village and wife to the chieftain. Others did not, though they dared not press their luck by voicing it. Ridley Ward was the best chieftain Hyrstow had had in many years. He was fair and honest and protected his village without question. Yrsa, with her streaming golden hair, deep blue eyes and towering, combat-honed figure, was the epitome of a match for the chieftain, though some villagers still harbored suspicion.

Brunhild issued Emma a tight, disapproving smile.

As she turned to leave, the older woman had to look up, and up some more to peer into Yrsa's face. The Viking woman showed all her teeth in what wouldn't really be considered a grin, as she stepped aside to let the smith's wife pass.

"Good day to you!" Yrsa said as Brunhild made her way through the short wooden gate that circled Branton's hut. Yrsa was smiling as she took the door from Emma and followed her inside.

As Emma passed the dough-strewn table to place the baby inside the cradle on the other end of the room, Yrsa strode to where Æffie played. With a genuine smile that transformed her face to breathtaking, Yrsa scooped up the little girl in both arms and gave her neck a rough nuzzle. Emma tried to hold back her wince but Æfflead giggled, smacking her flour covered hands against Yrsa's leather-clad shoulders.

"How are you today, Æffie?" Yrsa asked the toddler.

Æfflead's mossy eyes narrowed, and her little mouth pursed with her usual severity.

"That bad?" Yrsa asked with mock surprise. She jiggled the little girl in her arms then gently flicked her nose. Æfflead's laugh was like sunshine. So rarely did Emma see the child smile or laugh—she'd begun to think the Viking was the only one that could make her do so. Emma secretly hoped Yrsa would soon receive a verbal response from the girl since she had yet to speak.

"Would you care for some bread and honey?" Emma offered.

She moved to the tall cupboard against the west wall

that housed the family's food. Before Yrsa could answer, she withdrew a pot of honey and a half-cut loaf, placing them on the slim side table meant for food preparation before slipping a large knife through the dark bread.

Yrsa plopped Æfflead back on the floor and drew a chair from the table beside the door. As always, she moved as if she owned the place. Emma admired her self-possession.

"Thank you," Yrsa said.

She spread her legs to make room for the dagger and sword that hung on her belt, the metal of the larger weapon clanging against the chair as she moved. Drawn to her, Æfflead slapped a floury hand on Yrsa's trousered thigh. Yrsa tickled the child's chin then reached for the jug of watered ale on the table. She poured two cups and placed one at the end of the table closest to Emma. For her part, Emma sliced a thick wedge of bread and drizzled it with a smattering of honey. She passed it to Yrsa who took a large bite then tipped her head back as she chewed, savoring the sweet concoction.

"So," Yrsa started, eyes fixed on Emma. "Branton stayed in our hut last night."

Emma's spine straightened at the mention of her husband. She had wondered where he'd gone after their encounter. She had walked back to his hut, heart hammering in her chest, alone and shivering.

"He did?" Emma didn't know what to say so attempted aloofness. Yrsa rolled her eyes. She smacked a hand on the heavy wood table.

"He did. He stormed in like his backside was on fire,

drank a pitcher of ale with Ridley and fell asleep near the door. His drunken snores kept me up most of the night."

"I thought you and Ridley were residing in the hall now."

"We are. But the wedding festivities reminded us of our own vows and we thought 'what better place to play bride and groom than where it all started.' Hence the jug of ale. What we did not anticipate was Branton escaping to the same place."

Emma tried to suppress her grin. The thought of Yrsa being put out was only too delicious. Her friend liked to make a scene when inconvenienced. "Poor Ridley."

Yrsa arched a blonde brow, a conspiratorial gleam in her eye. "Indeed. He had to please me this morning, in a hurry, rather than slowly, leisurely drunk from the wedding."

The blush that overtook Emma was so furious it reached the tips of her ears. She pressed her lips together to impede the laugh that threatened. "Oh, I am sure it was a hardship for your husband."

"It seems to have been for yours." Yrsa's tone was straightforward, her features blank.

It was an invitation for an explanation if Emma wanted to offer one. Emma sucked a breath through her teeth. She wasn't ready to discuss Branton's lack of desire for her.

Other than the madness in the woods, which Emma tried not to think about. It proved more difficult than anticipated. The stinging between her legs every time she moved was a constant reminder.

"He's...grieving," was all she could say. She and Yrsa were friends, however their perspectives on love and life and death differed. Emma didn't have the luxury of a family member slain in battle on which she could swear an oath of vengeance. Her grief at losing Jon was mingled with the sting of abandonment at being made a widow. It was surprising in its fierceness and unrelenting in its loneliness. She had to trudge along the normal way, without glory or revenge. For there was no revenge against the illness that stole through her hut three years prior and claimed Jon. There was only the drive to keep herself and her daughter clothed and fed.

Branton didn't hide his broken heart. He wore it like a ragged flag on his back for everyone to see. What made a lump form in her throat was the fact that she knew what it was to lose a spouse. She and Jon had been well married prior to his death. And she'd had a full three years to reconcile it. Bran had mere months.

"Does he not want to find solace in your bed?"

Emma bit her lip. Everything about their joining screamed that Bran found her repulsive, only worthy enough to tangle with under the cover of darkness. She'd pressed him by bringing the cloak, she knew. However, she didn't want him to think he had to disappear into the forest, alone, every time he had a problem.

"He does not. It appears I am not one to garner male affection."

Something softened in Yrsa's face, perhaps a memory of Emma's short flirtation with her own husband before they were married. "I had hoped that maybe your wedding night would have been enough of an excuse for Branton to assuage his loneliness with you."

Emma huffed a little laugh, tucking a strand of hair behind her ear. Tate fussed in the cradle. "I would be lying if I didn't wish for the same, for his sake."

Yrsa's brow shot upward as she took another bite of bread. She scrunched up her nose as she chewed. "His sake? What about yours? Have you been with a man since Jon passed?"

"No," Emma said, sheepish. "It's that Branton has been so low. He's either off in the bush, saying he's going to cut but not bringing anything to show for it, or is abed. I had thought by fulfilling my marital duties, he could forget his grief for a time."

Yrsa snorted. Æffie laughed at the sound, clapping her dirty hands. The girl crawled under the table and popped up on the other side, near Emma's feet.

"You are his wife, not a mere distraction. He's damn well lucky to have you. As are the children. It's why he wanted to marry you. And you have to remember your own needs and pleasures. Bran isn't a hardship to look at. When he comes around, you should take full advantage of what those muscles have to offer."

"Yrsa!"

"What?" her friend said, laughter cupping the word. "You are beautiful, Emma. Don't pretend to not know it. Perhaps Branton is entrenched in his grief, but you should work at enticing him, for both your sakes. Undress quickly at night, rub his back after a long day, offer him your mouth—"

"Yrsa!" Emma tried for stern but it came out exasperated. After Branton's firm rejection last night, the last thing Emma would be doing is dropping her pride to be rejected again.

Before Emma could object further, Yrsa was rising, brushing the crumbs from her hands onto the table. "Someone is coming."

Surprise flew through Emma at Yrsa's hearing. She knew it was her duty as a sentry that honed the skill. Soon enough, heavy footsteps pounded the frozen dirt outside. Emma made for the door to see if it was one of her regular customers.

Æfflead, seeing that Yrsa was about to leave, heaved her arms up and stood on her tiptoes to be lifted. Emma was about to tell Yrsa she needn't spoil the child, but Yrsa scooped Æffie up with one arm and tickled her neck with her free hand. The girl tipped back her long dark hair, a humming noise coming from the back of her throat.

Before Emma could open it, the door swung open to reveal Branton on the threshold, his cloak tied loosely about his neck. He brought with him the scent of frost and birch. His hands dangled at his sides. Hands that had gripped Emma's hips as he drove into her the night previous—Emma halted the train of thought before her cheeks could fully redden.

Bran peered from beneath hooded brows as he took in the scene: Yrsa holding his second youngest; Emma at the door, hands pressed against her apron. Redness colored his cheekbones, though she didn't know if it was from the pinch of cold outside or the sight of her.

"Greetings to you," Yrsa said, her lips twisting in the most annoying manner.

Branton looked from her face to the smiling Æffie in her arms, and his gaze softened. "Hello, Yrsa."

"Sleep well?" Yrsa prodded. She offered the same deranged grin she'd given Brunhild Smith.

Æffie shoved her fingers between Yrsa's teeth, a laugh bubbling from her. Yrsa spit them out but rather than scold the child, she smacked a loud kiss on her chubby cheek then placed her on the floor. Æffie made a high-pitched sound of distress as Yrsa stepped around her, hand on the pommel of her sword as she made for the door. Yrsa sketched a mocking bow to Branton as he stepped inside to let her pass.

"I expect to bed my husband in private tonight," she said as she stepped across the threshold.

Branton looked ready to wring her neck. Little did Yrsa care. With long-legged strides, she swaggered out of the yard.

Æffie's whines had dissolved into a full-blown cry by the time Branton sealed the door. Tate whimpered from the cradle. With a short sigh, Emma went to the baby. She couldn't look at Bran without being reminded of the lustful madness that had overtaken them. Instead, she focused on the child he ignored more than the rest.

Tate nosed at her chubby fist, then attempted to fit the whole thing in her mouth, drool pouring forth. Two little white teeth grazed the plump flesh of her hand as she gummed it before spitting it out and wailing for more. Emma's heart dipped. Tate had fed twice that morning. If she kept feeding at the same rate, she'd need more goat's milk by the end of the day. Neil was usually off cutting with Branton in the woods or doing chores around the hut, and when Emma asked him to perform such a menial task as gathering milk for his sister, he didn't bother to hide his annoyance.

"Can we speak?" Branton asked. His voice was too deep for the room. It was jarring somehow, his blatant masculinity in the face of his wailing girls and new wife.

Emma scooped up Tate to hold like a shield in front of her. She wasn't proud of it. Sleep hadn't been easy and she'd spent the morning worrying how Branton would react when he next saw her.

Though, as much as they were strangers in the marital sense, she did know him. She'd gotten a taste of the pride he had in his children when he would wrestle with them in the grass after a long day's work. She'd been teased by him when she and Merthe had been asked to sup with their family. And recently, she'd witnessed his struggle to enter the main room of the house each day, dazed and quiet, while Emma helped get the children fed and clothed.

She nodded, trying to keep her face open.

"Last night..."

Æfflead wailed louder. Branton shoved a breath through his nose and picked her up. She wrapped her arms around his neck with such ferocity, something in Emma cracked a little. These people had lost the pillar of their life. Each of them was looking for something to root themselves to. Emma doubted she was a strong enough branch to carry them all.

He tried again as he rubbed Æffie's back. "Last night..."

Æffie chose that moment to stick her fingers in her father's mouth. To his credit, the corners of Bran's eyes crinkled with a grin. He plucked Æffie's hand from his mouth then placed her on a chair at the table, handing her Yrsa's half eaten slice of bread. Distracted, Æfflead happily chewed on the sweet treat. Branton tipped his head to the room at the back of the hut.

Emma's mouth went dry. She continued to make the slight humming noise that Tate liked as she placed the baby back in the cradle. Bran held the door open behind him and, beneath his stare, Emma couldn't help her flush.

Her mind suddenly trotted out the memory of Branton shoving into her like a knife, strong and true. She'd been wanton. Completely out of her mind with lust. Branton had been hard and hot and huge inside her. It had opened a chasm of longing in her that she didn't know existed. In the light of morning, she knew she was wretched, to want so badly of this man who was not for her. He'd told her as much, and she'd pushed him.

Branton closed the bedroom door behind her while Emma put as much distance between them as possible. She wrung her hands as she met with the wall on the opposite side of the room. There was something in the weight of his gaze that made her pulse thrum like the beating of a small bird's wings.

As he turned, Branton rubbed the back of his neck with his broad hand. It drew her eyes to the vambrace that encased his forearm. The leather had frayed around one of the buckles. She'd need to remedy that.

"I am sorry," he began.

"It's alright." Emma's words were at the ready. Better to dismiss what happened and be done with it.

"It is not. My behavior was inexcusable. Did I...hurt you?"

"No. You didn't. I...was enthusiastic about it."

The grimace that bit into Branton's features caused her heart to plummet.

"I am deeply regretful that I disrespected you. It will not happen again."

Emma stiffened. Sweat lined the back of her neck where her bun sat. She licked her lips as she paused to think. Bran caught the movement with his eye then glanced away as if she'd done something lewd.

"Branton, I did not feel disrespected. I thought...I don't know what I thought. Perhaps that you'd had a change of heart then needed some time to ponder it."

"I did not." The edge to the words bit, though they were not a surprise. He remained close to the door as he continued.

"I should not have taken you that way. And I apologize if I have given you the wrong impression. I love Freda. She was..." he swallowed heavily against the words that seemed to snag in his throat. "Emma, I cannot be the husband you wish for. I'm disgusted with myself for giving into my baser instincts. I laid awake all night thinking of how appalling I was."

Emma's head dipped beneath the weight of his words. Disgusted with himself? She knew he still loved his wife and that she was no substitute. But was she so displeasing that she disgusted him?

The shell around her pride dented. She was a grown woman who didn't need a man, as she had proven every day since Jon's death. A slight from her husband should not have injured her in such a manner.

She reached up to rub the ache that bloomed in her chest and replied, "I am sorry to have caused you such pain."

Suddenly, he was across the room, grasping her chin to tilt it upward. His thumb was calloused yet gentle, and Emma wished she could lean into his touch. Branton's eyes locked on hers.

"You haven't. Emma, you've been the one true help I've had these long months. You deserve so much better than I can offer. But, for my children, I am selfish. They need a mother as good as you."

Bran released her chin and Emma felt as if she could breathe. He looked away, to the candle on the bedside table, the floor, anywhere but her face. With a sigh, he scrubbed a hand down his thigh, as if to wash away the feel of her skin.

"I hate myself for trapping you in this marriage."

Her hand was circling his wrist before she could stop herself. His flinch made her drop it just as quickly. Still, she had to make him see that he needn't feel as if she'd had no other choice. Emma had made the decision for herself as much as for the person he loved so deeply. Her vow to Freda nearly tumbled through her teeth, but Bran's rare focus on her halted the confession. Emma's needs were rarely considered by others, and Branton's new worry for her caused a spark of selfishness to ignite within her.

"There is no need to think you trapped me, Branton. The widow tax, while I gladly paid it, had become too much. Merthe needs a dowry. And I love the children. Of course, I want to help with them."

The words were the plainest truth, and she hoped he would see it as such. There was more to it, but Emma knew she couldn't tell him of her promise to Freda the morning after their marriage's consummation. It was what Emma told herself for the time being, anyway.

Branton was nodding as he took a step back from her. His face had gone from pleading to stoic in a mere blink. He shifted from one foot to the next, eyes cast upon the floor. Unease lined Emma's belly. Despite her protest, could he want out of the marriage? It made her cross her arms over her chest to protect herself from his next words.

"I know. It is because you are such a good woman that I am prepared to...service you in the way a husband services his wife, if that is what you wish."

She froze like a rabbit about to be struck down by a dog. Had her own proposition from the previous night sounded so wretched? A bitter taste rose to the back of her throat at the thought of making him perform in a way he obviously detested.

"What I wish?"

His next words came slow, as if he'd chewed them all night.

"If you require, I can bed you. I cannot promise affection, however."

Pride and confusion and indignation swirled inside her. She felt hot all over, slimy in her own skin. The air in the room was suddenly stifling.

"Well, thank you so much for considering my wanton desire." Emma felt her face flush and twist as she spat the words. She planted her hands on her hips and glared up at him. Surprise etched along his features.

"Truly, thank you for being so gracious as to think of me." She snorted. "No. I won't make you have relations with me against your will, Branton. I will do right by our children and keep this house, but you needn't feel beholden to bed me when you clearly do not want to. I am not a monster sharpening my claws in the night."

Branton's eyes snapped to hers, the light blue darkening.

"I am simply trying to strike a bargain with you," he said through gritted teeth.

"A bargain?" Emma gave a mocking little laugh. She wished she was above such a trivial reaction, but no man's words had cut her so deep. "We already stuck one. When I agreed to be your wife, our bargain was made. I am sorry about what I proposed last night as I thought it was what was expected of me. No matter. I will fulfill my end of our agreement and care for the children. You do not have to worry about any other obligations to me."

"Fine," he bit out.

"Fine!"

He issued a glower hard enough to make a grown man quake before exiting the room. Emma heard his voice lighten as he bid goodbye to Æfflead followed by the bang of wood as the front door shut. All the energy coiled inside her disappeared. How, in one day, had it all gone so wrong so quickly? Emma was left with the urge to slump to the floor.

Then a knock sounded. Tate started to warble.

Emma did what she'd done her whole life. She straightened her spine, pasted on a smile, and went to help others.

CHAPTER

FOUR

There was rustling in the forest to the west. Branton halted his chopping and tipped his ear up to better hear if whatever made the sound was animal or person. The scrape of bush and the crunch of fallen branches had begun some time ago, halted, then shifted. He and Neil should have been the only ones in Hyrstow's wood that far in.

There it was—straight north, in the direction of the river. Branton straightened, eyes searching on the frosty boughs around them. He couldn't see anything delineating a person through the mess of pine and bare birch. A chill that had nothing to do with the cold wound around his spine.

"What is it, Father?" Neil asked, pausing for a moment, his gaze following the direction of Branton's. His chest rose and fell with exertion, his hands wrapped around his own ax. Neil's cloak, now too short for him and frayed at the edges, lay in a heap on the ground. A thin layer of sweat coated his skin despite the chilly weather.

"I don't know," Branton replied.

Neil shrugged, then continued to bundle the cut logs into the bavin. They were to bring the three-by-six foot bavins back to Hyrstow to be used for buildings. The Earl of Deircia had been generous with his allocation of Hyrstow's forest since the Viking raids. It gave Bran an excuse to be in the woods all day, even if what he brought back didn't constitute a day's work.

Branton tried to shrug off the feeling that he was being watched. He had other concerns as of late. Sliding the handle of his ax further into his palms to give himself better grip, Branton heaved it into the air overhead and brought it down into the felled tree before him.

"Branton!"

Ridley's deep voice cut through the copse of trees like an ax through old wood. There was a boom to it that he'd learned from having to give orders to his men.

Branton sighed, placed the head of his ax on the tree, and leaned his elbow on the knob to wait. The dangers of woodcutting often presented themselves in the most innocuous of ways, and having another man appear in the vicinity was one of them.

Within moments, Ridley walked through the trees. With his height, he wasn't difficult to spot. Not for the first time, Branton marveled at the fact that his friend had survived years as a knight without being struck down. He would have been the most obvious man on the battlefield. Perhaps that was the reason he was so good with a sword.

"What brings you out here, Rid?" Branton asked. Neil stopped his work, sniffing away the moisture that dripped from his nose. As Ridley approached, Neil inclined his head in greeting to their chief.

"Bran, Neil," Ridley nodded to each.

"To what do we owe the pleasure of such a visit?" Bran hitched his chin in the direction of the small cart he used to maneuver stacks of wood though the forest. It was slim, with a front wheel that allowed Bran to pivot among the trunks. Neil dug around in the bottom of the cart for the small cask of ale they'd brought along.

Ridley accepted the outstretched cask and took a drink. He handed it back to the boy and waved off the offer of bread.

"The earl has sent word. He's ordered to have the wood southwest of Guston felled."

Branton took a swig of the ale, relishing its hoppy bite as he considered Ridley's statement. The winter air cooled the sweat on his skin.

"When?"

"As soon as you can."

Neil looked sharply at Branton, the question as to whether Bran would bring him evident in his green eyes. He'd have to consider it on the way back. It was one thing to have his son help him with the cutting around Hyrstow, quite another to send him into territory recently overtaken by the Earl of Deircia.

"I'll need to finish up this section for the church. It'll

take another day. I'll need another to see if I can get Sam or Jory to come with me. Maybe Joseph can spare Ewan for a few days."

Ridley nodded, though his gaze was fixed on the swaying branches of the trees. "What of the wood I asked you for a few weeks ago?"

Branton's hackles rose. Ridley had asked him to cut wood for new fencing. It was a job that Ridley had given out of pity, knowing that Bran's income had been lean since Freda's death. There was plenty of work for a cutter in Hyrstow, though on the days he cut, Bran found it difficult to get much done. He was slower than normal and sometimes used his time in the forest to rage against God or hide the amount that he cried. Ridley must have known, however, and a resentment had built within Branton over the past months, like a film of scum over pond water, at the charity offered to him and his family. He should have been able to provide. The goodwill shoved his face into the dung heap of his own failure. He turned to face Ridley with his arms crossed over his chest.

"Haven't cut it yet."

Rather than get cross with him, Ridley's eyes softened, and his mouth drooped into a sympathetic frown that Bran had the sudden urge to punch off his face. He loosed a breath through his teeth to stanch his flare of anger. He knew it was unwarranted.

"I will," he insisted before Ridley could comment on it further. Bran knew Ridley was looking out for him. He knew that he needed smaller, manageable jobs to focus on. His family's food stores had dwindled over the winter. Meat was almost unheard of in their house, and any morsels of it were bought by Emma. The children's clothes were wearing thin, and his own needed mending. Yet heaving his sore body from the hard cot on the floor had become increasingly difficult. He didn't see much point in rising when he could escape into sleep and not feel the dry ache of loss that had turned his shattered heart to dust.

Ridley looked to the bavin of stacked wood. He scratched his chin with his thumb, as if carefully considering his words. "Are you cutting for my brother? Village jobs should take priority."

"Aye, but higher payment is my priority. Besides, Father Chisholm on behalf of the High Priest advised the church wishes to add to the priest's living quarters. This load should be a start. Joseph may have mentioned something."

"There are new people coming to Hyrstow each week looking for lodging. We've hosted as many as we can in the hall, but it is getting cramped. There is need for a tavern or inn, and Oswald knows this."

Bran shrugged, wrung out by the conversation. It was no concern of his, the swell of people that had begun to flock to Hyrstow in the past year. The High Priest, Ridley's brother Oswald, had been harping on the church's need to accommodate more priests for years now. Intake of novices sent by wealthier landowners garnered the church a good income. If there was room. And St. Paul's was currently full.

Ridley hooked his hands on his hips and speared Branton with a glance that betrayed nothing of what he was thinking. "All that aside, what if you used someone from near Guston? You could take your pick of farmhand."

"Do ye want me dead?" Branton admonished.

As far as he knew, the people of Guston did not take kindly to Hyrstow overtaking the land south of their border. He did not expect hospitality from the people left farming there. Those who'd decided to stay in the reclaimed territory hated Earl Lachlan's rule and caused a stir for Ridley who had been tasked with overseeing the taxes on their lands.

Ridley smiled back, but a tightness hugged his mouth. "Of course not. I thought it would be a good opportunity to increase relations with the town."

"And why would we need to do that, Rid? Lachlan is going to send a campaign to take Guston out as well?"

Ridley's ochre eyes narrowed, though his grin didn't falter. Neil looked between his chieftain and his father as if in fear they would come to blows. They wouldn't. Yet Branton felt the power in his friend at that moment. Ridley had offered up someone from Guston as a suggestion rather than giving an order. He'd learned a few things as a knight, that was for certain. And if the Earl of Deircia was about to take Guston for his own, Branton wanted nothing to do with it. It wasn't his battle. He would accept the order to cut the wood nearby, take it where it needed going and accept payment.

Regardless, he couldn't ignore a direct order from the

earl. He would have to finish the job for the church and go. It meant leaving Emma to move house by herself. As far as he knew, most of her things were at her own hut and, though they hadn't much discussed the matter, there had been the assumption that she would move to where his children needed her. Now he felt like a true dolt for not helping her to move her things sooner. Instead, he'd been focused on escaping the house as fast as he could after their argument.

"Emma will need help moving some of her belongings to my hut. Lord knows she and Merthe didn't have much after the Viking raid, but see if you can have someone help her when I'm gone. She'll have enough to do with all the children and her work."

Ridley issued him a wicked grin. "Dare I send Yrsa?"

Branton snorted. Ridley's own smile broke and suddenly they were having a hearty chuckle at the prospect of Yrsa degrading herself by moving house. In the months spent with them, she'd proven to be a terrible housekeeper and worse cook.

"No!" Neil protested. Loudly. "What about Uncle Grahame?"

Bran's laughter died on his lips. A chill wound its way up his spine at the thought of his golden-haired, green-eyed brother-in-law helping Emma. The jokes they would share as Grahame picked up a basket of her things. The way she might eye his lean muscles since she and Bran had vowed to not touch one another. She was a woman, not a nun, after all. A woman with physical needs. And who better to oblige than the one man in the village who could charm the scales off a snake.

Ridley was nodding and Neil grinning, and Branton suddenly had the urge to shout the woods down around them.

"Not Grahame," he said, his tone too sharp. "What about Wilfred?"

Ridley gave him a purposefully inquisitive look that Bran ignored. "You'll send Grahame's father but not the man himself?"

The fact that he didn't use Freda's name in conjunction with the Shepherd family wasn't lost on Bran. He knew his friend was trying to spare him grief, but the lack of her name being mentioned stung.

"Aye, I will. Golden Boy is busy with the sheep. Wilfred would love to help."

Branton didn't mention that he'd barely spoken to his father-in-law since Freda's death. It wasn't for the elder's lack of trying. Wilfred would be glad to help his daughter's family in any way, even if it was welcoming her replacement.

Bran's throat grew tight.

If Freda were there, she'd hit him upside the head and tell him to get Grahame *and* Wilfred to help, then have her mother over to cook while Emma organized. She wouldn't have her friend suffer a lack of comfort just because Branton was too proud to ask.

God, he missed Freda. She'd know what needed to be done.

Branton coughed around the tears that burned his

eyes and looked up to the treetops where bare, gray branches scraped the sky. Ridley took Neil by the shoulder, turning the boy, asking if he could see the hawk perched on a faraway log. There was no hawk, but by the time they turned back, Branton had gotten control of himself.

"Alright. I'll send for Wilfred. And Paul. I've heard Ingrid's been missing Emma as of late. Are you nearly done here?"

Neil shook his head. "Still have to finish bucking up this tree."

"Ah, well, in that case, my horse is back through the woods about fifty feet. Can you go get the food from the saddle, Neil?"

Neil nodded and ran off through the trees, his long, adolescent legs carrying him.

"Couldn't be more obvious about it, could you?" Bran asked. He hefted his ax and walked a ways from Ridley to one of the felled trees.

Ridley grinned, but Branton ignored him, instead chopping a deep groove into the wood. He had to move, to do something. It was too hard to withstand Ridley's pity.

"Staying in my hut again tonight?"

Ridley must not have spoken to his wife or he would have heard about her telling Branton he was unwelcome. Bran heaved the ax upward then brought the blade down. It gave a satisfying *thunk*.

"No. Emma and I have come to an agreement."

"Another one?"

Bran's jaw hardened. He didn't have the patience for Ridley's prodding.

"Indeed. She and I are man and wife in name and status. We can live side by side under the same roof."

Branton brought the ax upward again then sank it into the wood. The iron bit through the fresh trunk like a dog through meat.

"Like you did last night?"

"What do you really want to say, Rid?" Bran halted his cutting, spreading his hands wide along the smooth wooden handle, and turned to the other man. Ridley's mouth was cemented in a knowing sort of grin that made Branton want to throttle him.

"You wouldn't speak of your wedding night and refused to be under the same roof as Emma. Now you don't want Grahame to help her, and you'll be living with her in 'status' only? Forgive me, Bran. I know that your grief is a living thing, but it seems as if you do not know what you want."

Branton's lip curled to reveal teeth. He twisted the handle of the ax until his knuckles were painfully white.

"What of it, Rid? What gives you the right to come here and question me about my relationship with my... with Emma?"

Ridley held both hands up in a placating gesture. His sharp features softened as if he knew all too well what was going on in Bran's head. As if he could read the twisted urges that had grasped Bran last night and pitied him. That he knew of Emma's plight because they had a near-history.

Something black slithered through Bran's mind at the memory of Ridley and Emma dancing at the celebration last summer. If it weren't for Yrsa crashing into Ridley's life, he and Emma would have likely married.

"You know what? Do not answer. I do not care what you have to say on the matter. Just have someone other than Grahame help her while I'm gone."

Bran turned his back on Ridley and strode to the other end of the log. He hefted the ax and continued his work without looking back. Bran could hear the low-spoken apology from Neil, and Ridley's accepting murmur. He tried to ignore the scrape of embarrassment he felt along his skin that his son felt the need to make excuses for him.

"Neil. Get over here and help me," Branton commanded. His tone was sharp. He didn't mean for it to be. He didn't know how to tell Neil it wasn't his fault he was angry. Words seemed unable to pass by the knot that clogged his upper chest.

Neil rushed to join him. The sound of their tools cutting and scraping echoed through the birch and pine trees that arched to the sky. From above, fat flakes began to fall.

They didn't speak again until long after Ridley was gone.

"Mother, where would you like these?" Merthe asked. She held a pair of brass goblets, one in each hand. The brushed metal glinted in the sunlight streaming through the hut's door which had been propped open with a large rock. Unconventional in winter, but the hut was stifling with so many people moving in and out. Plus, Emma wanted to be able to watch for customers as she organized her things.

"You can put them in the chest by my bed for now."

Merthe walked around where Ginnie and Æffie played on the floor. She nearly ran into Fiona, Freda's mother, as they both tried to pass through the bedroom door.

"Goodness, dear! You gave me a start," Fiona said with a light chuckle, holding a hand to her bosom. Her softly wrinkled face bore a forgiving grin. Emma was glad for it. Fiona knew both Emma and Merthe from the market, as well as being Freda's friend, though they hadn't had many instances to get to know one another other than short, polite conversation. She lived further afield, past Hyrstow.

"Apologies, Mrs. Shepherd." Merthe was quick to amend with a little curtsy.

The older woman waved the gesture off then patted Merthe on the shoulder. It warmed Emma's heart to see the girl so accepted by the matron. She hoped the generosity of spirit would extend to herself.

"Please, don't call me that. I am Fiona to you. Have known ye since you were a wee babe," Fiona admonished, affection cradling her tone.

"Of course, Fiona. Thank you," Merthe said. She ducked her auburn head, a slight smile curling her lip.

It caused a sort of wistful sadness to creep into Emma's heart. Merthe had been joyful once. After Jon's death, she'd grown an edge that hadn't been there before. For such a willowy, pretty child, it was somewhat of a shock to others that she wasn't full of pleasant smiles and happy greetings. Though Emma had never required her to speak words of little consequence. Only in the last year or so, as her friendship with Yrsa grew and she felt more secure in her role as a helper with Freda's children, had the joyful Merthe peeked out again.

"Right, then, Emma. D'ye think we have everything sorted?" Fiona tucked a stray hair beneath the lip of the kerchief that encircled her head.

Rocking Tate on one hip, Emma froze her features into a bland grin. The hut was stuffed full. A sturdy shelf had been pushed against the wall beside the table which now housed stacks of pots and cups. Her herbs sat on a chair waiting to be hung. Blankets, Merthe's clothing and personal items, and Emma's sewing kit had been chucked onto the children's bed. Thankfully, the matter of her bed had been sorted first thing. She'd had Ridley bring it that morning to exchange it with Branton's.

"Most of it is here, yes," Emma hedged.

"There are some bowls and bags of flour left at your hut. Will you be bringing them here?"

Emma sighed. Exhaustion dug its claws in around her lower back. "No. The bread oven is there. I need most of my supplies to remain there, along with some bowls and kitchen things."

"T'will be hard to keep two huts," Fiona commented, moving forward to sift through a handful of utensils on the table. Her movements were efficient as she sorted the knives and spoons.

"Indeed. If my hut was larger, I would have suggested everyone move there. But it has the bread oven. I'll just have to go there in the early morning and stay for a good part of the day to bake."

"Have you planned for suppers and mending and other chores?"

Fiona's questions were practical, not meant as a slight, though they nipped. Perhaps it was beneficial that Branton now had two properties, however the prospect of keeping both homes daunted Emma. Before the marriage, she helped as much as she could with the cooking, cleaning, and baby, but the managing of food stores, procuring fabric for clothing and overseeing of all the children wasn't her responsibility. As his wife, those duties now fell to her. Neil was a large help with the live-stock—a horse, chickens, and four goats—and Merthe could help sew the clothing, but Emma had authority over every detail in both homes.

Emma broadened her smile in Fiona's direction so as not to appear overwhelmed.

"Of course. I have Merthe and Ginnie's help. It will all be taken care of."

Fiona moved forward, her hands clasped within the pockets of her apron. There was a mix of sadness and pity in the set of her mouth. Before she could say what she intended, Merthe returned to the main room. She went straight to the door, cloak in hand.

"I'll be back in a little while, Mum. Just going to collect the eggs at Yrsa's." Emma nodded absently as her daughter left.

Dusk would come soon, and she needed to prepare supper. Somewhere on the table was a bit of dried fish which she would serve with some bread, though in hind-sight, she should have had Ginnie make more of the pottage simmering on the fire. Neil ate like he was starving at every meal and Merthe wasn't far behind him. Perhaps they could have the bread, fish and finish what pottage was left.

"Emma?" Fiona prodded. Her hands were extended out for Tate, and she wore a smile that told Emma she'd been waiting a moment too long.

"Ah, sorry." Emma handed off the baby, whom Fiona accepted with a grin. Tate fussed a little at the transition, reaching for Emma before chewing on her fingers. Drool seeped out around her chubby fist.

"Shhh, Tatswip." Fiona bobbed the baby up and down.

Free of the small burden, Emma went to the table and hefted her large iron pot. The thing wasn't as large as the one Bran's family owned, so it hadn't been put to use. She'd need to find a place for it eventually. Instead of tackling that decision, Emma placed the heavy iron on the floor beside the door.

"Has Bran warmed up to her?" Fiona settled her stooped body onto one of the chairs at the table and arranged Tate on her lap. The baby jutted her legs out in protest of being forced to sit.

Emma knew Fiona was speaking of Tate. She carried the stack of three bowls she had in hand to the shelf. Knowing the other girls were in the room, she was mindful of her words.

"He's…been busy. What with the wedding and now the earl's contract to cut near Guston…" she trailed off, at a loss to what excuses she could give for Branton's coldness toward his youngest child.

Fiona offered a wan smile then focused on Tate. She cooed at the baby, smoothing wrinkly fingers overtop the plump skin of Tate's arms. Emma glanced at Ginnie, who was holding up a jug with a question in her gaze. She crossed the room to direct the girl to place it on the sideboard for the time being. When Emma turned back, Fiona was staring at her, her eyes misty.

"He may never like her, you know."

Emma didn't know what to say, so she nodded. She knew men weren't particularly soft toward their children. Her father hadn't been though she'd known that he worked hard to marry her off with a decent dowry. He may not have been affectionate but the rueful grin he'd given her every so often while she helped her mother sew in the evenings let her know he cared. The youngest of twelve, most of her surviving siblings had been gone from the home long before she'd taken her first steps. They were scattered across Northumbria now, between her hometown of White-bridge and south. When Emma was of marrying age, her cousin, Ingrid, who had wed a Hyrstow man, sent word to her parents of the Baker's son, Jon. By the next spring, her parents had seen her to Hyrstow with a small chest of fine threads, cloth, and coin as her dowry.

Fiona continued in her severe tone, "In his eyes, she's the reason Freda died."

A chill ran along Emma's bones. In the corner, she noticed Ginnie's ear twitch upward. The girls didn't need to hear this. They didn't need to associate Tate's life with their mother's death any more than they already did. Emma cleared her throat.

"It isn't true. Freda was near death delivering Æffie as well. It is a woman's burden, the chance that she will not live to see her children grow. Surely, Bran must know that."

Fiona nodded, though the brief smile that bracketed her face didn't travel to her eyes.

"I think he knows and does not care. He loved Freda very much."

Emma inclined her head. Though she liked Fiona and appreciated the woman's help, the emphasis on the last few words left no room for debate. Bran loved Freda. Emma was not Freda. End of story.

Rather than argue, Emma gathered the heap of her clothing from the pile on the children's bed and took it into Branton's bedroom. She dumped the pile on the bed and considered not moving it until the following day. She'd not slept there since Branton left earlier that week to fell the forest near Guston. After their last argument, she'd taken to sleeping beside Merthe on the children's bed against the north wall. She'd shared a bed with her daughter since Jon had passed. It felt unnatural to suddenly be thrust into one all alone. Other than Tate, all the children slept on the large bed in the main room. Neil against the wall, then Æffie, Ginnie and Merthe. After Bran's absence the night of the wedding, Emma had curled around her daughter for warmth and decided the family bed was as good a place for her as any since being a member of the family was what she'd been married for.

The door slammed. Emma heard Neil's voice from the other room.

"Gran! Why is the door hanging open? It's cold out there!"

"Emma wanted it that way." She could hear the shrug in the other woman's words.

"Does she not know how to run a house? The baby will catch her death."

"Don't be rude, Neil," Ginnie piped up. Æffie whined at her older sister's sharp tone.

"Come off it, Gin. I'm not. Everybody knows not to leave the door wide open."

"Don't say Tate will end up like Mother."

"Are you dull? Mother didn't die from cold. She died from that one." Neil must've paused to gesture to Tate but continued over Fiona's gasp of protest. "All I'm saying is I don't want the rest of us to meet the same end just because Emma does."

"She doesn't want that!" Ginnie shouted. "Emma loves us!"

Emma sighed. A bone-deep tiredness had taken up residence in her limbs over the past few days. Each of the four nights of Bran's absence carried a similar argument. Neil, either upset that his father had not brought him to Guston or chafing against the introduction of Emma and Merthe into their home, had no qualms voicing all the things Emma did wrong.

What none of them realized was that she wasn't simply the woman who had come to care for them. She'd lost a dear friend too.

Emma covered the gaping hole of loss she felt in her middle with a smile and strode back to the other room. Neil stood near the fireplace. He warmed his chapped, red hands over the heat as he glared at his sister. With exaggerated forcefulness, he rubbed his hands together to ease the chill. Emma had no doubt he was cold. Before Branton had gone, he'd left a towering section of logs for Neil to cut into more useable pieces. Neil seemed intent on completing all the work long before his father was to return.

"Hello Neil," Emma said brightly. She refused to indulge in his sullen attitude. Neil's frown smoothed to a grimace in greeting.

Between the two chairs, Ginnie had Æfflead in her arms. The older girl's large green eyes widened at the exchange between Emma and Neil.

"Well, let's get ready for supper, shall we?" Emma brushed her hands together and started for the table. Fiona rose, Tate tight in her arms.

"I should go."

"You're welcome to stay," Emma offered. She issued a wide smile to cover her internal calculation of how much food she should prepare for an extra mouth.

"Ah, dearie, thank you. I'll help with the children while you cook, but I won't stay. I'm sure Wilfred is already at home. I have to get back to feed him anyway."

"Will Uncle Grahame be there?" Neil asked, removing his cloak and hanging it on a peg near the door. He pushed his dark, curled hair back from his face. The question made him appear younger. It stripped him of his surliness.

"I don't know, sweets. He may be. He's been spending a lot of nights at the hall lately."

Neil nodded, his mouth turning downward at the news. "I'll walk you home, Gran. Then stay for supper if you don't mind. I won't eat much."

Fiona's gaze darted to Emma's. Emma nodded. She didn't want to stand between the boy and his grandparents. As it was, Fiona and Wilfred had much land and many sheep to care for, and it would be dark by the time Fiona returned home.

"Why don't you spend the night, Neil? It will be late after supper, and I don't want you traveling home in the dark," Emma suggested. She busied herself at the table, moving her cutlery into a nearby cabinet. The words felt right but came out sticky, as if she was trying too hard to accommodate him.

"I don't care about the dark," he was quick to retort.

Emma forced herself not to wince as she found room for the knives within the cabinet. Of course he would think she meant it as a slight.

"Though I will stay. That way I can help Grandfather with the flock in the morning."

"I want to stay at Gran's!" Ginnie said, coming to stand near the table. Neil shoved her in the shoulder. She punched him in the leg.

"That's enough out of you!" Fiona snapped. She gave each child a steely glare and resumed bobbing Tate. The baby's plump bottom lip turned downward, eyes brimming with tears. Emma made to reach for the baby out of habit but in that same moment, Æfflead tripped. She sprawled on the ground, hands flat on the straw covered floor. When she lifted her face and started to cry, Emma saw that her chin was scraped. She went to the child, propping Æffie on her knee to check her over for further injury.

It was then that Grahame and Merthe walked in. Merthe was staring up at Grahame with a wide smile, as if he'd hung the moon in the sky. Grahame halted whatever story he was telling, took one look around the hut—Fiona consoling a tearful Tate, Neil and Ginnie glaring at one another, Emma checking a sobbing Æfflead and the piles of extra items to be organized—and laughed.

"What is going on here?" Grahame asked as he strode into the hut. He gave Neil a hearty pat on the shoulder, dropped a kiss on Ginnie's head then turned to take Tate from his mother, which caused the baby to scream louder. He shook his head and made a face, sending his sandy curls flying. Surprised, Tate stopped crying and stared at him, her little mouth pursing into a frown.

"Oh, nothing to worry about," Fiona dismissed. She moved to the other side of the table where the root cellar lay buried in the floor. She opened it, popped down the short ladder and commanded Neil to come grab the items she held up. Emma finished consoling Æffie with a hug and kiss on the child's cheek, then stood. Grahame grinned at her and stepped forward to drop a heavy arm around her shoulders. She gave a gentle squeeze of his middle, mindful of Tate in his arms. He smelled of hops and leather.

"I've come to take Ma back home, but if my timing's off, I can head to the hall for some ale then come back," he said, releasing her. Emma shook her head.

"Nonsense. Now's as good a time as any. I was just about to prepare supper. Neil's going to walk with her."

"Can I come with you, Uncle?" Neil placed two potatoes on the table and came up to Grahame, a hopeful grin on his face.

Grahame gave her the same look Fiona had before, as if to check if it was alright before committing. She nodded and made a shooing motion with her hands behind Neil's back. Grahame grinned, a dimple appearing on one cheek, and clapped his nephew on the shoulder.

"Yes."

Despite Ginnie's protests of unfairness, the trio left soon thereafter, bundled in their cloaks and laden with bread that Emma insisted Fiona take as payment for her help. She and the girls had a quiet dinner. Merthe regaled them with a tale of being interrupted collecting eggs by Ridley's dog, Nod. She described how the big black, three-legged beast scared her at first, but that he simply wanted to be stroked behind his ears. Ginnie cooed over the tale, and Merthe, pleased by the reaction, smiled broadly. It stirred a ray of hope in Emma's chest. She'd not known how Merthe would feel, being an only child thrust into a life of stepsiblings and additional chores, though she appeared happy.

By the time supper was finished and cleaned up, Emma told the children a story then they all settled to bed. For once, Tate and Æffie settled quickly. A small gift which Emma took advantage of by retreating with a candle to the bedroom. Blessedly alone, she sorted through her things for a little while, glad she had them back. She hadn't been able to properly return home since the wedding and being at Branton's without her own items had been...odd. It still didn't feel real that his hut—Freda's hut—was now her home.

Emma touched her garments, the soft wools slipping through her fingers, and thought of her wedding night. Her mind trotted her back to it whenever she had a private moment.

Warmth spread through her chest and neck as she recalled Branton's wide hand tightening on her hip once he was seated inside her. It had felt as if Branton's cock would spear her in two with its girth. His pause as they adjusted to the sensation of one another had nearly driven her mad. She'd wanted to moan, to hike herself onto him further, but instead, she bit her lip against the invasion so as not to worry him. He'd had enough on his mind, and Emma hadn't been touched in an intimate way for so, so long. It shamed her to think of how greedy she'd been.

In spite of her tiredness, her mind corralled her to wonder what Branton would look like without clothes. Emma had felt the thickness of him, the angry, delicious heat of him. Her thoughts began to fragment as they hooked to the memory of how he felt moving inside her. It caused an urgent pulse between her legs.

"Stop it," she whispered to the empty room. It would be all too easy to relax into the bed and rub herself to make her feel as a man would. But she was nearly a stranger to the pleasure of her own hand since Merthe was with her near constantly. Not tonight.

Emma straightened, glancing behind her as if caught. Despite the deep void of loneliness she harbored, there was no way she would use thoughts of Branton's body to pleasure herself. She'd claimed not to be a monster and use him in such a manner. Well, she wouldn't in her own actions either. There was no point in thinking of him as anything other than someone she lived with.

Quickly, Emma readied for bed. She tried to ignore the guilt that pulled at her. Her impulses would not over-take her, she vowed. When she went out into the main room, she took Neil's empty spot on the bed, cuddling into Ginnie. The girl didn't stir. Emma was thankful for it.

She didn't sleep until her mind had wrung itself dry.

SIX

Bran's head nodded with the urge to sleep. He rearranged his backside in the saddle, sitting straighter to fend off the clutches of slumber. His arms and shoulders ached. In the past seven days, he'd hefted his ax more than he had in months. It begrudged him to learn how out of shape he was. He, Ewan Builder, and Sam Sawyer had worked from sun up to sun down felling trees, then deep into the night to buck up the lumber. Each night, they'd fallen asleep after devouring their rations of bread, cheese, and whatever small animals they could roast over the fire. The entire time, they looked over their shoulders, uneasy cutting forest on such newly reclaimed land. If the Earl of Bernira decided to send men to stop them, they would be slaughtered. Even in the daylight, there had been a rustling that Branton couldn't attribute to animals passing through. At night, the possibility of their throats being slit for revenge made him toss and turn until a restless sleep claimed him.

Only one man in Guston agreed to work with them. He'd been a mangy thing named Holbrook who lived in little more than a shed on the outskirts of town. He'd been all too happy to accept the promise of coin, and he'd worked as hard as any of them. He didn't bring any food and ravenously ate whatever they offered. Despite his dogged work ethic and bottomless appetite, the youth was quiet, somber. He bore a haunted look that caused one not to want to gaze upon him for too long.

Branton sent him back home the day before they finished up with the insinuation more of their men were arriving with carts to remove the wood. It was a necessary lie. The wood was wet, the mornings cold, yet the afternoons had warmed. The ground had begun to thaw. Half-frozen mud clung to their boots and the ends of their cloaks. Carts laden with their bounty would have sunk into the softly rutted roads. They'd need to wait to haul it home.

He, Sam and Ewan had covered the cut wood with deadfall and whatever leaves they could find. Hopefully anyone peering through the trees would think it was nothing.

Bran cracked his neck, trying to alleviate the tension that had settled there. To their right, forest gave way to bush then rolling fields. Ahead, damp grass encroached on the road, marking the end of Guston territory, newly claimed by Hyrstow. Not many traversed the hills that led to the Shepherd's land.

Sam, his sandy-ginger hair bright against the hills that rambled past, was slouching on his horse. He let out a mighty yawn, then shook himself a little, just as Bran had done a moment before. On Branton's other side, Ewan gazed out at the fields, not looking at anything.

Branton gave a short whistle. "Ewan."

The other man turned his head back to look at Bran. His mop of black hair had been tied back with a strip of cloth, and his cloak hung around his neck like a drunk friend.

"How'd ye fare in Guston last night?"

Ewan's sleepy eyes turned up with his devilish grin. He gave a loud guffaw then went into detail about the pretty maid he'd met on the road to the village's tavern. Branton didn't particularly care about Ewan's luck with women, but the other man's stories kept him from drifting off. By the time Ewan finished his tale—which involved the maid, her friend, a chicken, and a jug of ale —they were nearing the Shepherd homestead.

As the road curved southwest, he recognized the lone rowan tree atop the tall western hill. The branches reached out like long-fingered hands while the gray-tinged bark seemed to stare at him. Branton cast his eyes to his horse's mane as his throat clogged with grief. He and Freda had spent too many days of their young lives beneath the tree. It was where she'd demanded his affection; where their lives began to twine as one.

"Who is ahead?" Ewan asked.

Bran turned to find two figures in the bowl of the valley, one tall blonde, the other short with dark hair.

They were on foot, swathed in cloaks, the taller walking with a stick to coral the small band of sheep that were nearly the same dirty white as the melting snow. Even from a distance, Bran could make out the taller of the two reaching out to ruffle the shorter one's hair.

Something like the excitement he used to experience when returning home crept up on Branton. It was a surprise. He hadn't been away from home since the previous fall. He didn't think he'd care about where he was—when home, he didn't want to be there since memories of Freda plagued him—but he missed little things like Æfflead's tiny hands, the way Ginnie's eyes still lit up upon seeing him, and the wry twist of Neil's mouth. A warm meal, sleeping by the fire—those would be comforts after his trip.

"It's Grahame and Neil," he said to bury the homey sense that built in him.

Sam cupped his hand around his mouth and gave a little shout. The figures paused, turning to find the sound. When they spotted the horses, Neil lifted his arm in a wave. Bran half expected him to run to the cart, a wide smile locked on his face, like he used to do after Bran had been gone for long periods. But Neil wasn't a small child any longer. A wistfulness pulled at him as Neil simply stood with Grahame, waiting.

Grahame held out the wood staff to corral a sheep that attempted escape as the horses neared. He nodded once at the trio, his lips twisted upward.

"Father!" Neil said, his voice betraying excitement he tried to conceal in the presence of older company. It suddenly pained Bran that his son was a little boy no more. That he hadn't been in a long while, but Bran, in his grief, had somehow missed the transition. Neil's threadbare cloak was pushed off his shoulders and the knees of his trousers were worn through. He dismounted his horse, heedless of being the stoic father he wished he was.

"Neil," he said gruffly, hooking an arm around his son. Surprised at first, Neil's hands hung at his sides for a moment before his arms wrapped around his father's waist. "Missed ya, Son."

"Me too, Father," he said as he pulled away. Neil's eyes crinkled at the sides with his happiness. "I thought you'd be gone longer."

Bran felt his grin widen. "We got enough done."

Grahame's green gaze met Bran's overtop of Neil's head. A question wove itself between his sandy brows. Ewan swung himself from his own horse. His long face scrunched in an exaggerated wince.

"This one wanted to get home to his pretty wife." He clapped Grahame on the shoulder in greeting, which the other man reciprocated.

Bran cleared his throat so his words wouldn't carry the bite of annoyance. "I want no such thing. We cut plenty, then it was time to leave."

He wouldn't have the others believing lies about his and Emma's arrangement. The prospect that he was a regular newlywed, starved for the affection of his nubile wife was laughable. Not that Ewan and Sam had believed his protests when, earlier, they'd asked him what it was like to be married to one of the most beautiful women in the earldom. A red hot poke of anger had made him glower at them and tell them to mind their own damn business.

Grahame smirked at Bran, but he was gracious enough to maneuver the topic back to cutting. "Did you find help in town?"

"Only one lonely fella that lived on the outskirts agreed to work. His eyes lit up when he saw the wage we offered. I know we're a bit mangy looking, but you'd think we were lepers by the way the people glared at us."

"It's not like they knew we were from Hyrstow, either," Sam chimed in. He'd dismounted and searched for his water skin in his pack.

"Well, they would have figured it out if we were granted access to cut the forest, and they weren't," Bran muttered.

"Was it dangerous, Father?"

Neil's eyes were wide, his hand insistent on Bran's vambrace. There was something different about his tone. Deeper, perhaps, than it had been. Had a few days really made the difference? Or was it Bran's neglect? His gaze softened on his son.

"It wasn't," he answered. Neil opened his mouth to add something—likely to protest that Bran hadn't brought him along—so he cut him off. "Though it could have been. The people in Guston didn't like us there. Didn't want to sell us anything the one time we went to market. It was a good thing we had enough supplies."

"I've eaten enough rabbit and stale bread to last a lifetime," Ewan chimed in.

The men all laughed, but Grahame issued Branton a sharp look over the top of Neil's head. Bran shook his head to indicate he didn't want to get into it. As far as he knew, Grahame's family hadn't had an issue with their land butting against the out-lands of Guston. He didn't want to give cause for worry.

"How are the children?" Branton asked.

Neil's grin descended into a slight scowl of distaste. He rubbed his hand over the top of his head, tipping it back. "Whiny. Though Ginnie thinks Merthe is a new toy, she follows her around like a puppy. The younger ones are fine. Thankfully Uncle let me stay over for a few nights, so that I could get out of that den of women."

"Hey," Grahame warned, issuing his nephew a sharp look, "that den of women is to be respected for all the work they do. Especially Merthe and your new mother."

"She isn't my mother," Neil snapped, fisting his hands at his sides as if he wanted to punch the man he looked up to.

Bran clenched his teeth, caging the questions that arose about Emma. If Grahame hadn't relayed dire news upon seeing him, everything must have been alright at home. He didn't need to ask after her. He would keep to himself all the scenarios he thought of while away. Most were terrible imaginings of all that could befall his family. Pain, accidents, death.

At night, his mind shifted to memories of Emma staring up at him, expectant, as she offered to fulfill her wifely duties. Then he would recall the heart-shaped bow of her lips, her breath along his neck on their wedding night, the sigh when he thrust into her, the scent of lavender and bread and woman; each memory of her settled around him like a veil.

The black-as-night loathing he felt for thinking of a woman other than Freda was true torture. As if the despair of the past months an appetizer, the errant thoughts of Emma were the main course of his punishment.

"The house all settled?" he inquired.

"Yes, Father."

"Right. Well, shall we carry on?"

Grahame made a clicking sound in the back of his throat and held his staff horizontally to usher the sheep up the hill. The beasts bleated at having to move from the snow-touched brown grass where they grazed. Grahame had no patience for it. He clicked again, shoving the end of the staff at the bottom of the closest animal. It gave a snort then moved forward, bleating louder as it struck out along the worn path. The others followed, crying until they heard Grahame's soft murmurings to move along. Where Grahame coaxed, the sheep went without question.

Bran helped Neil up onto the horse as the others settled onto their own mounts. Branton opted to walk with Grahame up the slope.

They didn't have to say much as they walked afield. Grahame relayed the news of the past week. Some of the village's grain stores were found to be rotten, Merthe was Yrsa's shadow when she was allowed to be, and one of the Tanner sisters had been hired by Grahame's mother to help comb and weave the latest wool harvest. Grahame said the last part with his eyes intent on the sheep. Bran was grateful. The lance of pain that swiped at his insides and jostled them around like scrambled eggs had him looking at the sheep as well.

Freda used to help her mother with all the sorting, beating, greasing and combing that went with preparing the wool for sale. She would strike up the road that led to her parents' before daybreak, whatever babe was small at the time in a sling, the other children trailing behind, and would return three days later with the metallic, grassy scent of lanolin on her. Exhausted, she'd feed everyone scraps of bread and pottage and crisp ale sent from her parents, would put everyone to bed, then warm Bran in the way only a woman could.

"She's a bit nasty, Father," Neil reported, wrangling Bran from his thoughts.

"Who?" he asked, glancing up at Neil. Neil gave him the look of impatience he often issued.

"Isolde Tanner. She barely speaks, and when she does, watch out. She's like a bitter apple, all rotten on the inside."

"Neil," Grahame said, his voice sharp. He cut his nephew a look that told him to not continue his next words.

Bran wiped his palm over his mouth to cover the grin that poked out. It felt rusty. And a possibility revealed itself to Bran, one he found too delicious not to pester his brother-in-law about. He lifted an eyebrow at Grahame.

"The Tanner sisters are rather comely, aren't they?" He offered.

"I hadn't noticed," Grahame answered without missing a beat, though his grin belied otherwise. "'Tis a boon for Mother to have help."

Bran nodded. With all the children, and her work, he doubted Emma would have time to help in the way Freda had. And he wasn't sure he wanted her to. It struck too close to have her take over his wife's duties completely. The Shepherd farm was Freda and Grahame's. Like the rowan tree behind them, Freda's presence was here, in the fields, beneath the tree, in the bustling huts. Bran suspected it was why Neil loved spending time at his grandparents'.

As the men carried on, eventually leaving Grahame and the Shepherd's land, thoughts of Emma descended. They hounded him, like a relentless wind. How had she been managing with the children? Had she made any coin over the past weeks? Did she ever think about their time together in the forest?

The last question had been a shadow over his mind. Did she hate him? He didn't think so. Emma's disposition was like sunshine; even in the hardest of times, she didn't seem to let the world cow her, but that caused him to wonder even more what she thought of him. She could hide her true self behind her smile and gracious manner, he was sure. And for some reason, it pricked at him that he didn't know if he'd get a glimpse of the woman underneath.

As they proceeded to Hyrstow's border, the sun's fading golden light warmed the stone church that came into view. Home. A place he thought well to be rid of until he was away. As the party turned down through the road that ran next to Hyrstow's wood on the right, it caught Bran off-guard to realize he was curious about the woman he'd chained himself to. And what lay dormant beneath her smile.

SEVEN

"There wasn't anyone else?" Yrsa asked. She passed a warm bowl of soup over the table to Branton, then settled back into her chair, her own meal half eaten.

He'd returned, earlier than expected, his cheeks tinged pink from the air's crisp bite. The girls met him with hugs, and he'd been gracious enough to offer a false smile at Ridley and Yrsa's unexpected presence.

Emma had winced when his gaze roved to her, as if Yrsa showing up unannounced with Ridley in tow was something she had to apologize for. The clench of Branton's jaw betrayed his annoyance but he just looked away from her without comment.

The chair creaked as he reached for the bowl, his bulk pressing into its woven back. "There was not. Those in Guston stayed away. They were certainly not in favor of us."

Emma forced herself to continue slicing the loaf of bread she held steady on the cutting board. She stared at the scattered crumbs harder than she needed to, breath held, waiting for Branton to go on. He didn't look toward her as he spoke. She knew because she kept peeking at him from the corner of her eye.

Instead, his gaze traveled between Yrsa and Ridley, who sat across from him at the table. Ginnie was at his right, her little hand reaching out intermittently to pat his arm as she slurped her soup. Æfflead played at his feet, happily strumming his trouser leg. Neil was back from Grahame's, sitting on the mattress across the room, satisfied with the stories Branton had told him on the way back. Beside her, Merthe poured cups of ale while Tate fussed in her cradle.

The hearthfire popped and sizzled with the new wood Ridley had added while Emma bounced between slicing bread and stirring the thin broth. Branton had already devoured three of her buns which he'd layered with thick slabs of hard cheese. Though the cheese had been costly at market that week, Emma was pleased by his appetite.

"Did you see any of Eadric's men?" Ridley asked.

Suddenly, the back of Emma's neck prickled. She had a distinct sense of eyes on her. When she glanced back to the table, Branton was staring. She froze, her grin locked in place, as if she'd been caught doing something indecent. So slight she felt she was the only one to notice, the corners of his eyes crinkled as his lips curved upward in the smallest of grins. It was nothing, a throwaway acknowledgement, but Emma felt a flush creep up her neck.

"Bran," Ridley prompted. Branton held her gaze for a heartbeat longer then straightened.

"None. We stayed in the cold-as-all-hell forest. No one paid us any mind."

"Bread?" Emma offered, coming round to the table.

"Please," Bran said. He stood a little to accept the bread board Emma passed him over Ginnie's head. "Have a seat, Emma. The food will get cold before you've eaten anything."

Surprise widened her eyes. No one cared when she ate, let alone have it be warm. Her nourishment fell between the cracks of everyone else's needs. Lack of thought for herself failed to bother her like it used to when Merthe was a new babe.

"Here," Branton said, pulling out the chair beside him. He remained standing as Emma came around, then helped her push in the seat. Even after he seated himself his hand remained along the back of the woven fabric. If she leaned backward, she would come into contact with his warm fingers.

"Thank you," Emma said, giving Bran a grateful sideways glance. He'd already looked away.

"The farms we passed by appeared in good shape. One of the farmers poked his head out to ask if we were men of Hyrstow. When we confirmed, he asked after you," Branton continued.

Ridley ate his meal, though his hand stretched over to claim Yrsa's thigh. He nodded around a mouthful. "Aye, the land there has been a boon. Which farmer?"

As Ridley and Bran descended into a discussion about the farming plots on Hyrstow's acquired land, Emma ate. The soup was savory despite the slim cuts of vegetables. Her garden hadn't produced as much as she had hoped the previous fall. Despite her worries, Emma managed to enjoy the meal. All of the children were under one roof, not arguing, and Branton was back. The house felt snug with everyone inside, but Emma was grateful.

"What do you mean, 'if'?" Ridley asked Yrsa, his tone was sharp.

Emma's mind had drifted. She straightened, forgetting that Bran's hand was on the back of her chair. Between her shoulder blades she felt the hard curve of his thumb. She nearly pulled away, but then it scraped along her back, gentle as a feather. Still, it didn't distract her from the scowl that painted Yrsa's face.

"I mean that 'if' we have children, they are still a long way off."

"Not with the way you two carry on," Branton said under his breath. His eyes slid to Emma, as if to share in silent camaraderie. She couldn't help the way her mouth wove upward. Ridley and Yrsa's trysts were no secret. It was inevitable that she would be with child soon.

Yrsa looked down at her bowl, chewing her mouthful of carrot longer than necessary. Her voice was low as she spoke. "Maybe not. There is a herb from my homeland that I can take..."

Surprise then consternation colored Ridley's features. He removed his hand from her leg. "A herb? You would travel all the way back to your homeland to deny me a child?"

Yrsa straightened, her tone becoming guarded.

"I did not say that. I simply said that we don't know when we will have a child. It is the decision of the gods to plant a seedling in a woman. We've been lucky so far."

"How do you mean, 'lucky'?" Ridley became deathly still as his voice lowered.

Emma tensed. There was no need for such a private conversation at their table.

"That's not what I said."

"What then, Princess? You do not want a child?"

Color leached from Yrsa's face as her eyes darted from Emma to Branton. The room descended into quiet. Emma felt the need to move, to say something to alleviate the severity of Ridley's question but she couldn't think of something quick enough.

"Well?" Ridley demanded, his eyes locked on his wife.

"Ridley, I think—" Emma began, but the words were overpowered by Yrsa's answer.

"I do not want to speak of this here," she said.

"Yrsa..." Ridley held a warning in his tone that Emma had never heard before. "We shall discuss this outside. Come."

He rose abruptly from the table with Yrsa following. Æfflead whined at the departure.

"Thank you, Emma. Bran," Ridley said, nodding at each of them before opening the door for Yrsa.

Emma shot her friend a sympathetic smile, even as relief claimed her. She and the family didn't need to be privy to Ridley and Yrsa's private dealings.

"Well," Emma infused her voice with cheer, "the weather seems like it should be turning soon. My cousin, Ingrid, said she saw one of the rabbits near her hut has turned from white to brown."

No one commented as they chewed, nodding. Merthe offered a sympathetic little grin. Unfortunately, the sound of Ridley and Yrsa's argument didn't abate as quickly as she would have liked. Their raised voices could be heard as they walked away.

Emma could feel Branton's hand dig into the back of her chair.

"The soup is...good," he offered.

Ginnie nodded, her eyes wide, clearly still able to hear Ridley outside.

"I want to know why you would deny me children. Yrsa, we haven't even discussed this, and you've decided. Why?"

Yrsa's answer was shouted, as if she was stalking away. "Because I am not yet ready to die in a birthing bed."

Emma barely saw Merthe move to offer Ginnie a pat on the back, or a pale-faced Neil pull a crying Tate from the cradle. Emma only had eyes for Bran as he scraped his chair back, stood, and made for the door. His great shoulders heaved beneath his dark brown tunic as he pulled it open. The bang as it shut made them all jump.

"Bran!" Ridley protested from somewhere outside.

Emma was up and moving toward the door without fully realizing what she was doing.

"Merthe, please tend to the children."

Then she was racing outside, running through the yard to where Yrsa and Ridley stood near the gate. The fading dusk allowed her to see Branton's dark form as he stalked toward the woodshed. It was situated to the southeast, the last touch of humanity bracing the twilight-encrusted meadow beyond.

"Emma..." Yrsa began, regret clouding her features.

"Don't," Emma said, her tone lethal. Indignation as red as a hot coal burned in her chest. "*Do not say one more word* this evening. Your squabbles are not welcome here. Leave, now."

She barely saw them nod before she rushed toward the woodshed.

"Branton," she called, though her voice was strangled. Her throat was suddenly thick with tears.

The memories of Freda's last moments surfaced as she ran. Emma had held her friend's bloodied hand as Freda requested a promise. A vow to care for Branton and her children, no matter what the cost. And because the midwife had been trying to stanch the blood, and Freda's breaths were thinning, and panic was clawing at Emma's bones, she swore an oath from the depth of her soul.

When she turned the corner, what she saw threatened to make a new mark on her tender heart. Branton stood, braced against the shed, his face buried in his forearm while haunting, silent sobs wracked his shoulders.

For a moment, Emma doubted herself. She knew she shouldn't intrude on his suffering. She knew how unpredictable the depth grief could be. However, she also knew what it was to suffer alone. To feel as if no one in the entire world understood the hollow life after loss. The call to help, to provide any solace for Branton after such callous words were thrown, drove her forward.

Silent, she placed her hand on his shoulder. His body was warm beneath her palm and the very realness of it—of the hard flesh and soft wool—made her want to weep. Bran's love was gone. Yet, he was still here. Adrift.

With her.

Emma did not speak. Other than the tilt of his head toward her, Branton gave no indication he even cared that she was there. His face remained buried in his sleeve. Beneath her hand, she felt him tremble with how hard he tried to hold himself together. She had no idea how long they stood under the slope of the thatched shed roof.

It was wholly dark by the time Branton stepped back from the log wall. Emma removed her hand then clasped her upper arms to ward off the cold. It swept through her tunic and skirts. She hadn't bothered with a cloak and wore nothing but her shawl over her clothing. With a shuddering breath, Branton turned to her.

"I'm sorry," he began at the same time she said, "Don't worry."

She felt herself flush in embarrassment at interrupting him, overshadowing his apology. She waited for him to try again and when he didn't, she spoke.

"I'm—"

"It's—"

They halted, staring at one another in the darkness. It was nearly impossible to see Branton beneath the moonless night, but she felt as if he grinned at her. Rather than fumble over words again, they remained silent. As if pulled by an invisible string, he leaned toward her and she to him. Tentatively, his palm cupped her shoulder, easing along her back until his strong arms engulfed her.

Suddenly, she was moored. As if Branton's embrace was the thing to anchor her when she didn't know she'd been drifting away. Emma threaded her hands around his middle, clutching him back with a ferocity that scared her. His scent was like the deep forest amidst the snap of winter.

The foreign familiarity of it surprised her. But Bran had always been there. He'd been Freda's husband, and he had sung songs around the fire or told stories of his forest travels when she and Merthe had supped with them. He'd watched her and Freda work in tandem to prepare a meal and always had a teasing word to spare.

They had been a sort of family once. It was just different now.

"They don't know what it is to lose the other," Emma

finally said into Bran's shoulder. He shifted so that her words would not be muffled. She could sense his chin dipping downward to look at her, to listen. Emma released a rangy breath before plowing ahead.

"They have a love like a flame started with kindling. It's caught, and it burns brightly. But it could still go out if not fed more. Ridley may want a child. Yrsa may wish to live for herself for a time. Despite this, their love spats can stay in their own home and not in the presence of the children. Or you. I told them so."

Her voice carried an edge she rarely used. However, Emma knew she was right in this. Ridley and Yrsa would not be welcome at their home if they continued to spar so openly.

Bran ran a hand down Emma's back. The heat of it scraped along her clothing, easing the gooseflesh that had spread across her skin. He dragged it back up, then down again in gentle, calming strokes. A sigh escaped him. As if her words validated him. She kept on.

"You do not have to worry about forgetting her, Branton."

"I know," he mumbled, his voice thick.

Slowly, she tucked her palm against the cliff of muscle that was his chest. His stature seemed a mockery of hers. She was so petite, and he, so thick and wide. With conviction, she pressed where his heart beat beneath her hand.

"She'll stay with you, with us, for the rest of our lives. Everyone tells you to move on, to marry again so that you can do just that. What they don't say is how you'll see her every day in the faces of the children. And it makes you want to push them away and hold them tight all at once. How you'll think of the way she used to dance when you sang for her. Or that you'll remember her on the slope of the valley to her parent's house. She'll always be here, in this land, until you take your final rest together."

Branton's hand on her back stopped moving. He drew away, releasing her, and Emma knew she'd over-stepped. Her heart lodged in her throat at the prospect of offending him.

He shifted, dipping his face closer to hers, as if trying to catch a glimpse of her in the barely-there light.

"I've forgotten: you've lost her as well. And Jon."

The words were gifts. Acceptances of her own grief. Tears stung the backs of her eyes. Emma tried to bite them back with a grimace, but a squeak of a sob eeked out of her. Then she was being pulled back into Bran's embrace, his arms engulfing her so that she could bury her own tears in his chest. She shuddered in his grasp, wishing she were stronger. Emma had gone out to console him, but now she was the one in need of someone.

She never cried. She thought she'd used up all her tears when Jon died. Though Freda was her friend, women died in childbirth. Often. She hadn't shed a tear over it. Not because she wasn't devastated, but because there was no use for it. It wouldn't bring Freda back and wouldn't keep the children fed.

With a sucking breath through her nose to compose

herself, Emma straightened, though Branton's arms kept her caged for a moment longer than necessary. On a deep sigh that ran through her entire body, he let her go.

"Shall we head back? It's too cold for you to be out here." His voice sounded stable again.

Emma nodded, despite the fact that he couldn't see. He kept hold of her shoulder, trailing his hand along her arm then pulling her against him so her hand could nestle into the crook of his elbow. The warmth of his body was like a blanket and she couldn't help but lean into him.

Their gaits did not match, but Branton did not seem to mind their slow walk. When they met the glow seeping out from beneath the front door, he halted.

"Thank you, Emma. Truly. You've done me a kindness." His tone was like the brush of soft leather. Emma's heart beat faster.

Suddenly, the weight of him beside her, the way his hard arm felt curled around her own, made her think of their night between the trees. It called back the memories of him thrusting into her, of her claiming him by pushing back. The skin of her chest heated.

How rotten was her soul? She'd followed him to offer comfort. And here she was lusting after him.

Well, she wouldn't allow it.

Emma offered a small, polite smile. The one she gave everyone. But Branton wasn't just anyone, not anymore. And he seemed to recognize the change in her. He straightened, allowing her arm to slip free, clearing his throat. He opened the door, gesturing for her to step inside first, his blue eyes piercing under the brilliance of the fire. Emma forced herself to nod in thanks then looked away.

She'd promised Freda to care for her family. Not lust after a man so clearly not meant to be hers.

EIGHT

"Good, Sam. Again," Ridley commanded.

The hall was packed to the beams with as many men as could fit. Chairs that normally circled the central fireplace had been pushed nearer the large double doors while the two long tables which cut lengthwise through the space were shoved against the beds lining the walls. Flames roared, giving necessary light but with so many men moving about, the hall was sweltering. Once combat practice was complete, the furniture would be moved back into place and the men could go about their morning. Since the Viking raid the previous summer, Ridley had been on a mission to improve the quality of the men's fighting skill. It was arduous work, but bit by bit, the farmers of Hyrstow were becoming stronger, swifter.

Men with weapons in hand littered the space. Some were fortunate enough to hold swords, others axes, and a couple had makeshift wooden spears. Bran had a shield strapped to his arm and a mace cradled in both hands; the blunt, round head of the weapon heavy on his left side. He had to tense his stomach to balance the thing properly. He had no idea where Ridley had procured it from, but his friend had been grinning like a fool when he'd handed it to him that morning. Bran didn't bother with questions or thanks. He was still sore at Ridley for his little spat with Yrsa three days prior.

Plus, he'd had three long nights sleeping on the floor. His lower back ached and his hips were sore. He'd tossed and turned, unable to sink into the hug of slumber that erased everything. Maybe, if he wasn't so stubborn, he would acquiesce to sharing a bed with his wife. She'd offered to switch him places enough times.

As Ridley took Sam through the motions of an ax maneuver, Bran thought of his first evening home and the way Emma's mouth had twisted downward when he'd asked why she was settling herself with the children. What was left of his heart had tugged a little when she'd told him that she'd taken to sleeping with them in his absence. When he'd requested she sleep in their bedroom, she agreed, but not before folding her lip between her teeth in uncertainty. He'd made a point of throwing blankets on the floor when she entered the room so that she didn't think he'd want to share the bed. She'd relaxed a little. Until they had to undress.

Emma had pulled back the coverlet, fully clothed, but when she noticed Bran strip off his tunic, her eyes had caught on his half naked form. Resolute, he'd told himself her attention didn't matter. He hunkered down beneath his blanket and would have turned over if not for catching a glimpse of the way her shoulders set. In one fluid movement, her tunic was over her head, her skirts shucked a heartbeat after. Her underthings were light, like creamed honey, and the material had done little in the way of hiding the curve of her breast or the round flesh of her backside. Bran's mouth had gone utterly dry.

She'd quickly climbed beneath the heavy blanket. He could have sworn he'd seen her cheeks turn pink. Each night since, they'd performed the same dance of him bedding down, her cautious undressing, them trying not to look at one another.

Hate was a strong word for the situation, so he settled on dislike. He disliked that he had to force himself to look away. He disliked that she was so uncomfortable she had to dive beneath the blanket with a flush decorating her perfect skin. And he certainly disliked that in those awkward moments when it was just the two of them, he didn't think of Freda at all.

Scratch that, he *hated* that thoughts of Freda didn't hang about him like a cloak when he was with Emma. They did every other moment of the day. He wanted them to. He deserved to have her haunting him for the rest of his life.

Branton flexed his shoulders and turned his head to the side to crack his neck. He refocused on Ridley maneuvering Sam's arm to the left then telling him to strike down with the shield tied to his right. When finished, Ridley turned to the rest of the room to ensure that the men understood. When a question was posed Grahame yawned beside Branton, letting his head fall back with exaggeration. Bran nudged him in the ribs. He didn't want to be there any more than Grahame did. No, he would have rather stayed abed that morning, drifting in and out of the slumber that erased time and memory. It was only because Ridley came to his hut to apologize for his behavior that he rose and came for training.

"Thank you, Sam," Ridley said, dismissing the man.

Sam strode back to the group, his freckled cheeks red. His slim build slipped between the others with ease. Bran gave him a little nod as he passed, which Sam returned with a smile.

"One more maneuver, men. I'd like to see each of you pull that off cleanly."

Grahame scraped the back of his neck with his hand as he looked at Bran from beneath a furrowed brow.

"You'd think he would have let up by now," he muttered.

Bran squared up with Grahame, the mace a heavier weight than his ax. Grahame's shoulders drooped, his shiny sword and shield hanging in his hands. "Can you just pretend to knock me down so we can be done with it?"

"Not bloody likely. Rid will see right through it. Come on, let's go."

Grahame just narrowed his eyes at him. There were bags beneath.

"I've got better things to do. Namely, sleep while that witch Isolde is out of the house greasing wool. She's a nightmare, Bran. She helps Mother all day, doesn't speak unless to throw barbs at me because, in her words, I'm 'a male pig.' Mother just laughs to herself. She glares at me at the supper table and always has this sour look about her. I have half a mind to move into the hall for good."

As much as Branton detested whining, Grahame's brand was too irresistible not to indulge in. Grahame hadn't had a hard day in his life compared to most men, so the prospect of a pretty woman antagonizing him was only too good. Bran's mouth curved upward.

"Why are you smiling? Can't you commiserate with me like a normal person? Fuck, you're almost as bad as Rid on his high horse."

"What's pissed in your breakfast this morning?" Bran snorted.

Grahame only rolled his eyes. He held his sword's handle as if it were a toy, not a piece of steel that could damage a limb. Branton stepped toward him, swinging the mace downward, which Grahame barely bothered to lift his shield to. Bran eased off at the last moment so the round bludgeon skittered across the solid wood surface. Rather than appear cowed at his lack of trying, Grahame sneered.

Bran lifted his shield in case Grahame decided to actually use his sword then swiped the mace to the right. "What have *I* done? I'm not the one forcing everyone to train."

"No, you just mope about as if you're the only one that lost her, and you treat Emma as if she's lower than shit," he said. Sorrow tinged with malice lived in Grahame's green eyes.

The words were as effective as a sword strike to the temple. Branton's arms went slack, the weight of his implements pulling him downward. Of course, Grahame was right. Branton hadn't treated Emma well at all, for good reason. He'd been gruff with her every day since his return. As much as she had on her plate, he refused to help her when she rose early so that she could bake in the mornings at her own hut, the baby in tow. Instead, Branton had sunk further into himself, his mind cloudy with sleep, as he turned over and stared at the bed his wife died in. There was no way he could help Emma. An offer to help meant spending more time with her than necessary.

For all the bite in Grahame's words, Branton wished he could snarl a retort about Grahame not understanding, but Ridley's voice boomed through the room.

"Grahame! If you have time to chat, you must have executed the perfect maneuver. Would you like to show the rest of us?"

Bran folded his bottom lip between his teeth as he continued his own training. Heave left, bring the shield overhead. Shield down, swing right.

"I'd rather not," Grahame retorted. The words were buffered with a scoffing laugh—one only Grahame could get away with. If anyone else had spoken to Ridley in that manner, he would have them in the pillory. But not Hyrstow's Golden Boy.

Ridley's grin was carved of ice. If there was one thing

he took seriously, it was Hyrstow's safety. Under the watchful gazes of the men, he strolled around the fire pit toward Grahame. For all his casual reluctance, Grahame straightened. He wasn't as tall as Ridley—nobody in Hyrstow was—but he had a lithe grace wrapped in strength.

"Too easy for you, eh?"

Bran was the only one close enough to catch the way Grahame stiffened as Ridley prowled closer. But Grahame didn't falter. He made a show of yawning, stretching his hands out at his side, sword dangling, as his arms dropped back down. "Much."

There was a sharpness layered in the sarcasm that Bran wasn't sure he'd heard before. The way Grahame didn't avert his eyes from the warrior caused the back of Branton's neck to prickle. Had something changed between the two?

Branton's self-loathing curled around him like a pet. He wouldn't have noticed. He'd not noticed anything in months. But being near as Ridley came to stand in front of Grahame, the former's smile as brittle as frost upon water, told him something deeper was at play. As far as he knew, there was no reason for Grahame to take issue with Ridley. Grahame didn't take issue with anybody. And Ridley just wanted to be obeyed.

All of it gave Branton the sensation that he was trying to keep his head above water yet could not properly swim. It was a familiar feeling he tried to bury. Along with the blistering sorrow of Freda's death, the sense that he didn't know how to right himself caused him to retreat further. There was comfort in numbness.

"Well, I guess you're ready to face a true opponent. Tomorrow. After work, in the south meadow." The look Ridley leveled Graham with was one of unadulterated glee.

"What? You don't want to fight me here and be done with it?" Grahame protested as Ridley turned from him.

Ridley looked back over his shoulder, his brow hitched upward. "It is not I you'll be facing."

"Not you? Who then?"

Ridley tossed the name over his shoulder, a grin of pure amusement curling his mouth. "Yrsa."

CHAPTER

NINE

Emma held Æfflead's hand as she tried to rush through the tall, yellowed grass with Tate on her hip. The baby pulled at the strands of hair near her earlobe that had slipped out of her bun. Emma couldn't resist dropping a kiss on her chubby cheek. Tate giggled, her big blue eyes so much like her father's. Love for the girl swelled in Emma's chest. She carried deep affection for all of Freda and Branton's children, but having no mother, and a father that ignored her made Emma save a little more of her love for Tatswip.

She and the girls made their way to the south section of the meadow that spread like a wide mouth past the woodshed that housed the village's wood supply. People were already gathered in a ragged semi-circle in the center of the field. Remnants of snow bit at their feet but everyone's cloaks hung loose while they chatted about the upcoming spectacle. Some held cups of ale, others gestured toward Yrsa or Grahame, arguing good naturedly about who they thought would win.

In the center of the gaggle, with her long, white-blonde hair braided down her back, Yrsa stood in her leathers. A smile crowned her mouth. She held a wooden sword, one of the many implements Ridley had fashioned for training purposes. A shield sat in the limp grass at Yrsa's feet.

Grahame stood about twenty paces from her on the right side of the gathering, his face slightly pale. His own sword dangled in his loose-gripped hand, his left arm strapped to a shield. He'd discarded his cloak. Bronze skin peaked from the neck of his flaxen tunic, the leather strings of which opened to show the slope of his throat. Dark trousers encased his legs, which were braced shoulder width apart.

There were more women than men on Grahame's side of the meadow, Emma's cousin Ingrid, with her flock of children in tow, included. Though married to Paul, Ingrid wasn't shy about how attractive she found Grahame. Paul stood on the other side of the group, guffawing with Aeon Smith and Joseph Builder. There was a current of murmuring excitement to the gathered crowd that caused Emma to smile as she approached.

Briefly, she pondered why she'd never thought of Grahame as anything other than a friend. Indeed, she was a few years older and had been married with a child, but even after Jon's death she hadn't considered him an option. It was no secret that Grahame was popular with women. Even if she wanted a physical release, she and he had never shown an inkling of temptation toward one another. Grahame's bright green eyes, lean frame and perpetual grin didn't call to her.

"Emma," Branton's deep timbre snatched her attention. She scanned the crowd, her eyes hooking on the brawny figure standing in at the back. At his side, Neil shifted from foot to foot as if waiting to be permitted to push to the crowd's front.

Emma's smile fell. Branton's dark hair had grown shaggy, past his ears, meeting his beard. He hadn't cut it for months but, somehow, the look suited him. It lent a wildness to him, as if he'd been born of the forest and was merely living on borrowed time in the village. His dark cloak was pushed back from his shoulders, showcasing the breadth of his chest beneath his wheat-colored tunic.

Those standing next to him, Ewan Builder and Thomas Thatcher, moved aside as Branton edged out of the group to meet her. Neil took the opportunity to disappear. Gaze riveted on her, Bran slung his arms across his chest as he waited for her and the girls, his vambraces criss-crossing. Emma's heart kicked up a beat beneath his stare.

She tried for a small smile but the throb of her pulse was rather uncomfortable. Tate squirmed in her grasp while Æfflead tugged at her skirt, trying to keep up. The small crowd cheered as Ridley stalked to the front and stepped between Yrsa and Grahame. Despite the start of the proceedings, Branton's gaze did not leave her.

"Hello," Branton said, the tiniest of grins tipping his

mouth upward. Even the smallest of smiles changed his countenance from haunted to handsome.

"Hello," she said. Her face felt hot. He hadn't stopped staring.

Æfflead raised her arms to her father in greeting. His gaze jerked from Emma's face to focus on his daughter, lifting her. He spoke a few kind nothings into the girl's ear before turning back to the spectacle of Yrsa and Grahame. It allowed Emma to breathe again. Thomas dipped his head in greeting and moved over a couple of steps to make room for her and the little girls. Ginnie and Merthe were already at the front. They'd left much earlier than Emma, too excited to wait.

Two crows cawed to one another overhead while the wind tickled skin. There was a surge of excitement as Ridley spoke to Yrsa and Grahame in subdued tones then proceeded to the center of the group. Collectively, villagers craned their necks forward as Yrsa advanced, her sword and shield steady in hand. Grahame made a scoffing sound, his wooden sword swinging lazily, his own shield down.

"Last chance to let me out of this, Rid," he called.

Yrsa notched an eyebrow at Grahame while Ridley simply stood on the sidelines with his arms crossed. Emma could only see half of his face but it held both determination and mirth. He shrugged his big shoulders and made a hand gesture for them to continue. Grahame let out a low whistle through his teeth.

"You're really going to make me do this?"

"Scared, Saxon?" Yrsa quipped.

Emma was impressed she didn't call Grahame worse. Yrsa had a mouth like a band of bandits. The grin Grahame issued was wide and gleaming. If she'd been closer to more of the women, Emma was sure she would have heard a few sighs.

"Only that you'll fall in love with me and leave your husband."

A round of laughs and 'oh's' flew up from the crowd. Yrsa just shook out her sword arm. She'd had plenty of insults thrown her way since she settled in with Ridley. There were still those who thought her an enemy. Or, worse, a traitor to her own people. Emma had heard slips of insults passed behind her back at the market. The insinuation of Yrsa being quick to betray Hyrstow if the situation called for it must have hurt, but Yrsa handled the comments with her toothy grin and unwavering presence. Emma suspected the spar with Grahame to be more than a ploy to stifle Grahame's attitude. Rather, it smelled to Emma like another way for Yrsa to prove herself by providing entertainment.

"On with it!" Branton shouted from beside her, causing Emma to startle.

Tate too. Tears welled in her eyes, her little pink lips turning down into a wobbly frown.

"Shhh," Emma whispered, bouncing Tate on her hip while running a soothing hand up and down her back. Tate snuggled into Emma, nestling her head beneath her chin.

Beside her, Branton put Æfflead down, coaxing the little girl forward, past Ewan, to take Ginnie's hand at the front. He straightened, stepping back so close that his tunic's sleeve brushed Emma's.

A crash of wood on wood sounded, but Emma's attention was stolen by Branton's hand. It had come to rest on the small of her back. His wide palm, the heat of his spread fingers, pressed through her clothes like the sun after a long winter. Emma couldn't help her sharp inhale as he cupped her opposite elbow with his free hand, effectively bracketing her from behind. Tatswip's chin still quivered, and she looked up at her father with wide, terrified eyes.

"I'm sorry," he said to both of them in a soft voice. The words were like honey over gravel and they made something in Emma's heart cave a little. It was the longest she'd heard him address Tate, and even though it was in tandem with herself, she would take it as a good sign.

"It's alright. See? Father is sorry," Emma cooed. She pecked the crown of Tate's head. The baby's soft, short curls tickled Emma's nose. The baby calmed, the crisis of tears averted when the bark of wood on wood claimed her attention. She turned in Emma's arms, facing toward the racket.

Emma stole a look up at Bran.

He was staring. At her. Like she held all the answers in the heavens. Her cheeks prickled with heat. His palm on her elbow, his hand anchored to her back—it made her want to shrink and swell all at once.

As his gaze ate up her features, Emma felt his fingers flex. All her focus narrowed to the skin above her skirts.

The pads of Branton's fingers were five spots of heat that radiated outward, marking her. It rankled that all she wanted was to lean into him. He was so strong. So hard and vital. And the way Branton's gaze shifted from her eyes to her lips made her think he may have wanted the same.

A roar went up from the crowd. The noise forced them to rip their gazes from one another.

Yrsa had advanced to Grahame's side of the meadow. She'd thrust under Grahame's shield, earning a point in whatever game Ridley was playing. Grahame wore a sardonic smirk as if it didn't bother him in the least. He played to the crowd by letting his head hang, brassy curls glinting in the sun, then looked back up at Yrsa with rapt attention. He spoke, his voice low so it wouldn't carry, and whatever victory Yrsa had felt suddenly slipped off her features. Murder was left in its wake.

Yrsa struck out, once, twice, advancing with strength, forcing Grahame backward. His grin disappeared. In its place was a steely look of determination Emma didn't think she'd seen him wear before.

"There he goes," Bran muttered, "finally."

Emma was still in Bran's arms, as if he'd forgotten to let her go. She didn't shrug him off. They were two married people, after all, and no one else would likely think anything of it. Even if his touch was all she felt. It was as if there was no baby in her arms, no caress of breeze against her cheek. Only Branton's hands on her, making her feel like a dainty prize.

Standing in the middle of a field with people all

around was no time to lust after her husband. He didn't want her like that. He'd made it clear. And, as Emma continually told herself, she didn't desire him either. She was simply lonely and apparently so defunct that any speck of attention he paid her had her underclothes twisted.

Emma closed her eyes and drew a breath. Her throat felt like coarse wool as she swallowed. When she opened them, she glanced up to find Branton's gaze on her again. The heat in it, blue, like the hottest part of a flame, caused her nipples to tighten. And somehow, it was as if he knew it.

Ever so slightly, never breaking eye contact, Branton's head tipped to the side, studying her with a rapt interest he'd never unleashed on her before. Emma felt a flush creep from her neck down to her traitorous breasts. She offered a weak smile then straightened. He took the hint and his hands were gone. Emma felt their absence like the yanking away of a hot iron from a hide, branded all the same.

Ahead, the fight continued. Grahame was working to defend as Yrsa hacked at him. It appeared as if his shield was his only saving grace. Yrsa swiped three times, then once overhead, aiming for his right. With a curse Grahame blocked her blow with his sword. Ridley shouted something about the guard stance he'd taught them but both fighters ignored him. Sweat glinted on their brows. Each drew swift, heavy breaths. Finally, Grahame shoved beneath Yrsa's strike with his shield, sending her backward. The impact was hard enough that she nearly fell onto her buttocks. A couple of shouts wrought upward, though Emma wasn't sure if they were to cheer Grahame on or not. With gritted teeth, Yrsa gave him a little nod of acceptance. She was lighter, after all. If a man wanted, he could use brute strength against her. It was something Emma knew Yrsa hated but was aware of.

"Take the advantage!" Ridley bellowed at Grahame. Their friend had seemed to forget he had to move forward, that the number of strikes were what gained him points in the contest.

Yrsa did not. She walked toward Grahame, strides purposeful, shoulders squared. She stomped right up and shoved her own shield against his, the wood on wood cracking through the meadow. The Viking threw words at Grahame through her teeth.

Whispers went up between the spectators as to whether Grahame had it in him to truly hit a woman. Beside her, Branton scoffed. In the next moment, Yrsa's sword came down on Grahame's, hard enough that it sent his weapon flying. He grimaced for a heartbeat, then his features slicked into an oily grin. His shield rose against the next hit, but it was slow.

Emma watched in amazement as Grahame's head tipped to the side and he allowed the shield to fall beneath Yrsa's next blow. His smile slid wider, his arms open to her onslaught.

Branton's grunt of annoyance was mimicked through the crowd. Grahame was speaking, low enough for only Yrsa to hear, though his roguish grin did not slip. Emma was sure it was a look many women saw just prior to him slaking his thirst with a kiss. Yrsa appeared confused for a sliver of time, then her features hardened.

"We're doing this for you," Emma heard her say.

"I didn't ask you to," Grahame shot back.

Those around Emma shifted from foot to foot, eyeing one another warily. Someone grumbled about Grahame's pettiness over being bested by a woman. However, Emma's sense told her that what was brewing between Grahame and Yrsa and possibly even Grahame and Ridley was deeper than that. Emma had never seen Grahame throw such snark at them. She doubted anyone had.

Ridley peeled away from the group, hands fisted, shoulders bunched. If there was one thing he couldn't stand, it was the mockery of protection. Yrsa's golden eyebrows descended, her pretty mouth pinched. She looked from Grahame to Ridley then made a decision that drew gasps of surprise from the crowd.

Yrsa threw her sword and shield down. They each landed with a hard thump on the cold earth. She clenched her hands into fists then swung a huge arc with one arm. Grahame had the sense to duck to the side but Yrsa's other fist lodged in his gut, doubling him over.

"Oh," Branton muttered. His hand nestled itself against Emma's back again, as if he couldn't take the excitement without touching her. Her heart thrummed like a small bird's. A nagging need for more itched along her lower belly.

"Get up," Yrsa said, her voice carrying on the wind.

Grahame clutched his middle, glaring up at her through slitted eyes.

"I won't hit a female."

Emma's intake of breath made Branton wrap his other arm around her front again. He looked down at her, a question layered in his features, but Emma just shook her head and pressed her lips together. Yrsa hated being reduced to the weaker sex, even though she was one. Instead of snarling at him, however, Yrsa gave Grahame an open handed slap across his cheek. His face whipped to the side. As he stood, she stomped on his foot, then jabbed him with a fist to the upper thigh. The strike doubled him over, though he grinned through it.

"What is he doing?" Emma mused. Yrsa hit him in the shoulder to keep him bent over, then moved to bring her knee up under his jaw, but Ridley caught her before she could connect.

"Whatever it is, it's not good," Branton muttered. He'd bent to speak into her ear and the deep timbre of his voice tickled her sensitive skin. His body pressed from her shoulder to her elbow. Emma could feel the sculpted muscle of his chest, the slice of air between his hips and her skirt. She bit back the moan that threatened its way free.

As if acting of its own accord her body leaned back into him, ever so slightly. She told herself it was because she had to shift Tate's weight on her hip and Branton was in the position to cradle them. He didn't seem to mind. Rather, he shifted with her, removing his hand and aligning himself to her back so he could wrap his forearm around her ribcage. Anyone looking at them would see a husband giving his wife support as they stood to watch a long contest. Bran's body held hers so easily, his broad chest outstretching the expanse of her back.

Then his mouth was dipping to her ear again, speaking low. "I have half a mind to fight Yrsa just so the men here remember their place with the chieftain's woman. Grahame disrespecting her so openly doesn't bode well."

Emma nodded, her body going slack in Branton's arms. She agreed. Of course she agreed. But she couldn't exactly make her body shake itself free of the comfort of Branton's embrace.

Emma tipped her head back to speak into his ear. He leaned forward to hear. "You might get hurt."

As she spoke, her lips danced along the shell of Bran's ear. His skin was warm and smelled like the cold birch he'd cut that day. She had the sudden urge to swipe her tongue along the lobe.

Branton shivered. She felt it in his entire body, as if he were a large dog shaking out his fur. His arms clasped her tighter. And, if she didn't know better, the hard nudge along her backside wasn't the ax handle slung in his belt. He released a ragged breath before turning his lips to her ear.

"I'll be fine. Safer fighting her than if I stand here with you any longer." At the last part, Branton dipped his hips into her, pushing the evidence of that thick ridge against her backside.

The words were mean-spirited but said with humor. Emma let out a low chuckle. She couldn't help but lean her head back onto his shoulder, pressing her bottom into him in flirtation as she said, "You'd better go, then."

He clenched his eyes as she spoke, as if the words were taxing to hear. Against her back, his chest heaved.

All at once, his arms tightened and he flexed his hips forward, slowly. Emma's mind threatened to go blank. Her core pulsed, begging for the attention that her backside was receiving. She rolled her hips once to prove he wasn't the only depraved one. Branton's forehead dropped to the crown of her head and he let out a ragged curse that she felt in her ribs. Then he dropped his arms and stepped away.

Emma steeled her spine so she wouldn't fall back. She was panting. Tate sat in her arms, oblivious. Over a harsh swallow, Emma watched Branton adjust his lower half then shove through the crowd, arm up, shouting something about wanting to fight. Cheers went up around them as Ridley measured his friend's intention against Grahame's mocking joviality. Branton said some words to the three of them, and it was decided that Yrsa would fight him instead.

He didn't once look Emma's way as he picked up the discarded wood sword and swung it. Yrsa dodged, whipping around to offer a strike to Bran's midsection. His shield took the impact but he grunted from the force. He jabbed when Yrsa moved forward again. She threw a few taunting words at him, playing into the jubilant role of Viking maiden the crowd cheered for, then aimed another hit. The blow was strong and sure, striking hard against the shield. Branton made a show of shaking his head to which the crowd laughed. Then he lunged, thrusting the sword forward from beneath the protection of his shield. Yrsa maneuvered away, skipping from foot to foot, arms loose, a grin etching along her mouth at having a real opponent.

Emma tamped down her worry by telling herself they wouldn't truly hurt one another. That the clamminess of her hands was unnecessary.

It was when Branton circled Yrsa, and he faced the crowd head on that his gaze landed on Emma. There was something haunted in his stare, the grim set of his mouth. Emma fought the chill that skipped down her spine. Then he ripped his gaze to his opponent, clenching the handle of his sword as he gave a mighty thrust. Gasps went up at the force of his power but Yrsa kicked him in the leg and he stumbled. Surging forward, Yrsa got under his guard. She smashed her shield against Bran's once, twice, three times. Branton must not have been holding the iron bar on the inside well enough. With horror, Emma watched as the shield slipped from his grasp, thudding to the ground with aching finality.

After a few carefully aimed blows by Yrsa his sword lay on the ground too. But rather than stop fighting, Branton leaned in, his face as dark as the devil's and muttered something to Yrsa.

Emma strained to hear but couldn't make out the words. Though the straightening of Yrsa's shoulders and the curl of her nose in an indignant snarl was enough for

Emma to guess at what was said. Yrsa threw her weapons to the ground and swung a mighty fist at Branton's jaw. He appeared stunned for a moment, then came at Yrsa, meaty palms outstretched. She swung again, but while Branton watched her hand, he missed the kick to his inner thigh.

Emma's hand clapped over her mouth. Branton had been taking lessons with Ridley. He could defend himself; however, Yrsa was quick and daring. And though Branton was there to put up a fight, he didn't seem to mind taking what Yrsa delivered.

All anyone could do was watch as Branton let himself be beaten to a pulp by the Viking.

TEN

Branton's swollen skin felt tight in the firelight. After the fight, Ridley had passed him a rag, with which he'd toweled off most of the blood that drenched his face. He'd been able to sit through supper, though the heat of the flames from across the room invaded his every breath. The children had been quiet and Emma had hovered, asking if he needed assistance to clean his injuries. He'd refused.

He didn't want to be anywhere near Emma. Spectating with her had been a mistake. Looping his arms around her as she held the baby had been second nature. The scent of lavender and bread she carried on her clothing had begun to make him salivate. Even if her leaning back to speak into his ear caused his cock to fill with an unholy need. He suddenly craved to feel her lips against his ear, his neck, his throat. Thoughts of his hands roving her creamy skin, his own nose buried in her hair as she rode him invaded his mind. He wanted to elicit moans from her. To learn her. And by her reaction to him, he didn't think she would mind.

He'd betrayed Freda once already. He vowed not to again. And, what made everything worse, was the growing need not to hurt Emma.

So he did the thing he knew Yrsa wouldn't back down from. He leaned forward and taunted her ability to fight a man bare-handed, calling her filthy, Viking scum. And she beat him into submission like he deserved.

"Goodnight, Father," Ginnie whispered from the bed at the other end of the room. She lay on her side, Æfflead tucked beside her, already asleep. Neil lay on his back on Æffie's other side, a hand across his forehead, eyes closed. His chest rose and fell beneath the large blanket, but Bran could tell he was not yet asleep. Merthe, on Ginnie's other side, faced the wall. Her light brown hair draped across her shoulders, her breaths steady with sleep.

A pang of regret hit Bran. Merthe worked hard. Emma's marriage to Bran was to benefit both families; however, Bran wondered if Merthe saw it that way. The girl had been given tenfold the amount of responsibilities, compensated by a sliver of mattress in the corner of the room.

"G'night, dear," he said, standing from his seat at the table. He left his half-full mug of ale abandoned. His right leg ached and his face felt like it had been tenderized by a butcher's hammer. He put a log on the fire to keep the hut warm, then made his way to his room.

Emma was inside, already down to her shift, the

gauzy material loose around her hips. For once, her hair wasn't trapped in the usual confines of a bun. Lord, she had beautiful hair. So long it touched her backside, woven with strands the colors of beechwood, oak, and chestnut. It draped like a glossy curtain down her back.

Bran shook his head as he closed the door behind him. He was an absolute idiot, thinking of Emma's hair. Her *hair,* of all things. Branton swallowed his embarrassment as he turned to face the rest of the room.

The small fire near his cot flickered. A pot of water sat within the firestones. Before he could ask what it was for, Emma crossed to the fire, a cloth in hand, and dipped it into the liquid.

"Be careful!" Before he could think, he moved forward, pulling Emma up by the arm to save her from burning herself.

"It's fine. Not too hot, see?" She ran the wet cloth over the back of his hand. The water was a little warmer than room temperature, the moisture a comfort against his tight skin. Bran swallowed and released her. Embarrassment warmed his cheeks.

"Branton," Emma started, looking up at him. Her eyes were large, the color rich, like an elk's hide. "I want to clean your injuries. Can you sit on the bed, please?"

"I'm fine."

Emma's lips firmed into a line. It was something she did more often these days. As if to hold in her exasperation. The determination in her gaze did not falter, however. She placed her hand on his forearm, overtop his vambrace. Though it wasn't skin-to-skin, her touch felt like a manacle.

"Your wounds need tending. Please."

Bran's heart thudded heavily beneath his ribs. Emma didn't ask him for anything. Ever. It was as if she knew how unreliable he was so didn't bother.

"Fine," he huffed, shaking his arm so that she'd let go. She did, if only to allow him to step over to the bed and sit on the edge of it.

"Thank you," Emma said. Before he could stop her, she came to stand between his knees. Too late, he pushed his legs together to bar her from entering his space, which only caused his knees to hug the curves of hers. Immediately, Bran spread them wide apart, as if burned. Heat flushed through him. Emma's simple desire to help was being muddied by his inability to act with normalcy. He suddenly didn't know what to do with his hands. Did he put them on his legs? Let them lay on the bed helplessly? Secure them around her backside like he wanted to?

A hint of a laugh skipped out of her. It pulled him out of his head enough for him to glance upward. He couldn't help the manner in which his gaze wandered up the swell of her breasts which were at an extremely convenient height, then continued traveling up her flushed neck to meet her slightly pointed chin. His eyes locked on her grin, her plump pink lips spread wide.

"I don't often bite, you know," Emma said. Mirth cupped her tone.

"Often?" Branton asked. He meant to tease. The word came out hoarse.

Emma pulled that pretty bottom lip of hers through her teeth rather than answer. She peered down at him, eyes alight with something like mischief. For the first time, he craved a laugh from her. It had been an age since he'd heard it.

"Well, on the off chance I'm lucky enough to garner a bite, I hope it's not a deep one."

Emma's mouth dropped open in surprise, then curved upward, her cheeks high and round in the heart shape of her face. A laugh, deep and true, sprang from her belly and warmed the room. Branton couldn't help himself. He cupped the back of her thighs, anchoring her between his legs. A grin stretched his mouth, though he was sure it hung unevenly on his face.

As if his hands reminded her what she was doing, Emma gently unwrapped the strip of cloth that circled his head. Hardened blood had glued the material to his skin and Branton winced as she carefully removed it.

"She struck true," Emma said, eyes narrowing as she examined the cut.

"Aye," Branton grunted. The gash had split above his right eyebrow. He'd bled like a stuck pig, the red drops getting into his eye, burning like hell. The wound had stopped bleeding only after a strip of cloth someone had handed him was wrapped around his head. He'd worn the slouching material all evening.

Emma's movements were tentative, her touch gentle. Branton reminded himself he didn't deserve the kindness. With Emma's flesh in hand and her flowery scent clinging to his nostrils, he was acting the same as he did in the field. As if she'd singed him, he dropped his hands from her.

"You don't have to go easy on me," he said, gruffly.

Emma's features twisted into a question but rather than ask it, she retreated to the fire. Bran released an unsteady breath.

Emma was comfort and strength all wound together in a body to die for. Before their marriage he'd never looked at her as such a temptation, but since his return, the curve of her hip, the nape of her neck taunted him.

With the cloth, she removed the small iron pot by the handle and set it on the floor beside them. The delicate skin of her forearms strained with the weight. Branton forced himself still. She didn't need help.

With measured care, Emma dipped the cloth in the water, wrung it out, and stepped back between Branton's legs. He clenched his fists on his knees to stop himself from claiming her thighs again. They were soft with womanly sinew and they called to him like a siren's song.

She focused on cleaning the rest of his face before going back to the wound above his brow. While she worked, Branton closed his eyes. He did not want to observe the way her lips pursed when she pressed harder to clean the blood from his beard, nor the way her eyes crinkled with a wince when she looked back up at the gash. He certainly didn't want to focus on the near rasp of her nightgown against his chest.

"Why did you allow Yrsa to beat you today?"

Her lowered voice caused his eyes to snap open. Her earnest look compelled him to evade the question. If she knew the truth, she would think him mad.

"Who said I let her? I have a poor left hook."

Emma smirked. It tugged at something broken in Branton's chest. There was a wry side to this woman that he doubted many others saw.

"That may be, but you did Ridley a kindness today. You didn't have to."

"What kindness?" Bran had the inkling his friend was thankful he'd come forward, but he'd been too wound up by Emma prior to the fight, and too sore afterward to pay attention.

"Grahame gave up. I don't know why, but he did. And he said some nasty things to Yrsa in the process. You did too, I might add. She has a hard enough time garnering respect, and it doesn't help when her husband puts her on display to be mocked by his friends."

Branton swallowed against the sudden dryness in his throat. "I didn't mean to disrespect her."

"Oh no?" Emma pulled back to raise an elegant eyebrow at him. She propped a hand on her hip, full of provocation. The move caused the light material of her shift to clasp her breast.

"You challenged her to a bare-handed fight. Did you throw it?"

"No. Yrsa is a good opponent. I tried. But she is swift and ruthless when she needs to be. And after Grahame's mocking, she needed to show it today. I was happy to oblige."

Bran winced as Emma continued. The cloth scraped the inside of his wound.

"Why?"

The word was breathless, as if Emma's entire life hinged on his answer. A grin tickled his frown. She was never greedy. Not for herself. Only for the children. However, he suspected her nudging their discussion toward what happened between them that afternoon was out of pure selfishness.

Bran opened his hands then clenched them again. He was very glad to be sitting down. His cock had tented his trousers as soon as he'd grabbed her legs. How could he tell her his temptation drove him to seek punishment? It wasn't Emma's fault he couldn't keep his eyes off her. She was doing her part and caring for the children. It was no fault of hers that he missed his wife and desired her in the same breath. He knew it made him a twisted husk of a man.

Emma bent a little to catch his gaze. Freckles graced the bridge of her nose.

"Bran," she asked, "why?"

He yearned to push her away. But she was so damn beautiful in the golden firelight. Beautiful and kind. She cared. She'd shown it the other night when she'd come to comfort him. She was good. Well and truly an angel set on this earth to spread the love in her heart. And he was a demon, nearly ready to take her down to the depths of hell.

"Because having you in my arms felt...good. For once

I felt halfway whole. Not like a living ghost. And I don't deserve to feel that way."

Emma's eyes softened. Her hands found his shoulders, the warm strength of them a comfort he didn't earn. She squeezed once. Rather than offer platitudes however, she stood taller, dropping the cloth into the water beside them and stepping back. Bran nearly made a grab for her. She didn't look at him as she left the room. He heard her rummaging around in the kitchen area, then she was back with a knife and pawing through the meager chest of cloth she saved to make clothing. Carefully, she sliced a long, thin section of material before returning to her place between his legs.

He didn't speak, and neither did she. Emma wasn't frivolous with words. Branton was thankful for it.

"Here," she whispered. She wrapped the cloth as best she could around his head, then tied a knot on the side so he could lay on his back for sleep.

"Emma," he said, his voice low and broken as if rust had eaten it.

She placed her hands on her hips, mouth popping open on a large breath. "Branton, I—" she began. Her gaze bounced from him to the bed behind them to the floor and back up again.

"What is it you want to say?" He couldn't help it—he reached for her forearm. It was smooth and soft in his grasp. Chilled, though. She allowed him to pull her one step closer into the confines of his legs.

"You're not going to like it."

"I don't like anything anymore, so it doesn't matter much."

Emma made a little sound of exasperation in the back of her throat but spoke. "You always talk like that. Like you're this terrible beast that doesn't deserve the warmth of those around you."

"I don't. Look at me, Emma. I'm worse than broken. All I'm good for is cutting, if that. The rest...I'm glad to have you, even if you've chained yourself to a terrible marriage."

Her hands were on the sides of his face before he could speak further. They were surprisingly soft, scented with yeast and rye. Something in Branton's chest wound tight.

"Stop," she insisted, taking a step closer so that her chest nearly brushed his chin. "Stop."

Then her palms were sliding down his cheeks, around the back of his neck, and she was climbing on top of him, hitching her legs around his hips. Bran froze. She pressed her face into the side of his neck and hugged him as if she could drag him out of the depths of hell single-handedly.

"You matter, Bran."

The muffled words, spoken into his skin, cut through his soul like an ax through old wood. Suddenly his throat felt swollen. She was wrong, but he appreciated her faith in him. That she would offer comfort after he confessed he'd rather be beaten than desire her...Emma didn't deserve his surly treatment. She should have had a husband who doted on her, one who wanted her wholly.

Loathing, familiar and weighty, settled in his belly. She deserved more than he could give. Still, she clung to him. As if he were a raft in the middle of a storm. It made him want...something. To be better, maybe. To be a man worthy of such devotion.

Slowly, unsure if she would jump up if he did so, Branton wrapped his arms around Emma. Her breasts squashed into his chest, the clutch of her hips hooked over his in a way that would have made it so terribly easy to push into her if they weren't clothed. Her hair tickled while her breath scored his skin like a brand. For a long moment, they held one another, twisted together like two tragic angels, wings ripped from falling.

Emma murmured words into his skin, "You matter to us. You are good as you are. You matter."

Bran bit back his tears by burying his nose in Emma's flowing hair, all the while wishing he was a better man, one who would not forsake a woman as good as she to a hollow life of servitude.

Slowly, Emma drew back, her cheek grazing his, its softness a shock to his sensitized bruises. Instinctively, he brought his hands to her hips, his fingertips denting her flesh. The movement had her soft cradle nudging the length of him. Bran's cock jumped at the contact.

Emma's gasp shot through the room. It was sharp, so at odds with the woman herself. He had to hear it again.

In a moment of absolute madness, Branton flexed his hips into her. He was rewarded with a tattered sigh that he wanted to inhale.

Hands around his neck, Emma met his stare. The tip

of her pink tongue poked out to skim along her bottom lip. Bran was helpless. All he could do was watch it disappear into her mouth. Then her lips parted, eyes drifting to his mouth. For a moment, Bran was stunned. She wanted to kiss him. And he wanted to pry her lips open with his and taste her.

Freda.

Regret was like a hammer to his skull. He wasn't Emma's. He wasn't even his own. He was a slave to his past, to his wife, to his duty. And the clutch of Emma's body against his, the small shudder he felt go through her as her core nudged his hardness, anchored him to his resolve. He couldn't betray Freda.

Memories surfaced of their first kiss beneath the rowan tree on her parents' land. Of afternoons spent holding hands, lying on green hills, her midnight curls spread out like a crown.

Without a word, he pulled back. He could feel Emma's body tense as he ran his hands down her legs to settle on her knees, ready to push her away. God, she was such a petite thing. Curvy yet willowy in a way that made Bran think he could hold her weight forever. He caught the dip of her head, the pang of hurt that flashed across her face.

It gave him more reason to hate himself.

"I'm sorry," she said, unwinding her arms from his neck.

She tried to shove upward and he should have let her go. It would have been easier. But he didn't want her to think anything was her fault. He was the beast, not she.

He wanted to settle between her legs, to part her center and thrust inside her until she moaned his name. It was absolutely not acceptable.

And, though he wanted her to stay away, he found himself unable to simply dismiss her. They were partners. He could protect her from himself, from the wreckage he would inevitably cause.

Branton anchored his hands about her waist so that she couldn't rise. Unfortunately, the move pressed her further into the head of his cock. Branton had to stifle the growl that rumbled through him at how good she felt.

"Don't be sorry," he rasped.

A look of confusion swept her features.

"Emma…I can't help the craving I feel for you. It is like a weight around my neck. But don't you ever be sorry. You've done nothing wrong other than care for me and my family."

His skin felt strapped to his bones. It was too much: the heat between her legs, the lavender scent of her, the way she looked at him like he was all she wanted. She deserved so much more.

"Bran." She sighed. "I crave you as well. That is why I am sorry, for I know that you will never feel as I do for you."

If he could have broken more, he would have. But as it was, he was already bits of crumbled dust. Emma didn't know how far his depravity reached. All she knew was that he could barely rise from bed, that he couldn't care for his family. She didn't know of the time he used a knife on himself to ward off the shadows that enveloped him. She was good and pure. He should have sought to give her the world.

She moved to get up again, and he could see the embarrassment of rejection warming her cheeks. She didn't understand. Perhaps she never would.

"I'm so sorry, Emma. For the wreck of the man you've been left with. Thank you for caring for me tonight."

With that, he gently eased her hips backward, then took her hand to help her off his lap. As soon as she was free of him, she pulled her hand away, eyes anywhere but him.

"Goodnight," she said, quietly.

Bran nodded and stood. His damn cock was still trying to fight its way out of his pants. It was painfully hard, unaware that he wasn't going to do what it wanted.

Silently, he readied for bed, telling himself he was doing the right thing. Not only for Freda, but for Emma as well. If he and Emma could ignore the temptation of one another, it would go away. He was sure of it. They were simply a man and woman thrust together. It would pass. As he settled into his hard cot, his gaze traveled to the bed and the woman who lay there. She'd given him her back, rightly so.

Branton swallowed a sigh. He was her husband. It was his job to protect her. Something he hadn't been able to do for Freda. And if denying Emma protected her, he'd do it. Branton stared at her curled form long into the night, telling himself that doing the right thing mattered, even if it felt so wrong.

CHAPTER

ELEVEN

The forest was alive with sunshine. Small animals scurried through the underbrush, birds fluttered above, and the drip of melting ice echoed through the trees. It should have eased the cloud in Branton's head. But the spring weather only sought to make his mood darker.

With a grunt, Branton drove his ax into a felled tree. The blade split the stump halfway. He gritted his teeth, bringing the ax up then down again to finish the job. His arms shook with each impact. One wrong move and he could lose a limb.

Bran scoffed at the idea. He should be so lucky as to bleed out in the forest.

He and Emma had not spoken in a fortnight.

Indeed, they had communicated. Words issued over the children's heads, small pleasantries of the day, greetings and nods and goodnights when it was time for sleep. Nothing remained of the tenderness they'd shared the night she healed him.

Their days had gained a familiar rhythm. Emma woke early to prepare bread in her hut before dawn, then returned to Branton's to get the children ready for the day and complete chores. With the younger girls in hand, she slipped back to her hut to bake the loaves, then came back once again to clean, tend the animals, mend, and feed the children.

Bran could barely stand her industriousness. It cast a glaring light over his ineptitude. Which was why he couldn't get enough of the forest as of late. The soaring trees and rustling animals left him to wallow in all the ways he was failing his children. How he had failed Freda.

Neil had asked him if he could accompany him that morning, and Branton had refused. His mood was too stormy to risk his son seeing him in such a state. As much as he loved his boy, he knew he wasn't what was best for him. Neil needed someone to look up to. Not a broken man that continued to crumble. Bran had told him to help Emma set up her market stand. She'd been baking for two days straight to prepare. As he left, he ignored his son's disappointed glare.

Something to his left caused Branton to pause his chopping. He stood as still as he could, eyes fixed on the bare trunks around him for several breaths. Nothing. The back of his neck itched as he went back to work. It wasn't the first time he'd felt something observing him in the forest. He had half a mind to chase down whatever it was, but he couldn't summon the spirit to. If it was a threat, an animal would make itself known. And he had his ax.

The rustle of a larger animal through the underbrush to his back made him jump. Relief flooded him as a shaggy three-legged dog pushed past a hawthorn bush. Nod nosed around his fresh logs, gave a short bark then rounded back the way he came.

Branton grimaced. He didn't want to deal with a lecture from Ridley today. To his surprise, Grahame was the one who came through the curtain of trees.

"Hello, brother," Grahame said. The green tunic he wore emphasized the emerald shade of his eyes. Freda's eyes. He wore a rich brown cloak, tan trousers, and carried an ax. The gash from the fight had healed quickly, and Bran was able to properly convey his surprise with a raised eyebrow.

"To what do I owe the honor of a visit?" Branton asked.

He placed the head of his ax on the ground, leaning the handle against the stump he'd been using. As Grahame wove his way through the scattered logs, Bran clenched his tense hands into tight fists then shook them out.

Grahame shoved a hand through the unruly blonde curls that hung down over his forehead. He'd shorn the sides short, a choice Branton didn't understand. Grahame grinned, but it looked brittle. Shadows lay beneath his eyes, as if he hadn't had a good sleep in a few days.

"Father said he could spare me for a few hours. Said you've been holed up in the forest for days."

"Why does Wilfred have any cause to worry about where I spend my days?" Branton asked. He couldn't help the way his lip curled back.

Grahame held up his hands as if to say he was simply the messenger. Branton didn't believe it for a minute. His brother-in-law had always stuck his nose where it didn't belong. Rather than speak his mind, however, Grahame came to where Bran stood, plopped his rump down on one of the logs near Branton's feet.

"Is Ridley behind you?"

"No, why?"

"His black beast, Nod, keeps skulking around the forest. That, or I'm lucky enough to have something hunting me. Maybe it will put me out of my misery."

Grahame's eyes narrowed, causing his grin to take on a feral quality. "Don't you mean Lady Wolf's beast? Nod's taken quite a liking to her."

"You know calling her that only pumps up her pride?" Branton's hands found his hips as he fought the grin that picked at the corner of his mouth. Grahame bestowed the nickname on Yrsa after she proved herself to Hyrstow. It fit.

"That's why I do it. It's fun."

"Yeah, because Yrsa's a barrel 'o fun. And you were miserable to her during the fight so..." Branton let the words dangle, sarcasm layering his tone.

Grahame scratched his chest, then propped his elbows to his knees, threading his fingers together. He stared at his hands, shrugging as if he didn't care if he repaired his relationship with the Viking or not.

"Why are you here, Grahame? I doubt it's to chat about Yrsa's pet." Irritation was like hot coals in his belly. He'd come to the forest to bathe in his mood. Not to have to put on a front around the happiest person he knew.

"D'you remember Adara?"

Branton didn't bother to hide his surprise. He was prepared for Grahame to share a story about his latest female conquest or ask him to sup with Fiona and Wilf. But Grahame fiddled with his fingers, his gaze locked on his own hands, as if afraid of what Branton would say.

"Adara?" Branton asked to buy himself time.

He cast his memories back over the past few years, to think of any woman Grahame would have told him about with that name. When he couldn't think of one, he thought back even further, to their youth. Most of his life was overshadowed with memories of Freda. Of his children as weanlings. There were the times Ridley visited, and others when the hall was filled with food and drink on holidays.

"I knew her long ago. I think it was right before Neil was born."

Bran put his hands on his hips, trying to think of whom Grahame spoke. The months leading up to Neil's birth had been terrifying and exciting. Freda had been so gorgeous in pregnancy, her skin dewy and her hair thick. Branton pushed past the memory of his wife that made his throat clog. Grahame would have been around fourteen years of age at Neil's birth. Finally, his mind snagged on a memory.

"Was she that scraggly little thing that used to follow you around the field shepherding?"

Something haunted lived in Grahame's gaze as it snapped to Bran's. He nodded.

"She and I grew close that summer. She was staying with a cousin nearby. At the end of the season, she received word that she was to be married."

Bran cocked his head to the side. It wasn't like Grahame to be cryptic.

"And?" he asked.

Grahame let loose a long sigh that seemed to weigh his shoulders down.

Impatience urged him to smack Grahame up the side of his head. Instead, he ventured to guess what he was on about. "She would have been rather young for marriage at the time, no? Was she older than us? Or a noble?"

Grahame pressed his lips together. A tightness bracketed his mouth. "Aye, she's noble."

"Ah," Bran said.

His brother-in-law didn't have to say much else. Nobles married for strategy and family relations. Despite Adara being young, she was likely betrothed before she'd been born. She would have been married off as soon as her betrothed summoned her. By the sickly look on Grahame's face, Branton knew his assumption wasn't far off.

"Her husband is ill."

Bran's brows shot up. Not because he was surprised about Grahame's words but because of the hope layered in his tone.

"So?"

Grahame rolled his eyes up to where Bran loomed over him. He licked his lips then dropped his gaze to his boots. "Perhaps he won't survive. If he's ill enough..."

Bran swallowed and shut his eyes. He didn't have the wherewithal to deal with Grahame's problems. "Are you listening to yourself? Where did you hear this news? How do you know it's true? If he's ill—and that is a large *if*, by the way—you can't do anything about it. She's noble. You're not. Best you move on and focus on a woman that you can settle with, even if you don't care for her."

Grahame unfolded himself from the trunk and stood to his full height.

"Like you did with Emma?" His words were a knife buried in silk. Anger and hurt were lodged in his stare and Branton would have felt sorry for his comment if Grahame didn't look down his nose at him when he spoke his wife's name.

"Emma isn't your concern, now is she?" Bran said, his voice dangerously low. A rushing sound had taken up residence in his ears.

"She's not. And it's a good thing too, otherwise, I'd tell you what I really think about the way you're treating her."

Branton inched his chin up. He leveled a glare at Grahame that made the other man flinch. He knew he could take the conversation further. That he could cave to his curiosity and ask what Grahame's opinion truly was. The simple fact was that he didn't have to. Grahame liked most people and Emma was extremely likable. Anyone that wasn't a simpleton could see that Bran wasn't what was best for her.

Even if he wished he could be.

Branton shoved the errant thought down deep so it wouldn't spring up again. Though, his effort didn't seem to matter. It tickled the back of his mind any time he had a spare moment. His arms around her at the fight, Emma's help with his injuries, the clutch of her around him as he slid into her on their wedding night—despite his heart belonging to Freda, he found himself thinking of Emma too often. Hence his surliness and keeping to the woods for days.

"Good thing," Branton clipped the words with a nod in the direction Grahame had come. "If you're done asking me about married women, you'd best be on your way. I have work to do."

Grahame pressed his lips into a line. His features sharpened, knife-like beneath the dappled tree cover, and for a heartbeat, Branton thought he'd gone too far. But then Grahame cut him a smile. Warmth flooded back into his countenance as he clapped Branton on the shoulder.

"You're right. I'll keep my nose out of all of it," he said.

His voice was too cheery, but Branton let it slide. He didn't want to dig too deep, for his life was an open wound and Grahame's problems were the scratch beside it.

It was what he told himself, anyway. Once upon a time, he'd been a man his friends could come to. Not any longer. Another reason self-hate roiled in his belly. Even when he wanted to help, he couldn't.

Branton nodded as Grahame tapped his shoulder and strode around him to disappear through the trees. Before he left, Grahame turned, his mouth lifted in his usual grin.

"Thank you, brother."

The words hit Branton like a punch to the side. He didn't deserve Grahame's thanks. He'd not helped him with his problem, but rather had gotten angry about Emma.

But Grahame's questions burned in his mind. Emma had brought change whether she meant to or not. Branton didn't trust it. He'd found himself resenting their careful routine. A sliver of a question had begun to poke at him.

What if?

Branton picked up his ax but ended up holding the handle for too long, his gaze unfocused, his head a mess.

TWELVE

"Æfflead, can you say 'bun'? B-U-N." Emma held the soft roll before Æffie's face, drawing out the word as she tried to coax a word from her. Æfflead, a beatific smile on her little lips, only stared up at Emma with big, green eyes.

"B-UUU-NNNN," Emma said, slowing the word further.

Æfflead clapped then patted Emma's cheek. Emma's heart dipped. She'd been trying to get Æfflead to mutter anything other than grunts for several weeks, and nothing she did appeared to help. The girl was nearly three. She knew Æfflead was not simple. The girl had a keen gaze and took direction when she decided to.

With a sigh, Emma stood, rubbing her hands against her apron. She didn't know if the fine weather was to blame for the busyness of the market or if people were hungry for travel after winter's retreat. Stands stretched down the length of the square, beginning a few feet from the well and running across the open space to the square's northern tip. Those from surrounding farms and further had come to sell their wares or to stock up on supplies. The soft ground leading into Hyrstow was rife with the swells and valleys of footprints and wheel divots. The church's doors were open, giving access to prayer for those who sought it. Sunshine blessed the crowd, though the temperature still called for shawls about shoulders.

Though some were strangers, Emma saw a few people she recognized from out of town. Her uncle, Henry Armorer, Ingrid's father, had traveled the two days' ride from Whitebridge and stopped by Emma's bread stand to greet her. A wide smile had broken across Henry's thin face when Emma told him of her marriage. He'd been adamant that Emma's family should sup with him at Ingrid's that evening.

Emma had hesitated, unsure of Branton's interest in attending, so she told her uncle she would at least stop by later for a visit and story around the fire. He'd wrapped his long, strong arms around her in a deep hug and, for once, Emma felt like the cherished daughter she once was.

Emma's own father saw her to the altar then passed the following winter from a longstanding ailment of the joints which crept into his chest. Her mother remarried shortly after. Her parents had been simple farmers and the last of the family's coin had been sunk into Emma's dowry to Jon. It burned that her mother's new husband was three days in the opposite direction of Whitebridge.

It may as well have been across the world. Emma had seen her mother only once since she'd remarried and it had kindled a fire in her to always pay the widow's tax rather than be married off to whomever the village chieftain deemed appropriate.

Finally, the sun dipped from its apex to begin its descent.

"Two sceats for a loaf," Ginnie told the man bent over the bread display. A small table housed their offerings, bracketed on the right side by the cart. Lohlin Weaver took up the space to Emma's left, her own wares hung between, giving the illusion of a wall. The man narrowed his eyes at Ginnie, his lined face betraying displeasure at the price.

"Two sceats? That is the price at the earl's keep. It's not worth that much here."

"You haven't tasted this bread, though! It melts on your tongue. Light but filling, tasty yet solid enough to be used as a trencher. You won't regret the price."

The man patted the worn cap atop his head, mumbling to himself about the insolence of small children. Emma kept a careful eye on the way he spoke to Ginnie while she helped another lady wrap a loaf in the muslin she'd brought. Æfflead tugged on Emma's apron, trying for her attention, but Emma kept her smile fixed as she wished the woman well and greeted the next customer.

"Ye won't fetch me with a price like that," the man grumbled, "let me talk to your master. Where is he?"

The back of Emma's neck prickled. Since Jon's death,

the fact that she was female had influenced whether or not others bought her product. In Hyrstow, it was easier to sell her wares since those in the village knew she'd taken over her husband's business, though the weekly markets proved more of a challenge.

Emma straightened, excusing herself from her customer and moving over to stand behind Ginnie. The girl looked up at Emma with wide, uncertain eyes.

"I am the master of this stand," Emma said with a smile. The man narrowed his watery brown eyes at her, hitching his chin up when he saw she was a woman. He wasn't terribly tall but had a lanky, pointed countenance that turned impatient beneath his curled lip.

"You husband 'ere? I'll take five loaves if he'll give 'em to me for five sceats. He ain't got no business chargin' two." The man ran his tongue over his teeth as he shifted his gaze over Emma's form. It wasn't lewd, yet it made her want to shiver. As if she was something to look at while he was speaking, nothing more.

"I run this stand. The price is two sceats a loaf." Emma buffered the short words with a dimpled grin. She placed her hand on Ginnie's head to dismiss the girl, but Ginnie remained faithfully rooted to the spot.

"You? Well, no wonder the price is so high. A woman running her own stand? Ye likely don't even know the price is too much." The man tipped his head back as he spoke, raising his voice to ensure others heard. He smacked a proprietary hand down on the table between them catching the attention of a few other patrons.

Rage, swollen and red, twisted inside Emma. It was

ugly and hot and she wished she didn't care what others thought. But a stronger side, cunning and pointed, surfaced. Emma allowed her smile to slide wider as she gathered the loaf her other customer wanted and held it out to the woman while reaching for payment. The woman shot her a grateful look, dropping the coin in Emma's outstretched hand. The man glared at the exchange, angry to be ignored.

"Indeed I am aware of the proper price, sir. The earl decreed the fixed rate as it came down from the King himself. I am but a simple woman following the law."

The man harrumphed. His hand was still on her table, the dirt between his fingers embedded into his skin. Emma wanted to bash those fingers with a shoe. It would teach him a thing or two about how to treat others.

"I'll still only pay a sceat and a half for a loaf."

"Then I suggest you move along. I have other customers." Emma looked beyond to the next person in line. She startled when she saw it to be Bran. He was staring at the back of the man's head like he was about to put his fist in it. All Emma knew was that he couldn't start a fight in the middle of the market.

"Sir?" Emma asked pointedly at Bran. His gaze shifted to her, softening.

"What can I get for you? It's two sceats for a loaf," she said, hoping that Bran would catch on. She didn't want or need a savior. She'd run her business for three years without help. Three hard, rewarding years of proving again and again that she had what it took to do things herself. Patting her hands on her apron, she prayed the girls wouldn't squeal at the unexpected sight of their father.

"Two loaves please," he said, loudly to be heard in the moving crowd. The corner of his lips tweaked upward as he spoke: he would play along. Emma thanked the heavens.

"Wait your turn," the man in front of Branton threw over his shoulder, not seeing Bran's wide stature. He then narrowed his eyes on Emma and said, "I'll take five for one and a half each. You should do well to take my charity. It appears as if you need it more than I." He looked pointedly at Æfflead whose fists hooked into Emma's skirts, and Ginnie, who glared at the man with her arms crossed.

Emma dared not look at Branton. Rather, she grinned so wide that her eyes crinkled at the sides and her cheeks hurt.

In a voice of honey she said, "It is too kind that you are so concerned for my family. Indeed, the prices are regulated by the earl so hard working women such as myself are not taken advantage of by those more fortunate. Though, the fact that you are still haggling makes me ponder whether you need the bread to feed your family more than I need your coin."

The man's face twisted into a sour frown. He chewed on his words and while he did so, Emma couldn't help looking to Branton. He'd crossed his arms over his chest, leaning back slightly as he watched. Mirth curled the corners of his lips. Raw admiration shone in his gaze.

"Aye, give me the bread. Five loaves."

Emma tore her focus from her husband, nudging Ginnie to gather the loaves while she held her hand out. She didn't want to chance the man slipping away without payment. Begrudgingly, he dropped the appropriate coin into her palm. Ginnie handed him each loaf which he stuffed into a cloth bag. The man curled a lip, his nose wrinkling in distaste then turned, getting a full view of Branton. The man flinched as he beheld Branton's clenched jaw and murderous expression. Bran simply stared the man down without a word. The thorny man couldn't get away fast enough.

"Inspired work," Branton said. Emma preened at the compliment.

"Thank you, sir."

Emma gave a little curtsey, issuing a smile of her own. Behind him, someone coughed so Bran moved aside to allow the next customer. Emma's skin prickled as he watched her speak to the woman from a farm to the west. His steady gaze on her was like rays of sun warming her cheeks. She felt when it shifted to his daughters who had gone around the side of the cart to see him. Finishing up, Emma turned to find Bran had gone to one knee. His dark head had bent down to hear Ginnie better. Large arms were wrapped around their little waists, and he nodded along to whatever Ginnie was saying.

Something in Emma's throat swelled. So rarely was Branton tender with anyone. It hadn't always been that way. Bran had once been an affectionate person. He'd often grabbed at Freda's bottom or looped an arm around his friend's shoulders. He showered his children in hugs and rubbed their necks with his beard to elicit joyful squeals. When he sang—Branton had a boisterous, loud voice that carried a tune better than a traveling bard—he used to throw his arms in the air, clapping, taking up as much space as he could as he went 'round to whoever was listening, joining their arms or waving them in to take the next verse. Emma herself had been swept into his arms more than once in this friendly manner, her cheeks and stomach sore from laughing at his antics.

It pained her now to witness his conversation with the girls. As if a ghost was trying to enter the land of the living once more.

She hitched the belt she wore beneath her apron a little higher as she leaned against the cart. On it was the pouch where she kept her earnings. Some days, the pouch weighed heavily against the top of her thigh, though most were lighter. Thankfully, today was the former. Most of her stock was gone. Still, she would remain to advise potential buyers that she would be back the following week and where to find her hut within Hyrstow if they needed anything sooner.

"Are you finished in the woods?" Emma asked. He held Æfflead in one arm and clasped Ginnie's hand with the other. Hers was dwarfed in his giant palm.

"I am for today. Might need to head out again tomorrow."

The words were clipped so as to bar any further

questions. Emma was prepared for him to leave because of her inquiry, but instead, he hooked a dark brow, issuing her a grin the devil would have been proud of. "I quite liked seeing you take that man to the dirt earlier. I've never seen that side of you."

Emma's blush spread from her toes to the tips of her hair.

"It's always been there," she said as she stepped closer, "I just don't deign to trot that side of me out unless necessary. I haven't been able to keep a business afloat all these years without a little wit and ruthlessness."

Something warm lit in the depth of Bran's gaze. He cocked his head to the side. "No, I guess you haven't, have you? There is a lot I don't know about you."

Emma's heart thumped harder at the way he was looking at her, as if she were a puzzle to be solved. It thrilled and frightened her. No one had ever bothered to take the time to know her. She and Jon had fallen in love young, then had a child. They worked, they lived, and somehow, the person she was got buried under the mass of responsibility she carried. It wasn't unique, Emma didn't think. Women never were thought of as having their own desires. They were simply reflections of their husbands, and if you were lucky enough, you snagged a good man who bothered to help.

Her grin faltered at suddenly being the center of Branton's focus. "There is not anything to know. I am but a simple woman with not much to tell."

Bran set Æffie down gently and released Ginnie's

hand, his eyes not wavering from Emma's face. His frame dwarfed her as he closed the distance between them. Emma inhaled, reminding herself not to back away. She didn't trust herself with this renewed version of Bran. The sheer commanding strength he emitted caused too many salacious thoughts. Because of their shared bedroom, she knew of the hard-packed muscle that made up his chest, the dips in the terrain of his stomach. She felt like a squirrel caught in a snare, his woodsy scent pressing every part of her.

"Well now, I doubt that very much."

A rogue strand of hair escaped her bun and scraped across her cheek. Branton's hand rose as if to move it away, then dropped. His lips pressed into a line. He seemed to realize the way his neck arched toward her, how close his chest had come to hers. He cleared his throat as he straightened.

"How is the market? Will you be here long?"

Emma curled her finger around the strand of hair and tucked it back behind her ear. Bran tracked the movement. She swallowed around the dryness in her throat.

"It is busy. If it keeps up, I'll be sold out soon but will remain to let others know where to find me this week."

Bran nodded. "D'you need help packing up?"

Emma shook her head as she took a step back. She needed to get back to work. Needed to not be tempted by Branton's grin and the softness toward his children and his sudden inquiries. He hadn't cared to help her before. Though, she would admit since she'd healed him after the fight, their existence had become more pleasant. He still slept on the floor, which she planned to remedy, but he didn't ignore her as he once did. Answers were given to her questions, and though he was sometimes abed or gone throughout the days, his tone had warmed. Whatever had changed, she couldn't mess up their silent truce by bothering him.

"No, no. I'll be fine. Merthe is to come back with Tate at the end of the day, and she'll help me. Plus, Ginnie is here..." she trailed off. Ginnie beamed and nodded at her father like he'd missed her contribution all along.

"That's right," the girl chirped.

Bran took a step back to peer down at his daughter. "Of course. How could I doubt you? I just meant to offer my service to Emma, lest she be too tired after having been so ruthless all day."

Branton shot her a wink. One that made her knees feel like soup. As much as she wished she didn't have to be ruthless, a sliver of happiness crept into her heart at the thought of it providing Bran amusement.

"I am used to it. And if you're nice to me, you won't be one to feel my wrath."

Branton's brilliant blue eyes leveled against hers. The loose hair danced across her cheek again and he stepped forward, lower lip secured in his teeth. His calloused fingers swept along her cheekbone, caressing the sensitive shell of her ear as he hooked the hair around it. Emma's breath halted. His gaze remained riveted on her while his fingers skimmed down the side of her neck. Emma wanted to dissolve into a puddle at his feet.

"I think I would like to test the limits of your wrath," he murmured, his eyes glittering like gemstones. Emma sucked in a breath, momentarily at a loss for words. She tried to think of some response, anything to make her not seem like an open-mouthed fool, but his fingers still lingered on the back of her neck, scraping up and down her flesh.

"No one has bothered to test it," she said in a breathless voice she barely recognized, "so I don't know the depth of it."

"I find that hard to believe. Jon didn't test your limits?"

Emma shook her head. Bran's other hand settled on her waist. His gaze dropped to her mouth, his eyelids at half-mast. The clatter of the market around them, the sun and breeze, the children all fell away until all she could see and hear and smell was Branton.

"What about Ridley?" The question was quiet, albeit strained.

Emma huffed a short laugh. There had been a brief period before Yrsa came when she saw herself marrying the new chieftain. It wasn't that she presumed she would, it was just that he was close to her age and unwed. Plus the fact that he was tall and strong and one of the most attractive men she'd set eyes on. During their time together, however, there hadn't been a sense of desire. Though disappointed in her prospects dwindling when Ridley chose to wed the Viking, Emma later knew it was for the best. She and Ridley never had the fire that he and Yrsa had. Emma had resigned herself to never experiencing it.

Until now. Bran touching her was like throwing dried grass on embers.

"Ridley did not desire to test me, nor I him."

Bran's eyes darkened, his hand flexing on her hip. Emma's heart skittered toward her throat. He didn't care about what she had with Ridley, did he? Surely not. She spoke quickly, to redirect their conversation back to the beginning.

"Plus, I reserve my wrath only for those who deserve it."

"And who says I don't?" he murmured.

Emma couldn't help the puckering of her brow. Acting on instinct, she brought her hands to his arms, cupping the solid flesh. It was strong; bone and muscle. It reminded her that they were all rendered to dust once gone, but vital beings in the meantime. Bran didn't deserve one bit of her anger.

"Why would you?"

He looked away then, his smile twisting downward into something that pulled at her heart. She was about to place her hand on his cheek, to turn his face to hers so that he would meet her gaze, but the clearing of a female throat had Bran dropping his hands from her like he'd cut himself on her skin.

Fiona stood there, eyes wide, as if she'd swallowed something sour yet was masking it with a wavering smile. Isolde Tanner was behind her, a basket in hand, though her eyes did not stop scanning the crowd around them.

"Greetings, Emma. Branton. So glad to see you together." Fiona's words were wooden.

Branton ducked his head at his mother-in-law. He moved around to the front of the cart to embrace the woman, then issued Isolde a polite hello. Isolde simply stared at him. Rumor had it she no longer spoke to men.

Emma offered a short curtsy, her legs unsteady. She forced a smile, welcoming the women, keeping her gaze from Branton. He departed the market soon after.

She busied herself with rearranging what was left on her stand as Fiona told Emma she was leaving Isolde to help for the rest of the day. Emma nodded, taking pity on the young woman who wanted no one's sympathy. Isolde didn't say as much but didn't have to. Fury lay like flames behind her eyes. Emma wasn't sure if she wanted to hear what would come out of the woman's tight-lipped mouth, if prompted. She looked as if she would stake every man to the ground by his feet then burn him alive.

Rather than have Isolde talk with customers, Emma instructed her to bring the lower loaves from the bottom of the cart to the top, and to entertain Æfflead. Isolde offered her a tip of the lips in response, the closest thing Emma had seen of a smile.

As the day moved on, Fiona's surprised stare stuck like a barb in Emma's mind. As much as her heart had felt dusted off after Branton's soft words, they were not to be. Branton had said it himself: she had a ruthless side. And she was best at being ruthless with herself. Delicious thoughts of her husband were all she would allow herself because their arrangement was working. Despite the needs of Branton's family, the heavy pouch at her thigh held the promise of savings for Merthe. Emma would not risk their deal for anything.

THIRTEEN

Emma's surprise, when Branton returned to assist with her cart, reminded him what a terrible husband he was. The first time, she made a fuss about moving it from the line of stands herself despite Bran's insistence. As he removed the rocks that held the wheels and hitched the shafts around his hips, Emma paced, wringing her hands then patting them on her apron as if pressing them to her thighs would keep her from physically halting him. Branton would have liked to see her try.

That first time, as he'd moved the cart forward, the weight of it surprised him. Emma had brought it to market herself? Loaded with bread? For all these years? She didn't have a horse. Indeed, she was lucky to have a cart. She and Merthe had simply pulled the thing to and from the market without complaint.

It made Branton feel like a right scoundrel. That very morning he'd ridden the horse into the woods not bothering to offer it to Emma. They'd been married for weeks and he'd not helped her in any manner. So, after he'd finished mucking around in the garden to pass the time, he'd returned to the market and taken the cart home. The next week, he helped her load it, then hitched up the horse and took it to the square, returning later to bring it back. She'd protested, of course, but he'd done it anyway. Her pretty lips, the color of spring roses, had pressed into a line.

Three weeks later, after having unstrapped the horse and set it to graze Branton checked the garden he'd planted then entered his home, shaking out his cloak. His muscles ached and, for once, the errant thought that he deserved the pain of hefting his ax overhead didn't plague him.

Inside, a fire roared in the hearth, Merthe bounced the baby on one hip while shimmying her hips in a little dance to encourage Æfflead who was clapping along to a tune Ginnie hummed. Neil sat by the fire, arms crossed, his booted foot tapping against the floor while Ginnie grinned, scrunching her nose at Æffie.

Amidst it all was Emma. She patted the top of her leg in a rhythm to the wandering tune as she stirred the pot that simmered overtop the hearth's fire. Her hair had come loose from its bun, the glossy strands flowing down her back. The scent of whatever savory concoction in the pot was divine, and the smile that Emma wore nearly tugged the scraps of him together.

Before he could rethink it, Bran loosed a low, crooning melody into the room.

All activity halted. Each set of eyes shifted to the door. Æffie's mouth dropped open while Neil looked at him as if he'd grown a second head. He paused, his heart thumping too hard. His children appeared afraid to move. As if he was a dead man that had reappeared years after the burial.

Bran swallowed. He couldn't look at the tears that had welled in Ginnie's green eyes or the cautious curiosity of Æfflead's open stare.

The urge to run caused him to retreat a step. He could disappear back into the forest and not return until night had truly fallen.

Then Emma was moving toward him, her eyes locking him in place. Time slowed as she extended her hand. Silence hung in the room as she clasped the vambrace on his arm and time seemed to start again.

Her tone was low and off-key but she picked up the chorus of the tune he had sung. The melody drifted through the space, bare and solitary, while the children's wide eyes wrenched from him to settle upon her. Within a heartbeat, Ginnie began humming. Merthe sat with Tate in her lap and started clapping the baby's chubby hands together. She echoed her mother, her light, lilting voice causing Neil to jerk his gaze to her. He paused for a moment then began stamping his foot on the floor to the beat, issuing a deep hum that gave the tune some meat.

The back of Bran's neck itched. He wanted to pull the part of himself he'd just unspooled back in. But Emma's steady hand on his arm, her tentative smile graced by the dimple that dipped into her cheek, made him brave for the first time in months.

Chest tight, fighting against the sensation of *wrong* that had overtaken him at doing something he enjoyed, Branton caved to the pressure of his family, opened his mouth and sang.

Rich and true, the words tumbled forth of their own accord. It was as easy as breathing. Despite being locked away for months, his voice curved around the melody, carrying through the room.

Ginnie jumped up and ran to him, her little fingers digging into the cuff of his sleeve as she dragged him further into the house. Emma released her hold on his arm, though Bran felt the absence as Ginnie pulled him toward the fire. Neil rose from his seat as they approached, a look of wariness tightening his jaw. However, he kept humming.

The hope that shone in their eyes made Bran's voice crack. He swallowed hard against the lump that settled in his throat and forced himself to continue, even when he felt Freda's absence lurking like a shadow behind him. She would have danced, kicking her feet from side to side in a jig, hands above her head as she shouted the parts she knew. Freda wasn't one to bother memorizing the songs. She simply wanted to be a part of the music.

Suddenly, Ginnie's chin trembled as if she too felt the absence of her mother. Branton tried to buoy the song, but Neil turned his gaze to the floor, as if willing the silver that lined his eyes to dissipate. Emma sniffed, her features falling, and Merthe's own gaze darted to her mother. Branton felt the song dry on his tongue.

Æfflead moved toward Emma, arms raised to be hoisted up. Emma obliged, gathering the little girl in her arms, securing her on her hip. Between Branton and Emma, Æffie's leg bumped his hip and on a slip of breath, she murmured the words of the chorus.

The world stopped. Everyone's eyes stuck to Æffie as she let loose the first words she'd ever uttered.

"From the forest,
Out of the wood,
Here we are,
The feast is good."

Æfflead trailed off as she felt the weight of the room's stare. She looked first to Emma, who held her with a smile lacing her lips, then to her brother and sisters, all in various states of open mouths and grins. Finally, her large eyes tracked up to Branton's face, her eyebrows pinched.

Branton's heart lurched. Despite the brightness in her features, everyone had begun to wonder if Æfflead would be mute. She showed no inclination to speak and, after Freda's death, he was sorry to say that he'd barely noticed. Æfflead had been another person that needed him when he could barely support himself.

Looking at her now, hope wound through his chest like a log catching flame. He wanted her to speak. He wanted her to have a voice in a world that was hard and dirty. The desperate desire to hear her say the words again thundered through him. Gently, he took her hand in his. Her fingers splayed out barely covered the breadth of his palm. A frown fit itself in her mouth, worry coloring her eyes as if she feared what he would say.

"You have a beautiful voice, little love. Can we hear it again?"

Æfflead's gaze widened before she grinned, then nodded. Emma, as if she couldn't help it, hugged her tight. From Branton's right came Neil's stomping beat while Ginnie resumed her humming. Bran drew in breath and held it, looking to Æfflead. He sang a few lines before the chorus so that she could become accustomed to the tune again and, at the highest point of the song, Æfflead quietly joined in. Her voice was small yet clear, and the tinkling beauty of it drowned out everything else. Emma's singing was subdued beside him, but she had started bouncing Æffie to the melody while Branton swung her little arm to and fro. To his surprise, Æfflead knew most of the words, her tiny voice rising and falling with the main portions and finally settling out when the song finished.

For a moment, no one spoke. Then they were rushing to Æfflead, hugging her and kissing her chubby cheeks and patting her on the back. Merthe told her what a lovely voice she had and Ginnie was shouting "I knew it!" while Emma smiled over her head at Bran.

A hearty feeling rose within him, composed of pride and love and relief. He didn't give himself time to second-guess it. Instead, he grinned broadly back at Emma, triumph for Æfflead shining in his gaze.

Together they sang another easy song, which Æfflead

chimed in on in sections, then they took to the table for supper. Æffie didn't speak for the rest of the evening, despite Ginnie's attempts to get her to do so. Finally, Emma told Ginnie she was glad she was such an encouraging sister, but the child needed to rest after such a big event.

Gratitude for Emma coursed through Bran. She knew just what to say to halt Ginnie but not hurt her feelings. He watched as she rose from the table, removing the dishes as she went. Merthe fed the baby spoonfuls of broth which the little one smacked at playfully. As much as she tried to avoid the baby's chubby fists, Merthe ended up with liquid on her cheek and in her hair. As Emma moved about the kitchen, Bran could see the urge to help her mother written across Merthe's face.

"Here, let me," he said, standing. He reached for the bowls in front of Ginnie and Neil, stacking them on top of one another.

"You don't have to..." Merthe's hesitated over what to call him. He wasn't her father, nor did he desire to take the man's place. But she also didn't seem to feel comfortable calling him Cutter or any variation of the last name that denoted his job.

"Bran. You can call me Bran, Merthe. It's all right," he said as he reached across the table to stack her bowl on top of the others.

Merthe's eyes widened, but she nodded, a small smile settling itself within her mouth.

Regret gnawed at him. He'd been so wrapped in his grief that he'd not had the decency to tell his stepdaughter how to address him. Merthe was no shy child. She'd stood against Yrsa in the first Viking raid, helped with all the chores, looked after the young ones and managed to help her mother at market when needed. Her industriousness was a grand example of Emma's parenting. And yet she was timid around him.

"I insist," he said, softening his countenance. She ducked her head then turned her attention to the baby, as if unsure if he'd meant what he said. It only made him want to try to prove himself.

He gathered the bowls and came around the table to find Emma staring at him as she washed dishes in the large water basin. A sense of wariness seemed to tighten the set of her shoulders. As he strode to her, hands full of bowls, she tucked the look away and smiled broadly. Bran swallowed. He passed the bowls to her, his gaze snagging on her features.

Lord, she was beautiful. She was temptation incarnate, and Branton suddenly felt clunky, too large. He ached to settle his palm along the small of her back, to dip his nose into the skin behind her ear. He stepped closer and her eyes shot to his, a question layered in their depths. Her lavender scent, layered with woodsmoke from the confines of the hut, caused his mouth to water.

"Branton?"

He straightened, clearing his scratchy throat. It felt scratchy. Affection and desire, gratitude and sorrow swirled underneath his skin. He couldn't indulge in the feelings. He wouldn't. Despite how good a woman Emma was. Despite the thrumming desire that had taken hold of his faculties, she was not someone to fill the gap of his lust. He cared for her more than that.

With a step backward he managed to utter, "I am off to bed. Goodnight."

Choruses of goodnight followed him into his room where Branton sat on the edge of the bed for a long while, staring at the empty fire pit as his family went about their nighttime activities.

The harness he kept on himself had almost broken with the joy of Æfflead's speech. He'd need to keep a better leash on his feelings. There was no room for desire in his life. He would help Emma and try harder with the children. That was all he could do. For the shattered pieces of his heart had been buried with the woman he'd loved, and he didn't have the strength to unearth them.

CHAPTER

FOURTEEN

"Emma!"

Emma's heart surged into her throat as Yrsa jumped out from the tree-line a few paces ahead of her. Yrsa didn't seem to care about the death-grip Emma had on her basket of washing or the fact that Emma had frozen still as a statue. Rather, she strode toward Emma with a hopeful look, long legs eating up the dirt path that led through the bush to the river.

"I've been looking for you," Yrsa said.

It took Emma a moment to gather her words and unclench her fingers. For once, she was alone. Merthe and Ginnie had been left to care for the younger children, and Neil was off with Bran. She'd had a restless sleep, tossing and turning with memories of the way Branton had looked at her when he'd brought the dishes over a few nights previous. His eyes had devoured her as if starving. Following his tenderness with the children and Æfflead's songs, Emma felt a sense of contentment she hadn't experienced in so long, she didn't know what it was at first. Then Branton had peered down at her as if she were ripe for plucking, and Emma's feelings skidded into territory she knew she couldn't visit. In bed, her skin ached for the feel of his wide, calloused hands while he lay a mere few feet away. The evenings had not been restful. Emma had jumped at the chance to be by herself for a few minutes.

And here Yrsa stood with her bow in one hand, a quiver of arrows across her back. She wore her leathers, her hair, the color of golden moonlight, was braided down her back. Emma always wondered how the woman felt comfortable in trousers. Skirts were much easier to move around in.

"I have some items to add to your pile," Yrsa said.

Emma rolled her eyes. It was no secret that Yrsa abhorred womanly tasks. A favorite topic of gossip in the village was that poor chief Ridley had no proper woman to care for him. What they ignored was that Ridley was self-sufficient after travelling Deircia as a knight for years. He needed little but Yrsa by his side. Their household chores were done together, and Ridley would rather do them himself than have to redo her work.

Secretly, Emma had no idea how he put up with Yrsa's flagrant incapability, though she suspected Yrsa continued to prove her incompetency just so that she'd have help. Ridley was lucky that to receive a knightly pension from the earl. It meant they were wealthy enough to hire Merthe for washing or tending to animals or planting if Emma wasn't using her for the same.

Emma wasn't so proud as to not accept the wages from friends. All of it would go to Merthe's dowry.

"I have enough, thank you," Emma said with a tart shove of her nose in the air.

An odd tension had settled between her and Yrsa since Yrsa had beaten Branton's face in. Resentment had burrowed past Emma's defenses and settled within the cage of her ribs whenever she thought of Yrsa taking advantage of Branton's self-loathing to make a point. She made to walk past Yrsa, but the other woman caught her arm.

"Wait for me? I have some things. I'll come with you."

Emma tried to hide her surprise.

Yrsa only rolled her eyes in a self-deprecating manner. "I know, I know. But wait for me. We rarely get any time together."

Emma inclined her head then waited, shifting her basket to her other hip while Yrsa raced north, to her old hut. When Yrsa returned, she held a small bundle. Emma wasn't sure if Yrsa spoke true or if the pile was hastily thrown together so that she could talk with Emma.

The women made their way down into the forest, following the path north for a few paces then set off west to the rippling sounds of the water. Yrsa didn't speak. Emma led the way, and for once, having nothing to say was a comfort. A crow cawed, and the ground was not as sticky as it had been a few weeks ago. Though the sky was as gray as the scales of a fish, spring had arrived.

At the river's bank, Emma set down her basket. Yrsa

did the same then stepped to the edge of the water where it eddied in a small pool. Roots and grass underfoot made the spot perfect for perching and washing. Emma crouched, tucking her skirts between her legs, twisting them around then folding them back up again so that they did not get wet. Yrsa simply crouched, her trousers allowing her more freedom to move. She took a piece of cloth in her hands and thrust her hands down into the water.

Emma couldn't help the little grin that tipped the corner of her mouth upward. It wasn't like Yrsa to be so tight-lipped. They'd been polite to one another in passing, and Yrsa had shown up to collect Merthe at certain times throughout the week. Emma knew whatever iciness had infiltrated their friendship wouldn't last forever—most things didn't—however, she didn't get the sense that Yrsa knew that. As Yrsa gave her a sidelong glance, it struck Emma how *young* Yrsa was. Truly not that much older than Merthe. It was not that Emma was much older at age six and twenty, yet the loss of Jon and fending for herself as a widow had aged her.

"May I ask you something?" Yrsa started. She kept her dark blue eyes on the cloth she scrubbed vigorously. It was as if her movement was the only thing giving her courage to speak.

"Of course," Emma said, adding a smile to her tone. "Anything."

Yrsa halted, her teeth secured to her bottom lip. She shoved a breath out of her nostrils. "Everyone is angry at me."

"That doesn't sound like a question." Emma nudged Yrsa's upper arm with her own.

The Viking gave a little huff of a laugh.

"Are you angry with me?"

Emma considered as she plucked a bar of lye soap from the small pouch on her waist and scrubbed a particularly vicious stain from one of Ginnie's linens. The material was so threadbare Emma wondered how Ginnie wore it. She added the need for more material to her growing list of items to buy.

"Yrsa, I love you like a sister. I am lucky to have you."

Yrsa flinched, as if unused to hearing affectionate words from someone other than Ridley. Emma passed her the soap. The woman took to washing with a renewed sense of vigor.

Finally, she paused, turning her face up to the sky. "Are you certain?"

Emma wrung out her wet material three times, flapped it open then laid it over the edge of the basket to dry. "I am not angry with you, Yrsa. I am sorry if I've made you feel so. In truth, I have been busy. Too busy to walk through the forest or come for a meal or have you over. Æfflead started speaking…"

Yrsa gave her a startled look at that, her lips tipping upward but Emma continued. "It has been wonderful. As if she'd stored words inside her all this time and just needed a key to unlock her voice."

"What was the key?" Yrsa asked. She passed the bar of lye back to Emma and absently rubbed the soap's bubbles from the cloth. Before the bubbles were truly gone she was wringing it out then flapping it in the air as Emma had done.

Emma gave a small smile and collected the garment from Yrsa before it dried stiff as a plank of wood. She dunked it back in the frigid water, taking care to scour the bubbles away.

Yrsa gave her a grateful grin.

"Branton. He sang again."

Yrsa's mouth dropped open, her hands propped on her knees. She'd only heard Branton sing once before, at her wedding to Ridley. Branton's voice had always lent itself to celebration. Deep and full, it could overpower others in a chorus. Though he didn't pursue the life of a bard, he could have, Emma knew. His voice was swell enough that he could have likely stayed on in Earl Lachlan's keep as entertainment. Freda had told her so. Instead, he labored for his family and only trotted out his beautiful voice before the glow of a bonfire beside the beat of drums. It was a gift to all who heard it. Until Freda passed.

"It's true. The children and I were dancing around in the kitchen and he came in, beheld us all and...sang. Soon after, Æffie joined in. It was as if she was waiting for her chance to show us what she could do. Anyhow, we've all been trying to speak to her or sing with her to have her say more. Sometimes it works and others it doesn't, but you should see the sunny mood it's put Bran in. He still storms about the house, but there is a tenderness about him with the children. As if he'd forgotten they were there, and now he sees them again."

"Even Tatswip?"

Emma pursed her lips. She didn't want to speak ill of her husband, even when he lacked any warmth for his youngest. She answered Yrsa's question instead.

"Yrsa, I am not angry with you. I've already spoken my piece to you about you and Riley minding your arguments around Bran. And I do think you could have gone a little easier on him during sparring."

"Yes, but—"

"I understand the position you were in, truly. But he is my husband, and I must look out for him. Despite his volunteering for the fight, he...struggles. Freda's loss has broken him in a way I am not sure he can recover from. And to have you put him down like that—it gave him exactly what he wanted."

"Did it?" Yrsa asked. Her tone was gentle, as if she knew that Emma held an egg in hand and worried over dropping it. "I think what he thinks he wants and what he truly wants may be two different things."

Emma scoffed and took another piece of linen from the basket. The water had numbed her skin. "We didn't marry for any reason other than it would help the other manage. He told me straight away that we'd never be more than that. He loves Freda."

"Everyone loved Freda."

Emma paused her washing to look at her friend. Her tongue sharpened, ready to deliver a reprimand. Yrsa was too callous with words. She was too quick to judge the grief of others. Before she could speak, Yrsa interrupted.

"What I mean is, we all lost her. Freda was a bright light in the dimness, snuffed out too soon. I only knew her for a short while, but she was kind to me. She never had reservations about my allegiance to Hyrstow, even though Bran did. I miss her deeply, every day. And I didn't have the history you had with her. So, indeed, the piece of me that mourns her is nothing compared to what you or Bran is going through."

"Perhaps you should not have taken advantage of a man's weakness that day."

Yrsa inclined her head. "Perhaps. And perhaps he needed the help of a good healer. He may have a soft spot for her. "

Emma splashed a little water at Yrsa, cheeks warming. Her mind raked her over the memory of sitting on his lap. No part of him had been soft then.

Embarrassment tinged with regret hounded her thoughts. Bran may not hate her, however, more things were shoving them apart than together. Emma ducked her chin and focused on ringing out the linen. The water held on, stubborn against her ministrations. Her fingers were starting to smart with chill.

"I do not think that is the case."

"Why not? He loves Freda, but is there no room in his heart for you as well? It is my experience that hearts can grow."

Emma sucked in a breath and held it in her chest. She took her time arranging the washed garment over the lip of the basket. A chilly wind snaked up her back as she moved.

"Yrsa, Branton may not dislike me, but he will never... I was there when Freda died. I tried to help. Her last words to me..." Emma swallowed the rest of what she was about to say. She hadn't spoken of her promise to anyone else. The vow had grown since she'd made it all those months ago. She had sworn it to put Freda at ease and somehow ended up tangled in feelings for Branton. The longer she went without disclosing it, the more she could ignore her betrayal.

Yrsa had stopped washing. Her garment dripped fat drops into the river.

"Naught you mind," Emma finished.

Yrsa's features twisted into a scowl. Again, it struck Emma that, of course, Ridley fell in love with her. Yrsa was beautiful, even in anger.

"What did she say?"

"That is between me and the dead. And she was my good friend, so I will honor her wishes until my last breath."

Suddenly, Emma's chest felt too tight. She was back in that room, the fire stoked high so Freda and the babe wouldn't catch cold. Sweat had covered Emma's forearms, slid between her breasts. Emma helped the midwife press Freda's belly, trying to stanch the flow of blood. It wouldn't stop. Freda's tearful words had caught between groans of pain. Emma's fear Merthe wouldn't find Branton in time had clawed at her.

She hadn't.

Too late, Branton had barged into the room. His

desperate howl when he saw Freda in the bed had been something out of nightmares.

Yrsa's frozen hand on her forearm pulled her from the memory.

"Emma," she said.

Emma was brought back to her friend, the soaked cloth in her hands, the nagging of her legs as she sat on her haunches. She blew out a shaky breath. Emma returned to why Yrsa came with her to wash.

"Tell me why you think everyone is angry with you."

Yrsa must have seen the haunted look in Emma's eyes. She let go of her arm and allowed conversation to change direction. With a lick of her lips and a shrug of one shoulder, Yrsa transformed into the careless Viking Emma knew.

"Ridley is still angry about me not wanting a child. We haven't spoken of it since the fight at your home. We've simply let it lie, and we never do that. He hasn't pressed, but I can feel his disappointment. He wants a family."

Emma tried to catch Yrsa's gaze with a searching look. "And you do not?"

Yrsa wrung the cloth in her hands and placed the bundle on the ground beside her. She pushed up on her knees and stood, pacing a few steps.

"I do not know. A child is...a large responsibility. It is something that's loomed, but I trained for raids and set out to avenge my father, and I never truly thought fate would catch up with me. It was easier for me to believe I would die in battle than live. And now I am faced with living."

Yrsa focused anywhere but Emma as she spoke, her eyes darting to the river, the clothes, the bush beyond. Emma remained sitting. Yrsa flexed her hands at her sides then looked at the ground, toeing it.

"The living is much scarier, Emma. I..." Yrsa's voice became thick, and Emma had the urge to hug her but then Yrsa was speaking quickly, as if to get the words out before her teeth could clamp shut on them. "I have so much to lose. Ridley is more to me than any person I've ever known. Love doesn't describe the way I need him. He is the very reason my heart beats. I want time with him. To enjoy him. And the thought of having his child? Of course I want that. I want to *give* him that. But not at the expense of my life. Not yet. We've had such little time."

Tears had gathered at the corners of her eyes and one broke free as she looked down at Emma.

"I am a coward. I was prepared to meet my death by sword or ax, but the thought of perishing in a birthing bed scares me more than any death I could have met in a raid. Freda was strong. She had so much to live for. I do not want to miss out on the life of my child, of Ridley becoming a father, because I've succumbed to a bloody death I have no control over."

Yrsa ground the heel of her palm into her cheek where the tears had coursed down. She swayed to one side, then another, her lip trembling.

Emma's heart broke for her. She stood, brushing her

cold hands on her skirts to rid them of water, then stepped forward to wrap her arms around Yrsa's middle. The gesture seemed to take Yrsa off guard because she held her hands out for a few moments before she reciprocated.

Indeed, Yrsa was over an entire head taller than Emma, so Emma rested the side of her head on Yrsa's chest, but somehow she ended up holding her friend as Yrsa shook with tears. Eventually, Yrsa's ragged breathing mimicked her own and they stood together, gleaning warmth and strength from each other.

Finally, Emma pulled away, looking up to cup Yrsa's cheek. The Viking did not push her away.

"Have you spoken to Ridley about any of this?"

Yrsa gave an imperceptible shake of her head.

Emma leaned back to rub Yrsa's chilled arms with her hands.

"You should. Speak to him of your wish for more time. Tell him of your immeasurable love and your fears. The midwife can give you ingredients for tea to prevent a child. Ridley loves you, Yrsa. He wants a child with *you*. It is our plight as women to face the reaper every time our bellies swell. But as women, we do that every day. We could fall ill, become injured, or be attacked in a raid. Every day you and I and our families face death's possibility. Does it stop you from loving Ridley with your whole heart? The fact that he could be felled at any time?"

She licked her lips before replying, "No. It makes me love deeper, harder."

Emma nodded, stepping back, her point made. "The same is with children. Each breath is sweeter because it isn't forever. I cannot tell you that the birthing bed is a pleasant place. Some women are lucky enough to have a fine time of it. You are young and strong. It will be hard—it always is. You cannot control the outcome any more than you can control the movement of clouds across the sky. I am sorry for that."

Yrsa's lip trembled a final time before she nodded. She stepped back and crushed the heels of her palms into her eyes. Emma remained silent for her reply but an unknown female voice ripped through the wood at their backs.

"Are you women of Hyrstow?"

FIFTEEN

Emma and Yrsa whipped around, the latter palming her dagger before Emma even saw her move for it. Somehow she'd angled herself in front of Emma, blocking her body.

About forty yards were all that stood between the woman and Yrsa. Her hair, as dark and shiny as a raven's feathers swept away from her face in a half-do that showcased skin which glowed amidst the day's gloom. Her shapely brows curved over narrowed eyes, though it was impossible to tell the color from a distance. Her cloak was like a jewel-bright red and hemmed with delicate silver swirls. No farmer or simple merchant would have the means to wear such a vibrant color. Glinting at the base of her throat, a purple gem the size of a duck's egg held the clasp. She was flanked by two large trees, with no horse or footman, as if she'd appeared from nothing.

The hair on the back of Emma's neck stood. She and

Yrsa should have heard another person moving through the bush. Yrsa's stance indicated that she thought the same. Her dagger shone in the drab sunlight peeking through the low clouds. There were no bird sounds, no scurrying in the underbrush.

The woman did not move an inch as they appraised her. Clearly, she was of noble blood. Fear, irrational and persistent, wormed through Emma. She didn't know of any nobles near Hyrstow. The Earl of Deircia's keep was a day and a half ride away.

Despite her unease, Emma knew it was better for her to speak than Yrsa. She stepped forward, ignoring the downturn of Yrsa's mouth, and addressed the woman.

"We are of Hyrstow, my lady. May we be of service to you? You appear lost."

The woman's grin spread like ripples on still water. It emphasized the slight squareness of her jaw, though it softened the aspect of her nose, which belled at the tip. Her countenance reminded Emma of a hungry fox.

"Thank you for your concern. I have heard that a knight of the Earl of Deircia resides in Hyrstow. Do you know of him?"

At her side, Emma could sense Yrsa sharpen. She ran her tongue over her teeth, raising the dagger slightly, as she considered the woman's non-answer to Emma's question.

"Our chieftain was—and still remains—knighted by the earl," Emma hedged. She didn't want Yrsa to issue words led by her temper. Her Danish accent was thick enough that others sometimes still looked twice when she spoke.

Too late, Emma realized she should have possibly led with a mistruth. The woman's lips curled further. She took a step forward, revealing fine shoes.

"He knew my cousin. I wish to leave him with something on her behalf."

Yrsa stepped forward, her hand out. "I am his wife. I will give it to him."

The woman's eyes widened slightly but her grin didn't falter. "His wife? I had heard he had no relation other than the priest at St. Paul's."

A sinking feeling took root in Emma's belly. How was it this woman knew so well of Ridley? Was she an old lover? A friend of the earl's? Her mind raced over the possibilities.

"May I inquire as to whom we speak? We would be happy to relay a message." Emma suggested.

The woman's raven head tipped to the side in consideration. At the same time, her shoulders straightened. Too late, Emma realized that her hands were concealed in that crimson cloak and could be hiding any manner of things. Yrsa didn't, though. She looked down her nose at the woman who still stood a considerable distance away, her lip curling back to reveal teeth. The woman remained unperturbed. Every instinct in Emma's body lit up to grab Yrsa and run.

"My gratitude, but no message is needed. I am so glad to hear he's taken a wife. It was a delight to meet you."

The woman gave a slight dip in farewell then turned. As her cloak swirled around her, it opened to reveal empty hands. Emma let loose a sigh of relief as the woman walked between the trees. She disappeared through the newly budded branches, becoming one with the forest faster than Emma thought possible. When Yrsa made to follow, Emma caught her hand. Her friend looked back at her, impatience written across her face.

"You don't know who she has with her," Emma warned. Yrsa pressed her lips together but remained still. After a few silent moments where all Emma could feel was her own thudding pulse, the distant sound of a horse's neigh and the rustle of a settling atop a saddle emerged from the forest.

Finally, Yrsa whirled, sheathing her dagger and bending to pick up the basket.

"We must leave."

Emma didn't move. Moments ago, she wanted to run, to hide, but now that the woman was gone, she felt safe. There was still half a basket of washing to complete. Just because she'd felt skittish did not mean she could abandon her duties.

"I need to finish washing."

Yrsa's head snapped toward her. Her eyes were narrowed, her mouth arranged into a scowl. "You will do no such thing. You must come back with me. That woman could have men waiting in the bush."

Yrsa began walking back the way they'd come with the assumption that Emma would follow. Emma didn't move.

"Emma," Yrsa commanded, "we must go. I must tell the others about the woman. There may be a threat. I must alert Ridley or Aeon."

"I'm fine here, Yrsa. Truly. I do not think she will be back. I need to finish this before supper. I cannot tomorrow or the day after, and I've already left the washing too long as it is. You go. Alert the others if you need to."

Yrsa stood there, her feet tugging her in the direction of the village, torn between leaving and remaining to protect Emma.

"I'll be fine," Emma insisted. They had simply encountered a well-dressed woman who had known of Ridley. Despite the strangeness of the visit, meeting a woman in the woods in itself was not dire.

"Ridley's instructions are for the women to head to the water if there is a threat. I will move upstream, if that makes you feel better. I have so much to do when I return home later. You're right, you must alert the others, but I will be fine."

Yrsa's nostrils flared. She passed Emma the basket then hooked her head south, to ensure Emma followed through with her promise to move downriver, before turning off up the path.

Emma was already obeying. Carefully, she picked her way through the forest until she came to the lip of a curved, sandy inlet. The water seeped through the sand where she crouched down, leaching up into her shoes. It was a shock to her already cold feet but Emma arranged her washing anyway. The task needed doing. Then she had to get home to relieve Tate from Merthe. Merthe would help with supper so Emma could start preparing loaves for the next morning. It was something that Yrsa hadn't realized yet—rather, maybe she did and she ignored it—but the work of a woman, a mother, was never finished. Not that Emma would ever admit it to anyone else, but the extra responsibility of Bran's family nearly wore her to the bone by the day's end.

She washed quickly, ringing out each garment with frozen fingers. The birds had begun chirping again while the babble of the river and the whisper of the wind through budding leaves became a song. Emma relished the silence. It was so rare that she was alone, and yet her solitude did not halt the uneven skittering of her heart. And with every rustle of bush, she looked behind her, thinking she'd see the raven-haired woman with unkind eyes.

CHAPTER
SIXTEEN

Branton tore through the bush, hands batting away leaves and branches that thrashed him. He tried to take deeper breaths than the ones that barely filled his chest, but he couldn't. His vision tunneled, his mind trotting out images of Emma, blood covering her chest from a stab wound; Emma being yanked through the bush by her hair; Emma, broken and unblinking, face down in the river. Dead, just like Freda.

Yrsa said she'd told her to move upstream but Branton had ripped through the bush looking and looking, and she wasn't anywhere near the regular washing areas. How Yrsa could have left her alone....

Emma, with her wide smile and sparkling brown eyes that held just enough of herself back, it made him want to know more. He'd not had the chance. He hadn't bothered. Grief had swallowed him, and she'd been the only one to pry back the curtain to reveal the slivers of light. Ælflead talking, Ginnie helping, Neil surly yet beginning to tolerate more. And Branton had treated her like a slave, a nursemaid. Someone he expected things from and never appreciated. Bran felt like the shards of his heart had inflated only to collapse.

Did he even know if she wanted to do all of it? To be with him?

Branton growled his frustration as he turned from the last washing spot to run back in the direction of home. This was madness. Ridley had struck north with Yrsa and Aeon, though Yrsa claimed she'd heard the woman depart. The assurance of the woman's departure didn't halt the worry that charged through Branton's blood.

A low hanging branch nearly whipped him backward when he barreled into it. Annoyed with himself for not noticing, Bran plowed forward, ignoring the sting that branded his upper chest. He'd heal physical pain later. Once he found Emma. He would find her. He couldn't lose her...

The river ran beside him, cold and mocking with its incessant gurgling.

Then she was there, making her way through the forest, Nod at her heels as she walked in the direction of home.

"Emma!" Branton cried, almost tripping on his own feet as he clambered forward.

She turned, and Branton could see that she carried a full washing basket, her lips tinged blue. Her hair had been ruffled by the wind, tendrils floating around her face. She paused, her cloak pushed back enough to reveal the wet hem of her skirt.

The wave of relief that crashed upon Bran was something he should have given more heed but all he cared about was that Emma was wholly alive in front of him. Her brown eyes were wide as he strode to her, their depths clear.

"Bran? Are the children alright?"

He didn't stop to speak. Instead, he tore the basket from her hand, dropped it on the ground and took her in his arms. She released a sound of surprised protest, but then her frozen hands were curving around his middle, seeking warmth. Immediately, as if he'd practiced the move hundreds of times, he wrapped her within the confines of his cloak.

"You're fine. You're fine," he whispered into the crown of her head. Clear water and the yeasty scent that was uniquely Emma met his nose. Bran inhaled as much of her as he could to assuage the icy fear that had taken root in him.

"They're f-fine?" Her teeth chattered as she tried to push her face away from his chest to inquire about the children.

Indignation slammed through him. It was just like her to think of everyone but herself. Fear morphed into something ugly before he could rein it in.

"Yes, they're fine. If you were home, you'd know."

The shock that colored Emma's face was quickly hidden beneath a bland smile. It made Branton want to toss his guts. Could he never get a rise from her? Was there nothing for which she cared deeply enough to show her true concern?

"You seem upset, Branton. Why for?"

He allowed some distance by dropping his arms and taking a step back, her pretty blue lips be damned.

"Why? *Why?*"

He felt as if whatever tether of control he had on himself had come to its end then had been yanked, hard. He paced away, trying to gather himself back together, then turned, pointing a finger as he spoke through his teeth.

"Yrsa comes back to tell us of some noblewoman who appeared like a ghost in the woods and that *you stayed*, despite her urging to come back."

Emma's smile folded down at the corner, but it did not descend into a full frown. No, heaven forbid Emma express anything other than slight displeasure. Bran was sick with fear, and here she was, remaining in the forest when there was the possibility of being taken, or harmed, or raped by whatever monster accompanied the strange woman. Noble women did not wander the countryside alone, and what Yrsa told him about her sent a chill down his spine.

Solitary and strong. Like she owned the world and had no reason to be frightened of anything.

Emma was staring at him as if she was trying to parse out what to say in the face of his anger. She cupped her elbows, rubbing her hands along her upper arms for warmth. Well, the layers of her tunic and cloak would have to suffice because Bran wouldn't go near her without throttling her. He clenched his fists then paced away before turning like a great beast in a cage.

Emma's tone was even when she spoke. "I was nearly home when you stopped me. I had to get the washing done. There is no other time this week to do it. And believe me, I was not going to rush back only to send one of the children into the woods to finish up."

"You could have come to get me!" He exploded, taking two giant steps toward her. Though she trembled slightly, Emma stood her ground. Finally, something akin to fury twisted her features.

"And say what? That I needed your help to do the *washing*? That is mine and the children's work. You've made it perfectly clear that you are too busy to do such tasks."

"How?" he demanded. His nails bit into his palms, but he didn't care. He had to keep himself from touching her.

Emma shoved her fisted hands on her hips as she glared at him. "You disappear into the forest all day! There are times when you do not come back with anything to show for it. You return for supper when you feel so inclined. I didn't even know you were in the village this afternoon."

Branton flinched beneath the truth. He covered it with a scowl, but the wounds had been opened. She'd noticed. Of course she had. Emma had just spoken life into his daily escape. She didn't know that, earlier, he'd felt the pull to return home with his meager helping of wood so that he could enjoy some time with his family.

She didn't realize he'd witnessed Yrsa dart from the woods to the hall, her face white, and he'd immediately followed.

He took a step closer, allowing a sneer to decorate his face.

"I pictured you dead in the river, your skin blue, eyes open. Or gutted by a raider. You, taken and ravaged against your will and left to die in the cold."

Branton locked his eyes on a root at his feet as the words sawed from him. He clenched and unclenched his fists, trying to shove back the swelling sensation in his throat. He couldn't look at her. The way her dark hair caressed the heart shape of her face, her curves on display from her hands on her hips. Her beauty and her anger now directed at him, it was like staring into the sun for too long. As much as he wanted to see more of her, it *hurt*. He shouldn't have been so scared to lose her.

Then Emma's hand was on his chest, as if it had always had a place there. She stared up at him, her face washed of vexation. Only concern and something wary shone in the depths of her gaze. A tentative smile curved her generous lips. It nearly crippled him.

"You were that worried?" she asked, her voice thin.

The hand on his chest pressed harder, and Bran knew he was damned. He would have torn apart the forest to find her, and here she was, whole. And he was shouting at her as if she were nothing.

When she had somehow become everything.

"Emma," he breathed before he snaked his arm about her waist and crushed his lips to hers. They were unspeakably soft. Full and firm and wanting. Regret ripped through Branton for not having tasted her before.

If Emma was still angry with him, her mouth didn't reveal it. Her lips slanted beneath his, pursuing a better angle. She placed both frigid hands on either side of his face and kissed him with a ferocity that nearly made him crumble. There was no need to pry her lips with his tongue. She'd already opened to him, allowing him to seek out the hot cavern of her mouth. Branton devoured her, his tongue stroking hers in a desperate rhythm. A moan worked its way from somewhere deep in her chest. The sound had his cock, already thick by her proximity, hardening to iron.

He wound his free hand through the layers of their cloaks in search of the roundness of her ass. With a growl of satisfaction, he groped the plump flesh. Emma had a delectable backside. It was high and firm and made for his grip.

Emma gasped, the sound high as it slipped through their urgent mouths. Her skirt had rucked up, but not enough. She was caught with her legs pressed awkwardly to his thighs, her clothing binding her. Emma's grip on his face strengthened, as if she too were being worked into a frenzy. She began to rub herself on him, seeking his hardness. Such a wicked, wild thing.

"Branton, I...you..." she said between kisses. Then she was hooking her arms around his shoulder, nuzzling past his beard, licking and biting the skin of his neck as if she would devour him whole. Branton's cock strained against his trousers.

All he knew was that he thought he'd lost her. And now he had her. She was in his arms. She was alive.

Careful not to trip on the roots that covered the forest floor, Branton walked them toward the trunk of a thick tree. He hitched Emma up higher, his free hand loosening her skirts, before he pinned her between his body and the trunk. Emma hung onto his neck, her nails scoring beneath his cloak to find his skin. The contact made him shiver.

"Never leave me frantic like that again," he demanded against her lips. Branton knew he was acting like a mad man. Her reasons for remaining in the forest were sensible but he couldn't stand the thought of something happening to her.

Hands hungry, he worked her skirts up around her waist, the fabric finally giving way to the press of his thighs between hers. Her undergarments were damp. A groan worked its way through his chest at the knowledge that he made her wet. Before he could work his hand between them to reach her center, Emma's legs clamped around him, and she pulled back from his lips.

"I am not some fragile thing that cannot care for herself," she said, eyes blazing. "I have cared for myself and everyone else in my life for longer than I can remember. I am the keeper of this family. I know that, and it is about time you learned it too."

Her words were folded in a fierceness that Branton couldn't deny. As much as he wished to kiss the sharpness from her mouth, the rightness of what she'd said nearly brought him to his knees. Emma kept them all afloat. He told himself it was why he couldn't lose her.

With his cock screaming at him to take her, Branton forced himself to slow. He drew a strand of hair away from her face with a finger, trailing it down her neck and overtop her spread cloak. He placed his large hand over her bosom where her heart lay and stared into her sparkling eyes so that she could see the truth in his next words.

"You are the oak and we are the leaves. You are the sun and we are but the animals that bathe in your light. You are the mountains and us, the ice atop. Emma, you do not have to tell me that you are our keeper for you have kept my home and the hearts of my children intact when I could not. When I still cannot."

When he finished, a small grin curved her lips. With a gentleness he knew he wasn't worthy of, Emma stretched upward and placed a kiss on his brow. Then she said words that Branton didn't know he'd been hoping for.

"Bran, your heart shines when you allow it. I am honored to accept the smallest measure of your esteem."

He wanted to stop. A connection with Emma was not what he'd agreed to. He'd done everything in his power to prevent it. But she was always striving, proving herself, even to her own detriment. And he could not stand it one moment longer.

Her hand slid over the breadth of his shoulder then secured itself along his chin. She clenched her legs once, as if to assuage the relentless steel of his length, then grazed her nose along his. The touch was like the whisper of a butterfly's wings against his coarse, wind-burnt skin.

A rush of emotion had him turning his face up and taking her lips with his. He shut his eyes against the sting of tears that swelled.

Emma's hands were suddenly everywhere. Her lips moved against his, her tongue coaxing in a way that had Bran reeling. He clasped her to him harder, leveraging her against the tree so that his hands could knead her bottom while he sucked her lower lip between his teeth. Emma's gasp caught in his beard and wound its way into his skin. His cock urged him forward in search of the sweet release he knew lay just behind the barrier of her underclothes.

"Bran," Emma panted against his mouth, "I want you inside me. Against this tree. And I want to be on top of you. And I want to have you in the morning and evening and the damned middle of the day."

Branton growled into their kiss as he thrust against her, grinding against her core. Emma rubbed herself on him with the same enthusiasm, rocking forward then back in an enchanting rhythm that made Bran's skin taut. It was cold and dirty but this woman had a hold on him and he was a slave to the moment.

Without a thought other than he had to get inside her, he backed up from the tree and set her down. Emma, confusion awash on her beautiful face, watched him unhook his belt and shove his trousers down around his knees. She smiled, the break in her caution blinding, and reached beneath her skirt to shuck off her underthings.

"I want you, Emma. Now. There is no waiting to take you in the comfort of a bed. I know that it is one more strike against me, but I cannot bring myself to care."

Emma was already wrapping her hands around his shoulders so that he could lift her to him. He parted her skirts, allowing room for his body between her legs. Branton let out a deep sigh as he turned her back to the tree and settled her into place, hands around her hips.

As he worked himself between her legs, her warm center slick for him, he tried to get a reign on his control. But Emma moved against him, untethering his concentration. He'd have to remedy that.

Easing his hips back, he kept an arm about her back to steady her and dove another between their bodies. Emma made a noise in the back of her throat as his thumb sought the nub that would garner her pleasure. He dipped a kiss to her nose, then lips, then chin as he slowly ground his thumb into her flesh, back and forth. Emma's mouth went slack as he slid his fingers around her entrance, swirling the moisture up, then down, then around, and finally, in. She released a half-sigh, half-groan as his finger dipped deeper into her, all the while his thumb circling that precious nub.

When Emma's legs began to tremble, Bran couldn't help it, he looked between them. Below the folds of their hitched-up clothes, her cunt glowed, slick and swollen and completely needy as he thrust his finger into her. He shouldn't have looked. Because rather than draw out her pleasure like he intended, all he could think of was to get that hungry part of her on his cock.

Without a word, he withdrew his hand. Emma dug her fingers into his shoulders in response. It elicited such a sweet sting that Branton fumbled as he got ahold of himself.

"Hurry, Bran," she said, her voice a tattered mess. Desire, hot and hard, hit him in the gut. Branton wanted her begging. Wanted her to understand a fragment of what she was doing to him.

"One day I will make you wait, woman," he said, his voice like gravel. He positioned himself before her entrance, and as he slammed into her, said, "but today is not that day."

The moan Emma made as he sliced into her was the finest tune. She melted around him, her face going to the crook of his neck and her legs falling slack. He kept her up as he withdrew to the tip then slowly thrust forward.

Though it tore at each fiber of himself, he proceeded with care. Their first time had been so violent, he'd been so out of his mind with lust and anger that he'd ravaged her without thought. As he withdrew and rocked forward again, he wasn't sure how long he would be able to hold that intention, however.

"Christ, Emma, you clasp me like the tightest fist," he said into her hair.

Emma shuddered, anchoring her hands to Bran's shoulders so that she could lift her head. "That is only because you are like a giant inside me," she said, the words cupped in a moan.

Her thighs clamped him as if he were a horse as her hands scored along the muscles of his shoulders, his upper arms, his back. Branton couldn't get enough. Her touch was like the lick of a flame along candle wax, heating then melting.

"Oh, heavens, you are..."

"What?" He ground through his teeth as he flexed into her, hands splaying against her ass. Her head lolled back to rest upon the trunk behind her. "Tell me what I am."

With a breathy moan, her eyes pinched shut, her mouth slipping open before she answered, "I feel so full. This is too good. You feel..."

Branton couldn't help but drag out of her inch by inch, then hover at her entrance so that he could hear more of her dirty words. "It's what?"

Her eyes shot open, focusing in on Bran's own. They were glassy with lust. Lust *he* put there. Pride shot through him like a hawk diving for a meal. It was a feeling he wasn't familiar with. Emma ran a hand from his shoulder to settle on his chest, all the while giving a squeeze of her inner muscles that nearly sent Branton to the ground. A smile curled her lips.

"Your cock is divine. I am very lucky to enjoy it." She leaned in and kissed him then.

Branton forgot to breathe. Though Emma did enough of that for both of them. She panted into his mouth as he drove in and out of her, her lips moving against his, then opening with a moan as he hit a certain spot.

"There. Right there. Oh, Bran," she breathed, her eyes cinching shut.

Bran had to think of the coldest river bath in order to keep himself from meeting his release too soon. Emma's brows pinched, and her mouth fell open. She was close. As much as he wanted to spill into her, he would not be selfish for once. He would not rob this gorgeous creature of her pleasure.

Gritting his teeth, neck muscles straining, he gave three shallow thrusts, then drew the final one out at an agonizing pace. Emma's eyes snapped open to meet his, her hands tightening on his cloak. Branton craved her need. Wanted to draw it out forever so that all she would ever know was him. Emma's legs tightened around him as she tried to control his movements.

He gave her a feral grin. Then he shoved into her with one great stroke.

Emma's inner walls convulsed. She gave herself over to the pleasure, her entire body loosening and tightening all at once. Branton didn't bother holding back after. Mindless, he thrust in once, twice, then erupted, the pleasure of it blinding him, sucking his soul from hell. His body spasmed with his release, his thrusts shoving Emma into the bark of the tree.

When empty, he drew back to focus on the dazed woman in his arms. Emma's head lolled against the trunk, her hair a sweaty mess. Her cheeks were ripe, flushed against the air's bite. Her eyes were half-mast, and her swollen lips cradled a grin. Had she always been this beautiful? Only now, after their marriage contract, could he recognize that Emma was one of the most gorgeous women he'd ever laid eyes upon.

It made Bran want to take her again.

"Here," she said, bracing one hand on his shoulder, the other gripping his still hard length so that she could ease herself off him. Bran helped, his tunic falling around his body as he gently placed her on the ground. He told himself she wobbled as he set her down so he could keep his hands on the flare of her hips. Her grin was stuck on her face as she bent to pluck up her underclothes, tucking her arm beneath her skirts to clean herself with them. When she finished, she balled up the material and tossed it into the discarded basket. Once she was back together, Bran adjusted his clothing and settled his cloak.

Emma turned her face up, her slightly upturned nose wrinkling, lips still frozen in a smile.

Her palm settled on the center of his chest. "Thank you for coming to find me. I know that you were angry, and I am sorry for that, but it means something to me. It means that you care. And I haven't had someone care enough to look for me in a very long time."

The words jarred him. Surely that couldn't be true? She had Merthe and Ingrid and Yrsa...though, he supposed Merthe would have been worried but assumed her mother was alright. Ingrid was too busy with her own brood, and Yrsa would cut her way through the forest if she knew Emma to be lost, but her alliance would always be to Ridley. And Ridley's was to Hyrstow.

It struck him like a bolt of lightning how alone Emma

was. Freda had always kept Emma in mind. The whole thing made his throat ache. Emma may have been the only person in the village that knew the barren landscape of loneliness. Perhaps even deeper than Bran himself did.

He cleared his throat as he laid his hand over hers on his chest. He couldn't help but lean toward her as he said, "I will always search for you, Emma. I would scour this earth for you."

The words rang with a truth that Branton hadn't felt in ages. He almost wanted to take them back, as if doing so would fortify himself from his own flagellation. But the way Emma's eyes turned up slightly at the corners, as if the words were a greater promise than their marriage vows, let Branton know that he'd done right by voicing them.

His chest felt tight beneath the broken shards of his oath to Freda and his new vow to Emma. He'd failed and forged. Though, staring down at his wife, he considered perhaps both could be true: it was a betrayal of his first wife to care for his second, and his second wife was helping heal the scar left by the first.

One thing he knew unequivocally.

He would always look for Emma. She was his rock amidst the storm.

CHAPTER
SEVENTEEN

After the encounter with the woman in the woods, time moved too quickly for Emma to observe it. The weather turned, chilly nights giving way to bright mornings. Animals sang mating calls. The roads dried, though Bran continued to help take the cart to and from the market on Sæterdæg. Emma was busy with the house and the children, with her business and tending to the garden. Neil griped about doing women's work. For her part, Merthe worked quietly, though Emma caught her trying to trip Neil when she thought no one was looking. Emma didn't have time to fret about it. She was down to their last coin after buying fabric to outfit the growing children.

After their tryst in the forest, Branton withdrew. Emma would have liked it not to hurt. As much as she told herself she knew that he was trying to reconcile their joining, something had felt like it shifted between them when he'd torn apart the forest in search of her. His kind words had had a heat to them, his touch was like a rain after drought.

After the first day of him grousing at her to leave him alone when she let him know of meal times, she'd become tight-lipped. On the third, when he'd taken some bread and gone to cut, he told her he needed time to sort his head out. The week stretched into another with him barely speaking. Emma found herself using the funds she should have been setting away for Merthe's dowry to buy rye. There was a shortage due to an unhealthy crop last year, and Emma had to bite down hard on her sorrow that what she saved was being spent on high prices.

After a long morning of Branton laying about, she set her shoulders and entered the bedroom with a cold bucket of water in hand. He squinted at the light which poured in from the door, holding a hand up to shadow his face. His hair lay flat against his skull from lying on it. The blanket fell about his shoulders and Emma steeled herself at the gauntness that hollowed his cheeks.

"It is time to rise," Emma said, her tone leaving no room for argument. She strode over and dropped the bucket on the floor next to him. Water splashed over the edge, marring the shoulder of his tunic.

"Go away," Branton said. His voice was hoarse from misuse. It would have pained Emma if frustration and hurt hadn't pulled the threads of her composure.

"Get up," Emma said, evenly. "You need to wash and dress. Your tunic is laid out on the bed, ready. You should go see what Ridley requires or if the men are training. It will do you good to get out."

The roll of his eyes as he laid his head back down broke the tether of her restraint. Before he could bring the foul-smelling blanket back up to his shoulders, she snatched the edge of the cloth and whipped it away. Shock marred his features as he bent in on himself, in an attempt to keep the cold at bay. Emma's upper lip curled.

"Get out of bed, *now*. I've let you lay about, hating me, hating yourself, for the better part of a fortnight. It ends today, Branton."

She retreated a step and began folding the blanket even though she was going to have it washed by the day's end. The course fiber whispered through her fingers as Branton pushed himself into sitting.

"Stop nagging. I am the man of this house, and I—"

"I am the woman!" she thundered. With a toss, the blanket landed on the floor before the bed. Emma settled her hands on her hips, hitching her chin as she glared down at him. "I am the one keeping the children fed and stretching our money. I am the one bringing in an income and keeping the animals. I am the woman of this house. Your house. As such, I am ordering you to *get up*. If you do not, so help me..."

Emma clamped her lips shut, not knowing what she would do if he didn't heed her. He didn't know that. Rather than play her full hand, Emma turned on her heel and stomped out of the room. She set to making bread, measuring out the rye and water, mixing it.

By the time she set the dough to rise, Branton

emerged. His hair was damp, pushed back from his face as if he'd finger combed it. He wore a clean tunic. Wordlessly, she offered him a bowl of cooked oats, not bothering to look him in the face. He took it, set it on the table near her bread, and sat down. Ate.

"You could have warmed the water," he said around a mouthful.

Emma offered a little shrug as she lifted the door to the cellar. Inside, she released a low breath, cataloging the food she would need to buy at the market. Their stores had dwindled. She'd have to take the girls foraging.

When she set her foot upon the ladder to ascend, Bran was there, crouching, his hand out. She slipped her hand in his. Despite the warmth of the hut, his fingers were chilled. Stepping out, they stood to their full height, hands still linked.

"I plan to find Ridley, though I will be home for supper, Ruthless." His frown was deep, though his eyes remained locked on her, as if assessing what she would do.

Emma popped a hand on her hip. "Ruthless? I am a kind-hearted soul, I'll have you know. Everyone would agree."

"Ah, but I know better. I know firsthand how ruthless you can be." A hint of mirth lay in the words. He released her, turning to the door to grab his cloak off the hook. As he draped it around his shoulders, he turned back, opened his mouth. Nothing came out.

Emma waited. She wasn't sure if she wanted to hear what he would say.

"What is it?" she asked.

"I...we...I did not pull out of you in the forest. I was a beast and I worry..."

She wiped her hands on her apron even though they were dry. His sullenness, though rude, suddenly clicked into place. She should have thought to ease his mind sooner.

"I do not think I can grow with child again."

Branton's gaze flitted over her as he scratched the back of his head. "Explain."

"After Merthe, I was unable to make another child with Jon. She does not have any siblings that have passed. I was not even able to conceive one that disappeared from my womb before it had the chance to sprout."

"I see," Bran said. He shifted from one foot to another, as if he wished to comment on the matter further but didn't know how. Finally, he released a breath, eyes to the floor as he spoke. "Thank you. For always looking for me in the darkness, even when you don't know if I'll still be there."

He left.

Emma held her middle as emotion worked its way through her chest. She slumped into a chair, staring at the table top in silence.

Branton surveyed the mess of detritus before him. What was left of their tidy wood pile littered the ground. The small strips of yellowed cloth they'd tied around the bases of the outer trees to mark the site were thrown to the wayside. An insult, the material unwound and tossed to be trampled. Whoever the thief was wanted Branton to be sure the wood had been stolen.

Ewan and Sam looked from where the stacks of logs should have been, to him. Ewan kicked at a few wood chips, digging his toe into the damp earth. Soaked brown leaves stuck to his boot. A drizzle had begun at the outset of their journey and had yet to abate. Wetness leached past their cloaks, coating their skin.

"This isn't good," Ewan remarked, casting his gaze back up to Branton who scraped his hand over the back of his head, nodding.

"Aye."

"Should we cut more?" asked Sam. "We could bring down a few of the larger ones and buck them up. Wouldn't take more than a couple days."

Branton pressed a thumb to his lower lip, thinking. They needed the wood haul. It was madness, the fact that they had to bring the wood all the way to the keep, and Lachlan was a petty fool for ordering them to do so. There was plenty of closer forest to harvest. As far as Bran could see, this was all a pissing contest between the earls. And Hyrstow had nothing to gain other than the threat of retaliation from Bernira.

Branton didn't know why the earls feuded, nor did he care. Politics were not something he could control.

Unfortunately, neither was producing wagon loads of stolen wood.

"We can't cut more without order from the earl, despite my inclination to do so. Plus, the wood will be green. It was to be semi-dried by the time it arrived at the keep."

"But the theft..." Sam trailed off, scrubbing a hand over his chin. "We need to send something back to the earl, no?"

"Indeed. But we cannot cut more than allowed. Steeper penalties handed down from the king tie the earl's hands, or so I'm told."

"Then we should head into Guston, see who stole from us!" Ewan interjected, stepping forward. His sodden brown cloak flapped around him as his hands moved with emphasis. His dark hair stuck to his brow, his boots slick with mud.

"We cannot," Bran said, holding up a hand to stay the man's anger. "It is an insult. One to taunt us into demanding justice. It would not bode well for us to storm into town. Guston hasn't been conquered, after all."

Thomas Thatcher spat on the ground, his sandy blonde brows dropping as his face morphed into a scowl. His presence was a mockery as well as Jory Farmer's; they'd been brought to help with the large amount of logs. "We rely on payment for that wood. How else are we to get it?"

Branton's thumb circled the head of the small ax hanging from his belt. He needed the money for his family just as much as the other men, if not moreso. Ewan and Sam were afforded the comfort of the hall. Thomas and Jory, both of whom had families, stood by, glaring. However, Bran would not allow a conflict borne of frustration to become something more.

"Cool your head, Thomas. We will return to Hyrstow and relay the theft to Ridley. There is a possibility the earl will grant us further use of this wood, and we can cut more in time."

"Until then, what of our payment?"

Branton ground his teeth. If they did not return with wood, there would be no payment, though he dared not cut more in a forest that was under conflict. Lachlan may excuse the offense of taking more than their share—but may not. The Earl of Bernira certainly wouldn't. It was a danger to be in the woods. Ridley had claimed the area for the Earl of Deircia and, though there had been little repercussions from Bernira, both Bran and Ridley expected it to come. The shadow of a noose tightened about their necks the longer they remained in the forest.

"We'll consult with the chieftain about our payment." Branton began walking through the trees, back to the wagons that were stationed in the meadow beyond. He ignored the grumbling of the men behind him. They followed, not bothering to walk stealthily through the forest. It made the back of Bran's neck itch. The men were worried about payment, and if Bran was honest with himself, his mind was fixed on it too. That, and the possible punishment the earl would dish out for neglecting to provide the necessary wood. The earl was fair, but Bran knew that nobility could be fickle and that he could be blamed for not concealing the logs well enough or returning for them sooner.

Heaviness grew in the pit of his stomach, and by the time he'd walked to the horses that were hobbled by the trees, his worry about not receiving payment had spread through him like a spider's web.

Bran ground his teeth as he hitched up the horse. The beast neighed as it was backed up to the wooden planks. Bran ran a hand over its mane to calm it. He didn't speak as the others hitched up the second horse, grumbling as they went. Returning to Hyrstow and parsing out how he was going to support his family clogged his thoughts. There was no way he could continue to have Emma work herself to the bone.

Memories of her had been ever-present since leaving Hyrstow. He'd been a fool to cave to his dark mood. And Emma was so good as to drag him out of it.

The others seemed to sense his mood and clambered together onto the wagon, leaving him alone. Branton was fine with it. He'd begun to accept this new version of himself as a man who did not waste words when none were needed. The others could grumble to one another while he tried to push thoughts of Emma from his mind to focus on the worry of income. Plus, he needed to get the men out of Guston territory. The road next to the forest lay south of the town and was close enough that Branton's shoulders had taken up residence around his neck. For all he knew, the manor lord of the area could have men ready to slay them on the road back to Hyrstow territory.

After the Vikings had descended, Ridley had told Bran the story of his last assignment as a knight for before he was assigned chieftain of Hyrstow. There had been much bloodshed in the lands around the forest. One woman's death had turned Ridley from a knight to leading a life in Hyrstow. These lands were tainted with blood and sacrifice. He would not risk his men longer than he thought necessary.

As they began the journey home, the sun tried and failed to reach around the cloud that blocked it. Sam hooted with laughter at a lewd joke of Ewan's. The sound made the corner of Bran's lips lift. When Thomas joined Jory's guffaw, Bran's shoulders eased downward. It was against his inclination, but his creaking laughter escaped when Jory volleyed back a bawdy tale of a barmaid he once met in Eoforwic. There were worse things than being on the road with friends. It was something Bran was beginning to remember.

EIGHTEEN

"The tithe is gone?" Ridley sat like a king in one of the great hall's chairs. He tapped a finger on the armrest, looking at Branton's feet as he spoke, absorbing the information.

"I left it too long," Branton ventured. He ran a hand over the top of the small ax in his belt, avoiding Ridley's gaze. He was the reason the wood had been left uncollected. His inability to complete his duties had come back to bite his ass.

Ridley's brows drew together as his eyes sharpened on the fire before him.

"Perhaps. I will dispatch a herald to advise the earl. It is likely retaliation from Guston. I fear Lachlan should have had us press further when we were taking the land. Could've taken the town itself. My troop was weary, but it would have prevented further trouble. Or it would have caused more. There is no way to know."

Ridley scraped his thumb against his brow. Branton

knew he was allowing himself to muse only because he and Branton were alone. If the others had entered the hall, Ridley would have dispatched orders right away. It was why Branton had insisted he tell Ridley himself. He guessed that his friend needed some time.

"With the herald's message, can we request an allowance for more wood? I can take more men, more carts. We can have it felled and brought back in a fortnight."

Ridley's mouth inched upward as he regarded his friend. "We can. However, there is no guarantee that Lachlan will approve. Everything with Guston has felt... different. When Lachlan would normally keep the peace, he started this odd war with Bernira. He ordered the wood to dry. To not bring it back until later spring. It is almost as if he's baiting Guston."

Branton indicated a chair, and Ridley nodded for him to sit. He lumbered over to the heavy piece of furniture, its arms carved of sturdy oak and dressed with a fur cushion. A sigh of satisfaction slithered out.

Branton was prepared to let Ridley muddle over the details. His only job was to cut the wood and bring it where it needed to go. He needn't have any other concern. Though the way Ridley absently ran his hand through his hair, staring at the fire as if it held an answer, had him thinking there was more to Ridley's worry than met the eye.

"Has anyone seen the dark-haired noblewoman?" Bran asked. He'd been curious as to why the woman would appear and not return.

Ridley closed his eyes and pinched the bridge of his nose. "No. Did you see something amiss on the journey?"

Branton shook his head. He didn't think the woman had to do with the wood's theft, but it was a separate, strange occurrence that he didn't want Ridley forgetting about. A niggling doubt stuck in the back of his mind.

"No, though it's still strange. Woman shows up outta nowhere, seeming to know you and saying she'd be back."

"Indeed." Ridley's grimace was one of annoyance. He straightened, tawny eyes locked on Bran. "Well? Out with it. What do you want to say?"

Bran scratched the back of his neck. Questioning Ridley had never been an issue; however, something in their bond had weakened since he'd taken a step back from life. He wasn't sure if it was his place to do so any longer.

"I know you've said you don't remember her. But it's just us. Were you bedding a noble before you came home? Is there any reason she would come back? Could she have taken the lumber?"

Ridley let the words simmer. His gaze remained locked on Branton, silence hanging. If Branton didn't know his friend, he would have been intimidated. The weight of Ridley's gaze would have forced him to speak to fill the quiet, possibly revealing more. Instead, he held his friend's stare, countenance bored, as Ridley worked over the suggestion in his mind. Finally, Ridley pushed his hands to his knees and rose, stalking around to the back of the chair. He grasped the tall back, the hewn knobs on the edges.

"I've bedded women, Bran. Some of them noble, some not. I will not deny that I've satisfied my lust with willing partners, and I've told Yrsa the same. Though, I cannot think of one that would have traveled into the woods, spoken to Yrsa and Emma, then disappeared. No noblewoman has so much freedom that she can leave her home unattended for long. And I haven't bedded anyone from Guston. That is the only place where I can think that woman came from. And she hasn't returned to relay a message to me."

Ridley shrugged his big shoulders, releasing the chair's back. He stroked a hand over his beard, which he had cropped for the warmer spring weather. "I doubt a woman would have the authority to order the wood stolen."

Branton allowed his brows to shoot upwards, his mouth twitching into a scowl. It wasn't Ridley's inclination to underestimate women. Ridley seemed to understand Bran's surprise. He issued a wry grin, propping his forearms on the chair's back to gesture with his hands as he explained.

"Think about it, Bran. I do not know of many women in a position of power high enough to give an order like that. Not unless they are at an earl's court, even the queen's. And if they are at court, they do not care about the politics of little villages such as ours, believe me. The women of court are pious, hungry for the queen's recognition. They want prosperous marriages for their daughters and dukedoms for their sons. They are strategic, yes. Cunning? Of course. They have to be. But I doubt very much they are giving orders to have lumber stolen from somewhere as far north as Guston."

Branton ran his tongue across his teeth. He nodded, his mind casting back to the urgency he felt when he couldn't find Emma in the forest. It led to thoughts of the other things they did in the forest. He felt raw, gone too long after a wasted trip.

Putting his hands to his knees, he made to stand. The men would be coming in for supper soon.

"Well, I'll be off. I want to get home."

Ridley gave him queer look, like a mixture of humor and longing. He nodded, bracing his hands on his hips. "Thank you for coming to me as soon as you returned."

Two men entered, grinning when they saw Branton and Ridley. Before they could fully interrupt, Bran caught Ridley's attention with his parting words.

"Let me know as soon as you can about what the earl decides. I'm sure the church expected a portion of it. The men were expecting payment. It's a hefty amount we've lost. It's needed, Rid."

Ridley pressed his lips in a line as he nodded. Though he did not understand the burden of providing for hungry children, Bran knew Ridley would do his best for Hyrstow. There was a weight layered in his features that Branton swore wasn't there when he'd left for Guston. It tugged something in him, made him want to do a good deed for his friend.

"I'll tell the High Priest about the loss of the tithe," he blurted.

Ridley gave him a sharp look coupled with an arched brow.

Bran shrugged, his lower back aching from riding all day. "He won't be as angry with me as he will with you."

"You're right about that," Ridley said. He clapped Bran on the back and Bran took his leave.

As he walked out of the hall, he felt his shoulders hitch back up. The High Priest of Hyrstow wasn't one he enjoyed calling upon. But Ridley's relationship with his brother hadn't gotten better after he'd married. Not that the relations between brothers had ever been smooth. The nicest Oswald had been to his younger brother was likely when he'd almost been killed, along with their parents, in the raid on Hyrstow when the boys were young.

St. Paul's great wood doors loomed above him as he approached. They did not have the intricate carvings some cathedral doors boasted, but the planks were well hewn and sanded. Bran couldn't help the sense that he should knock. It was silly, but it struck him that he'd not entered the building since Freda's burial service. He hadn't found a reason to. God had forsaken his family the moment He'd taken its pillar away.

Chiding himself for hesitating, Bran pushed on the door. A priest was on his knees before the altar, hands clasped in prayer, head bowed to the great cross at the far end. Branton didn't want to disturb him. Awolf Tanner sat on a bench with Father Chisholm, deep in conversation. He didn't wish to interrupt, especially since he overheard Awolf refer to one of his daughters as being unable to wed. The church was quiet and he did not want to intrude on Awolf's misery.

Soon enough, Father Chisholm saw Branton hovering near the door. He patted Awolf on the arm, offering quiet suggestions of prayers for strength. They stood, the tanner towering over the priest. Branton nodded to Awolf as he passed. After the other man had left, Father Chisholm offered a kindly smile to Bran.

"My son, I have not seen you within these walls for much too long. Welcome back."

Branton shoved away the awkward sense that he didn't belong and offered a close-lipped smile. "Thank you, Father. I have come to ask an audience of the Reverend Father. I have news of the wood from the new northern lands."

Father Chisholm dipped his head and offered a smile that made him appear much older and wiser than his age, which was close to Branton's own. He gestured to the nearest bench. "I can notify the Reverend Father that you are here. Please, have a seat while you wait. If you've just returned, it may be a good time for rest and prayer."

Branton nodded as the priest shuffled away. He glanced around, warring with the sense that he didn't belong in the quiet sanctuary. The glass windows illuminated the room, a grandeur which no other building in the area had. Freshly washed stones crawled from the floor to the ceiling, finishing in huge beams that supported the cavernous roof. Pride tickled Branton's chest. His father and his father's father had worked on this church. They too had been cutters, settled in Hyrstow—almost unheard of for his profession at the time. Normally, cutters were nomads, living on the outskirts, taking wages where they could. It was a point of pride that his family had been integral in helping maintain the place of worship.

That he could not provide the requested wood dug beneath Bran's skin. The church's coffers were deeper than anywhere else in the area.

Branton didn't have much time to feel the regret. Father Chisholm approached, his lips twitching upward in an apologetic smile. "The Reverend Father is not taking visitors at this time."

"When will he?"

"I am unsure. It could be today or tomorrow. I welcome you to wait this afternoon to see if he is able to fit in your unannounced visit."

Branton scraped his hand across the back of his neck. His hair was getting too long. He'd have to see if Emma was any good with shears. The thought of her caused him to shake his head before he realized he was doing so.

"I need to get home to my wife. I can come back to see the Reverend Father."

Chisholm's eyes tightened. He looked as if he swallowed something sour but nodded all the same. "In my humble opinion, it may serve you to stay. Take the time within the church to pay penance for your absence. Your wife will be there when you return."

The words dug into him, sinking in teeth that wouldn't let go.

"That's what I thought with Freda."

The priest was kind enough to appear cowed at the words. He nodded in parting. Bran didn't hesitate to leave the expansive building behind. In the time Bran made his way to his home, a weary peace had settled in him. Indeed, he worried over the lost income. However, he looked forward to a warm meal with his family. He'd missed the children. Even the baby had taken up residence in his thoughts on the trip home. Her gurgling, drooly grin beneath eyes the color of his own made a small smile form on his lips.

Most of all, he wished to see Emma. He'd been a moody bastard since their copulation, then he'd had to travel to claim the cut wood. It had felt like an age had passed since he'd laid eyes on her, despite it only being a few days. They'd taken their marriage oath a little less than three months ago now. It humbled him to think that he'd gone from hating the prospect of a marriage to yearning for a look upon her face. Freda was with him every moment of the day, yet Emma called to him like a siren he could not escape.

NINETEEN

Branton kept glancing at her as he undressed. She knew, because she was doing the same to him. Their eyes locked, sheepishly at first, but with each passing moment their gazes grew bolder.

He'd returned without the cut wood, something Neil peppered him with questions about, but rather than impatience, Branton met the family with hugs. He claimed to have missed them, even though he was not gone long. It made Ginnie grin larger than Emma had seen as of late and caused Æfflead to run around the room saying, "miss us, miss us, miss us."

All the while, his sky-blue eyes hadn't traveled far from her. It caused Emma's pulse to throb beneath her skin. Emma had chided herself as she tucked the children into bed. Surely, Branton didn't mean that he'd missed her as well.

Though, alone now, she wasn't so sure. She stood on her side of the bed, brushing out her hair. It had grown longer and somehow felt thicker, despite the meager meals she ate. She hadn't been particularly hungry as of late. Not when there was so much to do. In Bran's absence she'd taken the time to sew a new tunic for Ginnie and had added a length of fabric to the cuffs of Neil's trousers to extend their life. She wished to buy cloth for Neil's cloak but didn't want to stretch their meager sceats. Now that Branton hadn't procured the wood, she was doubly glad she hadn't. Branton must have picked up on her inner calculations because he said, "Ridley is sending a herald to the earl to find out if we have the allowance to cut more of Guston's forest."

He sat on the bed, stripped to his underpants. She thought she would be immune to the sight of him by now. Previously, they'd resolutely faced away from one another for propriety's sake, but since the day in the woods, their discipline had worn. They hadn't seen one another fully nude, though seeing one another in their nightclothes had become almost routine.

Almost.

Because Emma could hardly take her eyes off the breadth of Bran's shoulders or the way his stomach muscles shifted as he stretched his arms overhead. Dark hair covered Branton's chest down to his navel and Emma thoroughly enjoyed the domineering sight of it.

"Ah," was all she said. Though the sight of Branton was distracting, her mind dragged her over the worry of money again.

"Can you use some Merthe's savings for the next

while? I'm sure if we can cut again, the earl will pay well."

Emma placed the brush on the small table beside the bed.

"If."

Branton's lips drooped, his hands hanging between his knees in defeat. He nodded.

"I've cut enough for Ridley as of late. I can request more in the meantime. He is in need of an inn. And I will follow up with the church. There is still a need for more living quarters."

The words were offerings on action Emma wished he'd taken earlier. She pressed her lips into a line to prevent herself from admitting so. Her gaze went to the bed, unfocused while she calculated how much she had saved and how much they would need to get through the hump of spring. As if sensing her discontent, Branton stood and changed the topic.

"You'll never guess who's taken a liking to Sigrid Tanner."

Emma lifted her chin to meet his gaze, her shock apparent on her face. "Well, come on, tell me what you know. You can't just drop that sort of information into the conversation and expect me not to be curious."

Branton turned, eyebrow arched. A wry smile decorated his lips as he stood and moved toward her. "I'm not dropping anything. It's Sam. He's been seen bringing flowers to her house. Ewan asked him about it on the road and he said he'd like to court her."

"And? Do you know if she reciprocates his feelings?"

Bran hitched a hand on his hip as he beheld her. Mirth lit a flame in his blue eyes. "Why so nosy, Ruthless? I thought you were too busy to worry about the village gossip."

Emma's mouth dropped open. Branton had stepped so close they were but a hand's breadth apart. She didn't know what to do with this sudden invasion of her space or his teasing attitude.

"I will have you know I am busy and still enjoy a little news now and then," she teased, smacking him lightly in the chest. He didn't move. Rather, he looked down at where she'd hit him, then at her face, his grin curling into a full blown smile.

Emma suddenly felt hot all over. The air was heavy with threat, but Emma stood her ground, her hands itching to score along Branton's naked torso.

Then he was dropping his shoulder, pulling her forward into him. In an instant, Emma was thrown over the meaty muscle, facing his backside, her legs dangling precariously against his chest.

"Bran!" She whisper-shouted so as not to wake the children. He landed a loud smack on her bottom in response. Emma squawked at the indignity of it, but Branton just laughed, the sound rich and gravely. Her own laugh slipped through her lips as she wiggled against his hold. It was futile. Branton's strong hands banded around the backs of her thighs like strips of iron.

"Are you feeling full of kindness now?" he asked, the deep timbre of his words dancing through the thin fabric of her nightgown.

"No, you big brute! You want to see ruthless? I'll give it to you!"

Emma wound up a fist and struck him in the round flesh of his backside. He must have anticipated the move, however, because he tightened his muscles. It was more like hitting a tree than a man.

"Ow."

He chuckled, his fingers gripping her legs like he was about to pry them open. His face turned to her hip and Emma felt his teeth denting her flesh before she was being righted, sliding down his front, her body absorbing the feel of all those swells and valleys of muscle.

"See? I told you. Ruthless," he said. One hand remained locked on her hip, the other came up to sweep the billowing hair from her face. Emma pretended to snarl but she couldn't hold the expression. At the sight of Bran's soft eyes, his smile, her worries abated, her mouth dissolved into a grin.

"Did you just bite me?"

Branton's throat bobbed, features slowly morphing from flirtatious to serious. His hands on her loosened enough that Emma covered them with her own to prevent their leaving. She tried not to take the swing of Bran's moods to heart, though it was difficult losing the grinning man. Emma was desperate to keep him.

"And? How did I taste?"

Bran's eyes widened, the blue glittering like jewels in the firelight. Again, Emma was struck by how damn gorgeous his eyes were. She tightened her hold on his hands, leaning into him lest he disappear into the cloud of his grief once again.

"You taste like I want another bite."

The flush that reddened her cheeks stole down to tighten her nipples into points against the fabric of her nightgown.

"Take one, then."

Bran's gaze darkened, hands flexing against her in the most delicious, proprietary manner.

"I promised myself I wouldn't do to you what I've done before," he rasped.

Emma's heart fell. So, it was back to him denying her, then.

"And what's that? Offer me pleasure?" The tart words were out of her mouth before she could catch them within her teeth.

"No." Bran shook his head. "I told myself I wouldn't just take you. You didn't have much of a choice both times we were together."

Emma released his hands to step back and put her fists on her hips. It was either that or hit him for being so dense.

"Did it not appear that you satisfied me both of those times?"

"No. But—"

"Then halt your worries. I am pleased to hear of your concern over my choice, however, there seems to be no other way in which to convince you that your physical interest in me is not one-sided. If you crave a release such as I do, then we can come to an arrangement where we need not be so cautious with one another."

If the sentiment startled him, he didn't show it. Instead, he absorbed her words like water seeping into dry ground. Finally, he clasped her hip in a big hand and drew her into him.

"Another arrangement? That's all?"

Emma was unprepared for the diminishing sensation the last words placed on their intimacy. Foolishly, she'd held out hope that perhaps Branton would care for her in his own way. But time and grief were strange things and though Bran proclaimed that she was invaluable to the family, it didn't mean she was invaluable to *him*.

Emma rolled her eyes to cover up the sting, bringing her hands up to smack against the round hardness of his upper arms. "Indeed. Us lying together to satisfy our needs does not need to complicate anything. You can be devoted to Freda. I can remain my own. We can indulge in one another's bodies without concern of offending the other, if you so choose."

The set of his lips in a line within his beard almost made her think she'd misread the situation, but then he was scooping her up, shelving her bottom on his forearms.

Emma didn't hesitate to open her thighs, hitching her legs about his waist. She skimmed her hands across the expanse of his shoulders, bringing them up to his face so that she could plant a kiss on his mouth. He ducked, instead placing a kiss on the bone that swept across the top of her chest. His lips were soft but his beard scratched, the sensation mixing with the solidness of his body between her legs.

After a taste of her, Bran ran his lips downward, across the swell of one breast, then the other. All the while, his hands worked, kneading her ass. Emma loved the rough way he handled her. As if he wasn't afraid to use her for his pleasure. And after having had him twice, Emma desperately wanted to be used.

Branton's lips found her nipple overtop her shift. The pebbled bud was begging for attention. Greed, flagrant and overpowering, took over. Her hands, acting of their own accord, secured around his neck while she pushed her chest up. She didn't bother pressing her lips shut over the groan that tumbled forth when he clamped his teeth around a nipple over the cloth.

"Bran," Emma mumbled against his hair. The strands were coarse yet comforting, just like the rest of him. When he released her breast to pay attention to the other, Emma's hips jerked forward to ride him. His cock was so hard against her, it felt as if it would punch through his underclothes.

"Stand up," he commanded around her breast.

Her brow pinched as she gazed down at him, unsure. He loosened his hold, allowing her to drift down his body. Her skin scraped against the barrier of her clothing, all the while molding to Bran's hard frame as he slid her down. His hands remained on her hips when she stood as if he didn't want to stop touching her. Emma was dizzy, her mouth watering, core aching as he appraised her.

"I want to unwrap you like a gift."

Emma couldn't help the grin that spread her cheeks wide. She didn't know if this tentative arrangement of pleasure would hold but decided to give in to the promise of it. Bran released her to crouch down, gathering the hem of her shift in his awaiting fingers. Like the slow rake of water over stone, he brought the material upward, first baring her lower legs, then her knees. Branton paused. Worry struck the smile from Emma's face. She could only see the expanse of his back, bent forward as he was. "What is it?"

Bran looked up at her with a notched eyebrow, his ragged breath tickling the skin of her knees. He looked sheepish as he said, "How is it that your knees are so divinely shaped? Your legs?"

The laugh that burst from Emma came from a deep place that she usually kept locked tight.

"I had no knowledge that knees could be shapely," she teased.

Bran's lips curled into a crooked smile as he crouched further, cupping her lower legs in his hands. Emma's breath hitched as he dipped his lips to one knee, then the other. Her shift remained gathered in his fist as he continued up her body. The scrape of his lips across the crown of bone, the heat of his hands, the warm caress of his breath, had Emma's eyes rolling back. When his lips met with the skin of her thigh, she had to bite her own lip to stop from crying out. Instead, she buried her hands in his hair.

"May I taste you, Emma?"

Emma looked down into eyes that burned like the center of a flame. The mound at the apex of her thighs quivered with want, drooling with hunger for him.

"Y-yes. Please. I would like that very much."

"Too proper," he snarled, nipping the inside of her thigh. "Tell me what you want."

"I want..." Emma couldn't possibly voice all the ways that she'd imagined him over the past few weeks. Embarrassment coloured her cheeks at the thoughts of his lips against hers while his hand lay like a necklace against her throat, or of his arms straining as he held her ankles in the air while he drove into her, or of his fingers working between her legs while he thrust into her from behind, his teeth on her shoulder as he did so.

"Tell me," he whispered against her flesh. His tongue scored the skin of her upper thigh a moment later and Emma wanted to dissolve.

"I want your mouth between my legs. I want your hands on me. I want you to take me on the bed, hard."

Branton's brilliant gaze widened for a speck of time before it descended into wickedness.

"Ruthless," he chuckled, the sound like a clap of lightning to her skin. Then he disappeared beneath her shift, his nose burying into her mound. Emma grasped his shoulders as his tongue slid along her slit. Gently, he lapped her, seeking out the bud between her legs.

The sensation was so decadent, and overwhelming, it was nearly uncomfortable. Emma couldn't help but flex her thighs, trying to push them together. Jon hadn't enjoyed pleasuring her this way. He'd done it a few times when he'd noticed how well she liked it, but in each instance, he told her how it took too much time when he was so primed with lust, he just wanted to enjoy her.

It was ridiculous she ask it of Bran. Though, the wet silk of his tongue, the manner in which he speared her; it was too delicious of a sensation to have him stop, despite knowing in the back of her mind he likely wanted to. As his tongue swirled around the bud, Emma pressed his shoulders, a silent order to have him move away.

"What?" Bran growled as he halted, his head like a boulder beneath the cloth of her shift. Emma was suddenly thankful the billowy material allowed for Bran's huge frame.

"You can stop. You don't have to keep going if it is not something you wish to do."

Fingers tightened on the back of her thighs. "What if this is exactly what I wish to do?"

The dead seriousness of his words sliced her doubt in two. She licked her lips and said in an unsteady voice, "Then continue."

Emma hadn't finished speaking before the warmth of his tongue tangled with the flesh of her core. Branton ate her like a man starving. She couldn't help but tremble. It felt too good to have such a man worship her. She had to place a hand over her mouth to cover the moan that tried to escape. There weren't words for the pairing of Bran's scratchy beard against her upper thighs and the skill of his tongue. Her skin felt as if it was on fire.

Emma's release was a snake coiling deep inside her, readying itself to strike. When Emma was at the precipice of pleasure, Bran moved his mouth away, drew back the skin of her mound, and bit her lightly above the nub. A bolt of shock went through Emma, so swift, she would have toppled over if Bran didn't have a hand locked around her thighs. Then he scraped his bottom teeth over her, his tongue flat and insistent against her, and she *melted*.

"Bran," she whimpered as she fragmented. She felt him grin against her skin. Rather than give her the moment's reprieve she thought she needed, he pushed a finger into her and pressed down with a long swipe of his tongue. Pleasure shot through her, as sharp and precise as the prick of a needle. She moaned, collapsing over his head while he continued to tongue her. When she tried to move away, too sensitive to take anymore, Bran drew back. Even as she shook, Bran's head remained beneath her nightshift. He'd removed his mouth from her to allow her to work through her satisfaction, but then she felt his teeth on her inner thigh and she thought she'd come again. His hands scraped up the backs of her legs, his lips drawing upward against her hip, stomach, between the softness of her breasts. When he settled between them, nuzzling the flesh then applying open mouthed kisses, Emma giggled.

"She speaks," Bran murmured, his head bobbing beneath the fabric.

"Those weren't words," Emma said. Her voice was lower, slower than normal. Bran sucked a nipple into his mouth. Emma hissed through her teeth. Damn the man, he knew how to pleasure a woman. A part of her was regretful she was only figuring this out now. They could have had months of pleasure if she had taken him up on his offer to service her.

It wouldn't have been the same.

Branton hadn't been ready. She wasn't sure he was ready now. Though the glint in his eye as he released her nipple and shook himself out from beneath her shift told her otherwise.

"You look hungry for me, Emma. Are you?"

"Y-yes," she said, voice thick.

A wicked grin spread Bran's lips. With his tousled hair and the press of the thick length of him against her body, Emma's heart tried to jump out of her chest. He was downright devilish. Handsome. And...

Mine.

Her heart tripped over the word and looked at it as if discovering possessiveness for the first time. Finally, her mind caught up. He wasn't hers. He never would be. She was always someone's second choice. But, in moments like these, she could pretend she was first.

"You're going to stand there and take what I give, understand?"

Emma sucked her bottom lip through her teeth and nodded. Then Bran went to work.

CHAPTER

TWENTY

"Lift your arms," Branton commanded as he clutched her shift in a fist and pulled upward. Emma obeyed. Her nether region pulsed, aching to be filled. She would do whatever Branton asked, as long as she could have more of him.

The material rasped over her heated skin, blinding her for a moment as it went over her head. Anticipation was a tingling feeling that wound through her chest and up her arms. She was entirely at Bran's mercy. When off, Emma found Branton's gaze devouring her body as if it were dessert.

"You've taken your pleasure. Now I seek mine. Get on the bed, eyes forward. On your hands and knees."

Excitement was a taut string in her middle. Her quickness betrayed how eager she was to comply. The soft stuffing of the mattress caved beneath her hands and knees while the blush that cloaked her was red hot.

But Bran didn't climb onto the bed behind her.

Emma heard rather than saw the rustle of his clothing as he discarded his underclothes. Her eyes begged for her to look. She wanted nothing more than to drink in the expanse of Branton's bare flesh, but her fear that he would reject her if she did not do as he ordered kept her gaze locked on the wood grain of the wall. Still, he didn't move to her. Just when she grew impatient enough to look back, she found him at the side of the bed, wearing only his vambraces.

Her mouth dropped open. Bran was like the statues she'd heard of in the king's castle. Though she knew his shoulders were wide and meaty, she'd not dared look upon him with such open abandon. They capped his body like round boulders. The muscles of his chest were proud and tight and hard. He stood on thickly muscled legs. His stomach? A lesson in brawn. And lower, his thick, veiny cock jutted next to her mouth. The crown was nearly purple and the girth of it made her clench her thighs together. *That* had been inside her? Moisture wept from the tip.

"What do you want, Emma?"

She couldn't help running her tongue along her top lip. Something deep in Branton's gaze flared. She might as well have shouted she wanted a taste. He wrapped a large hand around his shaft and moved closer.

"Are you hungry for me, Ruthless?"

Emma's arms nearly gave out at the suggestive words. As scandalous as it was for her to want him in such a manner, she did. She wanted to learn the feel of him this way. To see his undoing by her. Without hesitation, Emma leaned forward, lest he change his mind. Branton hummed appreciatively in the back of his throat.

"Take it into your mouth. And I'll see if I can't make that nice cunt of yours come again." His tone was like gravel. She wanted it hoarse from calling her name.

Emma leaned to her left, angling her head appropriately, licked her lips once, then slid them over Bran's meaty head. He tasted like sin and shadows, musky and warm. Above her, Branton let out a string of curses as she slid her mouth downward, taking more. When he hit the back of her throat, she backed off, swirling her tongue around the tip then down again. Lord, the girth of him stretched her mouth in a way that Emma had never experienced. She had to loosen her jaw, slathering him with her spit so that he could glide better along her tongue. His fingers drifted through her hair as she bobbed, back and forth, sucking at intervals then loosening her throat. As she hollowed her lips, Branton issued a strangled sound from deep in his chest and pulled away. Emma nearly fell on her face into the mattress.

"Devil knows I wasn't expecting *that*. You are too talented," he muttered. Then he was climbing onto the bed behind her. She was ready for him to take her hair in his hand and spear into her, however, he placed his hand on her lower back instead. Gently, he rubbed his palm in a circle over her heated skin before sliding it down to grip her hip.

"I need you now. Take it well for me."

"I will," she said with a glance behind her. The sight

of him, the expanse of his chest hair, dark and over-bearing in the firelight, caused desire to thrum through her like a wave.

Branton wasn't gentle. He didn't need to be. Sucking him had turned her core to liquid. He shoved into her opening as if he was powerless to stop himself. It was then that all Emma's sense left her. Branton stretched her so wide, made her so full, that when he pulled out, she hiked her ass backward to halt the loss. She could be filled by him forever.

He grunted a laugh and gave her a light smack across her buttocks. The sting made her gasp, but the sensation wasn't unpleasant.

"Still hungry, you greedy little thing. I shall have to satisfy you, then."

Emma couldn't help but clench around him as he pushed forward. He was right. She was greedy. She needed Bran inside of her like the crops need sun. A slave to her body, she would do whatever he told her from now on, if she could only share his bed for the rest of time.

Branton clutched her hips, his fingers digging deep as he thrust in and out of her. Again, Emma glanced over her shoulder, wanting to see his stomach muscles bunch with the strain of movement. The smacking sounds of sex filled the room and once Bran saw her looking between his body, the flames of desire in his eyes were set ablaze.

"Do you like watching your hungry cunt devour me? You take it so well." He skimmed one hand up the slope of her spine, then wrapped his fingers around her neck, pulling her back into his chest. The reposition caused him to go deeper.

"Bran," she gasped. His fingers pressed her neck on either side of her windpipe and Emma thought she would just about die from the pleasure of it. Her climax threatened, like fire set to burn an entire forest.

"Yes," she moaned, her throat working against his grip as he took up a punishing pace. In, out, again and again until he slid his other hand from her hip to the apex of her thighs and rubbed. Emma mumbled a string of incoherent words as her release overtook her, like a ship swept up in a storm, tipping over and emptying itself through her. Bran's body furiously jerked into hers, his thrusts shoving them further up the mattress, his fingers tightening around her neck. Her vision waned as his cock throbbed within her and Emma felt as if she was teetering between the clouds.

She wanted every night to be like this one. For all of Bran's misery, an inkling she was the one to bring him out of the darkness had sprouted in her mind. He cared for her, in his own way, and she him. They were good together. And despite all the times her hope soared only for him to destroy it, it was rekindled any time he looked at her. Freda had his yesterdays. Emma wanted his tomorrows.

It was selfish of her, but in that moment when they were still joined, his heart thundering against her back, it was too hard to remind herself she meant little to him.

With his pleasure complete, he released her throat,

wrapping his arm beneath her breasts to hold her up. Then he was nuzzling her neck, soothing the bruises that would come with his tongue. Their breaths heaved, sweat slicking their bodies as they tried to calm, Bran still seated to the hilt inside her. Her hair was a tangled mess between them. As she relaxed back into Bran's strong arms, she considered how good it felt to be conquered like a piece of rare land.

"Are you hurt?" Bran asked, his tone etched with concern.

"No," Emma said, a smile cradling the word. "I'm wonderful."

Bran's relief-filled laugh wove into her hair. "Thank God."

Gently, he withdrew. Emma bit back a whimper at the loss. She wanted to reach back for him but stopped herself. Branton took up a cloth from the nearby table, rinsed it in the small basin beside, and said, "Here, Emma, let me tend to you."

Still on her knees, Emma remained tight-lipped yet compliant as he pushed slightly on her lower back so that she moved onto all fours again. He cleaned the remnants of himself off her, one hand running over her backside in round, soothing motions.

When finished, he looked around the room, a bewildered look on his face.

"What is it?" Emma asked. She turned and sat on the bed, her lower half stinging a little as she did so.

"I seem to have become dull in a matter of minutes. I can't find my tunic."

He blinked hard, looking around the room while Emma stifled a giggle. He looked sharply at her.

"I'm sorry, I don't mean to laugh," she amended, covering her mouth with her hand. Bran's lips twisted up into his crooked smile.

"Don't apologize. I like the sound."

Finally, he found his tunic behind the chest on the side of the bed.

As he draped it over his head, Emma spoke what was on her heart. She wanted more of him. Wanted him to lay in comfort after what they'd just done.

"Sleep in the bed, Bran."

He looked up at her, one eyebrow arched in an unsaid question.

"I...do not know if it would be right," he said slowly. He looked to his cot, then her on the bed. His hands flexed into fists at his side.

"Please. I lie here every night thinking you'd rather be anywhere but beside me. I won't bother you if that is what worries you."

He shook out his shoulders as he paced to the door and back. His gaze raked over her. The glow of the fire emphasized the slight lines that had gathered around his eyes.

"You're not a bother, Emma. Ever. I'm sorry if I've caused you to think so."

"Then come share the bed. It is yours."

Bran put his hands on his hips and dropped his head, his chin touching his chest. He heaved a breath. Without looking at her he said, "Freda died in that bed."

Emma's entire being ached. The confession stained her lips; it was long overdue.

"She didn't. It is my bed from my hut. I had help moving it in while you were gone. There was never a good time to tell you. You seemed so resolute in your decision to stay away from me, and I didn't want to upset you further. I put the other one back in my hut for the time being. This one is a bit smaller, but not by too much."

Bran's shoulders seemed to crumble as she spoke. A glassy sheen grew over his eyes, a sliver of hope shining in them as he dragged his gaze from the mattress to her face.

"You did?" His voice was a cracked whisper.

Emma nodded. "I did. I'm sorry if that displeases you, but I wanted my own bed. Not the one my friend took her last breaths in."

Bran swallowed then turned away. His shoulders heaved, and he took a shuddering breath, head bowed. When he turned back, his eyes still shone, but he'd gotten control of his breathing.

"Aye, then I will sleep in the bed."

He ambled over, appearing lost as he pulled back the blanket. The mattress sagged under Bran's weight. A satisfied groan escaped him as he eased into its softness.

She turned her gaze ahead, spooling back into herself, her lax muscles stiffening. He would have second thoughts about what they'd just done. Might even hate her in the morning despite the promise they were just using the other to meet a physical need.

Emma's heart twisted in her chest.

"Goodnight." She said it in a voice that left no room for further discussion, rolling to face away from him. Branton didn't say anything as she lay her head on the pillow.

She refused to let it hurt.

Rather, she considered the depth and facets of feeling one person could have for another. And while she loved Jon and missed him, it occurred to her that she and he didn't have the tenderness for one another Branton and Freda had had. A bitter taste bit at the back of her mouth. Perhaps, she'd just gotten a taste of it, too late, with a man she could never truly claim.

TWENTY-ONE

The stirring of children in the next room roused them from sleep. Somehow Emma had fully come to rest atop Bran, as if she were a lizard climbing onto a large warm rock. Both of her legs were on either side of Branton's hips while her head lay on the center of his chest. He didn't mind. Rather, he'd wrapped his arms around her middle during sleep, locking her in place.

Clearing her throat, Emma moved upward to roll off him, but Bran caught her around the bottom, scooping her forward, putting them nose to nose.

"Bran! Wha..."

He winced. "Apologies. I didn't want you being prodded by a very eager part of me."

A little chuff of surprise sprang out. Bran scrunched his face, trying to hide the grin that was forming.

"It's alright. It is natural," she allowed. "Though,

after last night, I can see why your lower half would be inclined to think it would be getting attention today."

She had the audacity to wiggle. Branton squeezed the round flesh of her backside, a laughing groan escaping him. He sorely wished he could indulge in the previous night's activities again. He dropped his head back while he scored her center with his insistent appendage. As if on instinct, she arched into him. All his thoughts smeared into a mess of hands, lips, and skin.

"Bran," she breathed against his lips.

The way she said it, the tangle of her tongue over the 'N' in his name made him ache. It struck him that she wanted him just as much as he wanted her. It was wonderful.

"Tell me something of you. Something that no one else knows," he said softly.

Emma layered her hands on his chest. She placed her chin atop them.

"There isn't much to tell. You know me, Bran."

His throat suddenly felt thick. Indeed, he knew her, as a friend and a partner in their home. But did he truly know the woman beneath her duties?

"Humor me. Please."

He couldn't help running a hand over her lower back then tracing absently on her creamy skin.

"I hate potatoes," she said, dissolving into a giggle.

"Potatoes?"

"Potatoes! I know I should be thankful for whatever food graces our table but they are in everything and they taste like mush."

Bran's deep chuckle rumbled from him into her. He couldn't help it. Potatoes? How could such a practical woman dislike something so vital to their life? He suddenly craved to know more about her contradictions.

Before he could ask, the children's sniping at one another in the next room grew louder. Emma sighed, letting her head fall to Bran's chest. He clasped the back of it, hugging her to him as he made a noise of agreement in the back of his throat.

"We need to get up," he murmured, though longing colored his tone. His muscles were deliciously sore from their exertions.

Without warning, Emma placed a kiss on Bran's chest, atop his heart.

"What was that for?" he asked.

"Simply a thank you for last night."

Before he could respond, she lifted her leg and rolled off him. He let her go. He had to. The gift of her bed had nearly rendered him speechless. It was coupled with a deep affection for her that had shaken him. When he'd gotten ahold of himself enough to pull her to him, she'd already turned away.

Rather than take the time to light a fire, they bustled around the room in search of clothing. They didn't speak, though Bran wanted to. He wished to unspool Emma, to know her in more than kisses and urges.

As they completed their dressing, Bran stood before her. He sought her shoulders in the darkness, resting his hands atop them. He didn't know what to say other than he wanted her to know how grateful he was for her switching beds and that sharing her body with him was something he didn't take lightly.

Tate began to cry. Calming shushing sounds came from Merthe next. The smack of something on the floor, and Neil's muttering cut through the door.

Bran sighed through his nose. The silence between them grew stifling. He pressed her shoulders with his thumbs, as if to hold her there, with him, until he could think of how to name his gratitude.

"Don't speak," Emma whispered into the dark. She patted his vambrace in a dismissive gesture. "I know you were just doing your husbandly duties. I understand, and I thank you."

Branton remained silent as he dropped his hands from her. The children grew louder. He opened his mouth to halt Emma, but she ducked around him and went into the next room, leaving him staring after her for once.

THE REVEREND FATHER failed to call on him in the days that followed. Branton went back to the church twice to advise him of the stolen wood. It didn't matter. He was ignored. After two days, he imparted the news to Father Chisholm to relay the loss to the Reverend Father. The news had likely already spread through the village.

The rest of the week was spent cutting the Hyrstow forest in preparation for Ridley's inn. It was necessary work and yet salacious thoughts of Emma prompted him to remain close to home. Though there was barely time for it, they somehow ended up tangled in trysts. One in the woodshed, another in her hut when he caught her alone baking, a third time when she'd tracked him down in the forest to offer him some lunch. He took pleasure with her every evening, practically salivating any time he saw her. His lust drove him. At least, that's what he told himself it was. He resolutely shoved his guilt about betraying Freda to the corners of his mind, allowing it to eat at him when he was alone.

Days later, Neil caught up with him as he walked through the meadow to tell him Ridley needed him. Branton found his friend in his hut, poring over a book with a quill and ink. The bed, table, chairs and cabinet were the only items in the small space. It was a boon that Ridley had a space to work, however, Branton wondered how long he would keep his family's hut now.

"Nowhere for you to do that in the hall?" Branton said by way of greeting.

Ridley's grin made the corners of his eyes crinkle as he stood.

"Good to see you, Cutter. Indeed, my hut is the only place I can concentrate. If I am in the hall, the men find me with questions or ale. If I am in my personal quarters, Yrsa finds me for...other things."

Branton refused the seat offered to him as Ridley sat back down. "I have news from the earl."

"And?"

"He has issued a decree for more lumber harvested from Guston's woods. He wants it soon. The timing is sharp. I am to travel to his keep in three weeks' time. He wants it by then."

"Done. And I will accompany you to the earl's keep." The words were out of his mouth before Ridley finished speaking.

Ridley held up his hands. His smile revealed the white of his teeth. "I appreciate the eagerness, Bran, but it will be lots of work and travel. Once the cutting is brought back to Hyrstow, you can remain behind if you wish. I will take Ewan, Sam, Wilf, Jory, and Thomas. Grahame must stay back to finish lambing, otherwise, I'd bring him too."

Branton shook his head, arms crossed. "It's my work you're taking. After the first theft, I won't let it out of my sight."

Ridley's brows rose, his mouth twitching downward. He leaned back in his chair, stretching his long legs beneath the table and crossing them at the ankles. He pressed the tips of his fingers together.

"We will not let anything befall your lumber. I can broker the payment myself. I swear to you that I will bring back all the funds."

Bran ran his hand over the back of his neck. He was properly cowed that his friend thought he didn't trust him for payment. "I trust you, Rid. But it is a mark of my honor to see this lumber to the earl. He's given me more allowance than necessary on account of the theft. I have to prove to him that my services are worth it."

Ridley nodded, his forefinger against his lips as he thought.

"What of Emma?" Ridley asked.

"She understands if I have to leave," Bran answered immediately, though he wasn't as sure as his tone.

The hut's door opened, and Grahame strode through. He wore a cloak of fine wool, its wheat color bringing out the shine of his brassy hair.

"Greetings," Grahame said as he claimed the chair on the opposite side of the small table. There was a tension about his eyes, his usual grin pulled into a neutral line. Branton wondered what stress his brother-in-law could possibly have.

"Up to your neck in lambs?" Bran offered with a grin.

"Aye. Six so far, the little heathens. Had a good time this winter together is all I'll say. Haven't been able to get to Hyrstow all week."

Ridley clapped Grahame on the shoulder and gave it an encouraging squeeze. "Anything your family needs from the earl's keep?"

Grahame shook his head. He placed his elbows to his knees, hunkering into the conversation. "I'll ask and send word before you leave."

"Shouldn't you know by now?" Branton teased. "You're groomed to take over for your poor old dad, and you don't know what he needs for summer? I'm sure Fiona would like some nice needles, and Wilf could use a new cloak. Perhaps some fresh shoes for both."

Grahame's brow creased. He pushed off his arms saying, "Yes, they'll probably want those. I've been too busy chasing lambs and having Isolde Tanner scold me out of my own house to remember."

"Isolde? You're not bedding her, are you?" Ridley's tone was sharp, his eyes narrowed. "She's been through enough without hope of your flirtation."

Grahame lifted his hands in surrender. "I'm not. Christ. My gratitude to you for thinking I would further harm a damaged woman, though."

It was Branton's turn to lean forward. "Forgive Rid. Isolde has grown into a beautiful woman, and you have certain...proclivities toward..."

"Any woman you can get your hands on," Ridley finished for him. Bran winced.

Grahame's face contorted for less than a heartbeat before it slipped beneath a hooked brow and a devilish grin. Bran almost believed it, but the show of teeth was more feral than anything else. Grahame waved off the insult.

"I'm not one for goods as damaged as hers. And, don't worry. She'd sooner stab me in my sleep than bed me. It's a wonder she's left her sister at home to stay with us. All she asks is news of how Sigrid is doing."

"How is Sigrid doing?" Bran inquired. It surprised him that he cared. As if a great fog was lifting, he realized that people other than he had suffered over the past year.

Isolde still refused to speak with men—other than Grahame, apparently. Her work for Fiona was tireless. She wore her anger like armor, refusing to let anything or anyone dent it. Branton didn't blame her.

"Fine, as far as I know. Awolf hasn't said much, though I know he is trying to broker their marriages."

"Awolf's family is prosperous. What about Sigrid for yourself?" Ridley asked. He drummed his fingers on the chair's arm, impatient at the turn the conversation had taken but willing to endure it for his friends.

Grahame shook his head and stood. "I'm leaving if this is going to turn into talk of marriage. I hear enough of it from my mother. 'What about her?', 'have you considered her?' She's disappointed I'm not going with you to the earl's keep to find a bride of high standing."

"Well? What if you did? I'm sure your father will allow you the freedom to attend me. The ladies at the keep are always looking to secure a profitable marriage for their maidens."

Grahame's nose wrinkled. "Marriage to a child? No, thank you."

"What do you take me for?" Ridley said, exasperation leaking into his tone. He propped his forearm on the table to lean forward. "Not a child. You could broker a contract, wait until the maid has grown."

Grahame began to back up as he spoke. "My family wasn't good enough for anyone to agree to a betrothal when I was young, and I am thankful for it now. I have no mind for marriage. I am quite enjoying my time being the rake."

Branton remained silent as Grahame took his leave. Ridley's gaze remained locked on the door. He seemed to chew over his words before directing his attention back to Branton.

"We'll depart Frigedæg to miss the crowd of Saternesdæg's market."

Bran nodded. An itch had taken up residence in his center with the length of the conversation. He yearned for home. "Your brother hasn't deigned to see me. I've relayed the loss of the wood to Father Chisholm. I'm sure the news has gotten back to Oswald by now."

Ridley sighed, his mouth pulling downward. He absently drew a circle with a scarred finger on the table-top. "He is displeased. The herald also made it known the church is not to be given an allowance of the new wood to be cut."

"Even if it pays?" Branton asked.

Ridley clenched a fist, his gaze locked on the floor as he thought. "Oswald has greed for his church, but Lachlan purposefully gets in his way. It was impressed upon me to not let the church grow too powerful here, but who am I to stand in the way of people's belief in salvation?"

Bran scratched his forearm and forced himself not to shift from foot to foot. He wanted to get home and relay the news to his family that he was to be on the road for an extended period. It would mean Emma minding the children alone, though if he was being honest with himself, she'd been doing so all along. Or maybe it was the prospect of being gone for so long that made him feel as if he had ants in his boots.

"Perhaps there is more at play here than you are aware of. I've never known the earl to do something without reason. Though, with your overtaking lands near Guston and his weakening the church, the reason appears to be power," Branton suggested.

Ridley's mouth pressed into a line. He darted his gaze to Bran then the door, hearing something that Bran had missed. Without hesitation, he pasted a small grin across his lips and straightened just as Yrsa entered.

"There you both are. I heard there was a herald?" Yrsa asked. She patted him on the shoulder as she proceeded into the hut and came to stand beside Ridley.

"Indeed," Ridley answered, threading his fingers through his wife's.

"And? What is taking so long to discuss?"

"You know your husband. Long-winded. Brooding," Bran jested.

Yrsa barked a laugh. Ridley simply stood, his head nearly touching the hut's roof.

"Hilarious."

"He isn't wrong," Yrsa chided, though she ran her fingers over his scruffy jaw with affection. Ridley leaned into the touch like a great dog being petted.

Bran scoffed. He turned, ready to take his leave. "I'm going home. I will arrange for a party to cut on the morrow." He left without a look back. All he would find were Ridley's hands around his wife's waist. Branton didn't know how they got through the day.

Branton did some brooding of his own as he crossed the village to his hut. He and Emma were a partnership. They didn't have the luxury of frivolous touches or teasing comments filtered with love. She did her part, and he did his—albeit better than he had in the past, thanks to her. Their latest agreement to satisfy one another had given him something to look forward to.

Though there was still a distance between them, one he had come to resent.

You resent all of it.

The thought slithered through him, unbidden. It was the truth. He resented having to resort to petty agreements to enjoy Emma. The thought that she wanted the protection of the agreement burned him as well. He'd told her he couldn't be there for her in love. It was still true, though something had shifted.

As he neared his hut, he heard Ginnie's voice rise, accompanied by sobbing. Chickens clucked, fluttering their wings at the disturbance as Neil's angry tone sliced the air. Worry caught a hold of Branton's gut. He broke into a run and when he came around the corner of the hut, he couldn't piece together what his eyes told him.

TWENTY-TWO

Emma had to get off her hands and knees. She struggled to draw a breath as her stomach rolled. Her nails dug into the soil while she tried to mash her lips together against the onslaught. Bile swarmed her throat, then she was emptying it into the dirt beside the woodshed.

"What in God's name..."

Somehow Branton was there, appearing from nothing. He ran to her, falling to the ground beside her, a large hand wrapped around her upper arm, heedless of the muck that would ensconce his trousers.

"Emma? Are you alright?"

Emma wanted to sob with the relief of having him near. Her stomach gave a mighty roll. She opened her mouth to reply, but instead, her lunch splattered onto the dirt. The sour scent made her want to heave again. Branton didn't seem to care. He braced a hand on her back, soothing in its weight, and drew his finger around her ear to remove a strand of hair that had become stuck there. Emma spit, her saliva stringy and rotten.

She closed her eyes, forcing air through her nose. Clear, clean air, in and out. She had to get up. Had to compose herself. Branton was still beside her, Ginnie somewhere behind them, Tate in her arms, both girls crying.

"Is she injured?" Bran demanded.

She could feel his movement, sense him lifting his face to ask his children about her well-being. It made her want to throw up again.

"I'm fine," she managed to say, her voice reedy.

"Shhh," Bran said, his breath against her ear, then he was moving away from her and asking the children, "Is she sick? How long has she been like this? Did she eat something?"

The panicked anguish in his tone caused Emma's heart to tremble. She didn't want him to see her like this, to find out this way, but it hadn't occurred to her until that moment that seeing her in pain could remind him of Freda.

Ginnie's breath hitched in her throat. "She was fine and then not and now she's sick and..."

Branton hushed his daughter's cries and thanked her without leaving Emma's side. He didn't understand the full depth of what Emma had begun to suspect that very week. At first, she hadn't thought it was possible. Then, as time went on, pretending it wasn't real was easier than the truth.

"Bran," Emma said, her throat feeling like shredded

meat. She grabbed at his arm to steady herself as she straightened. Her entire body ached and she must have looked like death because his eyes narrowed on her face before he braced one arm behind her knees and another behind her shoulders. He lifted her as if she weighed nothing. Grateful, her body sagged into his. Exhaustion weighed her down. She allowed herself to tuck into him, her face pressed to his muscled chest. He was wood and leather, spice and sky. For one more moment she could cherish the way he held her before it all came crashing down.

Branton turned toward the house, ignoring Ginnie's tears. Halfway up the path, he stopped, body tensing beneath her. Emma lifted her head to see why.

Father Chisholm was at their door. The priest waited, hands tucked into the long sleeves of his robe. Emma sunk deeper into Branton's arms. She had no idea why the priest was there but couldn't deal with him on top of everything else.

"Father?" Branton said. His voice rumbled through her body, the vibration a comfort as it seeped into her skin.

"Greetings. The Reverend Father has decided to see you. He's sent me to find you to discuss his portion of the earl's request." The priest looked toward Emma in Branton's arms, offering her an unsure smile.

Embarrassment flooded her. She tried to push up and out of Bran's grasp so she could appear presentable, but his grip tightened around her legs and waist.

"Tell the Reverend Father I am indisposed. I will speak with him later."

Bran began walking toward their hut, his gaze dropping to Emma and scoring along her features like a gentle hand along her skin. The urge to bask in his concern was overwhelming. To be wrapped in his strength, his warmth, the kindness that he seemed to only save for her—it was temptation unto itself.

"Branton, I would advise you not to make the Reverend Father wait. He is granting an audience, and I've taken extra time to find you. I fear he will be impatient with—"

Branton's lip curled over his teeth as he stomped up to the door. "I don't care that Oswald doesn't want to wait. My wife is ill. I must tend to her." He shoved open their door with his shoulder leaving a shocked Father Chisholm in their wake.

Inside, Merthe was juggling a tearful Æfflead. The toddler was saying something unintelligible, snot and tears running down her red cheeks. At the sight of them, Emma sagged against Bran's chest, hitching her hand up under her chin to place it on his heart. The hard muscle twitched beneath her palm.

"Your mother needs to rest. Merthe, bring a cup of water when you can, please," was all he said as he walked into their bedroom and shut the door.

Inside, light poured in from the roof's vent. Rather than lay her on the bed, he sat on the edge with her in his arms. Gently, he pressed a kiss to the top of her head.

Emma wanted to melt. She wanted to rage despite

not having the strength to do so. It was unfair that she and Branton had come to an understanding in their marriage only for it to be stomped on so quickly. He would not be happy with the news she held. Emma tried to swallow back the acrid taste that stained her throat.

"Let me see you," Bran said, leaning back a little. His inky brows were pinched with concern, his mouth turned down at the corner. Hair was in his eyes, and he looked at her with such worry, such yearning, that Emma's heart squeezed. How was it that she'd grown to care for this beast of a man who was so torn in his feelings for her?

"Mother?" Merthe entered, a cup in hand.

Branton adjusted his arm against her back so she could sit higher. Merthe handed her the cup, her brown eyes fixed with concern. The rest of her was painted in lines—the grim slant of her lips, the stiffness of her back, the straightness of her arms as she stood with the outheld cup.

"Thank you, darling. I'm fine. I am," Emma said, taking the cup and patting Merthe's hand as she did so.

The skin around Merthe's eyes tightened. She watched her mother take a sip.

The water was warm after having sat in the pitcher all day, but Emma relished the clean taste. She swished it around in her mouth several times before swallowing and taking another drink. Merthe's eyes remained locked on her as Æfflead's whine came from the next room.

"I'll take care of her," Branton said. His breath tickled her ear, stirring the shorter hair around her face that had escaped her bun. Merthe shifted, her gaze switching to Bran's. She held his stare for a long moment, and in it, Emma could see the steely girl who had stood up to the Viking raider over a year ago.

"She needs you right now. Please don't let her down. But don't forget that we Baker women can fare well on our own if the need arises."

With those parting words, Merthe spun on her heel, her tunic twirling around her as she exited the room. Bran's mouth fell open then shut. Emma sipped her water, hiding the grin of pride that threatened to sneak out.

"What did I do to deserve a threat such as that?" he asked.

Emma was glad to hear that humor laced his tone. She straightened. "I believe she thinks that you will react unfavorably to my being ill."

She unfurled herself from his lap, placed the cup on the floor and pushed herself to her feet. Branton held her hand as she rose. It was a courtesy that struck her as kinder than she deserved. He didn't let go once she was steady. The press of his calloused fingers on the inside of her palm lent her strength she was otherwise lacking.

"Emma," he said with more command in his tone, blue eyes darkening. "Tell me what it is. I've come home to tell you I must leave to cut the Guston forest. I just dismissed the Reverend Father's summons. I find Ginnie crying with you on your hands and knees. Please, Ruthless, tell me what is the matter. If you are ill, please lie back down."

Emma held the gentle graze of his voice in her heart for a moment. A tear slipped down her cheek, then another. She brushed them back with an impatient palm. From the depths of her soul, she called from within her the strength she knew she would need for the words she was about to speak. She tried to guess his reaction, whether it be rage or coldness, harsh words or silence. She'd endured much in her life, but for some reason, this upcoming battle seemed like the most fearful she'd contend with.

"I appear to be with child."

TWENTY-THREE

Branton's mouth dropped open as he stared at his wife. His head felt as if it had been caught between an anvil and a blacksmith's hammer. He dropped her hand.

"You're sure?" was all he could utter. Surprise, outrage, fear, guilt, worry raced through him for dominance.

Emma's lips pursed as if trying to hold back a snide remark. Her hands tightened into fists.

"My monthly bleeding has been delayed for a while now—" she said.

"A while?"

"Yes, Branton. It has happened before, even when I wasn't with a man. If I'm overworked or don't eat enough, sometimes it doesn't come for a few months. I do not think it is out of the ordinary, and life has been... difficult as of late."

Her tone was steady, her teary eyes at half-mast as she looked down at him. Hope twinged in his chest.

"Perhaps that is all this is, then," he offered around the panic that seemed to lodge in the lower part of his throat.

Emma shook her head. "I've been sick this week in the same manner I was sick with Merthe."

"How could this happen?" Bran shut his eyes and cupped his palm over his mouth to stanch the flow of questions that swelled to his lips. He knew how. Their wedding night, against a tree. When he'd searched for her in the forest, so frantic he thought his chest would cave in if he didn't find her. Or was it later? Did a child take root while they gave in to their desire the past week? As he stumbled over timelines, he tried to force himself to recall how long it took Freda to know she was with child. She'd been pregnant with Neil when they'd married, then Ginnie a few years later, and with Æffie she'd been so tired and sick...Then there was Tatswip.

The baby had destroyed them both.

And now there was to be another.

Emma loosened her fists to put her hands on her hips. "Surely you understand how—"

Branton held up his hands to stop her. "I do. It's not what I meant. I simply...cannot fathom another child. Were you not taking any herbs? That is what I meant by 'how'."

A deep line appeared between her brows as her mouth melted into a frown. Branton hated the scorn wafting from her quickly crossed arms, her straightened spine. As if she abhorred the prospect of being with child as much as he did.

"I suppose those tasks were my responsibility, as it always falls to the woman to manage families, but no. I took no such precautions. I didn't think it possible. When we acted upon our urges, I did not have herbs ready. And I had no need of them before you."

Bran rubbed a hand down his face, wishing he could scrape off the layer of exhaustion that coated his skin.

Another birth. Another squalling mouth. A memory of Freda in death flew to the front of his mind. The black strands of her hair had been sweaty against the pillow. When Bran got to her he ran his hands through it, his face next to hers as he cried, begging her not to leave him. Blood had swamped the bed, but it had not flecked her hair. Suddenly, his head felt as if it were floating and something deep clawed at his ribs from inside.

"Bran?" Emma asked, her features flowing from resentful to worried. Her voice sounded as if it was coming through a tube. He sucked in a breath, but it didn't fill his lungs. Nothing would. He was hollow, sipping air like it was something he could drink rather than breathe. The blood would overtake Emma. It was his fault. All of it. She would be next to die in the birthing bed, and he would be alone, the children would need him, but she...she would suffer.

Bran's vision turned gray at the corners, dark spots blooming before his eyes as he tried to get a breath out so he could drink more in, but he couldn't make his throat work. Air just kept coming and coming until his head felt as if it would pop off his shoulders. Emma was speaking, though he couldn't discern what she said, then she was beside him, her hand on the back of his neck, shoving it down. He didn't have the will to fight. His head was pushed between his legs and held there, her strong hand on his neck, kneading the muscles in his upper back. He felt as if a knife was lodged in his chest, carving him up from the inside out. He knew one thing with absolute certainty. The babe in Emma would kill her. It would stretch her then rip her, and she would be gone from this earth. Tears of pain dripped from his eyes onto the straw floor but he sat there, unmoving, focusing only on righting his breath, so he didn't kill himself with panic.

Finally, his reedy breathing grew stronger while his vision cleared. Through it all, Emma's hand at his neck was unwavering. When he was able to draw enough air without feeling like his chest would burst, he sat up.

Emma's hand fell. He wanted to grab it, to clutch it to his chest. He wanted to take her to a proper healer at the earl's keep and have her take herbs to rid herself of the child that would inevitably be her doom. In the same moment, rage bled into his every pore. She'd told him she couldn't have another child. He'd believed her. And damn it, he wasn't strong enough to fight the anger flickering within him. The rush of it was easier to embrace than to think of the horrors of their future.

"Did you plan this?"

Emma flinched. She crossed her arms as she stared down at him, as if they could protect her. Her beautiful eyes and petite curves and unwavering duty to his family all seemed like some sort of scheme that she'd concocted. He had no idea to what end, but there was no other reason for him to have slipped up so badly. Lust had clouded him. Now, they both would pay for it.

"Well?" he demanded as he stood. Branton saw her eyes shutter, the edges of her lips whiten as he berated her. But he could not stop the words that flowed from him like smoke from an inferno. His lip curled as he spewed hate for himself onto her. He didn't even have to reach for the ugly words. "Did you conspire to have my child so soon after we'd been wed? Why? To show what a monster I am that I could not resist the temptation of your flesh despite being in love with Freda?"

"I cannot believe you speak to me in such a manner. I knew you would be unhappy. I braced for that. Believe me, I am not all that pleased by this turn of events myself, but to say that I conspired to paint you a monster? I did not imagine you so heartless."

Branton stood, his fists clenched as hard as his jaw. The knowledge she wasn't happy about carrying his child dug like a worm into his gut. Not that he expected her joy. But disappointing Emma, after all she had done for him, was a special kind of torture. One he continued to lash himself with as he glared down at her, breaths shooting through his nostrils like those of a bull.

"You can't fathom how heartless I am," he snarled.

She tightened the grip on her upper arms, her jaw hardening. "I have never known you to be heartless until this moment," she retorted, her tone lofty, as if to rise above the conversation.

Branton was stubborn enough to not allow it. If he couldn't keep her safe, he would drag her down to the depths of hell with him.

"Here is heartless for you," he voice rose while he pointed at her, "how do I know this child is mine? Perhaps you've lain with someone else. I may not be the sire—"

The loud clap of flesh hitting flesh ricocheted around the room before the pain in his cheek registered. The strike swept his head to the left. He reveled in the sting radiating along his cheekbone. When he turned back, Emma was clutching her smarting hand with the other, brown eyes narrowed to slits. She seethed as she spoke.

"How *dare* you. I stepped forward to help with your children. I agreed to marry you so they would have someone to care for them because Lord knows you weren't. I'm the one bringing Æfflead out of her shell and tending to Tate, whom you do not even acknowledge. I keep this home and bring in enough income to keep us afloat, and *how dare you* claim this child not to be yours. I have not lain with a man since Jon passed. Which is a hell of a lot longer than you did after Freda."

The words hurt more than any slap. They rooted down through his chest and made their home in his marrow. Branton wanted to weep at the truth of it. Instead, he pressed his lips into a line and made for the door.

"Where are you going?" Emma demanded.

The anger in her tone, the sheer threat of it, made him continue without a word. He did it to irk her, to break her, just as she'd stomped all over the broken shards of him.

"Branton," she hissed through gritted teeth.

He shook his head as he walked. She was a liar. She'd made him believe she was here to stay, but she'd leave him the same way Freda did. He continued out the door, grabbed his cloak off the hook and stomped out of the house. The warmth of the cloak as he settled it around his shoulders was a welcome reprieve from the wind that rushed him.

Evening had begun to fall, causing him to wonder about the length of time he and Emma had been shouting at one another. Huts passed as he stormed up the path to the central part of the village. There wasn't anyone about, for which he was glad.

In the northern section of the village, the men's hall loomed like a large, slumbering animal. He didn't bother knocking when he came to the timbered door he'd cut the wood for. Didn't stop when several heads looked up from where they were crouched over their bowls of steaming supper. Instead, he made for one of the empty mattresses at the far wall, near Ridley and Yrsa's quarters. Without a word, he huddled down in his cloak and shut his eyes.

Footsteps scraped the floor next to him. Bran cracked an eye to see Ewan standing there, his grin pointed, brow raised.

"Good night?" he asked.

Bran rolled over, giving Ewan his back in answer.

Ewan must have wanted entrance to the afterlife early because he toed Branton's boot with his own.

"Get up. There's ale. It's strong."

Bran scrunched his eyes closed and waited. Ewan huffed a sigh and eventually meandered back to wherever he sat near the fire. The din of conversation and the slurping of food and drink picked up. Laughter abounded as stories began around the fire. When Grahame entered, earning a cheer from the men, Branton grunted and got up. There would be no sleep so early. He rose from the bedroll and claimed a chair by the fire. Grahame's mouth lifted in a quizzical smile upon seeing him in the hall, but he continued to tell of a part of his flock disappearing into the forest and him having to scare off a wolf while the sheep bleated like tittering children. The men's laughter was uproarious.

Bran was passed a mug. He drank from it.

Ewan was asked to tell the tale of their journey with the failed wood tithe. Indeed, the man had a gift for storytelling because there were snakes and a bear and tense sneaking of the cart past an angry landowner on the journey. Bran couldn't help but roll his eyes and gulp his ale. It was refilled.

He drank again, finishing it so as not to have to speak to the other men who tried to include him in conversation. It was refilled.

He drank.

And drank.

Slowly, his thoughts about the child and Emma and the hate he felt for himself began to soften. Laughter was a distraction. Grahame refilled his mug and claimed a seat beside him. They drank deeply. Branton's senses became deliciously dulled. Grahame spun another tale, this time, one of spearing Vikings. Branton swallowed the bitter ale, happy to go along with Grahame's version of events even though he was sure there were fewer men than Grahame claimed, and the fight wasn't so close.

The room softened around the edges with the vermillion glow of the fire illuminating bearded, laughing faces.

Someone plucked a lyre and another began to drum. A hand slapped his back. Bran turned to find Jory grinning over him, demanding he sing. Bran refused at first. But another mug of ale was poured and he was suddenly grateful for the men surrounding him. They wouldn't abandon him like his women. As he listened to the bare instruments, he couldn't help himself. Bran stood, hands going up to calm the shouts of excitement.

"I've had enough listening to your plucky music. Play me something and I'll sing!"

The men stood as they cheered, dropping back into their seats and clapping along to the strummed tune. Bran took another swig from his mug, belched, and opened his mouth. An uproarious song about a victorious battle tumbled out.

He sang for what felt like mere minutes, his voice deep and strong and good. Another tune was struck, and he picked up the old lyrics lurking in his mind. He remembered them all. There was nothing that mattered other than his voice and the men and the ale. A strange part of him wondered why he didn't do it any more. He loved singing.

Before too long, his chest heaved as if he'd run miles, and his throat ached in the best way. Men were singing along, drowning him out and drinking their faces off. Only when the door opened to reveal the pitch black sky outside did Bran realize the late hour.

In the doorway was a woman. A gorgeous, silky-haired woman, slight of stature and large of heart. Her mouth was tight and her stance rigid as she pulled her cloak about her shoulders and peered into the group of men at the fire.

It was his woman. She'd come for him.

"Emma!" Grahame shouted from beside him, waving her in. "Have you come to claim your husband? He's been singing our ears off."

Emma's eyes were wary, though once they locked on him, they didn't falter. She'd come. Despite how angry she was with him, despite the mutinous little thing in her belly, she'd come for him. Bran's grin swelled. He shouted the chorus to the last song, lifting his voice to the rafters as she stepped into the hall and made her way toward him.

"Your man is drunk," Ewan said, hooking his arm around Emma's shoulders and pulling her toward Branton. A spike of jealousy ripped through Bran, but he shrugged it off. He knew Ewan meant no harm, knew Emma wouldn't betray him. She was a good woman. A loyal woman.

And he'd been stupid enough to accuse her otherwise.

He'd been a bastard. The soft cloud of the ale opened his eyes to how truly wretched he'd been. Accusing her... shouting...his hate turned inward, rotting him further.

Before she could make it all the way to him, he moved through the circle around the fire and went to his knees before her. Surprise decorated her features as gasps and hollers rose around the room. Ewan released her, his eyes alight with mirth at the spectacle.

"Emma. I'm a miserable, terrible bastard who shouldn't be allowed near you," Branton said.

The rest of the words he meant to offer were drowned out by whistles and catcalls. Emma blushed, her hand going to her cheek.

"I've come to bring you home," she bent over to say, though Bran could barely hear it over the noise.

His hand shot to his heart, and he leaned back as if her words were an arrow she'd released from a bow. It *was* his home. Her home. Theirs. And it would grow. A child. With her.

As worry and embarrassment carved her delicate features, Branton was suddenly elated at the thought of having another piece of such a woman.

"We're to have a baby!" He threw his hand up as he shouted to be heard over the crowd. Some of the cheering stopped, some grew louder. Bran swayed a little on his knees.

Suddenly, Emma was placing her hands on his shoulders, her face red, then someone wrapped a hand around his upper arm to pull him up. Everything was foggy. It was Grahame on his other side, his head under Bran's arm to steady him as he helped move him to the doorway. Emma remained silent amidst the congratulations, both her hands wrapped around his upper arm. She couldn't close her hands around the muscle, and he flexed it, wanting her to see just how big it was. He knew he wasn't the most handsome and that he'd been terrible. Maybe she'd forgive him if she thought him strong.

Emma looked up at him, a question in her eyes. Even though he saw two of her now, he smiled. With a twist of her lips, she squeezed his arm back. Graham helped shuffle him through the great doors.

Wait.

Bran's mind felt like mud. Did he just tell the entire hall that she was having a baby? He must have drunk more than he'd thought.

The night air felt nice, carrying a hint of warmth. Branton stopped to close his eyes and let the breeze brush his face. Grahame and Emma both halted beside him. Grahame had height over him but Bran was brawn, and he could wield it if he wished. Good thing he didn't wish. Emma and Grahame were his true friends, his wife and brother-in-law. With a hiccup, he began walking again.

Eventually, they got him home, though the fuzziness of his mind did not fade. Blackness rounded the corners of his vision, winking in and out. Or maybe he was winking in and out. He tested one eye, then realized both were closed. He opened them and found himself in his bed, Grahame gone, Emma lifting the blanket to lie down next to him.

His heart squeezed at the sight of her in her night-dress. He hated being away from her, he decided. She lay down with her back to him, so he hooked an arm around her middle. She released a sound of surprise as he dragged her into him, her back to his front.

"Do you hate me?" he asked, though he wasn't sure he wanted to hear the answer.

Emma didn't reply for a long moment. Then her short nails scratched along his forearm. A shiver of plea-sure worked its way through him.

"No. Do you hate me?" she whispered.

Bran propped himself up, prepared to argue. "Of course not. You're my Emma." Then his thoughts drifted to the baby growing in her, to the children. "You're our Emma."

She sighed as if the answer was more exhausting than if he'd admitted his hate for her. The softness of her fingers played along his arm. It made him sleepy. He just wanted to hold her, but he needed her to know something.

"I do not want another child."

She tensed in his arms. Her fingers stopped roaming. Bran's tongue felt too thick in his mouth. He needed her to understand, but it dawned on him that he was very drunk and very stupid and would never be able to explain himself. He tried again.

"I mean I didn't think we would have a child. Not

that I don't want *your* child, just...we are getting old for children."

Branton settled his head on the pillow beside her, so close his lips met her hair. He spoke so quietly he wasn't sure he'd said the words out loud at all.

"I don't want this babe to kill you. I just found you. I want to keep you for myself."

TWENTY-FOUR

Branton's head felt as if it had been sucked through his nose then shoved back in. His mouth was a dry field of scorched earth. It hurt to move and when he did, his belly sought to repay the disrespect he dealt it the previous night.

"...allow me to rouse him..." Emma was saying to someone in the next room. Branton cracked an eye to find the other side of the bed empty. Sun poured through the roof's vent, revealing blankets twisted about his legs. Emma entered, shutting the door behind her. She was fully dressed in a cream tunic, brown skirt, and apron tied tightly around her slim waist.

"The Reverend Father is at our table," she said through her teeth as she whipped the blanket from his waist. Bran tucked down into himself, cowering against the cool air that lit across his skin. He wore only his trousers. Emma gave his hip a light smack.

"Get up. Now, Branton. I am not one to joke about

something such as this. The *High Priest of Hyrstow* is sitting at our table, waiting to speak with you."

She moved to the other side of the bed and drew his tunic from where it lay discarded on the floor. Her movements were brusque, her spine too straight.

"Here?" Bran asked, his mind foggy. As he formed the word, the failures of the previous day came crashing back like a spilled cartload of lumber. He jolted up, having to pause to draw a deep breath, so he didn't lose his guts all over the bed.

"Yes," Emma said.

She came to him, urging his arms up with a gesture. She helped him shrug the tunic on, pulling it down and spreading it across his shoulders. Bran tried to help, but his movements were sluggish. When finished, she gently raked her hands through his hair, smoothing the mussed strands. Branton's eyes drifted closed. Though the movements were quick, he wanted to soak in her touch.

"Bran," Emma said. "Maybe the church will ask more of you. Or maybe the Reverend Father has other ideas on how to gain some coin from the earl. Please, you must hurry. We mustn't show him further disrespect by keeping him waiting."

Bran opened his eyes. Emma's deep brown ones stared back, willing him to understand. She worried her bottom lip. With a groan, he nodded and stood, vowing to himself he would try to make arrangements with the church. He could carry on a conversation without spewing yesterday's lunch all over Oswald's pristine robes.

When he made his way into the next room, he found Neil listening intently to Oswald at the table. Apprehension curled along Bran's insides. Oswald did not stop speaking as Branton came forward. He continued to look only to Neil, regaling him with a tale about the serpent that spoke into Mary's ear.

Only when he finished did he pat Neil's hand on the table between them and look at Bran. The High Priest had lost weight since Branton last saw him. Gone was some of the pudgy roundness he carried about his chin. The hair that sprouted around the base of his skull appeared dull. It caused him to wonder if the man had been eating well.

"Thank you for joining us today, Branton Cutter."

Bran didn't bother smiling. There was no love lost between him and the head of the church. Everyone knew the High Priest hated Ridley's wife. Bran had also stopped attending mass when Freda died. It wasn't a stretch to imagine Oswald's own dislike of him. He inclined his head and gestured for Neil to rise.

"Reverend Father," Bran bowed slightly, as he knew was expected, "thank you for coming all this way to grace us with your presence."

Emma bustled behind him, the sound of a knife echoing along a cutting board filling the hut.

Oswald managed to look down his nose at Bran, despite being seated.

"I was more than curious to find out what was of such importance the Head Cutter would demand an audience then so rudely dismiss one of my priests shortly thereafter."

Oswald's eyes were like chips of icy dirt. Bran swallowed, wishing for water. The back of his neck ached, his clothing irritating his skin.

"My humblest apologies, Father. My wife had taken ill. I sought to help remedy her, and Father Chisholm appeared at that time."

Oswald waved a jeweled hand at the words as if they were nothing.

"I then returned to the church to seek further audience but was not allowed a meeting," Branton explained. He wasn't going to let Oswald shame him in his own home.

Emma came to the head of the table and deposited a loaf of sliced bread and a dram of their best butter along with the last preserve of honey. She dipped her head in a bow as she backed away, barely lifting her eyes to the men. Branton hated it. Emma wasn't some meek woman to be waved away. She was an important member of the community and his household.

"What news have you that you deemed so unimportant? What could you wait to share?"

Branton clenched his jaw. "I told Father Chisholm to alert you. The lumber that was left near Guston for the spring tithe was stolen."

The twitch of Oswald's mouth upwards was barely perceptible, but it was there. He wove his fingers together and rested his hands on the table before him, leaning forward.

"Do you know of the thief?"

Bran's mind felt like it was moving through rotten mud, too slow to pick up any ulterior meaning. He managed to shrug.

"I do not. They left no clues and we didn't bother going to Guston to learn of rumors."

"The chieftain knows?"

"Yes."

The High Priest inclined his head. His gaze shot to the food between them. He plucked a slice of bread from the pile and slathered it with the honey, using up almost the entire tiny pot. The sight of food caused Bran's guts to churn. He needed this conversation over.

"Ridley sent a herald to the earl. We are to bring back more lumber. The church's share is my priority." The priest didn't need to know he was lying. Bran could feel his heartbeat throb in his head. He would have said just about anything in that moment to make Oswald leave.

A spot of honey bobbed on Oswald's lip as he chewed. His brows drew together as he shook his head. "No need to worry. I plan to find another source of wood. I've heard of a traveling cutter from Insmere that may have some. It may be faster for the church to procure his goods."

Oswald continued chewing, licking his thick fingers as he did so, pretending not to acknowledge he'd just told Branton, in his own home, that his work was not needed.

Suddenly, there was a rattle of dishes, as if Emma had put something abruptly down, and she dashed from the hut. Both men startled, watching the door slam behind her. The sound of her retching was not overshadowed by the barrier of the door.

Oswald brushed the crumbs from his fingers, a look of distaste dressing his mouth. Branton tried to wrangle his attention.

"The contracts of St. Paul's have fallen to my family in the past. My grandfather saw its creation, my father tended to it. I am to travel with the cut lumber to the earl's keep in a few weeks time. Allow me to negotiate on behalf of the church. I am happy to provide the lumber necessary for anything the church requires."

Oswald lifted his eyes, which held a mirth Branton was unaccustomed to seeing. It caused a shiver to rattle his spine.

"Don't worry for the church. St. Paul's prestige is only at its conception. There will be enough wood granted from other areas. You need not concern yourself."

Branton wove his hands together on the table. He swallowed back the bitter mark of his pride and bowed his head. "I would like to continue the relationship my family has with St. Paul's. The income is needed."

Oswald stood, waving his hand in a dismissive gesture as he spoke. "The church is in need of lumber now. I will see what my other contacts have. Your income will follow with other work, I am sure. God is both good and generous. Your worry about fulfilling an obligation to St. Paul's is not required."

The High Priest of Hyrstow issued a slight nod then

turned from the room, leaving Bran speechless amid the sounds of Emma's heaving.

No income from the church. Lost income from the previous tithe and a new mouth to feed soon enough. Sweat slicked his brow. His stomach turned. He was able to push up from his chair and dash out the door before he threw up all over the ground beside the outdoor fire pit.

When he finished losing the contents of his stomach, he put his hands to his knees and found Neil staring. He and Merthe appeared to have tended to the chickens, the basket between them was filled with eggs.

"Are you with child too?" Neil asked.

Branton had no idea when he'd found out. Neil's mouth was folded into an accusatory frown, however, there was a lightness to his son's eyes.

Bran wiped the back of his hand across his mouth. He grunted a laugh. "Yes. One made of too much ale."

Merthe's grin was slow, her eyes wary. He winced as he offered them a smile. "Have you seen your mother? She wasn't well when she came out here."

"I'm here," Emma said as she came round from behind the hut. Her features were drawn, her skin pale. The line of Merthe's mouth tightened as she watched her mother stumble over to Bran, though she didn't say anything. She simply ushered Æfflead up the path into the house. For once, Neil followed without comment.

Emma held her stomach as she walked to him. Her eyes watered, full lips downturned and damn it if Branton didn't want to right those lips. Despite the baby, his fear for her safety, their lack of money, all he craved in that moment was to hold her. And for her to hold him. Through the pounding of his head and the rawness of his throat, he closed the distance between them.

Emma craned her neck back to peer up at him, her gaze limned with worry.

"Are you well?" he asked, brushing a sweaty hair off the side of her neck. He thought she might recoil. He would have deserved it. Instead, she leaned into his touch, closing her eyes as if his fingers moving to knead the back of her neck was the most delicious thing she'd felt.

"Better now," she murmured. "I am not used to it. The sickness has overtaken me often in the mornings."

Bran couldn't help sliding his hand down her back to pull her to him. She wound her arms around his middle, releasing a small sigh only he could hear. He dropped his face to the crown of her head and took a deep breath of her hair. Lavender and grass, flour and his own scent from her lying beside him wafted.

Though every trouble seemed at their doorstep, Bran relaxed into her embrace. The weight of Oswald's rebuff was heavy. Though, in that moment, with this woman, a fortitude sprouted within he'd not felt for a long time.

"I'm sorry for yesterday," he said, squeezing her about the shoulders. She looked up at him with a raised eyebrow.

The corner of her mouth twitched. "You said terrible things to me."

Bran swallowed. He had. He'd thought terrible things

as well. He wasn't past thinking them again, either. But he didn't want to.

"Aye."

"You also said something I will carry in my heart for the rest of my life." Emma hugged him tighter, pressing her face to his tunic as if to draw from his strength.

"What was that?"

Emma unwound her hands from his middle and pressed them to his chest, clenching the material a little. Her nails dug into his flesh and he let out a small hiss at the pleasurable sensation.

"You told me that you just found me. That you want to keep me safe and keep me for yourself. I don't think anyone has bestowed a sentiment like that on me before."

Wisps of the memory returned. Of him speaking into her hair in the dark.

"It's true. I can't lose you, Emma. Surely, you must know that." He cupped her face with one hand. Emma looked away, lifting her shoulder in a shrug that broke his heart.

"I understand you don't want to lose me. I care for the children and would be hard to replace. I had a good birth with Merthe. I know that was long ago, but I promise I will do my best to remain on this earth to follow through with our bargain."

Talk of her remaining alive to keep their agreement sobered him. Before its mention, he was about to proclaim how she'd begun to repair a part of him he thought irrevocably broken.

Indeed, they'd had an agreement, several by now, but he was beginning to understand he wanted her to *want* to be with him as well. Instead, she reminded him of their alliance.

Branton dropped his hand from her back.

"Let us go inside and clean up. I must attend Ridley shortly."

Emma's head tipped to the side in question. She appeared as if she were chewing her words then nodded and accompanied him up the path. They must have been a sight: ill, sweaty, and pale.

Branton couldn't help slinging an arm about her shoulders as they walked side by side to the house. She leaned into him, her hand settling across his waist. The trust of the gesture sparked something in him. The breath of a challenge, the desire to conquer. His efforts may have been too late, but he would prove to her he was someone worth caring for. Someone worth the risk of her life for his child. Someone he should have been for her a long time ago.

TWENTY-FIVE

A wave of heat swept over Emma. She'd been baking at her old hut for hours. It was two days until the market, but this pregnancy had forced her to slow in her daily tasks. As of late, she'd needed a head start. Merthe was a godsend. One of them had to bake while the other had to tend the children, make food, and run the house. Today, Emma had claimed baking. She was faster at it and could craft the perfect crumb within the bread.

With a sigh, Emma pushed off from the table that housed her muslin-wrapped loaves. Being baked two days prior to market rather than one meant they wouldn't be as fresh, though she took comfort in the knowledge sales wouldn't plummet. Whether from the spring heat or the need for more household goods, people had swamped Hyrstow's market.

Drawing a deep breath, she patted the small heaviness she felt in her lower belly. Sickness plagued her every morning. She'd counted on her fingers how much time had passed since her last cycle and the frequency of her sickness, and every time she was met with the same realization: Branton had implanted his seed in her on their wedding night. As angry and impulsive as the act had been, her body had accepted it. As if a greater force had conspired to make something out of nothing.

Despite the hardship it would add, Emma felt a tenderness toward the little being growing inside her.

It was late afternoon, nearly time for supper. Emma unwound her apron from her hips, plopping it on the table with a tired sigh. The empty hut had become merely a place of work, not one with a sense of home. It was an odd shift, considering she'd just been absorbed into Branton's hut like she'd always lived there.

She needed to get home and alleviate Merthe, see if her daughter had begun supper. Rabbits were rife in the woods. Branton and Neil had brought a few home the previous night and there was enough meat for leftovers. Emma grabbed a large loaf as she departed, one that she had baked with dried lavender petals and honey, thinking it would be a nice accompaniment to the gravy she intended to make if Merthe had not already done so.

She smiled in greeting to those she passed on the way home, grateful for the day to be done. Propping her tired feet on a stool while she mended clothing by the fire would be a small delight after supper. The sun had begun to tuck itself behind the village, cresting the tree line to the west. A part of her, an embarrassingly large part, wished for the day's end so she and Branton could seek comfort in one another's bodies.

Branton was to leave to collect the tithe from the Guston wood the next morning. A small party of men would accompany him to cut and haul it back to Hyrstow. Emma had questioned the safety of taking as much wood as they wanted from a place that wasn't fully conquered. Branton was desperate for the money, however, and vowed to not let the wood out of his sight until it was delivered to the earl. Unease sat low in Emma's chest. The original lumber had been stolen. She thought it dangerous to go back but knew she could not deny his leave.

The Reverend Father's visit a few days prior had planted a seed in her mind. Though he'd so callously dismissed Branton, there was no denying the church would grow. It was no secret Oswald had grand plans for St. Paul's church. Word had spread that he'd written the earl on many occasions requesting the funds to expand. Emma believed those requests were ignored, but time would likely turn that around. More people were flocking to Hyrstow proper. Families continually petitioned to have their sons admitted as novices. Expansion meant more people. More people meant more food needed. She'd heard the priests ate little more than oats and onions in broth, abstaining from meat. The loaves they cooked were dry disks meant to satisfy hunger.

Emma could bake it. If the bread was unleavened, she could make more loaves faster, and likely tastier than whatever priest was on cook duty on a given day. Indeed, she would have the children to care for, and a baby to birth, but she'd never missed an opportunity before. She didn't quite know how to offer this proposal to Branton or the Reverend Father, but since she conjured it, the idea wouldn't lay still in her mind.

Her promise to Freda lay like a dare before her. Indeed, she provided care, but this could secure the family's prosperity. For as much as her vow had locked her into a life she was beginning to cherish, Emma wished she could enjoy it. Part of her resented the weight of the promise, the secret of it. However, it had brought her a life she'd never dreamed of. One full of hardship but also purpose. Of love.

Once home, she greeted the children with affectionate pats and relieved Merthe of Tate. The baby's cheeks had filled out into chubby pillows which Emma nuzzled as she held the little girl aloft. The household busied itself with the ceremony of supper and sat down without Bran. Emma knew him to be at the hall preparing for the next day's journey and did not expect him until late.

To everyone's surprise, he returned during the meal. When he came through the door, however, his face was drawn. Purplish bags squatted beneath his eyes. Emma rose from the table to get him a bowl of rabbit broth and bread, which he accepted gratefully as he settled next to Neil.

"Are you well, Father?" Ginnie asked. Her light brows were raised with a smile of hope.

"Well? Father?" Æfflead copied. The little girl had

taken to mimicking almost every word any of them said. Emma didn't stop her. That Æffie was saying any words at all was a miracle.

"I am. Thank you, darlings." He grinned, which satisfied them enough to begin a light conversation about their days.

"Are you so excited for a new baby, Father?" Ginnie asked after their bowls had been empty and talk had lulled.

Emma's movements slowed as she gathered the dishes. Beside Bran, Neil scoffed.

"Don't be so daft, Ginnie," Neil grumbled. He speared his sister with a look Emma was sure would make Ginnie cry. Neil's jawline had sharpened over the course of the past few months. He had a way of tipping it upward as he glared that reminded her slightly of a fox about to pounce.

"Neil," Bran admonished, "don't."

"What?"

Neil's shout surprised them all. He stood, hands against the table top, his chair scraping against the floor. He flung his arm out to point at Emma. "Well, Father? Answer her. Are you happy to have found a new wife so that you could forget about Mother? And a baby! Ginnie, you don't know this yet, but to get a baby in a woman's belly means that the man has to put his—"

"That's enough!" Branton said, his voice as sharp as Emma had ever heard it.

Neil's mouth clamped shut, but wetness fixed to his lashes.

Across the table, Merthe rose in her chair, hand out as if to catch his wrist. Her daughter's rounded eyes were fixed on Neil, worry naked in their depths. She looked ready to jump between the father and son.

Branton continued without notice of Merthe. "Emma has been nothing but helpful to this family. She deserves your respect. I suggest you stay your tongue, son."

Neil's throat bobbed, but he held his father's steely gaze.

"Do you love her? Is it the same as how you loved Mum?"

No one dared breathe. Even the fire guttered in the hearth. Grief and embarrassment, hope and reluctance clogged Emma's throat. She didn't know what to do. Her hands went clammy as her heart sped up. Branton couldn't admit feelings for her. It would be a betrayal to Freda, to his children. Emma was to be the stand-in, the nursemaid, the overseer of the house. To suggest anything else would cut too deep.

Since she was already with child, and they'd agreed to satisfy one another physically, she and Branton had marital relations each night. In small moments, there were even gestures of affection. Sharing the same bed, a light hand on the small of her back as he passed by her, close-lipped smiles from across the room after a long day. Emma couldn't help the way her heart raced when Bran's gaze locked on her. And no matter how much she yearned to hear him proclaim a deeper feeling for her, she knew that the children would only recognize companionship in competition with their mother's memory. She didn't want them to.

"Of course he doesn't, Neil."

Branton's head jerked up to meet her gaze. His blue eyes flared with something akin to anger.

"Love is not needed for a baby to be born. Though we are both pleased to add to your already wonderful family."

Tate gurgled, the noises running together as she smacked her hands on the tabletop. Distracted, Merthe began to play a patting hand game with her and the baby laughed. Æfflead grinned, patting Emma's arm. "Love. Love, love, love. I love her. Love her."

Emma swallowed and offered Æffie a crinkly smile. She loved them too. Loved each of them in their way. It was special, this bond that she'd built with each child, even temperamental Neil. The affection had surprised her—she'd loved them as her friend's children but, now, she could think of no other life than with them. They had woven themselves into her heart, and she'd had the very special duty of helping to repair theirs. She'd thought the love she had for Merthe was unique. What she didn't realize were the layers of love a step-parent could offer.

Neil shoved a breath out his nose. He glared at his father, then shot his contempt-filled stare around the table, fists balled at his sides. With a sneer, he grabbed his cloak from the hook and left.

Branton's gaze remained locked on Emma as she took the stack of dishes over to the sideboard and began washing. The girls moved about the room to help her, each falling into their assigned jobs with practiced ease. Branton's gaze followed her around the room like a hand against the back of her neck, heavy and seductive all at once. After a few minutes, he stood and came round to her, pressing his hand to her hip to corral her.

"I'm going out to speak to him," Bran said, dipping his mouth close to her ear.

Emma shivered as his breath coasted along her skin. She nodded, knowing father and son had to close the issue, but worried over the words they would spew in anger.

Emma caught Bran's wrist, her hand circling his vambrace before he could depart. "Be gentle with him. He's hurt, but until now has hidden it well. This baby... it's a surprise to all of us. He loved his mother. Maybe he just needs a little reassurance that I could never take her place."

Bran's brows drew together as she spoke. "I know that he loves Freda. But I do not take kindly to him insulting me, and you, in our own home."

Emma shook her head, placing her hand on Branton's chest as she did so. His heart thudded steadily beneath her palm. It never failed to astound her that she could so effectively feel his heartbeat through such a thick layer of muscle.

"Promise me that you will not scold him over this. He needed to say his piece. He knows what happens between a man and woman to make a baby, and it feels like a betrayal to have the knowledge of it thrown in his face. If you must, speak to him about respect, that we are friends, but do not force his feelings about another sibling."

Bran's grip on her hip tightened. The intensity of his stony gaze caused flames to lick her insides.

"Do you truly think I carry no love for you?"

Whatever words Emma was prepared to answer with died on her tongue. Branton dipped his mouth close to her ear so as not to be overheard. "It scares me, what I feel for you. We are different from what I had with Freda. She will always have my heart, but I feel as if you've begun to repair my soul. And I do not know how I feel about that other than I must have you know it."

Emma could do nothing but stare as he brushed a kiss to her cheek then turned, stopping to give a gentle pat of Tate's head before following Neil out the door.

TWENTY-SIX

Time had Bran around the throat. His shoulders ached from chopping, and his lower back was a mess of knots. All he wanted was to get home. Even Ewan had ceased with the bawdy jokes as the three wagons laden with wood approached Hyrstow. Birdsong cluttered the sky, and the sun had begun its descent a few hours prior. Grahame's property had come and gone, and they were on the road that led into town.

"Finally home, lads," Branton raised his voice over the clatter of the wagon wheels.

Ewan, Sam, Thomas, Jory, and Neil gave little hoots of appreciation. Bran couldn't help a glance back toward Neil sitting beside Sam in the middle cart. His son chatted amiably, Sam having humored him most of the trip.

When Branton followed Neil out of the hut the night prior to leaving, he didn't anticipate telling Neil to join him cutting and to attend the trip to the earl's keep. As he reiterated to his son his relationship with Emma was different than that of the one with Freda, it occurred to him that Neil was becoming a man. If he was confident enough to insult Emma and Bran with his temper, he was man enough to work further afield. Neil's frown had unfurled, and his eyes lit. Bringing him was a reward for bad behavior, but Branton knew, deep down, that loving someone meant concessions. And Neil had worked as hard as any man.

"How's the missus?" Ewan ventured.

Bran looked sidelong at his friend. Ewan was suddenly very focused on the road ahead. Branton chewed over the words that wanted to pour from his mouth. *I've missed her. I want to feel her against me so that I know she's been well in our time apart. I want to see the bright twinkle in her eye she saves for me.*

Instead, he said, "Fine."

Ewan made a scoffing sound but didn't press.

Relief pricked him as Hyrstow's hall came into view. The trip had gone well, they'd cleared more wood than he'd expected, but he was still eager to get home. To have a hot meal and see his girls.

His girls.

The sentiment scared him. Ginnie and Æffie, with their mother's looks and heart. Merthe, who so diligently played with his daughters and helped around the house. He was glad at the prospect of income to provide her with anything she might need. His wife, with her quiet understanding, the dash of steel in her spine that had begun to draw him out of his shell. And the baby,

Tatswip. He was even looking forward to the sight of her chubby legs, and the happy sound of her gurgling. How had one trip away created such a chasm of longing?

Branton mulled over the thought as the group entered Hyrstow. At the edge of Bran's land, near the woodshed, they halted. Laden with wood, the three wagons were arranged side by side like children in a bed. Branton doubted he would have a restful slumber that evening. He'd likely stir at any sound with the thought of theft. The unease would only lessen when he'd handed the load over to the earl.

The men were jovial at a job well done, tossing barbs and questions between them. Sam scratched his scraggly red-blonde beard after dismounting from the bench. "Tomorrow?"

Branton nodded. "Aye, tomorrow, lads. Don't fog your heads up with too much drink tonight."

Ewan guffawed while Jory snorted. They each patted one another on the shoulder as they went their separate ways. Sam gave Bran a little wave as he hauled his discarded cloak and waterskin over his shoulder.

"Father!" Ginnie shouted as he approached. A crown of flowers sat precariously on her head, the ends of the daisies slipping out of the weaving. She sat on the bench to the left of the front door as she tended the fire within the open stones. "Merthe taught us to make these today!"

"Did she now?" Branton said, a smile in his tone. "Did all of my girls get a flower crown?"

"We did!" Ginnie chirped, spinning.

"Is Emma home?"

"Yep! Inside. We supped already since we didn't know when you'd be back."

Branton left the children out front. For some reason, his hands felt clammy as he entered his hut.

"Welcome back," Emma said. A wide smile spread her cheeks, her brown eyes merry. Branton found himself looking Emma over despite it obvious she hadn't befallen any horror in his absence.

Emma sat on the mattress with Tate who was rolling around on the soft bedding, drool dripping from her bottom lip. Emma huffed as she crouched and made to stand. Branton was across the room and taking her hands in a heartbeat.

"Here," he said as he pulled at her strong hands. He towered over her as she rose, realizing too late how close he stood. Emma accepted the help, her breasts scraping along the front of him as she moved. Her lashes shuttered as she peered up, her lips pressing together as her cheeks flushed with color at the lack of space between their bodies.

"Hello," Branton said, his voice deep and quiet and full of dark promise.

Emma's smile only grew brighter, the press of her chest to his, insistent. Branton couldn't help himself. He ducked to press a kiss to her lips. Immediately, she yielded to him and rather than worry that he was being too forward with his wife, Branton's tongue swept along hers in an arc that left him wanting more. Between them, her hands released his, latching onto the fiber of his tunic. The scrape of her short nails into his flesh made him shiver.

God, this woman. How could one taste of her make him want to get on his knees and worship her altar?

He pulled away slightly to angle his mouth over hers again. She tasted of tea and milk and honey. A small, throaty moan reverberated from her into him. Bran's head swam with it.

From the floor, Tate's hand clamped onto Branton's boot. With a sound of surprise, Bran broke the kiss and looked down at the baby, who sat at their feet, grinning up at them. Sheepish, Branton released Emma.

"How are you, little one?" Branton offered. He bent to pick up his youngest daughter. To his surprise, she reached for him as he gathered her and stood. She was a wiggly weight in his arms.

"So? Everything went well?" Emma asked as she bustled over to the sideboard to fetch him a bowl of supper.

"Aye," he muttered.

The child in his arms looked up at him with the bluest eyes he'd ever beheld. Again it struck him like a pick to his heart how much Tate took after him. A living reminder that he was the cause of Freda's death. Her little mouth turned downward as she stared at him, wide-eyed. He thought her about to cry, which he didn't blame her for. He was a stranger to her. But then her small hand rested on his chest, the other tapping his beard, fingers entrenching themselves in the bushy hair.

A gurgle pushed its way out of her, followed by a smile so tentative, Bran nearly went to his knees.

She was part of him, yes. But the slope of her nose, the way her cheeks rose when she grinned was all Freda.

Something deep in Branton shifted like a boulder giving way beneath a heavy flow of water. It took him a heartbeat to realize it was a relief. He'd been holding on so long to the hate in his heart for—not her, exactly—but a sense of duty to Freda to pit himself against the thing that killed her.

As Tate gazed up at him, her fat little fingers working in the hair of his beard, the clean baby scent of her skin seeping into him, Bran knew he'd been so very wrong. When he looked up at Emma, her eyes bore a silvery sheen.

"Looks like me, eh?" he asked, though his tone was thicker than he intended.

Emma offered a trembling grin and nodded, her hand going to her middle. She turned and retrieved a slice of bread to be served with supper. When she finished, she came over, hands out, ready to take the baby from him so that he may sit and eat.

"I'll hold her for a time," he murmured, giving the baby a jiggle. Tate slapped his shoulder and offered a grin that revealed two bottom milk teeth.

"Of course," Emma said and pulled out Branton's chair so that he could settle more comfortably with Tate on his lap. As she moved away, he caught her hand and held it, hoping that she could see the thanks in his gaze.

This was what he'd been missing while he was away.

Emma's help. Her persistence in the face of his foolhardiness. She was his rock. Her mouth tilted up as her fingers tightened around his. Emma looked at their joined hands, a sort of hope simmering in her gaze.

"Thank you," he said, his throat suddenly clogged with emotion.

He could do this. He could be the father he remembered, the man he wanted to be. With Emma at his side, he knew he could be a better man for them all.

CHAPTER

TWENTY-SEVEN

"Em."

Branton's deep voice settled along her bones like an embrace. He stood near the door, shirtless, his eyes sparkling like fine gemstones in the firelight. The strings on his trousers had been loosened showing the dip of V-like grooves of his waist.

She was staring.

They'd retreated to the bedroom after Branton had answered all the children's questions about the wood near Guston and when he would leave for the earl's keep.

Tomorrow.

It felt too soon. He'd already been gone for a week, and though he'd made the journey to and from the Guston forest before, she would be counting the days of Branton's return.

Emma had tried to focus on their time together as a family. She'd nodded along, offering grins and platitudes but all she could think of was the way he'd looked at her

304

when he'd entered the hut, as if checking her over to ensure she was alright, hunger stark in his appraisal.

As if he'd wanted to see *her*. Not just the caregiver of his children, the keeper of the home. It was dangerous, the feeling of longing and lust mingling inside her. What made it so much worse was the spark of hope beneath.

"What?" she asked, her cheeks heating. Her fingers felt clumsy as she untied her apron. The fabric of her tunic loosened from around her middle, which had become firm and slightly rounded. A layer of tension seeped from her with the freedom.

"I like when you look at me like that," Bran said. He crossed to her.

Emma had to look up at him as he neared. She shivered, though not from cold. "Like what?"

"As if I am something you wish to eat," he murmured. He lifted a hand and traced the side of her face with a knuckle. The grin nestled in his beard was one that teased the desire simmering low in her belly.

Emma had never been one to give herself over to her own pleasures. Now that Branton had unleashed this wanton side of her, however, she didn't think she could come back from it. She didn't want to. Her heart dipped as she tried to bury the guilt that clawed at her.

"I was under the impression that you were the one that usually did the eating," she teased.

Brightness flared in Bran's blue gaze, like a flame getting more air. He didn't bother with niceties. His broad hand was suddenly on her backside, squeezing the flesh as he pulled her to him. His other hand went to her breast, cupping it, then circling his fingers around her nipple. The rough rightness of it all elicited a delicious, needy sensation within Emma that slid through her like oil.

Emma braced her hands on his upper arms and smiled. She loved how domineering he was with her. He was going to take her, use her up, and she craved it.

"Ah, you're right about that, my lady. I've been waiting for my feast all day. May I begin?"

"Please do," she said as she wound a hand through the hair at the base of his neck. The muscles were tight there. She kneaded the column of his neck for a moment, and Branton halted his ministrations. He closed his eyes and released a groan.

"It appears to me that you need attention of another kind," she teased.

He pressed her to him, his hard cock prodding her stomach. "I would like that. But only if you promise I still get my treat at the end."

Emma tossed back her head and laughed. The sharp sound danced around the room. She smacked her hand over her mouth when she realized how loud it was. When she looked back to Bran, his eyes had softened.

"I like it when you laugh. You don't do it nearly often enough."

"Perhaps I haven't had cause to," she retorted. She'd meant it in half jest, but when Bran glanced at his feet, Emma knew her blunder. Catching him by the cheek, Emma cupped the bristly hair of his jaw. "You seem to be the only one who can make me laugh like that."

Branton's smile took its time, winding upward, alighting his eyes. It made her knees weak when it should have told her to guard herself. Though tenderness had bloomed between them, it didn't mean he truly wanted her. She was a stand-in wife. Pathetic enough to be happy gobbling up the scraps of whatever affection Branton threw her. But then he was wrapping a thick arm about her shoulders, pulling her close. Her breasts squished against him as he spoke into her hair, the words rumbling through him into her.

"I'll take the job more seriously, then."

She smiled into his shoulder, the bare skin of it warm and hard. Bran's next words were a welcome surprise.

"How have you been feeling? With the baby, I mean."

"Still not well in the mornings, but thankfully I've not had any upset in the middle of the day. Just tired," she said, pulling back from him, her chin dipping down as she spoke.

Branton didn't seem to accept her quick dismissal. He plucked her chin between his thumb and forefinger, bringing her face up so she could see the tender look in his gaze.

"The babe is well?"

Emma nodded. Her heart sped up with the sentiment. Despite everything involving the man before her, she wanted this child. It was never part of her plan—Freda's promise—and yet Emma craved Bran's acceptance of their choices.

"As far as I can tell, yes."

"Good." Branton drew his fingers from her chin to

her ear, then he settled his palm along her jawline. "I know I was a brute about the baby. It is just that I...worry for you. You have come to mean more to me than..."

Branton's lips pursed as if the words he wanted wouldn't form. Emma became still as stone. She didn't want to interfere in any proclamations Bran made lest he change his mind.

"Another child, one with you, is a blessing. I don't think I've said so yet."

Despite all they'd been through, Bran's words made her feel treasured. It was as if he fought his own battle all day and kept the softest parts of himself to share with her. With a shake of her head, she pushed him away.

"Here," she said as she gestured to the bed. Branton gave her a confused look but obeyed. He sat where she instructed with his legs over the edge, then she climbed on the bed behind him, settling on her knees. Scars criss-crossed the map of skin before her. Not many, but enough to show the times he'd cheated death in the woods. Freda used to lament when Branton came home with scrapes and cuts from falling trees and debris, her scorn only echoing her fear for him.

His skin was warm when Emma put her hands on his shoulders. A shudder wracked him as she began kneading his taut upper back.

"That feels so good," he said on an exhale. His head dipped forward and his shoulders slumped as her thumbs pressed into the pop of muscle connecting his neck to his shoulder. Knots like a sailor's sat beneath the skin.

Emma took her time with the massage. She paid attention to one shoulder, the middle, then the next shoulder. Bran's small grunts and groans of pleasure were payment enough. Little by little, the tension eased from his body, and he became pliant, letting her move down one arm, past the round muscle to his forearm, then his hand. Scars were rooted in the skin of his forearm, most thick and faded, others fresh and red. Freda had told her they were from years of branches cutting him, splinters shoving their way into his skin. She moved beside him to massage the flesh of his palm and each of his fingers. Like a large, happy animal he released little groans as she hit certain spots. When she moved to his left arm, his eyes flew open.

"You don't have to do that side."

"It's fine. Just remove your vambrace." Emma kept her tone soothing. It wasn't lost on her that he never took the vambrace off. Even in bed, the leather remained.

His gaze remained rooted to the floor.

"I can't."

"Indeed, you can. I can help."

"No."

Emma flinched. She tried to rally by pasting a smile across her mouth but Bran glanced at her out of the side of his eye, his scowl damning her intentions.

"Don't," he growled, shifting his elbows to his knees. He ripped his gaze from her as if she'd harmed him.

It cut. She'd thought them past these disagreements. What a fool she was.

"Don't what?" she dared ask, picking an invisible

thread off her skirt. Her tunic was suddenly too hot against her skin.

"Pretend everything is alright."

"Why shouldn't I?" Emma said. She offered a smile she knew must have looked pathetic. Rather than have him chastise her further, she uncurled her legs and stood from the bed. If he didn't want to share his reasons with her, fine.

She told herself she didn't need to know all of Bran. Even if it hurt. What was the alternative? Her feelings for Branton had deepened, dangerously so. The light he'd allowed back into his eyes when he looked at her, the way his lips grazed over her heart when they were in bed, his care to haul her cart to and from the market; they were all treasures she tucked away for herself. Her affection and desire and need of this man who was so heartbroken for another...her feelings were her burden to carry. She would seal them away whenever she was required to. She'd been doing it all her life.

Branton's fingers were like a manacle around her wrist as she made to rise. "You're angry."

"I'm not. It is alright," she insisted, infusing cheer into her tone. She turned away from him, pulling on her arm to free her wrist. The damn man wouldn't let go.

"Would you stop yanking, woman," he said, his tone layered in shadow. Branton stood, following her about the small room. "I will not let go. Talk to me."

Anger burned a hole in Emma's gut. Talk to him! He refused to open up to her, and yet he commanded the opposite. His leaving, the constant need of the children,

Bran's affection amidst his moods—it was too much. Emma felt as if she were about to burst.

"You talk to me!" she shouted, turning on him and shoving his great body with her free hand. His muscled chest was a wall of stone. Emma's wrist crumpled.

She swore, long and low, squeezing her eyes against the splinter of pain. Branton released her.

"I've never heard you swear," he said.

Emma gave him a disgruntled look out of the corner of her eye. He laughed. It caused Emma's blood to froth. "Just because you haven't heard it doesn't mean I don't have cause to," she gritted through her teeth. She moved her injured hand to then fro then circled it around to ensure there wasn't any damage.

"Emma."

She ignored him, resolutely looking at the wrist cradled in her hand.

"Emma," he repeated, his voice low and soft. It did something to her insides. Then his hand was on her lower back, and he was turning toward her so he could capture her hands and examine her wrist.

"It's fine," she said.

Branton, shirtless, the hair of his chest grazing her arm while he tended to her was not something she wanted to focus on. She wanted to dwell in the pain to better retain her anger.

"Ruthless," he said, "let me look."

Flicking her gaze to his face, she scowled up at him. His brows were pinched, his lips a tight line, his touch feather-light. It was all she could do to hold onto the flame of her anger while the maleness of his woodsy scent surrounded her.

"I'm sorry."

Emma squinted at him, pursing her lips with suspicion. But she allowed him to take her arm in his hands. His calloused fingers scraped across her skin, making her shiver.

A man that large shouldn't have been able to manipulate her wrist so gently. As he massaged a feeling of relief wove itself into her flesh. His breaths fanned over her cheeks as he focused on her arm. Emma was suddenly overcome. It was one thing to be the object of Branton's desire, but quite another to harness his care.

The flame of ire she held flickered.

"Thank you, Bran. It feels better."

He wrenched his focus from her wrist to her face, his eyes boring into hers to see if she spoke the truth. Emma's chest felt tight beneath his haunted stare. He was so damn beautiful. And it wasn't just that his face was pleasing beneath his mop of nearly black hair. It was the soul beneath, tarnished from the weight of life, yet still trying. Her anger dissipated.

She cupped his cheek with her free hand and rose on her toes to place a kiss on his lips. Branton's surprise was only betrayed by his hesitation. Then his arm was wrapping around her back and his lips were dragging across hers in a kiss that stole Emma's breath. When it ended, he dropped his forehead to hers and released a long, hard breath.

"I wear the vambrace to cover the scar." His eyes

remained clenched shut as he spoke.

Emma straightened within his grasp. If he'd been hurt…if he felt the need to hide it from her…an indecipherable emotion welled, forming like a stone at the bottom of her throat.

Very carefully she asked, "What scar, Bran?"

Branton's hands tightened on her hips. He wouldn't look at her as he spoke words that nearly cleaved her in two. "The scar that resides on my arm from when I tried to end my life."

Absolute horror struck her between the shoulder blades. She didn't dare speak.

"It was a little while after Freda passed. I couldn't…I just…there was no life without her. I didn't want anything if she was no more. The children kept looking to me for solace, and I could barely get through the day. There was no point to anything and the days dragged on and I just wanted it all to stop. I *needed* the pain to stop."

A sob heaved through his great body, halting speech. Instinctively, Emma made a shushing sound of comfort, her arms weaving around his middle to press him to her. Deep, ragged breaths scorched her neck where he'd buried his face. Wetness mingled with her hair, digging into her skin.

Killing oneself was a cardinal sin. It meant a soul would be trapped in the depths of hell with no chance of escape. The thought horrified her. If Bran had succeeded, his soul would have perished forevermore. The sense of *wrongness*, the thought of him not with her, was almost too much to bear.

When he calmed, Emma turned her face to press a kiss to his hair. She ran her hands down the hard planes of his back, up again. Slowly, she drew away so she could look upon his face. His eyes were still shut, brow pinched, as if waiting for the blow of her reaction. Only when she scraped her hand along his bearded jaw, beckoning him to look at her with soft murmurs did he open his eyes.

"Now you know," he said. He released a shuddering breath. "You know how weak I am. I had a family to care for, and I still chose to end my darkness rather than fight for any speck of light. The only reason I am here is because Grahame found me and bandaged me up. The scar remains to remind me every day how selfish I am."

Emma was at a loss for words. Doubt, like a poison snake, slithered through her middle, coiling around her fears. She'd known Branton's melancholy to be dark. She'd known he needed help, but to leave the world, his children, in such a way... All this time, Branton had been scared of loss, and yet he was the one who might remove himself from the life they were building. The snake tightened its grip.

She must have been standing without responding for too long because Bran dropped his hands from her hips. He turned toward his side of the bed, neck bent, head drooping. Though worry clogged her limbs, Emma made herself move.

"Bran," she said, reaching out to run a hand along his back. He flinched, and Emma was sorry to have wounded him. "Please do not turn from me."

His fists clenched at his sides but his gaze remained toward the bed. "How can I face you? You, who are so pure? My soul is rotten compared to yours. I don't know how you can even look at me."

Emma seized Branton's left wrist, wrapped her hands around the vambrace and pulled him back around to look at her. He would not disappear from this world again. Freda wouldn't have allowed it. Neither would she.

"Do not speak of such things," she commanded. Something in her tone caused surprise to flit across Branton's face before he buried it in a scowl. It would not deter her. Something Emma had over others was her ability to endure.

She brought his arm in front of her, pressing both hands to the flesh above the leather.

"Thank you for telling me your darkest truth. I am glad you did not succeed. Your pain...it's real, Bran. I'm so sorry you felt there was no other way. I am glad Grahame stopped you. For I am the selfish one. Your surviving meant that we were able to strike our arrangement. Though I know it did not start out as anything other than a marriage pact, I am more than pleased with your effort at being a husband."

Bran's jaw rippled as his eyes scoured her face. "You think it is an effort, being a husband to you?"

It was Emma's turn to look away. She'd meant to console him, not draw the conversation back to herself. "That's not what I meant..."

But Bran wasn't listening. He slid his free hand along

her side, grazing her ribcage and settling on her mid-back.

"Emma, there is no effort being your partner. I am astounded every day when I wake to find you with me. One of the reasons I am so angry with my scar is it serves as a reminder that I could have stepped out of this life too early; I could have missed out on a life with you."

The words reached down and tugged on something deep in Emma's heart. She knew she couldn't compare to Branton's first wife. She knew the love they shared was something untouchable. But his recent affection, his help, had kindled something in her that she had no business feeling. She'd promised Freda to look after him. She'd never meant to fall in love with him.

Emma tried to form the right words. Her jaw moved up and down in an attempt to come back with any sort of response that didn't sound too desperate. She couldn't. So instead, she took a step into him, wrapping her arms around his neck. As if he'd done it a thousand times before, he pressed her to him, encircling her in his embrace, nuzzling into her hair. There weren't words for the mix of urgency and affection she had for this man who was breaking through her defenses and rebuilding her from the inside out. They stood there for an undetermined amount of time, holding one another.

He'd been there for her, even in his darkness. And she for him. Their fledgeling bond made Emma want to do more. It infused Emma with the strength she needed to carry out her plan. Even if it was sooner than she'd anticipated.

CHAPTER

TWENTY-EIGHT

The church's door handle was heavy in Emma's grasp. Balanced in her other hand, she held a warm loaf of bread wrapped in one of the nicest spare cloths she could find. She knew it likely wouldn't be returned, but the loss of it was minor if she could get a word with the Reverend Father.

Inside, a single priest was on his knees before the dais, his head bent in prayer. The dip of wide shoulders, the slight roundness to his cheeks, the dark ring of hair that crowned the bottom of his skull—Emma was surprised to find she'd conjured the Reverend Father into existence. She did not expect to come upon him so quickly and without persuasion. Candles flickered in the dim room, allowing some light despite the day's grayness.

The great wood door boomed as it closed amidst the near-silent church. Emma did not try to hide her footsteps as she proceeded up the aisle flanked by long benches. Frankincense and the sharp scent of thyme mingled, overpowering the unassuming odors of dust, stone, and sweat. Murmurs echoed from somewhere deeper in the building.

The High Priest did not break from his prayer to acknowledge her presence as she approached. The cavernous space, one in which she'd always felt comforted by the community of others, seemed oddly hollow.

At the front pew, Emma genuflected, keeping the bread aloft as she steadied herself with one hand on the bench beside her. Though the roundness of her stomach was small, she was beginning the stage of her pregnancy where everything felt off balance. As she came to stand, Emma could make out the similarities between the priest and his brother. Indeed, Oswald and Ridley did not resemble one another greatly, though the air of authority and broad stature marked them as relatives. She knew Ridley and Oswald carefully kept their distance, circling one another like starving dogs fighting over a bone. She couldn't help but wonder: if the Vikings hadn't raided, if Yrsa hadn't come, would Ridley and the High Priest have joined their influence? A prosperous village and an important church could make a mark in the earldom.

Emma didn't know what to do as she came to stand beside him. Interrupting a priest in prayer must have been some sort of sin. The pews behind them stood like sentinels Emma's sore feet wished she could retreat to. Though she guessed that, if she didn't impress her presence, Oswald would think her there simply to count her blessings. He was often detached and outright ignored the women of the congregation unless they were with their husbands. Indeed, when she'd brought Bran's children to church when he couldn't, not a glance was spared, no words of comfort offered.

Not that someone as high as the Reverend Father needed to deign her with acknowledgement, but she'd thought he might have said something comforting to the children. He and Ridley had grown up in Hyrstow with Bran and Freda and Grahame. He was older than Ridley, but she'd assumed there was some sort of kinship between them, even if she didn't see it with her own eyes.

Emma swallowed, not knowing what to do. The bread was like an anchor in her hands, the warmth of it seeping through the cloth. It gave her something to cling to.

She *had* to procure another income. Branton was to bring home coin from the earl, but they'd gone too long on her income alone. The day prior, she'd had to use up Merthe's meager dowry to pay Glennis Miller for rye. It was that or ask the stone-faced woman for credit. Humiliation burned her gut. She'd always been able to feed and clothe Merthe. The fact that she could barely do so for the rest of the family caused a twisted kind of shame to course through her.

Baking was going well with the increase in visitors to the market, though it wasn't enough to keep the whole family afloat. It was as if she was set against a writhing current that held her from shore. Emma had no idea if they would have enough to weather another winter, but with the baby on the way, she didn't want to risk finding out the hard way. And in light of Bran's confession...if there was a sliver of a chance he'd consider ending his life again, she wasn't sure she could rely on him as expected. The past few months had been hard enough. Approaching the church was a gamble, but she would do anything if it meant providing for her family.

Oswald didn't move. His breaths remained steady, eyes shut, as if she wasn't there.

At a loss, Emma looked around. Surely, another priest could relay her message once the Reverend was done praying. She should leave. Bow to the priest and vacate to the comfort of her husband before he left. She had no idea how long he would attend the earl. He could be gone for a fortnight or more.

Steeling herself, Emma knelt on the ground beside Oswald. The stones bit into her knees as she placed the bread safely on the floor in front of her and settled herself next to the High Priest. Clasping her hands, she dipped her head in prayer.

Emma didn't know how long they prayed in silence together. Oswald's breath was steady and strong. It lulled her into a sort of trance, one she knew she should keep up her guard against. Yrsa had told her of the terrible things Oswald had done and said to her in the back room of the church last year. But despite the warning that prodded the back of her mind, Emma was so tired, so very worn out from her pregnancy, she trusted her faith to protect her in the house of its making.

"Good day, Emma Baker. What has you joining me in silence? Surely, you are busy enough you do not have the time to luxuriate in the majesty of prayer."

The High Priest's voice was calm. Emma turned to find he stared straight ahead at the large cross propped against the far wall. Light dribbled through the round window of stained glass casting dim ribbons of color across the wood below it.

"I do not wish to interrupt your prayer, Father. I know that your time is sacred."

Oswald nodded, hands clasped, never wavering on his knees as if used to kneeling on hard ground.

"Indeed. I thank you for the flattery, but it is not necessary. Time is what God makes it. Now, please tell me why you've chosen to spend this time in His company with me."

Emma paused to collect the words that she would use to sway the other ruling power in Hyrstow.

"I would like to sell bread to the church. Sometimes, the priests come to purchase it at the market. The prices, while fair, are higher than if I supplied the church directly and sometimes I'm sold out by the time Father Chisholm comes calling. I propose for the church to purchase bread each week to ensure an appropriate amount can be baked. This will give the church priority. I understand that there are capable cooks within these walls, yet I believe a weekly delivery would allow those focused on the Lord more time for prayer."

Oswald put his clasped forefingers to his lips. "What compensation are you expecting for each loaf?"

"It depends how much you require. They sell for two sceats each at the market. If there is a larger order, I could reduce the price to one and a half sceats per loaf."

"And what of when you cannot bake any longer?" Oswald diverted his attention from the cross and looked pointedly at her middle. Emma swallowed around the dryness in her throat.

"My daughter, Merthe. She is apprenticing under me and will be able to fulfill whatever is required."

Her next words were borne out of haggling.

"I believe this could be a beneficial arrangement. Your priests would be guaranteed an amount of bread each week. It would fortify them for their sacred duties."

Oswald nodded. His dark eyes drifted to her face, though he did not speak. Instead, his head tilted to the side, reminding Emma of an owl. Her knees screamed at her while he weighed her words.

"Tell me, Emma Baker, does your husband know you are asking this of me?"

She pressed her hands to her thighs to keep herself steady. Her chest felt too hot in the airless room. "No."

"Why have you not told him?"

"I did not think it necessary. I run my business as I see fit, and Branton completes his work without my interference."

"Hmm. Is keeping information from your husband not a lie of omission?"

"I do not keep it from him," Emma felt the half truth

like old wood on her tongue. "In truth, I want to secure the deal with you first, then bring it to his attention."

"'For nothing is His that shall not be made manifest, not anything secret that shall not be made known and come to light.' Gospel of Luke."

The look Oswald gave her out of the corner of his eye made her feel as if she were a child in need of a firm reprimand. Emma hoped he didn't find out it was she who dug Yrsa out of the church's back room that year. Were his words acknowledgement that he knew her secret?

Sweat slicked her hairline as she inclined her head. He continued, his tone gentler.

"You would do well to disclose this proposal to your husband. Branton Cutter and I have known one another for a long time. I know that he feels wronged by my decision to source wood elsewhere, and I believe he will not be kind to you for what he may perceive as going behind his back."

Emma tried to hide her shock as she lifted her gaze to the High Priest. He was not chastising her nor outright denying her.

"You appear surprised." A small smile softened his face, the wrinkles at the corners of his eyes fanning across the skin. "I appreciate your sitting with me in prayer. Since my brother's return and the Viking raids, I am not often afforded kindness from those who bore witness to my wrath the day his bride was found. But you have always been a steady patron of this church. Go now, tell Branton of your plan to supply the church.

Return when you feel it is not a weight on your conscience to do so."

Emma nodded, swallowing bile at the gentle rejection. She'd failed. There was no way she could discuss the matter with Branton with any sort of acceptance on his part. It was why securing the deal before telling him was so important. She pushed herself up, strain shooting through her low back at the movement. Offering a small bow, she left the bread on the floor before Oswald as an offering.

Her heart was low as she mulled over her misstep on the walk home. They needed money.

With a deep breath out, she placed her hand on her middle, willing the stitch in her side to disappear. What she saw when she rounded the hut made her heart lodge in her throat. Branton, checked the wood laden wagons, tugging on the ropes securing each load. The muscles in his back bunched beneath his light tunic as he yanked, and, when finished, he patted the load as if for luck.

Emma's heart wouldn't slow. The sight of him, sweaty and intent in the mid-morning light was enough to make her mouth dry. Everything he'd shared with her the night previous came roaring back to mind. His confession, the way they'd held one another, how she took his mouth with hers to assuage the urgent need to feel him inside her. As if he understood her craving, he answered her with his tongue and lips and body. Their joining was slow and soft and thorough. It brought Emma more solidly into herself than she'd ever been.

Bran swiped a hand across his brow as he turned, his own eyes softening as they alighted on her.

"Hello, Ruthless," he offered, grinning as he braced an arm against a wagon. A light tan had returned to his cheeks in the past weeks. Emma was glad for it. A sudden, fierce longing swept through her. She would miss him.

"I have something I need to tell you before you depart. A requirement of service, if you will." She glanced around to check that there was no one to overhear. Merthe and Ginnie had been left to care for the younger two.

"Oh?" A dark eyebrow lifted with the question, though his grin didn't dip at her hesitant tone. His gaze was indulgent, and he reached for her, hand falling away when she didn't step into his embrace. Surprise, which he quickly stifled, ran across his face.

The words nested in her mouth. She didn't want to have to ask permission from her husband to provide for their family. The plan had been to broker the deal, then handle Branton's annoyance. A contract would have made what she was about to say so much easier. Now empty-handed, and having to relay her intentions, caused more worry than it should have.

"I plan on brokering a deal with the church to provide the priests with bread."

The slight twitch of his mouth within his dark beard was the only betrayal that Branton had heard. Emma placed her hands on her hips to shift the weight from her center and continued. "I planned on speaking to the High Priest about it and—"

Branton thrummed his hand on the wood beside him, the other clenching in a fist at his side. "Do not broker anything with the church."

TWENTY-NINE

"Pardon?" A scowl nipped at her mouth though she buried it in her question.

"Don't bother, Emma. Oswald won't hear you out. You know how he can be with women: dismissive."

Heat barreled into Emma's cheeks. She crossed her arms against the burden of his disapproval. "Just like you're being now?"

"What? No. I've known him a long time. I know how he'll react, especially to something unexpected."

Indignation made Emma scoff. She was tired of Bran's word as law. "He said the same of you."

Branton's eyes narrowed, his mouth twisting into something ugly. He slung his hands onto his hips, staring her down. "The same of me? Have you already gone to see him?"

Damn. Her ire had gotten the better of her. Too late; she'd have to continue. Heart pounding, Emma pressed her lips firmly together to think of her next words carefully before speaking.

"I did. Our money is gone, Bran. The children are growing and eating, and we're not saving anything anymore. I had to use the last of Merthe's dowry to pay Glennis. I don't make enough on my own to help all of us. I wanted to have everything with the church arranged before you left, so you could depart with good news. I wanted to show I can do more."

"Have I ever given you cause to believe I don't think you can?" he huffed, his blue eyes focusing on her so intently, that Emma wanted to cower.

Somehow she found words beneath her tongue. "No. It has been a tough year. The markets are unpredictable. I wish to secure us a steady contract to help us through lean times."

"Like right now." The words were bitter. Branton stood as still as death, awaiting her response.

Emma popped her hip to shift her weight. A bead of sweat slid down her back as resentment oozed through her. She was trying to do the right thing, and Branton seemed to purposefully misunderstand her.

"Yes. Well, no. You're taking the lumber to the earl, and that is wonderful. But I've stretched our food stores as much as I can. I've mended clothing items that are nearly rags. Neil's shoes do not fit and Merthe has only one tunic. I know we've overcome a slump and that you'll fetch a good price for the wood at the earl's keep, but I want to contribute more with a steadier income we could fall back on."

To his credit, Branton did not interrupt. Rather, he remained quiet for some time, his gaze having shifted to their feet. Surely he would see the idea as a good one once his pride was out of the way.

Branton bumped his closed fist against the side of the wagon before looking back down at her.

"What did Oswald say about your little venture?"

A bitter taste stuck to the back of her throat. How dare he diminish her efforts? She worked to swallow it down, placing her hands on her hips. The wagon's shadow stood over them.

"He advised I not keep things from you. He told me to return after we've discussed it, which is why I bring it up now, before you leave."

Bran made a scoffing sound. "He won't accept."

"Don't be so quick to judge. He may. I do not think he dislikes me as he does the rest of you."

Branton turned from the wagon to face the hut, his lips curled in a smile that was nothing less than cruel. "That may be true, but you're shackled to me. And he surely doesn't care for me. I would not be surprised if he had you tell me before rejecting your offer outright, just so that we would have this disagreement."

Emma threw her hands out at her sides to prevent herself from pulling out her hair. "Why would he care? Branton, listen to yourself. Your pride is halting you from seeing a potentially good income."

He angled toward her, as if to corral her next to the wagon.

"My pride? My pride is protecting this family from

getting into bed with someone who dismissed me in my own home. Someone who cannot be relied on, someone who wanted Yrsa dead not a year ago. Do you forget that?"

"You did too!" Emma shouted. As soon as the words were out, she wished she could claw them back.

Shock struck any emotion from Branton's countenance. She licked her lips, all her thoughts scrambling for purchase at once.

"Indeed, he did those things. But you told the High Priest where Yrsa was. You didn't trust her. We understand you did it out of concern for your family. So don't make it seem like my earning an income is a betrayal. Your concern for Yrsa should not rival your concern for me."

Bran ran a hand over his mouth, hard. "It doesn't."

"Really? Because it appears your grudge against the man who held her is challenging the very real proposal *I* have to help this family. You forget that *I* saved Yrsa. I dug her out of the church despite it being against my better interest."

Branton dragged a hand through his hair, yanking it at the roots as he stared down at her. "Is that what this is truly about? You're upset that she got Ridley and you didn't? Instead, all you got was a marriage with the most miserable man in the earldom."

The words cut her down, made her small, as intended. Emma had to gulp back the offense before she took a step closer, craning her neck to look up at Bran.

"I do not think that! But since you've brought up the

topic, I would be a monster to not feel the sting of rejection because I was not enough for him. Just like I am not enough for *you*."

Emma wished she could yank the reins of her mouth. They'd gone beyond the issue at hand, but shouting the words at Bran felt too good to stop. She'd not voiced her true feelings in years. There had never been a time, and there was no one to lament to. Branton was with her for better or worse, and he'd downright beckoned her worst.

"Why say that?"

He invaded her space, claiming every part of her vision. Her knees felt as if they would give way beneath her. She'd intended to discuss her plan with Bran, not reveal almost every damn part of her scarred heart. Ire flickered in his gaze when she didn't speak. "Emma, tell me."

Something in the challenge prodded her fury rather than stifled it.

She said in a tone of cold steel, "I'm always someone's second choice. It is my lot. Whether it be Yrsa or Freda or the children or you. I am the only one who has ever put myself first, and it is a lonely life I lead doing that, I assure you. But I can't compete against a ghost."

A long moment stretched between them. He was not going to deny what she said. She was his second. Everyone's second. She'd said the words she'd always feared and was not met with resistance. Her heart groaned under the weight of the sorrow she felt.

Fury banked in Branton's eyes, his jaw rippling

beneath his dark beard. He clenched and unclenched his fists.

"Fine. If it is not a betrayal to Yrsa, count it as one upon me. I am your husband, and I can provide for this family. The earl has granted me access to more of the wood. I can sell to him, we will expand into Guston—"

Branton was suddenly too close. They were nearly chest to chest, practically shouting in one another's faces. The field around them was quiet, as if the animals and birds deigned to keep their distance.

"At the expense of your safety! Do you not understand, Branton? I want to secure a reliable income for this *growing* family. The first tithe was stolen! We have no idea what the earl will offer. I am sorry if that hurts you, but I have scraped by on my own, and I have scraped by trying to hold this family together, and I am so tired..."

To her horror, tears flooded her eyes. Bran simply hefted a sigh. His hands worked at his sides, fingers clenching and unclenching.

"Tired of what, Emma? Say it. Tired of me? Tired of this life you agreed to?"

She shook her head, not yet trusting her voice. She pressed a hand to her belly and drew a mighty breath before saying the words that were like scars on her heart, "I'm tired of always worrying I will offend you by just *being*. I know I am not Freda. I am reminded of it every day. In the faces of her children. In the way I catch you looking at me when you think I don't notice. I'm constantly being compared to my dead friend. You know what? I miss her. So much. And yet, she was human too. She had faults. Possibly her main one was relying too heavily on those around her."

"Tell me what you speak of," he commanded, eyes narrowed. He grabbed her chin between his thumb and forefinger, his eyes chips of ice. He applied a small amount of pressure on her chin as he spoke, igniting her anger again. With a snarl she threw her arm up, knocking his hand away, then stepped forward, bringing them chest to chest. The words were fire she had to expel to quell. They formed without thought.

"She relied on you to do everything for her! She had Tate despite me offering her herbs to quell the pregnancy, saying she would birth her even though she knew it might kill her. She knew the birth would be bad, as Æfflead's had been. And she had me promise—"

Emma's hands flew to her mouth to stop the words from flowing out. Branton had gone wholly still.

His words were stark as bones picked clean in a field. "What did she have you promise?"

Emma shook her head. She staggered back a step, nearly tripping on a root at her feet. Branton's hand wrapped around her upper arm, catching her.

"What was it?" he growled into her face.

Tears were streaming down her cheeks, her face flushed with regret. She shook her head, lips clamped shut. She couldn't tell him. He wouldn't understand.

"Tell me." Branton gave her a little shake. "Emma, tell me what you promised my wife."

Freda's rightful title broke her.

"She h-had me promise to take care of you. She knew you wouldn't be able to go on without her. Said that you loved her too well, and you needed a wife to hold you to this life. She did it for you and the children. And I agreed."

Bran's hand dropped from her arm. The absence of it was worse than any brand. He paled, the knot at his throat working as he swallowed. "That was why you agreed to the marriage so readily?"

He took a step backward, as if each word he spoke was like a punch from her. Emma raised her hands, preparing to grab for his arm, but he stepped out of her reach. "Yes, but Bran, hear me out."

It was his turn to shake his head, his gaze drifting to the ground at her feet. "When you were there for us, for Tate and the children after…after she was gone. It wasn't because you wanted to? It was because you told her you would?"

Emma shook her head. Her breaths burned in her chest against the tears she tried and failed to hold at bay. "Both. It was both, Bran. I wanted to help. It also meant I could fulfill my promise."

She advanced on him, but he stepped back for every one of her steps forward. If only she could catch him, hold him to her.

"You gave hints that if we were married, it would benefit both of us."

"And it did! It did, Bran. I do not regret my choice. And we've grown closer since then."

The pleading in her tone did not affect him. He

backed away further, his mouth working over words before they slipped past his lips. "Freda always knew me so well. I needed someone. The fact that you both schemed together to make the decision for me..."

"That isn't how it went, Bran. Freda...there was so much blood. And Tate was squalling, and I had my hand on Freda's stomach, trying and trying to save her—to save my friend—and she was fighting but fading all the same. I wouldn't have denied her anything in that moment, Bran. I would have promised her the moon if only I could snag it from the sky."

Horror and pain streaked across Bran's face leaving his mouth a ragged line. "I forget your bond. I..." he halted, tunneling his fingers through his hair then bringing his hands up to cover his face before dragging them down.

"Was any of it real?" he asked, hoarsely.

"Bran..."

"Was it? Was any affection you felt for me true? Or has this all been a great lie? A noble one, aye, but a great one. Painting me the fool for having fallen in—" He smashed his hand over his mouth to stop his next words. The words that Emma craved so desperately to hear.

"Of course it was." Emma went to him, her hand landing on his vambrace. She had to make him understand that what he was so scared of admitting to her had been growing in her heart all along.

"Bran, I l—"

"Don't say it."

"But—"

He took a forceful step back, wrenching his arm away. "Don't. Everything you say from this moment on is tainted. It was my folly to develop affection for you in a marriage that was simply an arrangement. I will forever wonder if you are doing it for me or for your promise."

The words rocked through her like fingers burrowing into the cracks in her heart, pulling it apart. "But, Bran, I care so much for you. It is why I want a place in your heart. Why being your second choice hurts so."

"Do you? Or are you so loyal to Freda you'd make me believe you love me?"

Emma felt as if she couldn't breathe. Small, watery inhalations caught in her chest, tightening. Dizziness swamped her. He was one to speak of loyalty to Freda.

"You should talk," she gasped, holding her side, "I've done my best in this marriage, in these circumstances, and still, it was not enough. You've finally made me see that I'm alone in this." Love and fear and fury spilled through her words as her very spirit was torn in two.

"I...I need to leave." His eyes scoured her frame, landing on her middle. When they dragged back up to her face, the raw pain in his features made her flinch. She wanted to go to him, to wrap her arms around him all the while wishing to strike him for ever doubting her. He stepped back, his distance a solid wall.

"When I return, I will uphold my marriage as we originally agreed. But I will stay in the hall. I will provide for us. Do not broker an arrangement with Oswald. I forbid it."

THIRTY

Bran was seventeen when he'd first set eyes on Earl Lachlan's keep. Nestled within the crumbling stones of an old Roman wall, he'd never imagined the sheer magnitude of the place. His ears had been wet with blood and vengeance, his wife with child, awaiting his return.

Now, all these years later, he stared at the sprawling wood and stone structure with the same awe. The land within the stones spread like an emerald blanket up to the great keep's towering log wall. Guards peppered the lookouts, appearing as small as mice from a distance. The roof and towers of the stone keep peeking over a wall, the sheer size of the building astounding. He could barely believe Ridley had resided there for nearly half of his life.

"She's breathtaking, isn't she?" Ridley said from beside him. He sat astride a great chestnut stallion, his smile almost feral with excitement. The small band of men they'd brought had halted at the opening of the forest into the wide plain that ran to the keep.

Branton swept his eyes over the grasslands before the stone wall, thinking of how Emma would love the sight. As far as he knew, she'd never been far from Hyrstow once she'd settled there. He frowned at the thought. The day-and-a-half trek to the earl's keep had proven torturous. Branton couldn't stop replaying the argument with Emma in his mind. He'd been so wounded by the admission of her promise to Freda he'd barely considered anything else she'd said. The long trip with nothing but dirt roads and forest allowed him to scour every detail of their heated words.

She'd gone behind his back. Once with Freda, scheming after his welfare, or so she said. And again with Oswald, because apparently he couldn't keep his family in good standing.

You couldn't. You can't. Emma is the only reason your family lasted the winter.

Branton stretched his neck to loosen the tension in his shoulders. He was a proud man, he knew. It was a fault. But what hooked him around the knees and took him to the ground was his desire to help Emma as she had helped him. She'd seen him through the worst part of his life—his family's life—and still strived to provide, even when pregnant. It was his turn. All of it was his turn. He was well enough. Telling Emma his darkest truth, and her acceptance of it had loosened something in him. He was ready to bring the load of wood to Lachlan and demand a regular salary for more. To show himself invaluable so that Emma didn't have to work herself to the bone any longer.

And that was the crux of it. Emma was ruthless when she needed to be. She sacrificed her own happiness for others again and again. She was selfless. Would do whatever was needed for her child and her friend, and now, him. He had no idea if she actually loved him. If she would have chosen him for herself.

Against every intention, he loved her. More than he ever thought possible. There weren't words for all that he felt for her, this gentle woman who healed his heart and twined her soul with his. He'd been an idiot to bark his intention to stay in the hall. The thought of returning to a life where they were merely figureheads was like a scabbed over wound ripped open. As his ass grew sore on the wagon bench, the long hours inching by, his rage folded in on itself.

She thought she was always second. And it was his fault.

Indeed, he'd had no role in Ridley's casting Emma aside for Yrsa. But had he even inquired about her relationship with Jon? He'd been so snared by his grief, that he didn't bother wondering more about the woman who saved him. The best he had done was get up, dress, and work. Sometimes he would take her to bed and make her feel good. But others...

He swallowed down the block of ice that had grown

in his gut. She'd stationed herself in his life to fulfill her word. As if their growing bond was nothing but a lie.

Wasn't it?

They'd set out rules from the start. He and Emma were never supposed to love one another.

A second stab of pain lanced through him on the road, dragging him further into a spiral of shame. To have Emma agree to help him and his children through a promise given to a dying woman...Bran wished he'd been able to offer such a gift to Freda in her last moments. The fact that Emma did was a testament to her strength.

And he'd shit all over it.

"It is breathtaking, Father," Neil breathed beside him on the cart, bringing Branton back to the present. The boy's eyes were fixed on the two towers that rose on either side of the stone building, then danced past to the far off cliffs which lined the sea. They couldn't yet see the dark, foamy water thrashing below, but Branton knew the sight would be equally as impressive to his son.

"Let's get a move on," he said, flicking the reins.

Ridley spurred his horse to pull ahead. He would be the first to address the guards at the gate. The horses moved as one, plodding forward on the worn road that wound through the grass. Bran and Neil's wood-laden wagon went first, followed by Ewan and Thomas's. Wilfred commanded the final wagon. Bundles of wool, carefully combed and woven by Fiona, sat stacked on the bench beside him. On single horses, Jory and Sam brought up the rear.

Once granted entrance and through the sturdy doors

of the outer wall, Branton was assaulted with the busy life within the fortress. His attention was commanded everywhere, all at once. The scents of human sweat, wool, animal droppings, dirt, piss and cold stone clambered for attention. A press of carts and tables to the right made up a market area, and to the left lay the stables. Homes sprung up further past the stables, and somewhere hidden toward the back, Bran knew, was the blacksmith, miller, ale master, and woodhouse. A great dirt yard dominated the center. Past it, the green of a large garden poked through the swarm of bodies that moved to and fro. Beside the garden stood a great well, and behind that, the huge manor house built of wood and stone. Red banners with the earl's sigil hung between the two towers of the keep, the pop of color commanding amidst the grays and browns of everyday life.

"Father, this place stinks," Neil said, leaning over as his eyes scanned the innards of the fortress. Branton chuckled as he nodded.

"Aye, I remember thinking that the first time I visited. 'Tis still true today."

Ahead, Ridley halted to speak with one of the guards that had granted them entrance. He remained perched on his horse, every vision the knight in his silver mail and helmet, his sword strapped to his side. The man he spoke with wore a similar helmet, which boasted a stripe of metal that ran over his nose, leaving the lower half of his mouth free. He laughed, then pointed further into the fortress, indicating the open space near the well, clapping Ridley's lower leg with a gloved hand after he gave direction.

Ridley grinned back then struck forward, his shoulders shifting in a way that Branton barely recognized. Chin tilted high, he nudged his horse with one hand on his reins, the other at his side as he moved into the yard.

The rest followed close behind, halting their wagons and mounts when Ridley dismounted from his. Bran was only too glad to ease off the wooden bench. Immediately, an old, thin man with a ring of white hair around the back of his head came out of the keep to greet them. His long, sage tunic was trimmed in brown fur, and he wore a grin of affection.

"Sir Ridley!" The man said, his arms up as if expecting an embrace.

"Godwin! How is it you've come to look so well?" Ridley removed his helmet and tucked it under one arm, embracing the man and dwarfing him in the process. Godwin tapped Ridley's shoulders to be released then clasped his bearded face in both hands.

"I've been free of looking after you," he said, a smile creating even more wrinkles on his lined face. His hooked nose and wizened brow gave him the appearance of an elderly hawk.

Ridley turned, his arm still bracketing the man and said to the group, "May I introduce the Earl of Deircia's Steward, Godwin of Whitebridge. Godwin, here we have Branton, the Head Cutter for Hyrstow, his son Neil, his father-in-law Wilfred Shepherd, Ewan Builder, Thomas Thatcher, Sam Sawyer, Jory Farmer."

Godwin greeted them all with hearty handshakes and kind greetings. When he commented on Neil being a good young man of creditable stock, Neil issued Bran an uncertain look out the side of his eye.

Branton shrugged. He'd met Godwin years prior, and from what Ridley had shared of him, the older man was as complimentary as he was intelligent. Though slight, he was a staple of the earl's household and to be given the utmost respect.

After releasing the horses from the wagons and handing the reins over to the stable boys, they were led inside the keep. In the main hall, Branton tried not to stare. Wrought iron sconces lined the walls and gleaming beams of deep brown wood made up the high ceiling. Hung between huge, multi-colored tapestries were bows of greenery that offered a fresh, evergreen scent to the cool stone. Two long wood tables, each bracketed by benches, stood in the reception hall's center. Fat candles dripping wax were set at intervals, accompanied by plates and utensils set for visitors. At the tables' far end sat two large, finely hewn chairs.

"Father, this place…"

"I know, son." Branton clapped a hand on Neil's shoulder to ground the boy. The memory surfaced of when Ridley, with him and Grahame in tow, led the men who had killed his parents to this very spot and demanded an audience with the earl. They'd not been much older than Neil at the time. Branton couldn't help the wry smile that escaped at the brashness of it.

Ridley caught Bran's eyes and smirked. He strode

over, bracing his hands on his hips, a mischievous glint in his eye. "Been a while, hasn't it?"

"Aye. It's easy for me to forget the majesty of a place like this. Huge and bustling," Branton said. He crossed his arms. Though it smelled far cleaner inside the keep, the foreignness of it tugged at him.

"Why'd you leave a place like this?" Ewan asked, turning round, his arms splayed. They were given the view of his dark, shaggy hair as he looked to the ceiling.

"It wasn't where I was meant to stay," Ridley said, though Branton could have sworn there was a wistful air to his tone.

Bran notched a brow at his friend. Gone was the uncertain chieftain who only wanted to help his people and had fallen in love with a Viking. In his place was a proud knight awaiting the order of his earl. Bran saw it in the set of Ridley's shoulders, the tilt of his chin. He was suddenly glad for not having followed Ridley down the path of a soldier.

"Hangman!" A tall man with flowing, auburn hair strode into the room.

Lachlan, ruler of Deircia greeted them with sparkling hazel eyes and a huge grin. He wore a rich, brown doublet over deep green trousers. A mighty stag was stitched in the center of his chest in gold thread. The same thread embroidered a swirling design over his shoulders and around the cuffs of his fine shirt while a belt beaded in deep greens, reds, and purples was slung about his waist. A presence as loud and mighty as a great wind, Lachlan ignored the chairs at the head of the table and came to stand before them.

For a moment, Branton was glad Emma wasn't present. For he was sure that Lachlan could charm the underclothes off a nun if he wished. Only the deep love for his wife, Cathryn, stopped him from doing so, Branton was sure.

Ridley went to one knee and bowed his head all in one movement. Bran and the others followed suit, though they were not so clean and swift as their leader.

"Up, up. All of you, up," Lachlan said, waving a ringed hand. "There is no need to suffer such courtesy on my account. Come now."

Lachlan approached Ridley, arms spread for an embrace, which Ridley stepped into without hesitation. The two men clapped one another's backs, Ridley taller than his earl. Branton kept a careful eye on the exchange as he stepped forward to help Wilfred from his knees. The older man's joints popped, and he gave Bran a grateful smile.

Introductions were made, and the earl gestured for the men to sit to have refreshment at one of the tables. Godwin had retreated into a door behind the thrones, then returned with several servants carrying goblets, a pitcher of mead, bread, honey, cheese and jam. They each thanked the earl profusely for his hospitality and began to eat at his insistence.

As the men spoke of planting new crops and Wilfred's large flock, Neil whispered to his father, "Why does he call Ridley 'Hangman'?"

The earl's ears perked up at the question. He held up a hand to pause the conversation.

"What's that, lad?"

Neil looked uncertain but continued after Bran gave him an encouraging look. "Why is it you call Sir Ridley 'Hangman'?"

Lachlan's smile widened, his eyes crinkling at the corners as if the memory held great joy. "It's a rather endearing story. Would you like to tell it, Rid?"

Ridley peered into his goblet of mead, swirling the liquid while waving his hand in a gesture for Lachlan to tell the tale.

"Awww. The Hangman of Hyrstow is too humble," the earl laughed, his bearded jaw, redder than his hair, flapping. "Well, young Cutter, you may not know, but there was a raid on your village many years ago where much blood was shed. Ridley's parents were slaughtered, and he swore a blood oath to avenge them."

Branton swallowed, deciding too late that he didn't want his son hearing the story. Neil would have already heard rumors of the history throughout the village, especially after the latest Viking raid. Bran didn't quite trust the gleam in Lachlan's eye as he spoke.

"Years later, he and your father and uncle, I believe..." Lachlan paused to verify if he had the details correct.

Wilfred nodded along, his lips pursed. Idly, Branton wondered how much he actually knew of what they did.

"Well, they found the scoundrels who killed Ridley's parents and slaughtered them. Brought the leader of the raid to me. They were from Bernira territory, those cowards. Ridley had shown his usefulness; your father too."

Lachlan pointed at Branton with the sharp knife he'd speared a choice piece of cheese with. Neil's wide eyes shot to Branton's. It made Bran itch. He wasn't in a position to interrupt the earl, yet he didn't want his son to know of the manner in which he, Ridley, and Grahame killed those men. The men had deserved worse than they'd got, but his son had seen enough carnage in his short life. There was a soft part to Bran that wanted to protect Neil as much as he could.

"As you likely know, Ridley was too old to undergo all the ceremony of knighthood. He hadn't been a ward, nor a page; he was too old for both—a man already. But I took him into my ranks as a foot soldier. And he was given the *worst* jobs. But he didn't falter and never complained. About a year in, I'd taken a liking to the loyal fellow. He came with me on various trips. Once, an assassin saw fit to shoot an arrow into me. He got me, right here."

Lachlan pointed to his right shoulder. Neil's mouth dropped open.

"While I was lying on the ground, Ridley checked me over, deemed I would live, then was cocky enough to demand a reward if he brought the man to justice. I agreed through my teeth, Godwin fussing over me and swearing at him. Wouldn't you know it, Ridley brought him to me. Strung the man over a tree and hung him just enough to cut off his air without actually killing him. Then he went to carving—"

"I think that's quite enough while we eat, My Lord," Ridley said. His gaze held Lachlan's, not waning to Bran's or Neil's.

Bran threw up a prayer of thanks that Ridley put an end to it. He wasn't there to rehash old memories. He had to get payment and get home.

Nothing will be the same.

Yearning, as sharp as any stab of grief, hit him in the chest.

Wilfred cleared his throat, and Neil dug his elbow into Branton's side.

"Pardon?" Bran asked, at least remembering his manners in spite of drifting off. He straightened immediately, clasping his hands in his lap to keep his nervousness at bay.

"I asked if you thought the wood near Guston could take another harvest such as the one you've just brought?" Lachlan repeated, his eyes narrowing.

Bran took it as a good sign the humor didn't drop from his mouth.

"Yes. Several times before there would be a need to let the forest rest. I don't know if the people of Guston were allowed to cut it. There appears to be no chopping in the area I was in."

"And how large is it, would you say, Master Cutter?"

Bran didn't acknowledge the weighty title, rather he propped both arms on the table, hands clasped, and leaned forward. This was what he'd been waiting for. He couldn't mess it up.

"I'd say from the south to east, then east to west,

around thirteen thousand acres. I haven't traveled to the north but I've gone deep into what seemed the center of it. It is dense. I'd say the northwest side, further from Guston, could be a risk since it is squarely in Bernira territory."

Lachlan leaned back in his chair, one hand stroking his beard, the other splayed on his still-trim middle. "Has Guston given any more problems?"

"No. Just the stolen tithe. Though, I've only been through once."

"Has anyone traveled into Guston proper as of late?"

"No. Not since we went to fell the first set of trees. We entered Guston to see if anyone else would help for a wage. Only one man did."

"How persuasive were you?"

The question took Branton aback. He was ready with a reply about how soon they could cut whatever Lachlan needed, not his methods of persuasion.

"Was it you who offered work?" Lachlan continued.

"Aye," Bran nodded. He had no idea where Lachlan was headed with his questions.

For his part, Lachlan had the decency to appear gracious. He inclined his chin, a brow hooking over one eye. "I mean no offense, Cutter, but you look like the devil incarnate. If you were the one promising work deep in the forest, I don't doubt you were rejected."

At Lachlan's wide grin Jory's laughter shot through the room. The others paused for less than a heartbeat then were guffawing along with him. Bran looked across the table to find Jory doubled over, sucking deep breaths, tears at the corners of his eyes. He kept trying to speak, but words would not come around the jabs of laughter shaking him. Even Neil had his mouth buried behind his hand.

Bran dared crack a smile at his own expense. It felt worn and brittle from misuse.

"It was him," Ewan gasped, holding his belly. "Bran was the one to ask around at the tavern and in the square. I didn't think anything of it since he's High Cutter, but you're right, he has the look of someone who might slit your throat as soon as you disappear into the forest with him."

"Come now, my lord, let us continue," Ridley said. He propped his arm on the table and leaned forward, his grin sharpening.

Bran wondered if Ridley would ever bring Yrsa to Lachlan's keep. She would like this pointed, wolfish version that only seemed to appear before his earl.

"You're right, my boy. Let us be on with it. Cutter, I will pay thirty sceats for the three cords of wood you've brought. Now, Ridley, we can adjourn, and I'd like to speak with you in private."

Bran's head snapped up with the dismissal. "My lord. If I may, I would like to discuss further arrangements for the Guston forest."

Lachlan's ruddy brows shot up as he locked his gaze on Bran. A lesser man would have quaked beneath the icy stare. "Pray tell, what do you feel is of such import that you supersede my time?"

"I would like the exclusive right to cut the Guston

forest for the next year. I know what the forest can take, and when it needs to grow. I will ensure it is not over-harvested. I will bring you the best of it and propose a salary of twenty sceats a cord."

Lachlan straightened, peaking his fingers over his belly as he regarded Branton with a shrewd gaze. Bran withstood the stare without flinching. He knew the amount was high but he risked his chance with a man who seemed to have a soft spot for Hyrstow.

"Seeing as I hold the lands in question, I do not see why you think you can demand such a price."

Bran didn't hesitate. "I know the land. My last wife's farm lay on the southeast side of the forest, near Hyrstow. I'm good at what I do. And, like you said, I'm scary enough for others not to cross me."

A smirk played at the corner of Lachlan's lip. He brought his steepled fingers to his mouth while his hazel eyes scoured Branton. Bran withstood the measurement without balking.

"Your last wife? Do you have another?" Lachlan's eyes narrowed on Ridley as if he failed to reveal a detail of import.

Neil cast his head down, and Wilfred fidgeted. The scar across Branton's heart rippled, threatening to break open. He swallowed.

"Indeed. My first wife passed in the birthing bed last year. I've remarried." He didn't say that the marriage was a sham, nor that Emma had never loved him.

Lachlan's mouth turned downward, his features

painting themselves with pity. "Sorry to hear. Glad you've moved on."

"I wouldn't quite say that m'lord. But I know I can serve the earldom better than any other. I will protect your interests, as they are mine."

The corner of Lachlan's mouth curling upward was the only indication he liked any of what Bran had just said. He was pressing his luck, and they both knew it. Lachlan was not a weak man.

"I will give you an allowance to cut the Guston forest for one year. Compensation will be fifteen sceats per cord. Hire who you will to help you procure that amount. Every three months you will bring me three cords of the best. You may keep an additional cart for Hyrstow, and, since Guston will have need of wood, you may sell one cartload every two fortnights for the same amount. That money will be brought back to me as tithe. Underwood can be collected by you and sold to whomever you see fit as payment for the hassle of Guston.

"Now, if the others would be so kind as to take their leave," Lachlan looked pointedly at Bran, "the Hangman and I can move on to private matters."

The bench scraped across the stone floor as everyone stood to heed the order. Branton's heart beat erratically with the taste of victory. Forty-five sceats were enough to keep himself and two men employed to cut the forest. It was large enough to ease his mind, though he knew Emma would still have to work. It begrudged him to think her plan with the church had some merit.

Even if he didn't return home to Emma, perhaps he

could prove through his hard work how much he cared for her. How, despite her reservations about his love, he did have a depth of feeling for her that rivaled sense. She was his wife. And he was ready to be there in every way that mattered.

CHAPTER
THIRTY-ONE

"There," Yrsa said as she set down the small cart in the center of the square. Despite the early hour, people milled about, many not from Hyrstow, awaiting the market and seeking the church for prayer. Emma wondered how long the market would be able to stand amidst the heavy blanket of cloud that hung above.

"Thank you. I could have managed."

Yrsa stood to her full height after securing a piece of wood beneath the cart's wheel. She wiped the grime from her hands on her legs, grimacing at Emma's words.

"I know you could have. But I am your friend. That means you don't have to."

Emma felt her bottom lip wobble at Yrsa's straightforward sincerity. She bit it, hard enough to taste blood. Tears had plagued her since Bran had left days ago, and she was exhausted from expending all of herself on her broken heart. She thought she could withstand anything. Her constant tearfulness made her realize it wasn't true.

Her first mistake was thinking that Bran would have understood the promise to Freda. She was Emma's friend, after all, and he should have gleaned the importance of that friendship, for both women. Yet she did not anticipate his surprise and hurt. After all that they had shared, the thirst they had quenched with one another's bodies, the family they had made, Emma had believed Branton would have felt her love. She knew he may have been uneasy with her vow but didn't think he would take it so far as to withdraw his affection completely.

He was right; she had lied. Sheltered him from the truth when she didn't think he could take it. But Bran was not a child. He wasn't someone to be protected and coddled. And, because she had done so with everyone else, it was exactly what she'd done to him.

"Well, thank you again," Emma said, her voice wobbly. She busied herself with arranging the bread on the table that faced the aisle. Carts and tables were hoisted on either side of them. Yrsa hung around, scooping up Æfflead and showing her things from the small purse at her waist while Emma and Ginnie worked. Finally, Yrsa stood to take her leave as well.

"I will come by later to help bring it back."

Emma gave a slight eye roll with the implication she was unable to care for herself, but Yrsa caught her off guard by placing both calloused hands on either side of Emma's upper arms.

"I promise, Emma. I will come back. You may think

yourself alone, but you are not. Ridley spoke of a disagreement between you and Bran before he left. Considering I've barely seen you all week, I take it you're more wounded than you'd like to admit. I'm here if you need anything at all. Your family has somehow become mine."

Emma's throat suddenly felt as if a lump of dough had lodged in it. She nodded, offering Yrsa a limp smile. Her friend bent to kiss her cheek then strode off. Emma was left holding her belly, trying to think of a way she could right the life that felt so upside down.

Once the cart was fully arranged, she offered Æfflead and Ginnie half a bun each. Since she hadn't been able to sleep well without Bran beside her, she'd made use of her time by baking a batch of buns spun with crushed hazelnut and rosemary sprigs. The girls took the morsels and devoured them within moments. As Æffie reached for another, a stout, hooded man in a dark cloak approached.

A strange feeling pricked the back of Emma's neck. There was a familiarity to his shape though Emma couldn't place him. His head remained down, his shaved chin nearly touching his chest. He came to stand at the table she'd arranged in front of the cart as a display, leaning into the worn wood. A bag lay against his hip and the unrefined fabric of the dark cloak denoted a humble existence. It wasn't until he spoke that Emma's heartbeat lessened.

"Mrs. Baker," Oswald said, lifting his head enough to look into her eyes, "are you intending to remain long at the market today?" He'd pitched his voice low, as if to mask it.

Emma tried to hide the surprise that splashed across her features. It was unusual for the High Priest to be out on market days, let alone asking questions of her. She pasted on her customary grin in the hope he'd further considered her deal.

"I intend to be here for the day, as usual. Would you like to have something from my stand before the rush starts? If you are intending to come back later, there may not be much left."

Oswald's gaze shuttered, his mouth curling downward. It confused Emma to think that she'd offended him already.

"There looks to be rain. It may be best for you to close early."

The weight behind the words caused the back of Emma's shoulders to hitch. As far as she knew, the High Priest didn't share concern over those who sold their wares. Her mind felt sluggish, her lack of sleep not allowing her to make sense of the suggestion.

"Alas, but I must remain until I've sold everything or until the day is done. Though, if you are inclined to discuss my previous offer, I can have Ginnie or Merthe hold the cart while we confer."

Emma knew Bran didn't want her to make deals with Oswald, however he'd made it very clear they were no longer man and wife in the way she wanted. She had no idea if his discussion with the earl would garner him more work and didn't want to lose the opportunity with the church.

A family walked by, and Oswald stiffened, his eyes shifting to the side as if to avoid discovery. He turned away from where people entered the funnel of market stands.

"I do not want to discuss any deal. Though I implore you to not leave your children unattended."

Emma placed a hand on her hip and cocked her head to the side. She had no idea what Oswald was on about, and if he was not to buy from her, he needed to move along.

"Indeed, thank you, Rev—"

"Shh!" He held his hand up to silence her before she could address him. With a furtive glance around the square, he rucked up his hood further. "You are a nice woman. Please heed me. Do not remain at market. The day is to be a long one."

Emma murmured a confused "thank you" as Oswald departed. Hands tucked within the cloak, he stole to the south, through the line of carts and tables, then veered around the stands and struck northwest, in the direction of the men's hall. Emma stood still as a post driven into the ground as she watched him. He acknowledged no one else and ducked his head if anyone looked in his direction. Emma rubbed her upper arms to ward off the chill that clung to her skin.

"Mother!" Ælflead said, tugging hard on Emma's skirt. It snapped Emma out of her reverie, allowing her to refocus on her task. She had work to do regardless of the

Reverend Father's vague warnings. As she reached down to hug Æffie, she breathed in the little girl's woodsmoke and wool scent. The delicate bones of the small body pulled Emma back to herself and her responsibilities. She straightened, ready to greet the day's customers.

BRAN'S HEAD WAS THICK. The taste of horse shit lined his mouth. After a few days in the keep under the watchful eye of Lachlan's hospitality, the men of Hyrstow had been given a send off for the ages. Deer roast cooked to perfection, vegetables, bread, thick slabs of cheese, golden butter, cooked apples, and mead, lots and lots of mead, was served. Bran's stomach turned over and the need to expel the meal assaulted him.

His shoulder pinched painfully as hard boards surged beneath him. He was a dead weight in what turned out to be the wagon's bed. A barrel of ale squatted at his back though the scent of alcohol could have been wafting from him. When he cracked an eye, it took him a moment to orient himself. Dimness swathed him and his mind glazed until he realized a tarp of thick cloth had been thrown over the sides of the wagon to cover it.

A murky memory of falling asleep in the back of the wagon rather than his cot drifted in, with it, the shame of the way he'd unburdened himself to Ridley. After too much drink, he'd lamented the curse of women and the havoc they wreaked on his heart. He recalled Ridley slapping him heartily on the back and asking if Emma's promise to Freda was truly a betrayal if it brought Freda peace in her last moments. Was it so bad if Emma ended up his wife, which was what Branton seemed to want most anyway? The means begot the end was what Branton gathered.

Ridley had told him to sleep it off, that his situation would seem better in the morning, especially since Bran had a nice pouch of sceats in hand after the sale of his wood.

The wagon hit a rock, and Bran hissed, his head throbbing. Men chatted around him, and the light that slipped through the seams of the tarp indicated daytime. With a great sigh, Bran crawled to the edge of the wagon and pushed at the tarp. The corner flap gave way, allowing him to sit up, blinking against the dappled sunlight that poured through the forest canopy. They appeared to be traveling on the south road, plodding through the woods at a steady rate. The high slope to their left let Bran know they were halfway through Deircia's Kingswood, over half a day's trek from the keep.

"Good morning, Father," Neil chirped from the front seat.

Wilfred sat beside him, his gnarled hands on the reins. Something rustled in the trees on the high bank, but before Branton could make out what it was, Neil laughed, delighted at his father's misery. Bran offered a grimace.

"Let your father alone," Wilf nudged Neil's arm. "You'll have your turn to feel as he does soon enough."

"Yes, well I don't think I'll ever nurse a broken heart

quite like he does," Neil scoffed as he turned, his grin stretching.

Bran steadied himself and took a swipe over the wagon's edge to bop him on the shoulder. "What's that supposed to mean?"

"Just that you spent the better part of last night talking about Emma and how she 'holds your soul' and 'there won't be another' and…"

"Is that Bran?" Ewan hollered from behind. "Jory, you owe me three sceats! I knew he'd wake before midday. Though the way you were going on about Emma, Christ-almighty, I thought we'd never hear the end of it."

"You've got that right!" Jory shouted.

"Alright, alright, that's enough," Bran groaned, blushing to the tips of his ears. Apparently his lament to Ridley wasn't the only one. Branton braced a hand on the back of the bench to steady himself as his knees began to scream at him from continued rest on the jolting wood.

"What?" Neil asked, narrowing his eyes. "You don't love her?"

Bran scowled. His head *hurt*. It was so foggy, he felt as if there was something looming in the forest, though the sunshine betrayed nothing out of sorts. He considered swearing off drink for the next year while he also decided not to honor Neil's question with an answer. Instead, he changed tactics. "I'll always love your mother."

"Dad, I know. You've said," Neil rolled his eyes heavenward. "I believe ya. But I see the way you are with

Emma. How you look at her. It's different from mum and the same. I understand."

"How do I look at Emma?"

"Like you're parched and she's water." Ridley's voice came from ahead.

Bran looked further, to find Ridley halting his steed to allow it to come beside the wagon. The path was wide enough for the wagon and horse to remain abreast, though Bran wished it wasn't so. His friend looked at him with a thinly veiled expression of mirth.

"Alright." Bran tried to rein in his embarrassment. He was a prideful fool, he knew. Emma was the best thing that had happened to him, promise or no.

Jory rode up behind Ridley, his grin wide, blue eyes dancing. He opened his mouth to offer his own comment, but his head snapped back, the ends of his shaggy blonde hair tickling the back of his cloak. A thin, long pole stuck out of Jory's open mouth. Blood welled. Gurgling erupted from him. Stupefied, Branton watched him fall backwards onto the horse, his body going limp as a second arrow lodged in his chest.

"Bandits!" Ewan roared.

Ewan drew the short sword at his side and reined his horse over to Jory's. Blood pumped from Jory's mouth, his hands going slack, his face too white. Ridley was already ahead, sword drawn, shield up to deflect any arrows aimed for Neil. Branton ducked as an arrow flew past his head. It lodged with a thunk into the wood near Wilf's back. The older man snapped the reins, spurring the horses forward.

"Move!" Ridley shouted, his sword leveled at the unseen threats.

Branton whipped the tarp away as he took hold of Neil by the scruff of the neck and yanked him backwards over the bench's lip and into the wagon's bed. As Neil's feet slipped over the side an arrow struck one of the horses. The beast screeched and the cart shuddered as it missed a step.

"Get low," Branton commanded as Neil lay down among the casks of ale and bolts of cloth and tools. They were still moving, still able to escape. Bran covered Neil with his own body, craning his neck to see where the attack was coming from. The cart slowed, the injured horse making a terrible keening sound. It forced the other horses to slow with it. Ridley shouted orders for Wilf to speed up while Ewan commanded Jory to respond.

The wagon's thick boards obscured Bran's vision. Shouts and the skittering of sticks and detritus from the embankment indicated a group to their left. The wagon was still moving. He peeked over its wooden lip to find seven men with bows drawn and short swords at the ready as they barreled toward them.

Ducking back down, he heard Ridley grunt and the clang of metal. Cursing. Someone shouting to retreat and other, foreign voices commanding their group to halt. Branton shoved Neil's head down further, pressing him closer to the ale.

"Stay down," he growled as he frantically searched for his ax, a knife, a sword, anything in the wagon's bed, but there was nothing. Neil's breaths came fast and hard beneath him. The scent of wood and panic shoved up his nose. His hands roved over the limited space in the back of the wagon, merely skimming wood grain, fabric, Neil. His rush made him sloppy until, finally, Bran's hand landed on an iron pot. He grabbed hold of one side, sitting up to gain leverage on whatever came his way.

Three of the bandits had brought up the rear, one of them catching the reins of Jory's now-vacant horse. Ewan, atop his steed, was fighting off a man below. His desperate strikes weren't connecting, though they kept the bandit at bay. Yet another had an arrow drawn and aimed squarely at Sam's chest. The younger man sat frozen on the second wagon's bench, wide-eyed, his lips moving in a silent prayer. Thomas was lying on the ground next to the third wagon, face down, his head bloodied.

A pained shout ripped from a man toward the front of their party. It took Bran half a moment to realize Ridley had dismounted and plunged his short sword through the belly of one of the bandits. With a hard kick, Ridley booted the man off his blade as another came at him from the right. Ridley caught the man with an elbow to the ribs then whirled, his sword cleaving through the air as the man backed away. Behind him, a weathered, sharp-eyed man closed in. Ridley swung his sword in a short arc to keep the men back. The only worry he betrayed was a glance back at the wagon to see where Neil was.

To Bran's right, another bandit climbed onto the

bench of his wagon, ax raised against Wilf. His father-in-law had his knife in hand, his jaw clenched and his eyes narrowed.

Bran's heart beat fast and his hands shook with the need to inflict damage. Rage, so deep it opened a chasm inside him, poured forth as he surged up, windmilling his arms, striking the bandit nearest him on the bench behind the ear. The man sagged forward into Wilf. Ready, the older man buried his knife in the man's gut as he fell.

Then Bran was up, his sole focus on the man with the bow pointed at Sam. He was across the wagon in two strides, flinging himself into the air. The man turned as Bran dropped. His arrow loosed without full pull, and it skittered away into the ground without harming man or horse. The bandit made a sound of surprise as Bran's much larger body took him to the ground. For a tilting moment, Bran thought he would fall upon a knife or other weapon. The bandit raised his arm against Bran's side as they collapsed into the damp earth, though the crunching sound of bone indicated it to be a poor idea. Bran thrust his hand down, curling his fingers around the knife handle on the man's belt and brought it up, ready to slide it into the man's body.

Cold steel kissed Bran's throat as he reared back.

He froze, heart hammering, knife in hand.

"You'll stop now," a gravelly voice said from above.

The bandit Branton straddled whined in pain.

"Get off 'im," said the man holding a sword to his neck.

Bran's gaze followed the length of steel up a grungy, wool-encased arm, to a grimy, bearded face. The man's age was difficult to determine—he could have been twenty or forty, years of hard living making him look old regardless. Old and unmerciful. Like a whetstone, ready to grind something down.

Silence met the roaring in Bran's ears. Somehow, the fight had halted. Fear trickled into Branton. Where the hell was Ridley?

"I have a right mind to slit your throat," the man remarked, more to himself than anyone else, "Hugo is my best archer. What'll I do without his arm now?"

Below him, Hugo dragged himself from beneath Bran, clutching his arm with his good hand, hissing in pain. Bran wished he could have clamped his legs closed on the man's neck.

The bandit with the sword turned to glance behind him. He shouted toward the topmost corner of the wagon, "Have you got the knight?"

"Yes!" Came the reply.

Branton's blood ran cold. He didn't know if that meant that Ridley was dead or had a sword on him. Bran risked a glance toward the wagon. There was a body in silver mail on the ground in front of the wheels. Ridley. He noted only one set of legs standing by his fallen form. Neil appeared to have heeded Bran's advice and remained hidden under the tarp.

From Bran's left, Ewan's howl cut the air. The sound ricocheted off the trees above them, clawing toward the sky. He fell to the ground with a thud, clutching his leg, his face pinched with pain.

"Tell me what goods you're carrying," the man with the sword demanded.

Branton made a show of pursing his lips into a line. The man notched an eyebrow then nodded to the man opposite who jabbed his sword into Ewan's arm. Ewan screamed.

"Drink, food, cloth, tools," Bran spat.

"Coin?"

Bran remained silent, refusing to glance down at the full pouch on his belt. He knew it would be found, but he wasn't going to hand it over to them.

"You do know we'll just kill all of you to find it?" the man asked in a bored tone. He scratched a large boil on his forehead.

Ewan groaned. Branton could glimpse him through the horse's legs of the second wagon. He wouldn't be walking any time soon.

God above, he hoped for Neil to remain quiet. And if all their throats were cut, perhaps his son could jump from the cart and run into the bush and hide. He could make it back to the earl's keep by following the path.

Bran's mouth went dry at the thought of his son being hunted and picked apart by these men. It caused a fire in his gut, one that charged his limbs with the need to move, to flay their skin and burn their bones.

He grinned at the man holding the sword to his throat. The man's brow descended at the show of teeth. "What are you smiling at?"

Bran huffed a laugh, knowing that mirth in the face of death made others feel unsteady.

"You won't live through this, you know that?" he asked.

The man's eyes narrowed and the steel bit into Bran's neck a little further. Pain flared, hot and angry. The warm slip of his own blood on his skin made him pause.

"Where'd you say you boys were headed?"

"Hyrstow." Branton answered freely. The measure of time these men were taking told him they were perhaps not willing to spill the blood of a knight. Or that they wanted something else, possibly a piece of information.

The man chuckled, the noise grating. "Hyrstow? Probably won't be much left of it, after the raid."

Branton's heart stopped.

"What raid?"

The men bent toward him, grinning, his yellowed teeth and rotten breath shoving into Bran's face. "Ah, you didn't hear? Guston's revenge."

THIRTY-TWO

A shift in the air caused Emma to scent dozens of bodies on the breeze. More people than usual perused the market, though few were buying. She wasn't sure if it was due to the impending rain, or the bustling in and out of St. Paul's. Several people throughout the market wore hoods up against the wind, shadowed eyes peeking from beneath as they passed. More men than normal, too.

As she considered the merit of shutting the stand down early, a hooded figure in a finely spun dark blue cloak glanced at her stand. Emma was hard pressed to see the face inside, though hair as dark as midnight cascaded from the hood's mouth.

"The Viking woman, is she here?" The voice belonging to the figure was certainly female, though pitched in a manner to sound different than it likely was.

Apprehension like a splinter in her side made Emma reach out to pat the crown of Tatswip's head from where she rested in Merthe's arms. Merthe had brought lunch for them and remained at the stand with Tate, ready to help pack up if the storm unleashed.

"Who is asking?"

The woman ignored Emma's question, slithering through the crowd, her cloaked head snapping right and left in search of Yrsa.

Something rotten curdled Emma's gut. There were too many people, too much shoving required to send one of the children through the crowd to alert Yrsa that someone was looking for her. Emma sighed, telling herself that Bran's departure had filled her head with unnecessary doom.

"Mother?" Merthe asked.

A man strode up, plucked a loaf from their stand and took a huge bite. He watched her as he chewed, open mouthed, as if challenging her to say something.

Anger spiked through her so fast, Emma crossed the small space behind the table within half a heartbeat to demand payment. She glared into pockmarked skin and dark, almost black eyes.

"That's two sceats."

The man made a show of leaning down to look her in the eye. The table between them did nothing to mask the scent of sour onion and unwashed male. He chewed her bread, enjoying the way she crossed her hands over her chest, and when finished, took another bite as if daring her to say something else. It was then she truly noticed the hooded figures. They were everywhere.

A shout blasted from the north end of the stalls, one

of incoherent warning. Time seemed to slow as she brought her gaze back to the man before her. He grinned, parting his cloak to reveal a wicked knife on his belt. A chill shoved through Emma as the man clasped the weapon's handle. She backed up, bumping into Merthe, her hands already up in a protective gesture.

Eyes locked on the man, she said, "Merthe. Keep hold of Tate. Come!"

Ginnie, who clutched Æffie near the cart's wheel, shrieked. Emma whirled, expecting the knife to bury in her back as she scooped up Æffie and shouted, "Run!"

At the same moment screams rang out among the square. Men, women, and children scattered as the wooden structures were overturned. Merthe and Tate came up against the cart blocking them from the other side. To their left, Athil Thatcher scrambled through the opening between her cart and theirs. Emma dared look over her shoulder. The man was climbing over her table, knife in hand. Bread littered the ground.

"Move!" she shouted at her children, ensuring they remained in front of her. She could almost feel the steel lodging into her. Merthe's keen instinct led them between carts and tables overturned all around them. Emma hitched Æffie up on her hip for a better hold, her stomach pinching as she did so. Food and goods were stomped beneath feet as villagers scattered. Panic clogged the air. Cloaked men poured in from the south entrance, crushing people in a bottleneck of damaged tables and fabric. Fingers closed around tunics and skirts, yanking women back and down. Screams carried, along with the coppery tang of blood on the wind.

Too many yards away stood the church, its doors closed. An old man banged on the slab of wood to no answer. To Emma's right, people swarmed, crushing one another in an effort to escape the threat of weapons. In front of them, a man thrust a sword at Mrs. Smith. Emma covered Æfflead's eyes as the blade disappeared into the woman.

Ginnie stopped short, screaming. Ahead, Merthe halted while sheltering Tate in her arms. Emma caught Ginnie around the wrist, yanking her back, into her own body. Murhred Butcher rushed the man holding Mrs. Smith. Emma couldn't get the girls around them.

A high-pitched whistle cut through the noise, drawing Emma's attention to the north end of the market where a raven-haired woman stood with a sword in hand, her dark hood thrown back, eyes locked on Merthe.

It was the woman from the forest.

Between one blink and the next, Emma let go of Ginnie and grabbed Merthe's sleeve with one hand. "Come!"

Emma had no idea if the man was still behind them, but she dared hope he wouldn't expect her to double back. Before she could doubt her choice, Emma swung Æffie around to her back, ensuring the girl's hands were twined about her throat.

The man behind them was kicking at overturned stands, looking beneath a swath of fabric that had fallen.

Emma barrelled for him. He looked up, mouth opening in shock, and Emma shoved her outstretched hands into his chest. His arms, full of knife and food, flailed upward as she pushed him with all the force she could muster. She could only pray that Merthe could get around her.

The man's filthy oath rang in her ears as the over-turned table caught his ankles. He went down with a crash, though the noise of it was overpowered by Æffie crying against her ear.

"Merthe! Go west!" Emma shouted.

Merthe glanced back at Emma, fear naked in her wide eyes. Tate squalled in her grasp. A crash like an ax through wood careened through the air. Emma flinched as she grabbed Ginnie's hand and began to run through the village. The market was in ruins.

Emma followed Merthe out of the square into the lattice-work of huts. Animals brayed from their pens. The clash of swords, thumps of wood, and the pounding of feet vied for Emma's attention as she tried to antici-pate where to run. She had to get the girls to safety.

Every instinct told her to run home. It lay to the south, but a scream of terror sucked hope from her. She rucked Æffie up on her back to alleviate the pain shooting into her hips from the weight. Ginnie clutched her hand, snot and tears running down her red cheeks. To their right, the door to the men's hall hung open like a missing tooth. Emma didn't get a count on the raiders, but she hoped there were enough men in Hyrstow to fight them off. Some had gone with Ridley and Bran—

she couldn't remember how many were left to defend the village.

Couldn't remember if mostly women and children were left like lambs to slaughter.

Metal rang against metal to their left, close enough she would have gasped in surprise had Æfflead's wrists not been choking her.

She picked up their pace, turning north when Ginnie tripped. The girl tried to catch herself but went hard to her knees. Merthe turned, mouth open on a ragged breath. She bent to help Ginnie up as Emma grabbed the girl's other arm. Cold sweat poured down Emma's face. They had to keep moving. Despite the pain in her belly, her back, her legs, Emma had to keep the children moving.

"My foot, my foot!" Ginnie wailed, collapsing as they tried to pull her up.

"It's alright, love. We have to keep going." Emma curled her arm around Ginnie's waist, though, as she crouched then hefted upward, Æfflead loosened her hold.

"Oh!" Emma grunted. She had to release Ginnie lest she drop Æffie. Panic that someone was at their back threatened to drown her.

"Mother!" Merthe shouted, her cheeks stained with silent tears. Tate sobbed in one arm, the other was wrapped around Ginnie, who struggled to stand. Breaths sawed in and out of them. The rain began.

Emma knelt beside Ginnie, ensuring Æfflead

wouldn't fall by twisting an arm around her back beneath the girl's bottom.

"The hall. Go."

Merthe nodded. Emma rose, practically dragging Ginnie as the girl sobbed, hopping on one foot. Their steps were staggered, too slow. Emma gritted her teeth, willing the raiders to stay away. She ground her feet into the dirt with every step, determined.

Finally, finally, they reached it. Merthe moved toward the door but Emma held her arm out to bar the way.

"I'll check." She laboriously set Æfflead down then peeked around the door. The glow of the fire's coals illuminated the empty chairs, and beds neatly made up along the far walls. Deeper inside, the door to Yrsa and Ridley's chambers appeared closed. It was silent.

"Quick," Emma commanded. She swept a hand back, allowing Merthe to carry Tate inside first. Æffie followed, then Emma hefted Ginnie across the threshold. Her belly burned with the strain.

"To Yrsa's room. Hurry."

With Emma's support, Ginnie hopped to the rear of the hall, her foot banging against the wood boards with a thump that felt like Emma's hammering heart. Merthe helped usher her into the back suite. The room was dark, the light from the roof's vent dim. Tate and Æffie clung to one another at the foot of the bed that jutted into the center of the room.

"Here," she said, pulling Ginnie over to the right, wedging her in the corner between the bed and the wall.

Merthe was there a moment later with Æffie, settling her as best she could. Emma plucked Tate off the ground and hugged the baby to her chest, shushing her gently a few times before placing her in Ginnie's arms. Tatswip stopped wailing at Emma's touch, though she twisted to be free.

Next, Emma ripped the blankets from the beds. She threw them over the crouched girls, hoping to give them extra cover. She spoke the words that were like daggers to her heart. Somehow, Emma managed to keep her voice steady.

"Ginnie, sweets, you need to keep hold of the girls for me. I have to look for a weapon and I need you to be big and strong and help me keep them safe, okay? You must stay quiet. No matter what you hear, do not come out. Stay hidden. Merthe, come with me."

The girls tried to stifle their crying as Ginnie held Tate. They were unsuccessful. She kissed each of their small heads then moved out of the room. Their panicked tears grated on Emma's nerves only because she knew the noise would draw the attention of the raiders.

Once the door was shut, Emma moved to the closest bed and pushed it across the doorway. Cold sweat formed along her hair line. The hard packed straw itched through its sheet as she shoved. Upon seeing her intention, Merthe helped drag the unruly straw mattress. Huffing, they moved a second mattress overtop of the first.

"Merthe. Look for a blade. An ax. Anything."

Emma ran to the long table in the center of the hall,

hands skimming over the surface. Merthe searched the walls for any weapons held aloft. Emma could hear her daughter's panicked, shallow breaths. The sound nearly broke her.

When her hands scored along the handle of a knife, Emma nearly wept with relief.

"Merthe, come," she said, gesturing to the open door. Merthe came up behind her, clasping her arm as if afraid Emma would propel herself outside.

"Mother, no. You can't."

Emma tried to draw a breath, but it caught in her throat.

What she had to do clawed against every one of her instincts. It made her want to cry—to rage—against the forces that had landed Hyrstow in danger once again. Instead, she faced Merthe and pasted a small smile across her lips.

"Merthe. Listen to me. I need you to take this," she shoved the handle of the knife into her daughter's hands. Merthe grasped it, already so capable with a weapon thanks to Yrsa. The blade was long and blunt. Made for rendering meat. It would serve Merthe well.

Emma opened her mouth to speak but couldn't over the knot formed there.

"Mother…" Merthe began but Emma found her words and spoke over her, clasping her hands around her daughter's. The rain struck the thatched roof with a multitude of small thuds.

"You must run to Grahame's. He may be home. He

can help me get the children to safety. I cannot carry Ginnie and Æfflead and Tate. We need *help*."

Merthe's lips trembled as her eyes filled. She shook her head, a sob wracking her body. Emma placed her hands on her daughter's shoulders. She shook her a little, though not unkindly.

"You must go swiftly, Merthe. I do not know where these raiders come from or why they are here. Move through the forest. Get to the other side to alert Grahame. Then stay at the Shepherds'. My love, I need you. "

Merthe nodded, then shook her head, tears flowing down her cheeks in earnest. Emma pulled her into her chest. She pressed her child to her as if she could meld her once again with her own flesh. Merthe hugged her back, her grip strong.

Emma sniffed loudly and forced herself to release Merthe.

"Stay low and quiet. Take your time and if you see raiders, hide. Do not allow yourself to be caught." The lump in her throat suddenly prevented her speech.

Merthe shoved the tears from her cheeks with the heel of her hand. She nodded, standing taller.

"Go. And do not return until you've received word that it is safe."

"I will."

Emma turned and poked her head out the door. In the distance, a man with a large knife walked across one of the pathways then disappeared behind a hut closer to the square. The rest of the homes appeared unharmed. A different sort of unease wrapped around the back of Emma's neck.

The raiders weren't sacking the village. They were staying near the square. Why?

It didn't matter. No one walked near the hall. It was Merthe's chance.

"Swift and sure, my love. Go." When Emma pressed a kiss to Merthe's cheek, she thought her heart would cleave in two.

Merthe nodded once, determination set in her beautiful features, then disappeared around the door.

Emma heaved it closed. She turned, placing her back against the hardwood. Tears slipped down her cheeks, her knees threatening to give out. Her heart refused to slow, even as she pressed her hands to her chest and sucked deep breaths.

Had she done the right thing? Or had she sent her daughter to her death? Fear, cold and punishing, gripped Emma's guts and squeezed.

She had to protect the children. They were her babies now and she would not let them down.

With a ragged breath, she pushed herself from the door. It needed to be barricaded. She raced to the other side of the room where the great chairs stood around the fire. Emma huffed, shoving her shoulder into the back of one, scraping it toward the door. It moved mere inches. Emma hated her weakness.

The hall's door swung inward. Emma's heart shoved to her throat as she ducked behind the chair. She steeled herself, knowing she may have only a moment of surprise to throw herself upon the raider. Footsteps sounded, though they were not the heavy stride of a male pleased with his domination. Emma peeked around the corner of the chair and locked eyes with a tall, blonde Viking. Emma nearly sagged to the floor.

"Emma," Yrsa said as she shut the door. Her sword hung on her hip, and she held her dagger in hand. A smear of blood draped across her brown tunic but she was whole. Within a few strides, she knelt in front of Emma, gathering her into a hug that Emma wanted to melt into.

"Shhh," Yrsa said into her hair. Emma felt the flat of Yrsa's dagger against her back. "You're shaking. Where are the girls?"

She felt Yrsa look past her shoulder for them.

"They are here. Locked in your room. I had to send Merthe for help. I couldn't leave them all. Oh God, Yrsa, I sent her out—"

Tears clogged Emma's throat, preventing further speech.

Yrsa nodded then raised her voice slightly for the girls to hear, "It's Yrsa young ones. I will guard you with my life. Do not come out. Stay hidden, no matter what you hear."

Stifled sobs of relief poured from the other side of the room, and Emma thought she might break at the sound of her children's terror. Then Yrsa was grabbing her hand and folding Emma's fingers around her dagger's gilded handle.

"Take this. Do you know how to use it?"

Emma nodded, blood rushing beneath her skin. She didn't know, but she felt that if anyone came at her children she could rip them apart with her bare hands. Yrsa caught Emma's gaze with her own. Yrsa's stormy blue eyes were steady, her breaths even.

"We can do this, Emma. I'm here."

As the words met the air, a roar sounded outside and the door was kicked open.

Time slowed as a dark haired man barreled into the room, his ax held high. He was broad of chest, and though blood coated one leg, he appeared overjoyed to find the two women. A wiry man followed him inside. The second, with hair like dirty dishwater, grinned. Emma cowered. She clutched the dagger to her belly, the handle awkward in her palm. Yrsa released Emma and uncurled to her full height. Her brows dipped with determination, her mouth a line. She straightened her shoulders, drawing her sword, blonde hair flowing down her leathered back.

"What have we here?" the first man asked. His grin belied a lack of teeth despite his youthful appearance.

As if Yrsa hadn't heard a word, she set into motion. The second man's eyes locked on her, his smile spreading as if Yrsa were a present tied with a bow. Emma could only watch, mouth open, as the Viking strode forward with steady steps. Both men grinned, lowering their weapons at her approach.

Halfway between Emma and the men, Yrsa grabbed an abandoned plate from the fireside table, barely stopping as she did so.

"Are you to prepare me supper?" the first raider jested. Laughter echoed through the great room. "We can eat after we've had some fun!"

Yrsa didn't stop. She turned the plate in her hand and threw it like a disc into the first man's face. He roared as the dish cracked into the bridge of his nose. The sickly crunch of broken bone was overshadowed by the other man's grunt of rage as he threw his sword arm up to stop Yrsa's blow. Crimson decorated her blade as she drew it back then swept low, to the side to avoid the strike of the first man's ax. His nose poured blood but he'd recovered from his surprise. In a blink, Yrsa slashed into the back of the wiry man's thigh. He jumped forward, nearly knocking into the first man.

Emma was frozen. Her heart was trying to punch its way out of her as she watched Yrsa. All the while, her legs burned with the need to run, run, *run* to safety. She knew she was no match for the men but couldn't leave Yrsa to fight alone.

Yrsa and the wiry man parried and thrust, their movements synced. He was a strong fighter, despite his injury. Yrsa growled as the man's blade whispered past her bad shoulder. She wasn't as strong on her right from a previous injury, Emma knew, and the longer the fight went on, the quicker the man was learning where to strike.

Emma stood there, dumbfounded, while the first man stomped toward her. Lank hair hung over ruddy brows that were twisted downward with malice. He swung his ax in the air with enough force to strike her head from her body.

A strangled sound escaped Emma as she darted to the side. It was chased by the gust of breath that shoved out of her as she hit the chair beside her. Feet tangled together, Emma fell, hard. Her arm and shoulder absorbed the impact of the planked floor. The dagger skidded out of her grasp. When she twisted to see the man bearing down on her, pain like the branches of a tree reached through her belly.

"Nice little missus," the man sneered as he loomed. Emma did the only thing she could think of. She kicked out with her foot. By sheer luck, she hit the man in the knee. His leg buckled. The victory was short-lived. He dropped to the floor at her feet, hands grabbing for her thrashing legs.

"Why do women put up such a fight?"

Emma heard her name shouted from across the room but she was too busy kicking at the man to look at Yrsa. Blood ran from the man's nose into his mouth and past his beard. His stench, like that of vomit and blood, assaulted Emma while his large hand clamped around her ankle. He yanked her into him, his hands climbing her legs. His fingers dug trenches in her flesh. Emma bit down on her scream, still mindful of the children next door. She shoved at his face but he kept coming, hands clawing, finding their way upward.

Desperate, Emma jammed a thumb into the man's eye, wrapping clawed fingers around the side of his face. The jelly of his eyeball caved beneath the pressure. Bellowing, he released her and she scrambled back, hand searching for the handle of the dagger. Her fingers nudged the metal just out of reach. She just had to arch back a little further and she'd have it...

A fist met her head. Once, twice.

Then his other fist met with her side.

The world halted. Pain like nothing she'd ever felt radiated from her belly down into her legs. Her face was on fire while her lips went numb. Shadows decorated the edges of her vision. Sounds echoed, but she couldn't connect them with what they meant. She curled into herself. A roaring in her ears like that of a storm on the ocean held her.

The hideous man kept coming. His dirty face twisted with a grin and Emma knew she had to get away but his hands were everywhere. He was climbing up her body, yanking her legs down. Vomit rose to her mouth as he tried to roll her over. She remained tightly bunched, her legs pressed to her belly for protection.

Then he was drawing back, his head at an awkward angle. The column of his throat was exposed while his eyes flew wide, searching. Everything around her moved as if through water. Something shiny glinted at the man's neck, then a red seam opened along his skin. Rain the color of black rubies fell onto her as the man's mouth opened and closed like a fish.

From behind him, a beautiful, golden face was twisted with rage. Yrsa gripped the raider's hair in one hand while her other continued its slice upward. She felt the man bucking, writhing to escape but it was too late. The red rain on Emma was warm. She turned her face into the floor to avoid the sticky feeling of it. Her breaths came out in gasping little pants, her body trying to recover from the pain still dancing through her.

Suddenly, the weight of the man was gone, shoved off by Yrsa.

"Emma!" Yrsa was shouting, though it sounded as if her voice was in the clouds. Yrsa shook her shoulder. "Emma, are you hurt?"

Emma uncurled enough to allow Yrsa to run bloody fingers through her hair. The tenderness with which her friend touched her after such violence struck Emma dumb. In the face of death, how could one be so gentle? But women could. Women always could carry life's violence with grace. The thought brought Emma back to herself. She had to get up. Had to help the children.

"Emma, please, speak."

Emma unfurled herself with a wince. Yrsa held her hand, steadying her as she rose to sit.

"I was hit...I have to get to the girls." Emma shoved the words through her teeth as she made to stand. The pain in her head made it swim. Yrsa looped an arm about her waist which Emma leaned gratefully into.

"You must hide in my room. I will guard you. Here, you dropped this."

Yrsa sewed the dagger into Emma's grip a second time. Tears welled behind Emma's eyes as a sob caught her throat.

"Thank you," she whispered as she clutched the handle. They had survived. They had survived. They had—

It happened so fast Emma could barely blink.

One moment Yrsa was helping her to the other side of the room and the next, Yrsa was being pulled backwards by her hair by a tall, snarling, gray-haired raider.

Emma screamed.

Yrsa threw her elbow back, striking out with a blow that didn't land. The man hit Yrsa between the shoulder blades then kicked her leg out from under her. Yrsa went to the ground, her knees barking on the planked floor. The man grinned and threw a meaty fist into the back of Yrsa's head. She lurched forward, her hands smashing into the ground, eyes glazed. He grabbed hold of Yrsa's hair again, tangling his fingers in the strands, laughing as he wrenched her head back to expose her neck. The glint of a blade shone at his side.

The man's mirth rang about the walls before Emma's mind locked onto the fact that he was going to kill Yrsa before her eyes. This man, no, these men—these pigs— had come to destroy them.

She would not allow it. This was her home. Her family. Her life and blood and heart. Damn these men, but she would *not* yield to them.

Emma ran, her grip on the dagger strong. Yrsa's eyes widened.

The raider swiped his fist at Emma. She ducked around the man. With all the rage and fear and strength in her body, she drove the dagger into the man's side, withdrew it, then struck again. It eased into him like a blade through dough.

Roaring, the man scooped his arm back in an arc to grab for her. Emma skipped to the side, pain spearing her stomach with the swift movement, but she did not relent. She wrenched the weapon from his body, striking again. It hit a rib, causing her wrist to balk. Again, he swiped at her and she evaded him, moving to the side, while jabbing beneath his unfocused reach. The blade struck true, sliding into his side. Blood welled, slicking her hands as she moved the blade back and forth.

It was only when he'd slumped to his knees, eyes glazing with death's mark, did Emma stop moving, stop striking with the dagger.

Great, heaving breaths wracked her. Blood was in her mouth; it dripped down her clothes. But the fire that roared in her limbs called for release. She kicked the man. Punched her foot into his side again and again as tears streamed in cleansing rivers down her cheeks until she felt arms close around her. Emma used the momentum of her kick to shove the arms away until Yrsa's wild scent hit her, and she realized her friend was pulling her from the body.

"Shhh," Yrsa was saying against her ear, her arms wrapping around Emma's shoulders.

Emma collapsed into Yrsa's arms. Cries came from the adjoining room, and though Emma hated to hear it, she did not dare go to the children.

"It is alright, we are alright," Emma shouted, infusing steel she didn't feel into her tone.

Yrsa and Emma stood together for a long time, arms entwined, watching the door for more intruders. As time crept by, Emma's shoulders unhitched from around her neck. The pain in her belly had dulled under the weight of her rage. Yrsa retrieved her sword and the weapons from the men on the floor. Then she and Emma moved to one of the beds along the wall, their slowness belying the tenderness of their injuries. They didn't speak as the rain abated and dusk stole in. When the door cracked open, Yrsa jumped up, weapons ready.

Grahame poked his head around the door. Fear touched his eyes as he scoured the hall.

"Yrsa. Emma. Are you alright?"

Yrsa's arms dropped, and Emma moved to stand with her. Grahame crossed the hall, sweeping them both into a single hug. They clung to him, each burying their noses into his shoulders.

"Merthe?" Emma choked out, tears streaming down her cheeks once again.

"Safe. With Ma. The raiders didn't come for us. They've gone, the village is clear. Where are the girls?"

"Here," Yrsa released him. She stepped back to reveal the beds shoved against her door.

"Uncle!" Ginnie's voice rang out. He moved around

the women, shoving the beds out of the way in one quick push.

Ginnie stood there with her fists clenched. Her chin trembled as Æfflead held a tearful Tate. Grahame petted Ginnie's head, murmuring praise, and plucked the baby up. Ginnie hobbled to Emma and secured herself to her leg. Yrsa bent to pick up Æffie. The little girl wrapped arms and legs around Yrsa's neck and waist as if she'd never let go.

Grahame glanced at the men on the floor. A sad grin curled his lips. "I think you ladies had the highest kill count."

Emma wanted to meet his eyes, to grin back in triumph, but pain like a knife wedged through her lower back. It struck her down, taking her to the discarded bed. As shadows entered her vision, Emma realized they hadn't truly won.

THIRTY-FOUR

*G*uston's *revenge.* The thought nearly swallowed Branton whole.

His girls.

His life.

Emma.

Before he could think it through, Bran raised his palm to the blade, shoving it away from his neck. He clamped down on his scream of pain as he grabbed the bandit's forearm with his other hand. The man lost his balance, his grasp on his sword loosening. The bandit swore, kicking up dirt as he tried to catch himself.

It was just enough time.

Bran was up, ready to fight, before the man could fully turn the weapon on him again. That was the thing about swords. They were long and cumbersome if tipped. Bran thumbed his hatchet out of the holster on his belt. The wood met with his palm like the embrace of a long-lost love. He didn't know if the other men noticed;

he only moved. Favoring his left, Bran swung with the surety of someone who had spent their entire life with the weight of an ax in hand. The curved edge connected with the man's outstretched arm, digging into the meat below the elbow. A cross between a hiss and a yelp erupted from the man's lips. His teeth clenched as if to absorb the wound rather than turn from it.

Foliage skittered behind Bran. He turned to find the man he'd jumped on, Hugo, had risen to his knees. His arm hung at an awkward angle, but he surprised Bran by reaching for the large knife on his belt. Bran didn't give him time to draw it.

With a great step forward, Bran swung his ax up. The man saw the hit and lifted his good arm to block the blow. The flat end of the ax head hit him in the hand, crumpling fingers. The man yelled, pain wrinkling his features. Arm upraised, Bran used his momentum downward to lodge his blade in the man's shoulder. He howled, falling, taking the weapon with him.

"Hoy!" A shout came from the front of the wagon. Neil and Wilf were standing atop the bench, swiping knives at the man who stood over Ridley. They kept him at bay but the man was taller than both. He had the reach, and when he struck out with his short sword, it tore through Neil's tunic.

Branton swore his heart stopped as the blade cleaved through the fabric. As it came away clean, the only thought in his mind was murder. Arms pumping, breaths sawing in and out, Bran ran straight for the bandit brandishing the blade. Bran moved with all of his speed, feinting to the right then dropping his shoulder. He slammed into the bandit, his shoulder striking the man's middle. Air shot from the man as he fell backward with Branton's weight crashing atop him.

Bran pummeled the man's face, blood raining down as the slice in Bran's hand wept. He barely noticed the pain. Rather, it felt supremely good to lodge his fist into the man's face over and over and over until the man's mouth and nose were nothing but pulpy messes of broken bones and cut flesh.

His name was said behind him, but Bran did not stop until a hand rested against his back. He reared, ready to attack whoever dared cross him only to find it to be Wilf. His father-in-law's green eyes were wide, his mouth opened in fear of Branton himself. He retreated a step, allowing Bran to see past the cart's rear where the other men he'd attacked lay on the ground. Sam and a weary-looking Thomas were tying one of the bandits with the horse's reins. Ewan had somehow crawled over to retrieve the sword dropped during Bran's scuffle and sat, holding it trained on the leader. The trees were silent. The only sounds were the heaving breaths of the men.

Bran harnessed the killing rage coursing through his body. It took effort to tamp it down. He forced himself to release the unconscious man he straddled. Behind Wilf, Neil stood next to the cart. His hands were clasped around his elbows, face pale as he watched his father.

"It's done," Wilf said, his features grave.

Bran leaned back on his haunches then came to standing. He strode to Neil, examining him as he approached, then swept the boy into a tight hug. Neil hugged Bran back with a strength he'd not known his son to possess.

"Are you alright?" He asked, his voice thick. He buried his nose into the boy's hair, hands roaming over his shoulders, arms, back to check for injury.

Neil nodded into Branton's chest, trembling. A sob wrenched from his son, shuddering through them both. Branton cupped Neil's head with his good hand and found it in himself to make calming, shushing noises to soothe.

"It's over. It's over, son."

He wished he could hold his boy forever but forced himself to release him to shout, "Don't kill the leader."

He spared a glance at Sam who nodded, then made his way to Ridley who sat with his back to the wagon's wheel, his forearm across his knee, staring at the ground. The back of his head was matted with blood. Bran made a wide circle around Ridley's front so that his friend could see his approach. Two men lay slain beside him.

"Rid," Bran said. His voice felt unsteady, as if he hadn't used it in years.

Ridley stared into the distance. His eyes narrowed on the ground in front of him before dragging up to Bran.

"They got us," Ridley muttered, stunned. "I dispatched one but the other…he hit me in the head. I could barely manage him. He had the training of a knight."

Bran leaned down to clap a steadying hand on Ridley's shoulder.

"They didn't get all of us," Branton said.

Ridley tried to rise, but he was unsteady. Bran hefted one of Ridley's arms around his shoulders and helped his friend to stand. He leaned heavily against the wagon for a moment before he got his bearings.

"Pass me my sword. I will keep guard if more come," Ridley commanded, sounding more like himself.

Branton did as he was told then walked to the rear of the wagon to relieve Ewan of his sword. Ewan's face was a mask of pain, his left arm and leg bloodied.

"Thomas. Ewan needs you," Bran ordered, before turning to the injured bandit who had held him at sword-point.

Bran's blood felt like it was racing through him without anywhere to go after such an abrupt end to the fight. There must have been a feral glint in his eye because the bandit cowered.

"What's planned for Hyrstow?" Branton asked, his voice as cold as it had ever been.

The man clutched his forearm in an attempt to stanch the blood to no avail. Bone jutted like a crooked tree branch. His lip was curled in pain and rage, though there was a gleam in his eyes that set Bran's teeth on edge.

"We heard of a raid."

"*When?*" Bran's gut felt like it was folding in on itself. If there was rumor of a raid, they had to get home. If they knew when, they could leave the wagons, take the horses and travel without stopping to be there by midnight.

If they didn't stop, Bran could protect the girls. *His girls.*

The man grunted a laugh, the sound a creaky wheeze. "Last week. Men from Guston overtook the market and swarmed the town."

The world stopped. Tilted. Scrambled to realign.

"Y-you said Guston was to have revenge," he shouted.

The man let loose a wad of spit. It landed in the leaf-strewn dirt near Bran's toe.

"I said there won't be much left of it. Guston *had* its revenge," the bandit snarled, his thin lips creasing into a detestable grin.

"How do you know?" Sam asked, stepping forward.

"Let me live and I'll tell ye."

Bran kicked the man in the leg. He hissed, hunching forward.

"Just came from near there," he shouted through spittle. "I heard it from a man from Guston. Sacked the market good."

Bile climbed Bran's throat.

Last week.

The children. Emma. Grahame, Yrsa, Fiona.

They hadn't been there. *He* hadn't been there.

Again.

Bran was blind to his action as he dropped the sword and crashed forward, wrapping his hands around the man's neck. Roaring washed through his ears, drowning out everything other than the feel of grimy flesh between his palms. He would squeeze the man's throat as hard as his heart was being crushed inside his chest.

Thomas stepped forward, hand out to halt Bran as dozens of questions about Hyrstow were hurtled. They rained around them, the importance of each a barb in Bran's side. He loosened his bloody grip.

"What was the reason for the raid?"

Wilfred's voice rang clear through the forest, his even tone smashing Bran upside the head. Damn it all to hell, they needed the bandit alive. Bran snarled before flinging the bandit to the ground. The man sputtered and choked on air as it rushed back into him.

Bran shoved himself up, hands on his hips, trying to draw deep breaths through his nose. He swayed, as if the anchor of rage leached from him. It was replaced by the burning whip of fear.

"Revenge. Revenge on behalf of Lady Clayton," the man said through snot and tears. He clutched his arm, burying his face into the ground, as if to disappear into the dirt and dried leaves.

"Who? What revenge?" Bran thundered, his voice cracking on the last word. He clenched his fists. His left hand throbbed as blood drooled between his fingers. It was good. The pain grounded him.

"I don't know! I don't. Please."

Bran snorted, eyes landing on the carnage around them. Ridley had an arm around Neil's shoulders near the wagon. And beside them, on the ground...

Jory.

He lay, eyes open, unseeing, at the leaves above.

A tightness built in Bran's throat. He turned, busying himself by tending to Ewan while Ridley stepped forward to fire questions at the bandit. The piece of shit had no good answers, nothing that could quell the sudden urgency of the men as they reassessed what needed to be done to get home as soon as they could.

A gash ran down the meaty length of Ewan's leg. Blood leaked from it but not at a rate Bran thought he would perish from. Bran placed his hand on Ewan's leg to stanch the flow.

"Got me good," Ewan said. He tried to infuse a chuckle into his tone, as if getting assaulted with a sword was his own fault.

"If we tie it, can you walk?" Bran asked. Ewan shook his head, his face turning white beneath his unruly beard. Bran lay a comforting hand on Ewan's shoulder despite the urgent yank on his soul calling him to Hyrstow. Sam stood next to Ridley, his face ablaze with simmering hatred for the man on the ground who still deflected answers. With shaking, hasty hands Neil packed the few items that had fallen from the wagon. Thomas quietly murmured to the upset horses, his own eyes hollow. As fast as each moved to get on their way, there was a dull shock about them, as if their motions were battered in wool.

Bran had to practically leash himself to the spot lest he grab one of the horses and fly home as fast as it could carry him. He couldn't leave when the others needed him. It wouldn't matter.

A week. A damned week had passed.

Wilf came forward, a shredded tunic in one hand, a water skin in the other. He crouched beside Ewan, tying the strip around his leg. Ewan hissed when Wilf tightened the wrapping.

"Something's wrong with my foot. Came down on it funny when I fell off the horse."

"We have to get back. Hurry," Bran said through clenched teeth, their dalliance almost too much to bear. He bent to lift Ewan himself but Wilf stopped him.

"Your hand."

Annoyed at the prospect of halting for something as silly as his hand, Bran glowered at his father-in-law. Wilf's lined features remained unruffled. In his grasp was another strip of cloth he must have poached from the wagon. The gash was wide, filled with fiery pain. He allowed Wilf to wrap his hand then set to work getting Ewan into the cart. He and Thomas stationed themselves on either side of the injured man and, while Ewan looped his arms about their shoulders, they each hefted a leg. Bran knew they did a hasty job of it by how hard Ewan grunted, clenching his jaw in pain. Bran had only a shred of sympathy. They had no idea how Hyrstow fared and would not know until they were home.

"Let's go!" Bran roared after Ewan was shuffled into the back of the first wagon.

Ridley slid his gaze to Bran at the command, his lips tight, but he nodded all the same. Without preamble, he drew his sword back then shoved it into the bandit's chest, ignoring the man's scream. He continued to deliver the same fate to the others. Bran kept moving, pointing at Jory's horse, ordering Neil to grab hold of the reins so his son didn't have to see the life slip from the man. Neil obeyed, his face ashen.

Next, Bran strode to where Sam and Thomas were standing beside Jory's body. The two men stared at their friend in silence. The arrows stuck out of his mouth and chest like dead trees.

"Come on, lads," Branton said, patting Thomas on the shoulder. The man emitted a strangled, choking sound he pushed back with a hand against his mouth. Sam's blue gaze darted from Jory to Bran then back again.

With a deep sigh, Branton bent on one knee, snapped the thin, protruding wood as close to Jory's open mouth as he could, then threw the end away. He did the same with the second. Jory's wife would have a hard enough time with his death without seeing the blatant manner in which he was slain.

"Thomas, grab his feet."

With Bran's hands under Jory's armpits, the two men hefted his body onto the second wagon, laying him between a box of tools and a drum of mead. He was like a sack of stones. When finished, Bran hopped down, ready to be off. Out of the corner of his eye, he saw Thomas, crouched in the wagon's bed, silently brush his hand over Jory's eyelids.

Pure, undiluted hatred for the men who harmed them shot through Branton like the arrow that had killed Jory. He flexed his fingers to measure the motion. It hurt. He stormed to the front of the wagon, needing to move.

His shoulders hitched around his neck, the pain in his hand coming to the forefront of his mind. They had to get back. Had to see the state of Hyrstow.

Ridley, still looking a little unsteady, climbed up beside Neil and shoved the dead bandit slumped there onto the ground. Bran had Neil climb up to settle in the bench's middle. Wilf took the reins and sat on Neil's other side, pushing the boy closer to Ridley so the blood stain wouldn't mar his clothing.

"We need to go. Now," Branton said, his patience a thread.

The others were moving as quickly as they could yet, it still wasn't enough. Sam tied Ewan's horse to the second wagon and Thomas searched the dead bandits for weapons and coin. Bran felt no remorse over the removal of the dead men's valuables.

"Bran," Ridley said.

Branton grabbed the reins of Ridley's steed and walked around to where Ridley sat. He was glad to see his friend's near-golden eyes alert. The sharp line of his mouth had fallen, along with his dark brow.

"Grahame was there. Yrsa was too. We left enough men. I have no mind to guess why we were raided, but trust your family is safe."

Bran's eyes narrowed as he looked up at his friend. To be so confident in his woman was a luxury Bran couldn't fathom.

"Blind trust has gotten me nothing. I wasn't there when Freda died, and if Emma..."

Bran couldn't get the next words past his dry lips.

"Try not to think like—" Ridley began.

Branton didn't allow him to finish. Rather, he swung up into the saddle, readying himself to leave. He straightened as they began to move out.

Emma would have protected the children. He knew it with his whole being. She was smart, careful, and she would have gotten the children to safety.

But would she have done the same for herself? She'd admitted she thought herself always second. Expendable. Would she have fought to protect herself?

The icy fingers of absolute dread clutched his spine.

Wordlessly, he squeezed his legs to urge the beast forward. It heeded his command, settling into a fast trot Bran knew the wagon would have a hard time keeping pace with. He didn't care. An image of Emma, hurt, bleeding, unseeing like Jory, burned in his mind.

She was his. He was hers, despite his protestations prior to leaving.

For all of Branton's wishes, worry slicked his insides with the knowledge he could not tear through the fabric of time to save her.

THIRTY-FIVE

They traveled through the night. Ridley remained awake, taking turns with Wilf on the reins while Neil dozed against Ridley's shoulder. A few times Bran saw him grit his teeth and, if getting to Hyrstow hadn't been so urgent, he would have insisted Ridley rest. Thomas and Sam guided the second and third wagons. For his part, Ewan didn't utter a complaint, though Bran knew the ride must have pained him greatly. Every bump, every jostle, would have spiked through his injured leg, but to his credit, Ewan pressed his lips together and closed his eyes, eventually drifting into a fitful slumber.

Bran remained on Ridley's horse, his head on a swivel, prepared for more violence. Bleary-eyed and restless, he forced himself straighter in the saddle as the night wore on. He couldn't bring himself to take a few moments respite in the wagon while the possibility of his family's harm haunted him.

Eventually, they had to stop to water the horses. Each moment they weren't moving was agony. Branton prowled around the edge of the small lake without taking food or water. Just a few months ago, he couldn't fathom getting out of bed much less traveling so quickly. The others gave him a wide berth until they were moving again.

A few hours past dawn, the party broke from the winding road through the trees and the south meadow came into sight. Bran couldn't stop himself from kicking the horse into a full gallop. The others rushed too, the sounds of the wagon's wheels churning against the solid ground. From a distance, Hyrstow appeared whole. Nothing had burned and small structures like gates and sheds remained intact. Closer, they could hear the village rumble; people talking as they walked between huts, beasts moving about their pens.

The sounds didn't appease Bran's worry.

He yanked hard on the horse's bit when he reached his home and practically threw himself from the beast once it stopped before the gate. He ran, bursting through the front door, startling everyone inside.

Merthe's head jerked up. She sat before a small fire, her usually tidy hair in an unkempt braid. Shadows lived beneath her eyes. In her arms, Tatswip slept while Æfflead and Ginnie played quietly on the floor beside her. They wore no bandages and carried no scars. Ginnie screeched at his abrupt entrance, but it turned to happy shrieks once she understood it to be her father.

A rush of sharp, sweet relief stung Bran. They were whole. All safe.

Bran ran in, going to his knees before them.

"My girls," he said, spreading his arms wide. The crushing sense of foreboding eased off his chest like a rock slipping free of a ledge.

"Father!" The girls shouted as they barrelled into his arms, though Ginnie favored one leg. Tears sparkled along their cheeks. They either didn't notice or didn't mind the blood that had hardened his tunic.

Bran's heart swelled with gratitude as he held their warm little bodies. Tears pooled in his eyes which he shut tight to prevent starting a flow that he wasn't sure he could stop.

They'd made it. His children had made it through.

"Merthe. Are you well?" He looked at his stepdaughter, searching for anything amiss. Æffie and Ginnie clung to his neck and shoulder, so he had to awkwardly look up at where she sat in Emma's fireside chair. She offered him a tired smile, her hand rubbing Tate's leg which sprawled across hers.

"I am," she said.

"Your mother?" Bran patted the girls on the back so they'd release him.

He was already moving, eager to find Emma. If the children were well, she wouldn't be far.

Bran strode to the bedroom. It was empty. Cold. Not even a fire was lit to warm it. He retreated, reaching for any reason why she wasn't there.

"Is she baking at her hut?"

The pocket of silence wasn't long, yet it was filled with a reluctance that set Bran's teeth on edge. He turned back to the room. No one hurried for an answer.

"She's at Grandmother's," Ginnie said.

"Why?"

"She..." the wobble of Merthe's lip prevented her from speaking.

Bran went to her, kneeling before her to look into her face. The fear he saw in her pinched eyebrows and twisted lips caused his limbs to lock up. He forced himself to gentle his voice.

"What is it, dear? I've heard of the raid. It was all I could do to get back to you. I am so sorry I wasn't here."

Merthe nodded. Æfflead released a sob.

"She and Yrsa and the younger girls hid in the hall. Ginnie hurt her leg, she couldn't walk. Mother wouldn't leave her. She told me to run to the Shepherd's for help. Men came..."

The words caught in her throat. Bran ran a hand down her arm to calm her. She'd been told to run for help? In the face of raiders? The strength of the girl...

"Mother and Yrsa fought the men off."

"They did?" Bran tried to temper his voice. He could swear the girls could hear the pounding of his heart. If Emma fought, it meant she was okay. Unless the baby...

"Merthe, dear, why is she at Fiona's?"

Merthe's watery eyes met his. The despair in them made Branton want to crumble. It brought him back to Freda. To the way he was fetched by Merthe, the same tearful look marking her.

Branton wiped his hand across his mouth to stop himself from shouting. She wasn't dead. Emma couldn't be dead. He couldn't lose her, not after he'd rejected her so thoroughly. Not after he'd had the space to realize Ridley was right. She was his and he, hers.

She couldn't leave this earth, leave him, without knowing she was the sun he grew beneath, the water that sustained him. She was the beating heart of his family, of his life. Emma couldn't be sent to her death knowing only Branton's scorn.

Merthe went on.

"She was hurt. She's not a warrior like Yrsa. The men hit her, hurt her. I don't know exactly how since I was off getting Grahame and the little girls were told to hide. She fainted after it was over. She hasn't been right since, and Fiona said it was best she stay with her to rest. I've been caring for the others and Yrsa has been in and out to stay with us in the evenings but she's been run ragged helping everyone else after the raid."

Merthe's face crumpled. Instantly, Bran engulfed her and Tate in a hug. She was chilled, despite the fire. Tenderness for his step-daughter overwhelmed him. She'd taken on so much, just like her mother.

"Shhhh, I'm here now. You have my word: I will care for all of you."

A great sniffle broke from Merthe, her tears soaking through Branton's blood flecked shoulder. Tatswip squirmed in her grasp, nuzzling into his arm. It cracked something vital in him to have to leave, but he had to go to Emma. The need to look upon her, to discover what

Merthe meant by "not right" wrapped itself around him like a great wave, threatening to drown him. He'd been teetering on a sharp edge the entire way back. Seeing the girls safe allowed him a step back from it, but the thought of something dire with Emma brought him closer.

"I have to go to her," he said, giving the girls in his arms a squeeze. "Can you stay here? I have to see her."

Merthe nodded, petting Tate's head then kissing the crown. "Mother was brave. She would have fought to the death for us."

"Yrsa too!" Ginnie exclaimed, throwing her arms around Bran's shoulders as he released Merthe and Tate. Bran scooped her into his lap and pressed her little body tight to him. His gratitude for their safety was quickly overshadowed by the panic winding in his chest like a coiling snake.

Emma was hurt.

"I must go," he said, his voice thick. He disentangled Ginnie's arms from around his neck and stood. As if sensing the wildness in his fear, the children heeded him. Branton grabbed the reins of Ridley's horse and set off toward the Shepherd homestead at a gallop.

Emma had fought. Had been struck.

After Freda, Branton thought he could not withstand more loss. As he kicked the horse to go faster, urging it across fields, he realized how stupid he was for thinking the worst in his life had already happened.

Since he'd learned about the pregnancy, he'd been so

desperate for Emma not to die in childbirth that he hadn't considered that she might die another way.

Time seemed to pull him backward despite his mad dash to the Shepherd farm. Giving the horse a final kick, he raced to the hut on top of the hill.

Fiona jumped as he hurtled himself through the door. Bran took two steps in, scanning the well-appointed homestead. Fiona's eyes were wide as she took in the dried blood that covered him from head to toe.

"Where is my wife?" he demanded, searching his mother-in-law's face for any indication of Emma's whereabouts. Fiona's lined face lightened when she saw him but closed off just as quickly. She went to him, clasping his arm to prevent him from entering her close-doored bedroom.

"Where is she? Where is Emma?" A pleading quality leached into his tone.

"She's safe," Fiona soothed, brushing a hand over his arm.

"I need to see her. I need—"

Fiona squeezed his arm. "She is in my room. But, Branton, you look as if you've spilled the blood of ten men! I need you to collect yourself. Emma needs you to be strong. Can you do that for her?"

Every instinct in Branton screamed at him to rip his arm away and go to his wife, regardless of how he looked. Another part knew the words to be true. He had to be strong, for he had no idea what he was about to see.

He couldn't do what he'd always done and expect Emma to piece the parts of him back together.

She needed him now. He would not falter.

"I can," he breathed, placing his injured hand over Fiona's on his arm.

His mother-in-law peered up into his face, her light brow tenting. "She's done her best, Bran. Everyone did. The raiders disguised themselves as visitors to the market. The stalls were ransacked. Brunhild Smith was killed. Awolf was injured. Emma protected all of the children. And now, she needs to protect herself by resting. I know there was an argument before you left. Will it be too much for her to see you?"

Bran ground his teeth. "Has she asked for me at all?"

Fiona shook her head and withdrew her hand.

"She hasn't said much, I'm afraid. From what I've gathered, she was struck in the head and middle. She takes the broth that I feed her and can get up to use the chamber pot with some help to steady her. She's weak, Bran. Weaker than I've ever seen her."

Bran nodded, not trusting himself to speak.

Weak. He wanted to crumble. He took a step toward the room, laying a hand on Fiona's slight shoulder. He chewed the inside of his cheek before replying, "I vow not to upset her."

Fiona inclined her head then swept her hand toward the door in a gesture of allowance. Bran drew in a breath. He tried assuaging his fear about Emma's health by asking himself if it would matter if she lost the baby, if her mind wasn't the same, if she would be bedridden. The questions didn't work. They all mattered. Everything about Emma mattered. He wanted her unharmed.

The creak of the door clapped through the quiet chamber. The room was dressed in reds and yellows from the flames in the corner pit. Emma lay curled on her side in the middle of the mattress, a blanket pulled to her chin. Her eyes remained closed as he entered, and he would have thought her asleep if not for the quickness of her breaths.

He stepped to the left side of the bed where she faced and knelt to behold her. "Emma."

Her eyes flew open at the sound of his voice. It took a moment for them to adjust, the rich brown widening at his appearance.

"I'm alright. We were ambushed in the forest. That's when we learned of the raid here. We fought our way free. I rushed here to see you, wife."

Bran was careful to use the title they'd pledged in their marriage. He needed her to know he still wanted her as a wife, a partner. She seemed to shrink into the blanket.

Tentatively, Bran put a hand on the bump of her hip.

"Emma, love. Can you tell me how you're doing?"

She stared at him, unblinking, for longer than he felt comfortable with, but Bran withstood it. He scraped his thumb back and forth across the blanket, trying to work warmth into her skin. His chest ached with the need to hear her speak.

"The children are fine. Neil as well. I've been told you

did a marvelous job protecting everyone," he said, keeping his tone soft.

Emma looked past him, her throat working as she swallowed. Still, she remained silent.

"Do you need some water?" he asked, inwardly cursing himself for not offering water straight away. He was up and out the door before Emma could react. He requested water from Fiona, confirming first that she could, in fact, drink, before returning to Emma's side with a cup in hand.

Relief pounded through him as she tried to push herself up with one hand while scooting her inner elbow underneath her.

"Here, let me help you," he murmured. He placed the cup on the straw-covered floorboards beside him then moved to stand behind Emma to cup her shoulders with his palms and assist her into a sitting position. Her body shook with the exertion so he kept a hand on her back to brace her as he reached for the cup. The cut on his hand throbbed. It was a small price to pay.

Emma took the cup in both hands and drank deeply. All the while, Bran wanted to rage at how unsteady she was. When she'd finished, Bran relieved her of the cup, and knelt on the floor beside the bed, his hand on her back as she leaned forward, elbows on her knees. Her silence clung worse than smoke. Had her head injury been so bad as to rob her of the faculty to speak?

Emma rested her forehead on her crossed forearms and blew out a breath. She closed her eyes. Bran was at a loss. She didn't seem to fear him. Almost as if to test her comfort with him, he swept a piece of hair behind her ear. Her hair lay undone against her back and some strands were hardened together, as if she'd not been able to bathe. A muscle ticked in Bran's jaw.

Had the memory of him been struck from her mind? As much as he wished at times to begin again, to be better, he didn't want Emma to lack memory of all they'd shared.

"I am glad you are well." Her voice was thin as an overused piece of muslin. Bran had to lean in to hear. "You can go now."

"Go? I only just got here."

Emma turned her face to him, resting her cheek on her forearms. There was a sadness haunting her features. "I am not the wife you expected. If you only wait until I am back on my feet, I can serve your household as you see fit."

She then dipped her forehead back to her arms, blowing out a shaky breath. Bran felt his insides plummet. What was she on about serving his household? She was no slave.

"Emma, you are my wife. I want you better. I want—"

"Me to be true? In the most honest sense? You know all my secrets and still, you were ready to leave our marriage." The words were toneless. As if she'd thought long and hard about what she would say to him and arrived at the very answer he'd suggested.

Marriage in name only.

Bran had been angry. Impossibly hurt by the

prospect of Emma not truly loving him. But not once did he want her gone.

"You misunderstand. I lo—"

"Don't," she whispered. "Don't say what you are about to without real thought. You've proven to me over and over that you love Freda. I never doubted you do. Though I was foolish enough to dream that, maybe, you would cherish me as you did her. I know now I was wrong. Please don't make me a promise of care unless you mean it. For I do not think I can stand another whipping of your scorn."

Bran straightened, feeling as if he'd been struck across the face. Indeed, he'd been cruel prior to leaving, but he'd expected Emma to rejoice in their reunion after the raid as he wanted to. The next words out of her dry lips sank any hope.

"I love you, Bran. With everything I have. And you've broken me over and over again. Please, just go."

Slowly, as if each movement took a great deal out of her, Emma lowered herself to the bed and turned from him. She minded her middle, which told Bran she hadn't lost the baby. It was the only comfort. An icy feeling of dread stole around him, making it difficult for him to stand. He wanted to lie down next to her, to hold her to him, to kiss her and tell her he loved her until she believed him.

She wouldn't. Not just from him rushing to see her. Emma was a woman of action. Like her care for him and his family after Freda's death. Like the comfort she'd given him when he hadn't deserved it. Like the promises she made and carried through with. Words would not sway her. And Branton had been full to the brim of words he realized, and had shown very little in the way of action toward her. He'd treated her like a whore, not a wife.

He'd fallen in love, but maybe he hadn't given her reason to love him back.

Feeling as if his heart had been scraped out from his ribs, he stood and left the room, closing the door behind him. He bid goodbye to Fiona with the promise to return the following day. Though his throat felt as if sand lay along his windpipe, he made his way home with a singular thought carrying him there.

He was broken but he would heal. For those he loved and for himself. There was no other way. He couldn't keep blaming the woman he loved for his misfortune. Couldn't sustain a life of despair.

He would prove himself. He had to.

THIRTY-SIX

The days blurred. Emma's head and body ached. She dwelled in the darkness of Fiona's bedroom, too glad to allow her responsibilities to fall away. She wouldn't have been able to focus on them anyway. Her mind was foggy after the raid. She'd been put in bed, bathed, clothed, and yet she couldn't pull her mind out of the mist.

Was this what Bran had felt when Freda died? This fathomless dark that swept her into the bonds of sleep? In slumber, she was able to escape. It was only there where she was not such a failure as a wife. There she could see Freda, who smiled at her, who drifted with her.

Bones aching, joints burning, everything hurt from laying about for so long. It didn't compare to the pain engulfing her heart.

Seeing Bran alive and well and calling her wife had crushed her. It had built like the drop of a stone in water, rippling outward until it became a wave crashing upon the shore. She recognized Bran as the wave, relentless in his need for her. It was chased by the ripples of his scorn. She was the shore, constantly being battered by her attachment to him.

She loved him. With all her heart and soul, she was his. She always would be.

It drove her deeper under the blankets.

She should have gotten up, dressed, gone home to care for her children. She couldn't call on strength for any of those things. The baby in her womb had begun to move, letting her know she'd protected it from the worst. Tears of joy stained her pillow the entire morning she first felt its movement. The gratitude and love amid her heartbreak were almost too much for her to bear.

It was only her and the little babe for days on end.

Fiona and Wilf had graciously moved their sleeping quarters to Grahame's room, while Isolde occupied the spare room. She knew the lack of Grahame and Isolde's bickering must have meant he'd taken up residence with the sheep or in the men's hall. Isolde, being at the Shepherd farm during the raid, tended to Emma's needs. She brought Emma food and water, sat her up when she needed to eat, and helped her use the chamber pot. The stone-faced woman didn't say much, and Emma didn't have the energy to venture conversation. They simply worked together.

Bran came and went, always in the mornings. Emma pretended to sleep. She overheard his low conversations with Fiona, telling her about the children and how he was making out with the responsibilities of the home. He was now dealing with his children himself—something he couldn't bring himself to do after Freda's death. A wisp of satisfaction curled within her that he could. It meant he didn't need her in the way he claimed.

It meant her family would be alright if she never came to be right herself.

Merthe often came to visit, and Emma did her best to sit up and carry on conversation when her daughter was near.

One morning, around a fortnight after the attack, Merthe commented on the state of the church, as a result of Oswald's abandonment of Hyrstow. It snagged Emma's attention.

"What abandonment?"

Merthe looked up from the socks she was darning, her mouth forming an 'O' as if surprised Emma didn't know. "The Reverend Father. He left us. Some folks remember seeing him leave the market just before the raid. He hasn't been seen since."

"Was he killed?" Emma dared ask. She didn't like Oswald but didn't wish a death dealt by raiders on anyone.

Merthe's lips formed a line, as if contemplating what she should tell her ill mother before shaking her head. "They don't think so. It appears he just left. Some of the church's silver chalices were taken, but Ridley can't be sure if it was raiders or not."

Emma sat with the knowledge for a moment, turning over a murky memory. She saw the Reverend Father the morning of the raid. He'd come to her stand, and told her to leave. A warning, perhaps? Why would he have done so? Emma couldn't imagine he would have known the raid was to happen.

Her thoughts felt muddled, her tongue thick in her mouth as she asked, "Who is acting as the High Priest then?"

"Father Chisholm. Branton's been tending to the church's needs and says the Father is doing his best to service everyone going in and out. There are still many visitors, despite the raid."

Emma swallowed around the lump in her throat. "Why is Bran tending to the church? Has he an income there?"

Merthe pursed her lips and laid down her sewing, staring at her mother. Weighing. "Bran isn't getting anything. He secured good payment and a contract from the earl. He brings Tate and Æfflead with him and spends time there helping fix things and talking to the Reverend."

Merthe shrugged. "He might pray a little sometimes. At night, I hear him in the bedroom talking to himself."

"Talking to himself?"

"More like talking to Freda. And you. He talks about his day, about how much he misses you both."

Tears pricked Emma's eyes and she expelled a breath to ward off the feelings that threatened to bring her fully back into the world. She folded her hands in her lap, now further away because of her expanding middle. Hope for Branton flickered within her. Even if they were not together, it meant he was doing something for others, for himself.

"Well, it sounds as if he is well. I'm happy for him."

Merthe gave her a long look that Emma couldn't quite interpret.

"Are you coming home soon?"

Emma chewed on her answer. She wanted to. Her heart ached to be with the children. She longed for the comfort of her own home, to be held by the man she loved.

"I don't know."

"Mother," Merthe put a hand on Emma's leg. The weight of it was a comfort. "Are you strong enough? The baby?"

"I'm not sure. I can feel him move. He kicks and rolls." Merthe's face lit up and Emma marveled at how lovely her daughter was. Generous, caring, forgiving and unfailingly reliable. Emma didn't know how she was so lucky.

"Him?" Merthe asked, one eyebrow raised.

Emma nodded. "It is a guess. I plan to come home when I can. I just..." she let the words fall, unsure of how to explain her relationship with Bran to her daughter.

She had to return, she knew. Despite everything, life moved on.

"He loves you," Merthe blurted, dropping her sewing. She didn't bother to retrieve it. Rather, she sat next to Emma, gathering her mother's hand in her smaller ones.

Tears sprang to Emma's eyes at the sweet gesture.

"Please, Mother. We miss you. Please come home."

Emma tried to smile, though her lips wobbled too much for it to form. Voice unsteady, she said, "I love you, my sweet. And the others. I wish to come home when I can. I do not feel strong enough. Even if you think Branton loves me, we broke one another's trust in various ways. I don't know if two people can come back from that."

Merthe bit her lip but said no more. They sat together in silence for a long time before Fiona came in to take Merthe home.

Isolde Tanner wore her customary grim frown as she helped Emma from the bed. She'd declared Emma's tunic smelled wretched and promptly took it upon herself to strip her and force her into one of her own garments.

"It's not necessary to wallow," Isolde muttered.

Emma stood on shaky legs as Isolde pulled a tunic smelling of wool and rosemary over her head. The fabric itched her tender skin but she wasn't one to complain, especially to someone as stern as Isolde.

"Thank you," Emma murmured. Isolde put an arm around her back to steady her as she sat back down. Her hips were sore, shoulders too. Movement would help. But everything was stiff from non-use.

Isolde remained silent, though the brackets around her mouth softened a little. Once in bed, Isolde fussed with the blanket, ensuring it was folded gently around

Emma's middle, then proceeded to pour her a glass of water from the pitcher near the bedside.

The liquid was cool and fresh, reviving Emma from the stupor she'd been in prior to the other woman's arrival. When she thought Isolde had finished, the woman surprised her by nestling down on the bed beside her, taking a hairbrush from her apron pocket, and working the matted ends of Emma's hair.

"It's easier if you keep up with these little things," Isolde said, her tone not leaving any room for dispute.

"I know," Emma admitted.

Isolde made a scoffing noise in the back of her throat, as if Emma would keep better care of herself if she did what she claimed to know.

"Has Grahame said anything about me being here? I don't hear him in the other room anymore. I am sorry to have displaced him."

Isolde captured another section of hair and began to work through the snarls. She didn't say anything for a few moments.

"He's staying at the hall."

Emma nodded, allowing herself to relax into the luxury of being cared for. She closed her eyes.

"You must start walking around the room," Isolde said from behind her.

Emma turned to glance at Isolde. The other woman's eyes were narrowed in the room's soft glow. Her light brown strands had been tamed by a gray kerchief. Her nose, a bump marring the pretty slope, wrinkled.

"It will not get easier unless you try."

Emma nodded, marveling that the woman who had been kidnapped and assaulted was offering her encouragement, in her own way.

"Thank you," she said again, reaching up to pat Isolde's wrist. "I appreciate your kindness. You don't need to be so, but I accept it and value it all the same."

Isolde's chin crumpled a little beneath the sincere words. Yet, within the blink of an eye, her mouth straightened, as if she felt nothing at all. Emma turned away, allowing Isolde the privacy of continuing to brush without the heavy tone the conversation had adopted. Isolde combed in silence, using gentle hands to untangle.

"My sister was the only one to show me such kindness after we were returned. I...remained abed for a long while afterward. The Viking woman, Yrsa, came to visit, but I couldn't see her. She was too much like those who took me. I couldn't stand it, even if I knew she meant well. I told her to not return. Sigrid changed too. One of the Vikings looked out for her, you see. She was not... used. And, though she would never say, I think she developed feelings for the Viking."

The disgust in Isolde's tone made Emma's stomach churn, though she didn't dare speak. There was nothing to be said to alleviate the brutality she imagined Isolde to have endured. The woman moved her brushing to the top of Emma's head, her busy hands buffering the sorrow of her story.

"It is the reason I stay here. The love I have for my sister is deep. Yet I could not remain in a home filled with her pining. Grahame's teasing words and grumblings about my attitude are much preferred to her quiet sympathy. I slowly gained my strength. I began to care for myself. And now, I know. I am the only person who will care for me. You've always been kind. For that I thank you. And it is why I urge you to become well. You are strong, Emma. Your husband asks after you whenever he sees me, usually with a child in tow. He bears the weight of my scorn each time."

Emma's throat tightened. During Branton's visits, her hands ached to run along his shoulders, to cup his tired yet joyful face. Indeed, she didn't allow herself to say much to her husband when he attended her, lest her feelings for him come spilling out.

She missed him in her bones. His flinty looks when she took liberties with her business, the tight smiles he let slip when she tended to the children. She even missed his temper, his shortness with her, if it meant he spoke true. Branton wasn't one to hide things, and his gentle conversations during his visits didn't quite align with the man she loved.

"Whether you return to your husband or no, you can take care of yourself," Isolde said.

When she finished brushing, Emma reached back to clasp her hand. Isolde allowed it, squeezing Emma's bones just enough to encourage. A tear slipped down Emma's cheek. Her smile felt brittle, yet she offered it to Isolde all the same.

"You have given me a gift," she said, her voice thick. "Thank you for trusting me with your story."

Isolde slipped her hand from Emma's grasp and

stood. Her mouth didn't curl upward in acknowledgement nor did she bob her head in thanks. The same blank look she always wore settled along her features.

"Repay my kindness by living, Emma."

Isolde left, closing the door behind her without a look back.

Emma put her arms around her legs. Bitter tears of longing stained her cheeks as she settled further into the bed.

She couldn't stay at the Shepherds' forever. There was no escaping her responsibilities. She missed the children. The love she had for Branton, however, felt as if it would crush her. She could not continue to hope for a return of affection on his whim. He needed to right himself before he could right their marriage, and she knew that day may never come.

With misery in her heart, Emma closed her eyes and tried to dream. Nightmares with heart-shredding claws met her instead.

THIRTY-SEVEN

Bran exited the church, bidding goodbye to Father Chisholm. His smile felt strung up by fraying threads. The church hadn't been much affected by the raid, thankfully. Damage was contained to the market stalls.

"Thank you, again, and please know that I am praying for the healthy recovery of your wife." Chrisholm wove his fingers together as he stood at the church's threshold.

Bran nodded, raising his hand in a wave of thanks.

In the square, Ridley and Grahame stood at the well, filling water skins. He ran to catch up with them.

"Brother," Grahame said with a crooked grin as he approached.

It was good to see. There hadn't been many offerings of mirth between the men since the raid. Villagers worked to rebuild market carts and tables, and a funeral had been held for Brunhild and Jory. Aeon Smith was beside himself, not opening his blacksmithing shop. For his own part, Bran had done his best to help others make repairs.

"So?" Bran posed the question to Ridley. They'd been waiting for word from the earl. It was expected any day now.

Ridley kept his features closed off. "Word has come. We are not to retaliate. Not until we know the motive behind the attack."

Grahame tightened the top of his water skin and slung the slim cord around his head and across his shoulder. His grin twisted into something ugly. "Motive? It could be anything! Guston could be angry you'd taken their lands. The Earl of Bernira could have decided he wants Hyrstow for himself. The reason doesn't matter other than it means war."

Ridley's eyebrows rose at Grahame's declaration. Bran, too, was surprised. Thomas, who was thatching a nearby roof, poked his head up from his work, eyes narrowed toward the outburst. A crow flew overhead, cawing. It drew their attention to the bright, early summer sky.

Ridley held out his hand, palm down, in a gesture of calm. His own mouth folded downward. "Hyrstow is not made of soldiers. We've suffered enough. And there isn't any way to determine who called for the raid."

"We know enough," Grahame retorted, crossing his arms. The tan fabric of his tunic stretched across his chest. His friend's fingers dug into his upper arms as he spoke. "We've heard rumors it was the Claytons. The bandits said as much to you. Yrsa recalls seeing the woman from the river at the raid."

"What?" Bran tried to keep up with the conversation. He'd been too busy with his family and the manual work of helping others to pay much attention to the political fallout Ridley had had to deal with.

"The Claytons are a prominent family near Guston. I do not have a force behind me to wage battle with them, regardless of your desire to," Ridley said to Grahame.

Grahame scraped a hand down his face, his jaw clenched.

Something didn't sit well with Branton, though he couldn't grasp it. The reason behind the raid, Grahame's knowledge, would have mattered more to Bran if he didn't have a slew of things to do.

It was an important day. One he hoped he'd remember for years to come.

He clapped Ridley on the shoulder in farewell. "I have to go. When you two want to share what the plan is with Guston and the Clayton's, I'll be at Fiona's."

Grahame winced. "Is Emma still not speaking to you?"

Branton cracked his neck to ward off the sensation of ants crawling up his back. He felt it whenever he thought of Emma not returning. He clenched his fists.

"She is not. Though I resolve to change that today."

"How?"

Bran let out a low breath. "I'm going to bring her to the rowan tree, if she'll let me."

Grahame gave Bran a look of surprise cradled in

sorrow. He scrunched his nose up as if trying to ward off the emotion that hit him. "I sometimes will myself to forget how you and Freda would sit under the tree and stare at the fields. How she would wait for you there when you were off cutting."

A lump formed in Bran's throat. He clapped his hand on Grahame's shoulder, sorry to remind him of his own loss. "Aye, we spent many wonderful afternoons there."

The men parted ways, Grahame stalking off to the hall while Ridley walked with Bran in the direction of his hut. Yrsa sat at the outside fire, stirring a pot with Æfflead at her feet. Nod slumbered in the corner of the yard, and Tate bounced in Ginnie's lap. Branton went in to kiss his girls before he asked after Emma.

"She's well today," Yrsa said, a grin laid in her words.

Hope glinted like a jewel inside of him. Despite the rocky start to their friendship, Bran had come to love the swaggering Viking. She'd helped Emma and the children in their time of need. And she did him a favor by checking on Emma that morning to see if she was of the mind to hear him out. Branton ensured the girls were fine to stay with Yrsa, then he took his leave.

By the time he made it to Fiona and Wilf's, the afternoon sun was a ball of vermillion dipping to the earth. The roadside was awash with yellow, red, and purple flowers. He picked a handful, which he clutched in his fist like a nervous boy. He tried to think of all the things he needed to say to Emma, but his intentions and his words would not connect. All he was left with were the awkward mutterings of a fool.

Fiona allowed him entry, a smile on her face. He hugged her, murmuring his overdue thanks in her ear for all she'd done for Emma. She smelled as she always did, of lanolin and wool. He told her how grateful he was she and Freda had been so close, how he loved that his children had such a strong grandmother; things he should have told her long ago, when Freda had still been alive. Fiona crumbled into him, quietly crying into his tunic as he softly rubbed her back. It must have taken some time because when he looked up, Emma stood in the doorway of the bedroom, arms crossed, a shawl about her shoulders and a curious look on her face.

The sight of her standing took his breath away. Over the past fortnight, he'd only witnessed her curled in bed, barely speaking. Now, though her face was pale, there was a sharpness to her countenance Bran thanked the heavens for. Her eyes were huge in her face, though wary. Her lips glistened as if she'd just licked them, and her hair appeared as if it had been recently washed, the long strands hanging past her breasts.

Disengaging from the hug, he offered Fiona the flowers in his hand. She accepted them, the tears staining her cheeks trailing down to her smile. Then Branton looked to his wife, the woman who held his soul, and offered his hand.

She bit her lip, hesitating.

"I'd like to show you something," he said softly.

There must have been the right amount of pleading in his tone because after a long outward breath, Emma slid her hand into his. It was small and chilled. All he wanted to do was warm it and her.

With time, he told himself. It was what he'd repeated to himself days on end since he'd returned.

He led her to the door where he bent to assist her with her shoes. The slip of her dainty feet into his hands and the curves of her legs made his mouth water. He'd not touched her in so long. And though her skin was pale, shadows beneath her eyes, belly slightly swollen, she was the most beautiful thing he'd seen.

"It's a little ways up the hill. Are you able to walk? We can go slow or I can carry you."

Emma's gaze dipped to his chest where she would have to be cradled if she chose the second option. Her chin lifted. She shook her head and in a low voice replied, "I can walk. The fresh air will do me well. You'll have to be patient."

They walked out of the yard, through the gate and turned to the right. The grass had shifted to a brilliant green, the blades appearing soft in the soft golden light. Branton was keenly aware of every part of Emma's body that touched him. From her hand on his forearm where her elbow was linked under his, to the press of her skirt along his legs, every bit of pressure, every lean into his frame for support made him itch to take her fully into his arms.

Their progress was slow up the hill, then down again. The rowan tree was further from the house than he would have liked, but that was what made he and Freda choose it as their spot all those years ago. Emma stopped to breathe several times. Worry speared Bran. Emma sometimes held her side as if she had a stitch but would not admit so, the stubborn woman.

At the base of the treed hill, Bran offered to carry her a second time. She merely issued a 'tsking' sound and continued walking. It fortified Bran that she was being so obstinate. It meant she was getting better. And even if she decided they would only be man and wife according to their original agreement after today, there was a simple happiness in knowing she was well.

At the hill's peak, Emma looked up at the rowan tree with a look of trepidation. The branches were heavy with leaves. She clung to his arm. He caught himself leaning ever so slightly into her, trying to catch a whiff of her hair.

"This is pretty. I don't know if I've ever been this far afield," she said, her voice hushed. She cast her gaze to the sheep-dotted greenery of the valley below, careful not to look up at him. Bran tried to tell himself it didn't sting.

"Why did you bring me here?"

"Ah, Emma, always one to cut to the quick of it," Bran said, his lips curling upward. He gestured for her to sit, but she shook her head.

"I've been in bed for more than a fortnight. I'd like to stretch my legs a little."

Beneath the branches, Bran nodded, turning to face her so he could take her hands in his. He ran his thumbs across the backs, the skin so soft, he couldn't resist turning her hand over to kiss her palm. When he pulled away, a frown marred Emma's face. He swallowed, trying to collect himself, and hoped beyond all hope he was doing the right thing.

"I've brought you here for two reasons," he said softly. His heartbeat was like a drum inside his ears. "The first is to bring you to a place that is as dear to me as my own home. Beneath this tree, my love for Freda bloomed."

Emma's eyebrows pinched together as her lips softened. He took it as a good sign she was willing to listen.

"She was always Grahame's impetuous older sister until one day, she wasn't. I'll never forget the look on her face, full of anger and hurt, when she told me to kiss her or leave her alone for good. I was just her brother's scrubby friend. No prospects other than cutting, which, as you know, can be a dangerous, less fruitful job."

Emma ducked her head in acknowledgement, and Bran felt his eyes get misty at the memory of Freda stamping her foot and demanding more of him than he even knew at the time. They'd been little more than children. God, how he'd loved her.

He let the memory wash over him. The bite of them had eased a little. Not completely, but when memories arose, he didn't try to stuff them down as before. Freda was still with him, every day. He never wanted to lose reminders of her, even if they pained him.

When he'd married Emma, he'd been flaying himself open every day when the memories of her became too much. Now he didn't want to abandon them. And Emma had never asked him to.

"Freda and I spent many an evening beneath these branches. We fell in love, grew together. Since her death, I couldn't look at this tree. I've had to pass it each time I've gone to cut near Guston, and each time, I hurried by."

Emma squeezed his hands as he spoke. She was with him. She wouldn't abandon him while he said his piece. Bran blew out a breath. His words felt clumsy.

"I've fought against a life without her for so long, and, yet you made me grow. It's been slow—slow and unforgiving. I've not been a good husband to you, Emma. I've expected too much. Right away, I wanted you to fix my family and myself, when I truly needed to face my grief. I just held on to you like a man drowning at sea."

Emma reached up and swept the pad of her thumb over Bran's cheek. It came away wet. A breeze stirred their hair, and a sheep bleated further afield. Bran felt as if he was nearing a precipice he'd never be able to retreat from.

"I agreed to the marriage, Bran. You didn't force me into it. Neither did Freda. I promised my friend I would care for you and the children. However, my feelings for you were never out of pity or promise."

Bran caught her wrist and kissed her thumb. He then lay her hand against the side of his face so she cupped his cheek, lacing his fingers with hers to hold it there.

"I've said Freda has my heart and that you have my soul. And yet, that is unfair. I've pitted you against her. My heart will always be broken for the woman I've lost, but it is *my* heart. After I returned, when you rejected me,

I realized I could not put all of myself onto another person. I had to be good in my own right."

"Oh, Bran, I never wanted you to feel unsupported." Emma pressed his cheek harder. She took a step closer and spoke quiet words that made Bran's love for her grow. "I wasn't well. Those days after the raid are a blur. I've always cared for everyone else. I needed time. I needed to heal and to think. And though I don't know what will happen with us, I know you are a good man. You'll do right by your family and me."

Branton drew a great, shuddering breath. He was too tempted to scoop her up, to plant a kiss on her perfect lips but knew he wasn't finished.

"I know. And, knowing how strong you were, I let you take on everything. The children, my grief, the household, our income. It all got dumped on you. This time apart, while it hollowed me out more than you could possibly know, it brought me back to myself. It made me realize the second thing I came here to tell you."

Emma drew her hand back and placed it on the small swell of her belly, as if to guard herself against his final decree. She pasted on the face she wore for strength. It nearly made him crumble, that she was so ready to guard herself against him. His hands were clammy, and his skin felt tight. Bran knelt, the grass soft beneath his bones, bending to the queen of his life. Emma gasped as he took her hand in both of his.

"Emma. You are not a stand-in wife. You deserve your own happiness, something I have robbed you of with my anger and grief and impatience. I regret having caused you pain because I love you. Do you hear me? I am in love with your heart. I am in love with the way you know just what to do. I am in love with your kindness, your ruthlessness, and your will. I burn for you, wife."

He'd said it. His gut felt like it had moved into his chest, he was so overcome with uncertainty at what she would say.

It was almost painful to watch her features lighten. Hope limned her gaze. Emma's light laugh was like honey dripping into his very being. Her wide grin dimpled her cheeks. Branton swallowed, hard. He knew what he had to say next would be the worst.

"I am prepared to live without you, if you so choose. I do not want to, but I will. Or, if you merely want to continue our original agreement of being married in name only, I will respect your wishes. Your well-being matters to me, Emma. As does my own. These past weeks without you have allowed me to care for my children in ways I haven't had to before. I've reconnected with others in the village and my friends. Your rejection broke me in the best way because it allowed me to become a better man. One that knows he loves you with the entirety of his being."

Emma swiped wetness from her cheek with the back of her hand. As he spoke, her countenance shifted from hopeful to sad to joyful. She chuckled, the sound husky and warm. "I know. Merthe has told me you talk to yourself at night, or rather, to Freda and me."

Bran felt his cheeks redden. He met Emma's gaze.

The final question made him sweat, his heart racing. "I have been. It helps me not go mad, talking to you."

Bran licked his lips, his grip on Emma's hand tightening. She could refuse him. He would let her if it meant she would be happy. "I have not respected your decisions in the past. And I want to, going forward. I ask you this question with love in my heart and a promise to heed your wishes: Emma, would you come home to me?"

Emma bit her bottom lip, pulling it through her teeth. She looked up to the singing branches of the rowan tree then closed her eyes, as if listening. Bran felt his life hanging in the balance. She drew a breath through her nose before she nodded, then dropped to her knees in front of him. His hands went to her waist to steady her.

"Bran, I love you. I know that love hasn't been easy. I took on everything."

She paused, looking across the fields to Hyrstow as if a far off song called to her. Bran shook, his limbs primed for rejection. A vow of love did not mean a marriage. When she continued, her voice wavered as if she had to speak around a lump. "I let you treat me the way you did. At times, it was wonderful. Others were awful. I so deeply wanted to be what was right for you. I can't be Freda. I was alone for a long time, Bran. Alone and lonely and you gave me a taste of love. Of companionship. And when you came, I worked hard to not be a second choice."

"You're not," Bran interrupted. He couldn't help it, he

stroked his thumbs up and down her sides to anchor them both.

Emma gifted him a swift grin. "We both want what is best for the other. I've realized that I have to let you in as well. So, know this." Emma took in a deep breath, her luminous brown eyes piercing him with a raw intensity he'd never witnessed before. As if she was allowing him to peer into her soul. "I am in love with you, Branton Cutter. Of my own free will, despite any promises I've made to myself or anyone else. I too, am prepared to survive without you, if you so choose, but I would rather live and fight and be with the man I love. Life will not be easy. I must bring this child into the world, and nothing is guaranteed. But I will do my best to remain in this life with you, and I promise my love and devotion."

Bran didn't need to hear another word. He hauled her against him, claiming her mouth in a punishing kiss. She wound her arms around his neck, securing him to her as if afraid he would let her go. The press of her belly between them and the life within only made him want her more. Emma moaned as he nipped her lower lip with his teeth. He relished the sound. His free hand ran over the mound of her hip to her bottom where he could secure it in his palm. A hunger so deep, so biting, caught fire within him. When they broke away, they were panting.

"I love you, wife. I accept your vow and make one of my own. Through hardship and sorrow, happiness and truth, I swear myself to you from this day, until the end of everything. I choose you foremost and forever."

Emma let loose a breathy laugh, cupping his face in her hands, before she covered him with kisses. "I love you, husband. And I claim you as mine."

Elation swooped through Branton like a bird in the wind. When he sought her mouth again, the stroke of Emma's tongue against his beckoned him to lay her down and settle between her legs. Emma clawed at his shoulders, laughing and kissing and causing him momentary madness as he rooted around to lift her skirt. He was unbearably hard for her. The little gasps and groans that left her as he sewed kisses into her neck were the sweetest sounds. When he was finally able to get through their clothes to reveal his shaft weeping with need for her, Branton paused, wanting to savor the moment.

Emma stared up at him, love shining in her eyes then reached down and gripped his hard length. The feel of her tight fist was the harshest delicacy. He pushed forward into it, slowly. Emma bit her lip as she guided him, rubbing him against her wetness. She held his gaze as he filled her, inch by desperate inch. Desire and trust and a yearning he didn't feel worthy of shone in her stare.

With a kiss, he began to move. Emma hiked her legs around his hips, locking him inside her as if she never wanted to let go. Bran trembled with the weight of their shared love. Of their new beginning. And as they came together beneath the branches of the rowan tree, Branton knew their love would bind them until the end of time.

EPILOGUE

Emma sat on the ground, laughing at the men that pulled ropes back and forth in a tug-o-war for the ages. A cacophony of grunts and oaths crowded the air as the men heaved. Clouds like fluffy candy swam overhead and the sweet scent of summer grass drifted on the welcome breeze. Emma had to sit on her bottom, legs splayed before her, hands behind her, to take some of the weight off her back. Tate sat between her legs, clapping. The baby rolled inside her belly, cheerful amid the happiness in Emma's heart.

Hyrstow's games had begun in the morning, had carried on through the day, and were only now tapering off before the drinking began at supper. Though, if they were honest about it, the drinking had begun when the sun had hitched across the midpoint of the sky.

Æfflead sat beside Emma, stewing mad because Emma wouldn't let her join the tug-of-war. Apparently the threat of getting crushed underfoot was not a deterrent for the child. Ginnie sat on Emma's other side, cheering on Bran, Neil, Grahame, and Sam. They were set against Ridley, Murhred, Wilfred, and Thomas. Both teams were well matched, but Ridley's inched toward the line, despite how hard the men's muscles bulged against their adversaries.

"Who's winning?" Merthe asked as she plopped down beside Æffie.

"Bran's side," Emma responded with a grin. She'd tried to wipe the self-satisfied smirk of a content woman off of her face many times in the days that followed her and Bran's impromptu vow renewal, but she hadn't been successful so had stopped trying.

"Where were you?"

"Looking for Yrsa. Couldn't find her. Is she here?"

Emma shook her head and shrugged.

Bran had his shirt off, his glorious muscles on display as he dug his heels into the ground. Teeth gritted, the swells and valleys of his stomach strained as his arms pulled. Emma could hardly wait to get her husband home. She knew just how she would trace those muscles with her tongue.

"Go Neil!" Merthe shouted, snapping Emma out of her reverie.

Neil's head snapped up, his gaze locking with Merthe's. The slip of attention caused him to trip slightly into Sam's elbow, which loosened Sam's grasp just enough to allow the rope to slide through his hands. Merthe's palm flew to her mouth as Neil and Sam tried to catch the rope, but the slack coupled with the renewed yank from the other end caused Bran and Grahame to slide. Bran's legs went out from under him, leaving Grahame the only one with a sturdy grasp. He let out a pathetic groan, knowing he was beat, then let the rope go. Ridley, Thomas, Wilf and Murhred fell on their backsides as the rope suddenly gave way.

"No!" Bran shouted at his friend. He pounded the ground with his fist, his brow pinching. "Why didn't you hold on? You could've held them off while we adjusted. You should have made them fight to pull you across the line!"

Grahame stood to his full height, leaning down to offer Bran his hand. "And rip my hands apart yanking? No thank you. You may want raw meat for palms but I don't."

Bran adjusted the cloth wrapping his palms and took Grahame's hand, chuckling. The slice in his hand had mostly healed, yet he still wore a protective covering. Emma surmised he wasn't pulling at his full capacity, as a result. The men congratulated one another with a slew of insults and hearty pats on the back. When they broke apart, Ridley went off in search of Yrsa and Grahame strode over to Isolde, who stood by Fiona. Though stone faced, Isolde didn't outright snarl at Grahame, which was an improvement. Fiona hugged Wilf, then gestured in the direction of their farm.

Isolde had been a surprise. She had approached Emma after her return home with a proposition: since she had no prospects and was tired of lodging with Grahame, Isolde suggested she apprentice under

Emma. She requested to live in Emma's old hut and man the bread oven. Though Emma wouldn't count her a friend, she trusted the woman needed space. Emma also knew she couldn't keep running herself ragged. So she taught Isolde how to make herbed loaves, dessert buns and how to time all the baking to ensure the bread was ready for morning. The arrangement was made on a temporary basis, to ensure it worked well for both. Isolde didn't need much other than distraction. She still was financially cared for by her father. Plus, Emma needed help. She prayed the plan would work. Especially since Father Chisholm had taken her up on the proposition of baking for the church.

Bran clasped Neil around the back of the neck, whispering something in his son's ear that made Neil scowl and shake his father off. Neil had grown an ungodly amount in the time between spring and late-summer. He was nearly as tall as Bran, though not as broad, but Emma could see the beginnings of it. He would be a large lad one day. She'd been doing enough sewing of new clothes to note it.

"Alas, Ruthless, I have failed."

"You were wonderful, Father!" Ginnie said, jumping up.

He picked her up beneath the arms and swung her around in a huge circle. Ginnie giggled, tipping her head back to let her long, dark hair soar. Emma just sat there, hand on her stomach as Tate patted the bulge. The baby would be with them in four months. Four more months of uncertainty. Thankfully, Tate had begun to sleep through the night in earnest.

When Bran put Ginnie down, he obliged to twirl the other two girls, then sat down next to Emma claiming his dizziness. He put his ear against her belly, his large hand on the underside. It was a posture he'd adopted that made Emma's heart swell. After a few moments of listening, he turned his head and spoke low words into the mound. When finished, he leaned up to claim Emma's lips in a kiss that made all the children shriek.

"What? I kiss her every day. One would think you'd be used to it by now."

Emma smiled as Merthe and Neil turned their gazes to the ground. The little girls screamed again as they jumped on their father, little fists play punching as they roughhoused. Emma leaned back on her arm, deliriously happy.

After their vows, not everything had been content. Bran had gone to cut the Guston forest a month after she'd returned home. Emma had spent several sleepless nights waiting for his safe return. Finally, he made it back to her. And though she knew he garnered a good income for the wood he'd cut and brought back, she feared for the next time he would have to go.

It was something they both had to live with. The way Bran watched her, the manner in which he cradled her belly at night, she knew he was equally terrified of the birth. It was faith that kept them going. Faith in one another. Faith in their bond.

Soon, Bran's arm snaked around her back. He got to

his knees, giving her enough support to do the same, then stood slowly so she could lean on him. Emma was thankful he wasn't as tall as his friends, for it allowed her to lean into him all the easier.

"Shall we retire, Wife?"

"You always call me that now," she teased, looping her arms around his neck. Merthe had scooped up Tate and had begun walking ahead with the children.

Bran remained rooted on the spot, his hands settling on her backside.

"Aye, because I love that you're mine."

She looked up into his blue eyes and saw desire simmering in their depths.

"And I feel the same," she said. She stood on her toes and planted a kiss on his mouth.

"Bran!" Grahame's alarmed shout echoed through the meadow. Emma and Bran parted to find Grahame running toward them. He was pale, his eyes wide. Fear flared inside Emma. And, indeed, when Ridley broke from between the huts, running to the hall with a look of murder on his face, Bran's grip on her tightened.

"What is it?" Emma asked.

"Yrsa's gone."

"What d'you mean? She left?"

Grahame shook his head, his face pinched and pale. "We think taken. Ridley's going to check the hall."

Emma pushed away from Bran, but he held fast.

"What do you mean, taken?"

A desperate, keening cry like the call of a dying wolf wrought the air. It came from the direction of the hall.

Emma glanced at Bran, then they were rushing toward the sound as fast as they could run.

Ridley knelt on the dirt path outside, a swath of white-blonde hair clutched in his hand and a piece of parchment in the other. Emma's heart lurched.

"Ridley," Bran said as he approached.

Ridley looked up at them, his eyes rimmed red, tears streaming down his cheeks. He simply held up the letter then clutched the hair to his chest. Emma felt her guts shrink.

Neither she nor Bran could read so they did not reach for the parchment. Grahame took it, his gaze scanning what he could.

"It's from Lady Clayton. It says..." he swallowed, then tried again. "It says she's taken Ridley Ward's bride for the payment of an eg-egre..."

Ridley spoke, repeating the words of the letter in a tone so like death it made Emma's bones quake. "'Egregious personal debt owed. There will be no negotiation of this debt; however, if Ridley Ward would like to plead for his bride's life, he may do so by sending Grahame Shepherd to the Clayton stronghold. There is to be no retaliation lest the same measures be taken out on his wife.'"

Emma's blood chilled. She tore her eyes from Ridley to look at Grahame, who stood staring in the direction of his home, the letter crumpled in his hand. His tanned face was ashen, his words hollow. "May Yrsa's gods save her."

ACKNOWLEDGMENTS

To my husband, Mark, for treating my authorship as the career I foresee it to be and not only a hobby. Thank you for managing the kids, the house, and our business in the times I've been preparing this book.

To my friends, Jill and Robyn, for listening to my constant book updates throughout the year. Growing different businesses together is something I will always cherish.

A huge thank you to my beta readers: Heather, May-Lin, Stevi, Rebecca, Kristin and Samantha. Your feedback was invaluable. To my ARC reader team - your early support has meant so much.

Deep thanks to my editor, Tracey, and all her expertise.

Finally, thank you to YOU, the reader, who has taken a chance by supporting my work. My gratitude forever.

ABOUT THE AUTHOR

C.A. Fray is the Amazon #1 Bestselling Author of the steamy medieval romances, His Viking Captive and His Saxon Wife.

C.A. grew up with her nose buried in books. She is a mother to three boys and maintains her sanity by writing tension-filled medieval romance. She has a house full of plants, runs a business with her husband, drinks too much coffee and still has her face buried in all kinds of books.

www.ingramcontent.com/pod-product-compliance
Lightning Source LLC
Chambersburg PA
CBHW061540190726
48289CB00004B/1112